WARLORD

James Steel is a writer and journalist based in the UK.

By the same author:

December
Legacy

JAMES STEEL

Warlord

AVON

This novel is entirely a work of fiction. The names, characters and incidents portrayed in it are the work of the author's imagination. Any resemblance to actual persons, living or dead, events or localities is entirely coincidental.

AVON

A division of HarperCollins*Publishers*
77–85 Fulham Palace Road,
London W6 8JB

www.harpercollins.co.uk

A Paperback Original 2011

2

A catalogue record for this book is
available from the British Library

ISBN-13: 978-1-84756-161-9

Set in Minion by Palimpsest Book Production Limited,
Falkirk, Stirlingshire

Printed and bound in Great Britain by
Clays Ltd, St Ives plc

Mixed Sources
Product group from well-managed
forests and other controlled sources
www.fsc.org   Cert no. SW-COC-001806
© 1996 Forest Stewardship Council

FSC is a non-profit international organization established
to promote the responsible management of the world's forests.
Products carrying the FSC label are independently certified
to assure consumers that they come from forests that are managed
to meet the social, economic and ecological needs
of present and future generations.

Find out more about HarperCollins and the environment at
www.harpercollins.co.uk/green

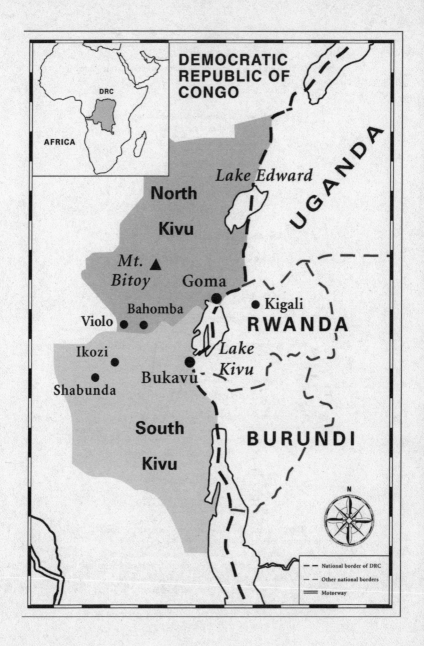

'There is no book on the Congo, we must write one ourselves.'

Congo Mercenary
Colonel Mike Hoare,
Commander of 5 Commando mercenary regiment,
deployed in eastern Congo, 1964.

In the Beginning

Chapter One

Eve Mapendo sees the figure lit by moonlight.

It has the body of a muscular man stripped to the waist and the head of a kudu, a dark antelope head with two heavy horns spiralling out of it like madness.

The creature stands in an opening in the forest on the hillside above her, at the front of a file of soldiers. They wear black cloth hoods over their heads with ragged holes cut for eyes and mouths. They stand in complete silence; the silver light frosts the surface of every leaf around them.

The horned head turns in her direction, the large eyes darkened by the shadow of its heavy brows.

Her pupils dilate wide as the adrenaline hits them. She clenches her throat muscles and painfully chokes off a scream. It cannot see her in the shadows of the doorway of her shack but she feels its gaze bear down on her like a hard hand gripping her shoulder, pushing her until she crouches on the ground.

The creature unslings the assault rifle from its shoulder, cocks the weapon and gestures to the soldiers to fan out and

5

move down the hill towards the refugee camp. They disappear into the trees.

A whimper of fear escapes her and the baby stirs inside the shack.

She knows what the creature is and she knows what it wants.

Joseph bares his teeth and screams at his enemy.

It's his first proper firefight and he wants to prove to his platoon leader, Lieutenant Karuta, that he can fight. He's fourteen or fifteen, maybe sixteen – he doesn't know. He was born in a refugee camp during a war and he never knew his parents.

He sees the enemy soldiers darting in and out of the trees across the small valley, a hundred metres from him now, firing wild bursts from their AK-47s and shouting insults. They are wearing a ragtag of green uniforms and coloured tee shirts. The bushes next to him twitch and shudder with the impact of their bullets, cut branches and leaves tumble down around him. The men in his platoon fire back with a cacophony of gunfire.

He glances across at Lieutenant Karuta who is yelling away and firing his rifle in long bursts, spraying bullets. Joseph brings his AK up to his shoulder and squints through the circular sight on the muzzle. The rifle is old and heavy, its metal parts scratched and its wooden stock stained a dark brown by the sweat of many tense hands that have clutched it during the decades of Congo's wars. He's often cursed its weight as the platoon trudged up and down the countless hills in the bush, but now it feels light and vital in his hands, an extension of himself growing out of his shoulder.

He pulls the trigger and the gun chatters, slamming back

hard into his collarbone. It clicks empty and he quickly ducks down, presses the magazine release, yanks it out, flips it over and shoves the spare one, strapped to it with duct tape, into the port. This is his first big firefight but he's practised these moves over and over again.

He doesn't know who the enemy are: one of the poisonous alphabet soup of groups in Kivu – PARECO, AFL-NALU, FJPC, one of the government FARDC brigades, even a rival FDLR battalion or one of the many *mai-mai* militias from the different tribal groups: Lendu, Hema, Nandi, Tutsi. No one knows what the hell is going on out in the bush.

This lot look like a local *mai-mai* militia. Joseph's platoon of soldiers are from the Democratic Forces for the Liberation of Rwanda, more commonly known by their French acronym, the FDLR. They bumped into the *mai-mai* by accident as they were coming down the valley side into the village and the fighting broke out in a confused way.

An RPG whooshes off near him, the white fire of the propellant shoots across the valley and the rocket explodes against a tree. The enemy gunfire slackens and they begin to withdraw. This is subsistence warfare and no one actually wants to get killed – what's the point? You can't steal, eat or rape if you're dead.

The FDLR soldiers that he is with start yelling and cheering. Lieutenant Karuta is next to him and Joseph looks at his excited face, eyes filled with laughter. The lieutenant is his father figure. His own father was an FDLR soldier killed when he was a baby, somewhere in the middle of the big Congo war. No one knows where or when – over five million people died so it's not like anyone paid much attention to him.

Lieutenant Karuta is forty and a *génocidaire* from the old days in Rwanda. He is a big man in green army fatigues with a wispy beard patched with white that he grows to distinguish himself from the young men under his command.

He waves his rifle joyfully in the air and Joseph joins in. The village is theirs; they must get there before the peasants run off.

They charge down the valley side, jumping over tangles of vines and bursting through bamboo thickets. The ragged line of cheering fighters rushes out of the shade of the trees and into the sunshine. They hold their rifles over their heads as they bound through the waist-high grass towards the collection of round mud huts with thatched conical roofs on the flat land at the bottom of the valley. Villagers burst out of the huts and start running around screaming in panic. Women try to grab their kids, old men stumble and fall, chickens fly up, goats run around bleating. Joseph is laughing with excitement. He's hungry after weeks in the deep bush living on pineapples and snails.

A woman in a red and blue wrap bursts up from a clump of grass to his right, squawking like a parrot, flapping one arm and dragging a goat on a string with the other. Lieutenant Karuta is onto her, changing direction and chasing fast as she flees down a path into a field of head-high maize. Joseph stumbles, recovers and follows him.

He rushes down the narrow path, the tall green stems blurring past him on either side. Lieutenant Karuta catches up with the woman quickly, kicks the goat out of the way and shoves her in the back so she goes sprawling. The goat runs on over her and the lieutenant has a moment of indecision – do I grab the goat or her?

But her shrieks excite him and he looks down at her on the ground in front of him. 'Get the goat!' he shouts to Joseph who squeezes past him and races down the path. The screaming starts.

Weird high-pitched animal shrieks come out of the night from all around the refugee camp. It turns her blood to cold liquid fear in her veins.

Eve crouches inside her shack clutching her baby, thinking, 'No human being can make that sound.'

She is nineteen, with a broad face, oval eyes, a blunt nose and smooth brown skin. Short and stocky, she wears a patterned *pagne* wrapped around her body and a plastic cross on a string round her neck. Her free hand clutches it involuntarily.

She and her nine-month-old daughter, Marie, are alone in a shelter at the edge of the camp. She has blown out her tiny candle and crouches in terror in the darkness at the back of the hut. It is ten feet long by four feet high; the walls are made of palm leaves woven onto sticks that are fixed to a frame of branches and she can hear everything outside. A piece of blue and white UNHCR plastic sheeting completes the curved roof. Her boyfriend, Gabriel, proudly made a door for her out of a corrugated iron sheet tied onto the branch frame with some electrical flex he found. He showed her how to tie it shut before he left – 'That will keep you safe!'

The camp mongrels started barking at the attackers as they came near but this turns to frightened whimpering once the screaming starts. She can hear the soldiers shouting now in Swahili, 'Over there! Look in that one over there!' 'Open up! Open the door!'

Screams of fear come from her neighbours in return.

'Open the door, or I'll kill you!'

Some confused banging and shouting.

'Where is it? Where is the albino?'

More sobbing and crying and then the dull sound of blows and screaming.

Her blood pounds so loud in her ears, she is sure they can hear it. She tries to still her heart – if she can make herself very quiet and very small she might escape. They want her baby but she can't give it up. Marie starts crying and she forces her hand over her mouth, pressing her face into her breast and smelling her milky baby smell one last time.

The shouting nearby has gone quiet. She hears footsteps approaching the hut. The thin corrugated iron sheet is all there is between her and them. A hand grabs the edge of it and tries to open the door but the flex holds it fast to the branch frame. There is a grunt of anger and then the iron bangs loudly as a machete hacks at the flex. Heaving, banging, tearing, they pull the door off its flimsy hinges and throw it to one side.

The demonic figure silhouetted in the moonlight is half man and half animal. The kudu head and horns look huge. It is stripped to the waist and muscular and in the flat silver light she can see the artery in its neck, beating fast just under the rim of the headdress. It is breathing hard and beads of sweat roll down its chest. The smell of the forest pours into the hut, musty and damp.

Eve cowers on the floor and looks up, wide-eyed in terror. Her hand moves to hold the baby tighter and Marie lets out a loud wail.

The creature holds its Kalashnikov in its right hand and stretches out its left to her. Eve makes a noise of denial, just a whimper. The Kudu is enraged and bellows at her before ducking its long horns under the roof and grabbing her arm. Its fingers are like steel, biting deep into her flesh, dragging her out of the doorway, clutching the baby in one arm. She is screaming now with fear, 'No! No! No!'

As soon as she is out in the open, a soldier in a black

10

cloth hood shouts excitedly at the sight of the pale baby and hits her in the back with the butt of his rifle. A rib cracks and she makes an *oof* sound as the air is forced out of her.

She loses her grip on the child and the Kudu grabs it by one arm and lifts it up in the air. It throws back its horned head and howls in triumph. The other members of the gang all join in howling and firing their rifles in the air.

Eve lies winded on the ground until they finish celebrating. The baby is taken away and then they look down at her. Rough hands grab her under her arms and throw her on her back and tear off her *pagne*. As the first man presses his heavy weight on her stomach, something inside her says, 'This isn't happening.'

But the tearing and jabbing continues and she thinks, 'Why are you doing this to me, God? Why have you made this terrible country?'

Chapter Two

'We are going to make a new country, Mr Devereux.'

The Chinese businessman looks at him closely to gauge his reaction.

Alex Devereux has the face of a man with strong feelings deeply controlled.

Dark tides run just under the surface but you will never find out what drives them.

His eyes lock onto the businessman's and flicker with interest before a shutter comes down and he glances away to look out of the window over the lawns of his country house.

Alex has a stern cast to his face, the habit of command engraved on his features by his time as a major in the Household Cavalry and his subsequent career as a mercenary commander. He is six foot four, broad shouldered, lean and fit, running every day up and down the hills of his Herefordshire estate – 'exercising his demons' he calls it.

Outwardly he is dressed like a modern gentleman with jeans, loafers and button-down shirt, black hair neatly trimmed; he's just turned forty and there is some salt and pepper at the temples. But there is a lot more to him than that.

At the moment he is very relaxed with one arm thrown

over the back of the old Chesterfield and his long legs stretched out in front of him. It's April, a shower is thrashing the rose bushes about outside, and it's cold so he's lit a log fire in the oak-panelled drawing room of Akerley, the Devereux country house where he lives alone. His family has been there nearly a thousand years, since Guy D'Evereux was granted the land by William the Conqueror. He is currently restoring the house with money from his Russian adventures but it is still always freezing cold.

He looks back at Mr Fang Xei Dong and says, 'That sounds interesting,' without any feeling.

It is a measure of how much more relaxed he is about life than before his success that he can be so detached about such a huge project. He refused to go up to London for the meeting and only agreed to it if it was at Akerley. It is also a measure of how interested in him the businessman must be that he agreed to the demand, arriving just after lunch in the back of a chauffeur-driven Mercedes.

Alex was surprised by Fang when his long limbs unfolded themselves like a daddy longlegs from the car door. He is northern Chinese, as tall as the Englishman, with wavy black hair, blue eyes and an angular face with cheekbones that seem painfully large. His skin is smooth and he looks to be about thirty.

When he arrived he strode up the imposing stone steps of the house towards Alex, full of confidence, completely unfazed by his first time in the heart of the English country-side. He thrust his hand out, 'Hello, my name is Fang Xei Dong but my business name is Simon Jones.'

His English is American-accented but it still has the flat, staccato Chinese diction. He clearly knows that no Westerner will ever get the sliding tones of his name right and doesn't want them to embarrass them with untoward mispronunciations. He cheerfully laughs off Alex's polite attempts at saying his name. 'Don't worry, in Congo I am called Monsieur Wu. It's the only Chinese name they can pronounce.'

He talks in rapid bursts, his long arms often reaching forwards as he speaks, as if trying to get hold of some perceived future.

He wears the casual uniform of the modern global businessman: neatly pressed chinos, button-down blue shirt with a pen in his top pocket and iPod earphones hanging down over his top button, a casual black blazer and loafers. When he settles himself in the drawing room he sets out an iPad and two BlackBerries on the coffee table in front of him that beep and chirrup frequently.

He sits forward on the leather armchair now and pushes his narrow-lensed titanium glasses back up his nose with a rapid unconscious dab of his hand; they slip off the bridge of his nose because his head jerks about as he speaks.

'This operation is completely covert at the moment but I understand from my contacts in the defence community that you are used to operating in this manner?'

Alex just narrows his eyes in response.

'I am referring to your operation in Central African Republic, which I understand was a Battlegroup level command?'

Alex nods. He is very cagey about his past activities. His CAR mission has achieved legendary status in the mercenary community but they don't know the half of it. Any mention of the word Russia or any possible operations he was involved in there and he clams up completely.

Fang is reassured by his discretion.

'This operation will require that level of skill and more. To be candid with you, we realise that it is . . .' he pauses

'... unconventional, from an international relations point of view, and we would prefer to work with a discreet operator such as yourself rather than one of the big defence contractors. They are much more ... conventional,' he finishes, sounding evasive.

Alex knows that by conventional he means law-abiding. He nods politely in acceptance of the point but winces internally. It wasn't the sort of reputation he had sought at the start of his career. He had always wanted to be able to serve his country for his whole life; major general was what he had been hoping for. Somehow things just didn't work out like that.

Fang blasts on regardless. 'I represent a consortium of Chinese business interests that will lease Kivu Province off the Congolese government for ninety-nine years. Under the terms of the lease it will effectively be ours to do what we want with.'

He stretches out his arms and says with a note of wonder in his voice, 'In Operation Tiananmen we are going to set up a new country and bring order out of anarchy!'

Alex looks at him quizzically. 'Is that Tiananmen as in Square?'

'Yes, it means "the mandate of heaven".'

'What's that?'

'It's the ancient Confucian right to rule, the basic authority that any government has to have in order to form a country. And you are going to establish it, Mr Devereux. It is our new vision for the world.'

Gabriel Mwamba is twenty-one and in love.

He is an itinerant salesman, pushing his *tshkudu* cargo-scooter uphill along a narrow track through the forest, breathing hard and sweating, beads of it stand out in his black, wiry hair like little pearls. The tendons across his shoulders and neck stand out and feel like red-hot wires.

He has covered thirty miles in two days over the hills; today he started out at 4am. To dull the pain he is thinking about Eve and how he is going to impress her when he gets back to the refugee camp where she lives. He is an ugly man and knows it, so he realises he has to compensate for it in other ways – he will be a successful businessman.

When he met Eve last year he liked the look of her, small and stocky with good firm breasts and smooth skin. When he heard of her rejection by her husband because of her albino baby, he knew she was the one for him. A fellow outcast. She looked so sad and he just wanted to put a smile on her face.

His own features have been carelessly assembled: his jaw is too big, he has tombstone teeth, puffed-out cheeks and heavy eyebrows. His body looks odd, composed of a series of bulges: a large head, powerful shoulders, protruding stomach and bulging calf muscles. It's all out of proportion with his short legs, a broad trunk and long arms. Because he knows he looks unusual his face has an anxious, eager-to-please look that irritates people and leads them to be crueller to him than they would otherwise be. However, Gabriel is an optimist with big plans and he never gives up.

He has been reading a French translation of a self-help book – *I Can Make You a Millionaire!* – written by an American business guru. He has absorbed a lot about spotting opportunities in the market and is sure he is onto one now. Market intelligence is key to these breakthroughs and he listens to his battered transistor radio once a day (to preserve the batteries, which are expensive) to catch the main radio bulletin from Radio Okapi, the UN radio station that broadcasts throughout Kivu.

The local Pakistani UN commander was on the bulletin talking in very bad French about the success of their recent operation against the FDLR and how they had opened up the road into the village of Pangi and installed a Joint Protection Team to allow the market to be held there on Saturday.

Immediately Gabriel knew this was his opportunity. He got together all his money and bought a load of consumer goods off another trader who hadn't heard the news and was selling them cheap. Pangi had been inaccessible for months so they would be crying out for what he had to offer, and that meant profit. As the self-help book put it: 'Adversity is spelt OPPORTUNITY!' It's a big investment but he is going to make a killing.

The *tshkudu* he pushes is loaded up with old USAID sacks containing cheap Chinese-manufactured goods: soap, matches, batteries, condoms, combs, print dresses, needles and thread, some tins of tuna (way past their sell-by date), boxes of smuggled Ugandan Supermatch cigarettes and six umbrellas in a bundle. He also has sacks of charcoal from the charcoal trading network throughout the province – he is following one of their secret paths through the woods.

It is heading downhill now into Pangi. The *tshkudu* is heavy and tugging at his grip. It's six feet long and made of planks – he built it himself. He hauls back on the handlebars to prevent it from running away from him, digging the toes of his flip-flops into the mud. The trail comes out of the trees and onto a dirt road leading to the village, where he passes the local massacre memorial. The date and number of people killed are scorched with a poker onto a wooden board nailed to a tree: 20 July 1999, 187 people. He doesn't give it a second look; every village has one from the war.

He is looking to the future and full of hope. At the moment he is a small-time trader, but one day he will graduate to be one of *les grosses légumes* – the big vegetables, the businessmen in the regional capitals of Goma or Bukavu, running an internet café or a trucking company.

A jolt of fear goes through Gabriel and he stops daydreaming. His step falters and he wants to run away but they have seen him already and to show fear would invite an attack. Three soldiers with Kalashnikovs are lounging at the side of the road on a log, smoking and staring at him through their sunglasses. Like everyone in Kivu, Gabriel is well practised at avoiding attention from the police or the army: his head drops, his eyes look at the ground and his body seems to halve in size as he pushes the *tshkudu* towards them.

The UN commander said there would be a Joint Protection Team in place but there don't seem to be any Pakistani soldiers around. That the three men are wearing the plain, dark green uniform of the government army, the FARDC, is bad enough, but what makes them even more of a threat is that they have the distinctive blue shoulder flashes of the 64th Brigade. The Congolese army is made up of militia groups that have been integrated into it over the years and the 64th Brigade is a former *mai-mai* group, a tribal militia of the Shi people in South Kivu.

Gabriel is terrified of them because he is a Hunde, a member of the Rwandan tribe brought into the province by the Belgians during the colonial era as cheap labour. They are hated by the '*originaires*', the indigenous Congolese peoples.

If he can just get past this group then he can blend into the market, do his business and sneak out with the crowd at the end of the day. His eyes are wide with fear but he keeps them lowered as he passes the soldiers. Their heads turn and they watch him intently.

Sophie Cecil-Black is feeling carsick and frazzled.

The white Land Cruiser swings round another switchback on the dirt road up the hill and her head swoons horribly.

They've been doing this since six o'clock this morning and it's early afternoon now. Up three thousand feet from Goma to Masisi and then down three thousand feet into the Oso valley and then up another three thousand feet to here.

God, one more swing and I am going to puke.

Saliva pours into her mouth but she tenses her throat muscles and forces the vomit back down.

She looks out of the window. Everywhere around her are stunning views out over rugged hills covered with grassland and small fields. It reminds her of a family holiday to Switzerland in the summer, but she is not in the mood to appreciate the beauty now.

Sophie is thirty-one, six foot tall and slim with straight brown hair, a striking face and a strident manner. Some men think she is very beautiful, others think she is very ugly. It's the Cecil-Black nose that makes the difference: secretly she used to want to file down the prominent bridge of it when she was a teenager but she has learned to live with it now. She wears a tight green GAP tee shirt, hipster jeans and green Croc shoes.

The Cecil-Blacks are a branch of the Cecil family who ran the British government from the time of Elizabeth I. Sophie went to Benenden, her father is a stockbroker and her mother is very concerned that she is over thirty and not married. Sophie couldn't care less about that: she knows she is called to higher things and has been doing her best to break the mould of being a safe, Home Counties girl ever since she refused to join the Brownies aged seven. She has a first in PPE from Oxford, a Masters in Development Economics from the School of Oriental and African Studies and an ethnic tattoo across the small of her back.

She is now a project manager with an American humanitarian aid charity, Hope Street, which has a large presence in Kivu and specialises in work with street kids, schooling and training them but she also does general humanitarian work. She leads a team of fifteen people based in Goma, where they have a large training facility.

One of her team, Natalie Zielinski, is sitting in the backseat. She doesn't get carsick. She's a small, bubbly Texan with brown, frizzy hair in a bob that never quite works. Sophie likes her optimism, but sometimes finds her irritating.

Nicolas, their Congolese driver, is a slim, self-effacing young man, very glad to have such a cushy job driving for an NGO, it's a lot easier and safer than the backbreaking life of the peasants in the bush. He is quiet and calm with the soft manner of a lot of Congolese men. He drives smoothly but even that can't iron out the constant bumping from side to side on the dirt road and those horrible lurching turns.

They started so early because they need to get a load of vaccines to a remote clinic before they go off in the heat. Several thousand dollars worth of polio, hepatitis, measles and other vaccines are packed into coolboxes in the back of the jeep. Once they get them to the clinic at Tshabura they can go into the solar-powered fridge and will be fine for the big vaccination day that they have set up later that week. The clinic is at the head of the Bilati valley and local field workers have spread the word around the farms and villages there, as well as advertising it on Radio Okapi. They are expecting two hundred children to be brought in to be inoculated.

The other reason they started at six is that Tshabura is on the edge of the area under the nominal control of the UN forces. The security situation in Kivu is always volatile; they listen to the radio every morning for the UN security update, like a weather forecast. At the moment their route is Condition Bravo – some caution is warranted, no immediate threat but follow normal security procedures. Condition Echo means evacuate urgently to save your life but it doesn't happen often. Lawlessness is just part of everyday life in Kivu and Sophie has become used to the daily list of rapes, muggings and burglaries, as well as keeping track of which roads are closed due to militia activity.

After a prolonged security assessment and unsuccessful wrangling with the UN to do the delivery by helicopter, Sophie got fed up with waiting and decided that they could race there in the daytime, get to the clinic, stay overnight in their compound and then race back the next day. White NGO workers are generally safe in Kivu, apart from the usual hassling for bribes from the police and army, but she doesn't want to be out on the roads after dark when armed groups roam at will.

All these factors are weighing on her mind and she's also irate because they are behind schedule. They had a puncture on a track that had been washed out by heavy rain and then lost an hour getting over the river at Pinga where a truck had got a wheel stuck in a hole in the old metal bridge.

The car at last comes to the top of the hill and Nicolas pulls up so Natalie can look around the surrounding area and check the map. She scans either side of the jeep and all she can see are lines of green hills in bright sunshine receding into the distance. It is completely quiet but for the noise of a breeze buffeting the car.

'Daniel Boone would get lost out here,' she mutters, as

she looks back and forth between the map and the view. 'One hill begins to look much the same as another.' The map has proved inaccurate already that day and there are no signposts anywhere.

'Look, can we just get on with it, please,' Sophie snaps.

'OK, OK,' Natalie says cheerfully. 'We're on the right route.'

Chapter Three

Alex is struggling to get a grip on the scale of the project that Fang has just outlined.

He stops being relaxed and sits forward, the fingers of one hand pressed to his temple.

'Hang on; the Congolese government is going to *lease* you Kivu Province?'

Fang nods confidently. 'Yes, just like the British government leased Hong Kong from China for ninety-nine years.'

'OK. How many people live there?'

'Well, that is a good question actually. No one really knows because surveys are from before the war, but we think about six million.'

'Six million people?' Alex looks incredulous but Fang looks back at him unfazed.

'Yes.'

Alex shakes his head. '*Why* is the government going to do that?'

'Well, Kivu is actually an embarrassment to the government in Kinshasa. The President promised to bring peace to the country when he got elected but he has failed to end the fighting, or deliver on any of his other Cinq Chantiers policies.

'The government has no control there. I mean, look at

the distances: Congo is the size of western Europe and trying to run Kivu from Kinshasa is like trying to run Turkey from London. Plus there are no road or rail links between the two areas.

'The government had to get the Rwandan army in to try and defeat the FDLR but that failed. Now they throw their hands up and say it is a Rwandan problem and the Rwandans do the same back to them. No one takes responsibility for it so the whole problem just festers on and will never get solved. I mean, the whole of Congo is just . . .' Fang waves his arms around trying to communicate the depth of the exasperation he feels about the country '. . . completely dysfunctional, the country makes no sense. The only reason it exists is as the area of land that Stanley was able to stake out.'

He begins ticking points off on his fingers: 'The country makes absolutely no sense on a geographic, economic, linguistic or ethnic level. There are over two hundred different ethnic groups in it and the Belgians practised divide and rule policies that exacerbated the differences between them. The only things they have in common are music, Primus beer and suffering.'

Alex is nodding in agreement with this. He has had some dealings with the place and is aware of its legendary chaos.

'OK, they don't control Kivu so they might as well get some money off you for it, right?'

Fang clearly doesn't want to be drawn into detail on money but nods. 'Yes, we are talking very significant sums here. China is already the largest investor in the Democratic Republic of Congo with a nine billion dollar deal and we have been able to leverage this to give us more influence.'

Alex nods; he can well imagine what 'influence' billions

24

of dollars of hard cash could get you amongst Kinshasa's famously rapacious elites.

Fang continues to justify the project. 'Actually the deal is not that unusual if you look around at the land purchases that are going on at the moment. UAE has bought six thousand square miles of southern Sudan, South Africa has bought a huge area of Republic of Congo, Daiwoo Logistics tried to buy half the agricultural land in Madagascar . . .'

'Is that the one where the government was overthrown because of it?'

Fang nods, unfazed by Alex's implied scepticism about his own project. 'Yes, but that was different. No one in the rest of Congo cares about what happens in Kivu; when you go to Kinshasa there is nothing on the TV or in the papers about it.'

'Hmm.' Alex is still not reassured – the more he begins to get to grips with the project the more he can see problems with it.

Fang continues, 'So your role would be to . . .'

Alex holds up a hand to stop the tide of enthusiasm. 'Hang on, who said anything about me actually being involved? This is a huge and very risky project and I am very comfortable at the moment. I'm not looking to take on any new work.'

Fang is momentarily checked and nods. 'OK, I can see that this is a highly unusual project that will take a while for you to absorb.' Then he just storms on anyway. 'The role of the military partner in the consortium would be to neutralise the FDLR.'

Alex feels he has made his point and that he can continue the discussion on a hypothetical basis. 'The Hutus?'

'Yes. After they conducted the Rwandan genocide in 1994

against the Tutsis they were driven out by the returning Tutsi army in exile and a million Hutu refugees fled across the border to Kivu.'

'And have destabilised the province ever since.'

'Yes. The genocide was twenty years ago now but their leadership have successfully maintained their ideology of Hutu power and indoctrinated a new generation of fighters. Their continued presence means that there are about thirty armed groups in Kivu but the FDLR is the main cause of the instability that breeds the others. Defeat them and the other militias would agree to negotiate; there would be no need for them to exist if a strong authority was established.'

'So it's a bit like Israel having the SS sitting on its border?'

'Yes, the Hutus killed eight hundred thousand civilians in a hundred days with machetes so Rwanda's government doesn't feel comfortable with them there. They will be our partners in the consortium.' Fang's mind is racing ahead already. 'How long would it take to set up a Battlegroup operation to deal with them?'

Alex takes a deep breath and considers the issue for a moment. 'Well, for the sort of air mobile strike warfare you would need, you would want to start the campaign at the beginning of the dry season in May, so next year, that would be thirteen months.'

'Is that long enough set-up time?'

'Yes, that would be fine.'

Fang makes a note on his iPad.

Alex continues, 'But look, President Kagame is safe now, isn't he? Why does he need to be involved with all this?' He's aware of the Rwandan leader's reputation for ruthless efficiency and running the country with an iron grip.

'Well, yes and no. The FDLR is not capable of reinvading

26

Rwanda right now but he is still a Tutsi in charge of a country that is eighty-five per cent Hutu. If he were assassinated like the last president in 1994 then the whole thing would start again. He is not the sort of guy who is prepared to have that level of threat right on his border.'

'So are you saying that the Rwandan military are on board on the project?'

Fang looks momentarily uncomfortable.

'This is a very delicate area.' He clears his throat. 'As I think you know, the Rwandans were involved in atrocities when they were in Kivu that attracted . . .'

One of the BlackBerries in front of him rings. He cuts off in mid-flow and answers it aggressively in Chinese and then starts listening with occasional grunts. He gets up and walks over to the window and looks out over the rose garden. He suddenly lets forth a tirade of angry instructions, jabbing his free hand into the air.

Joseph wrestles the goat to the ground and holds its head down.

He then faces the dilemma of how to hold both his rifle and the goat. The goat's string has snapped; he looks back and forth between the two. Should he hitch his rifle on his chest and hold the goat on his shoulders?

Eventually he settles on dragging it by a horn in one hand with his rifle in the other. He sets off down the path in the maize field, back towards the village where he can hear shouting, screaming and gunshots as the hungry FDLR troops set about the civilians.

There is the noise of a struggle going on ahead. As he comes through the maize he sees Lieutenant Karuta wrestling with the woman on the ground. She is putting up a fierce resistance. The goat bleats and Karuta looks up, his face puffy and angry with frustrated lust. Joseph stands and stares at him.

Karuta rolls off the woman and grabs his rifle off the ground and points it at her. She lies on her back looking up at them, eyes wide in terror.

'Cover her!' he orders Joseph, who holds his rifle by its pistol grip and the goat in the other hand. She stares at the muzzle just above her face as Karuta pulls out a knife, gets hold of her feet and quickly slits her hamstrings. She screams in agony.

He puts the knife away and straightens his uniform. 'Come on, she'll keep for dessert. Let's have dinner first.' He walks off down the path towards the village.

When they get back there the lieutenant organises the looting of food and three women are tied to trees. He sends out a patrol under the command of Corporal Habiyakare, another old génocidaire. They are to scout around the small valley to check that the mai-mai have gone. Meanwhile the men slaughter the goat and start cooking it whilst eating foufou and drinking the farmers' home-brewed beer from gourds.

An hour later the patrol returns, dragging a thirteen-year-old boy with them. He is barefoot, wears shorts and a ragged tee shirt, is crying and looks terrified.

Corporal Habiyakare reports back. 'Lieutenant Karuta, we have captured a prisoner!'

Karuta's eyes are already reddened from drinking; he is in a boisterous mood.

'Bring the prisoner over here, we will interrogate him!'

The boy is dragged into the middle of the village and stripped to his red underpants. His belt is used to tie his elbows behind his back so tightly that his chest sticks out painfully. Karuta sits on a wonky wooden chair in front of him but the boy falls over in tears. The men gather round and laugh and clap as they drink the beer.

The corporal drags the boy to his feet.

'What is the charge against the prisoner?' asks the lieutenant.

'Sir, we found him hiding in the woods, spying on our soldiers. He was armed with this axe.'

'What have you got to say for yourself?'

The boy sniffles and mutters, 'I was chopping wood.'

'You were chopping wood! You think I am a fucking idiot! You are a spy!'

'No! Not spy!'

'You were spying on my men!'

'No, not . . .'

'Shut up!'

'No spy . . .'

'Shut up! You are a spy! You work for Rwanda! Look at his feet, he is a Rwandan!'

The crowd pushes forward and looks at the boy's feet; none of the younger soldiers has ever been to Rwanda so they accept the older *génocidaire*'s word.

'Not Rwandan!' the boy screams in a high-pitched shriek.

'You will admit it! Beat him!' The lieutenant gestures to the crowd of men who push the boy to the ground and start kicking him. Others run off and pull supple branches off trees, then run back in, push through the crowd and start whipping the boy.

He curls up in a ball but his hands are behind his back and the blows rain down all over him.

'You are a Rwandan spy! Confess!'

He cannot speak under the torrent of blows; raw red and pink gashes open up all over his dark skin from the slashing branches.

A soldier pushes the others back and jumps on him, his Wellington boots landing on his hip with a heavy thud. The man springs off laughing and others take running jumps onto the boy.

'OK, OK!' Lieutenant Karuta waves his hand: laughing, the men back off.

The boy lies still, covered with dust, his pants wet with urine.

'OK, come on.' Karuta shakes his head, grinning at the enthusiasm of his men. 'On your feet, boy.'

The boy doesn't move.

'Get him on his feet.' He gestures to Corporal Habiyakare, who gets hold of the belt holding his elbows together and yanks him up. The boy stirs and sways on his feet.

'Over here, heh.' Karuta points casually to the ground at the edge of the cleared area between two huts.

The boy senses something bad and starts struggling. Habiyakare tries to drag him backwards by the belt but the boy becomes desperate so the corporal kicks his legs out from under him and pulls him along by the belt. The boy shrieks with pain and fear in a high-pitched cracked voice.

Lieutenant Karuta walks ahead with his Kalashnikov and the crowd of men follow, grinning in anticipation.

'Here!' Karuta points to a spot on the ground and the corporal throws the boy forward and jumps out of the way.

In one smooth action the lieutenant hefts his assault rifle by its pistol grip so that the weapon is held upright in his right hand. He cocks it with a flourish with his left and then fires a long burst at point-blank range into the boy. His body bounces on the ground and a red mist appears over it briefly.

The men give a huge roar of approval and Karuta turns and brandishes his weapon with a broad grin.

He starts call and response, shouting, 'Hutu power!'

'*Hutu power!*' the men respond, raising their guns in the air and punching out the words with their fists.

'Free Rwanda!'

'*Free Rwanda!*'

Chapter Four

'Come on, we've got to hurry up.'

Sophie can hear the tetchiness in her voice. Nicolas, as ever, takes it in his stride, nods obediently and pushes the Land Cruiser on faster.

It's four o'clock and the vaccines in the back are getting warmer by the minute. Their medical technician recommended that they get them to the clinic by late afternoon or else they would be ruined and the whole inoculation event would have to be reorganised. It will be a big waste of money and effort and a loss of face for the charity in the local community if they can't deliver on their promises. Sophie hates not getting things right. At least the tension is making her forget her carsickness; she sits forward and swigs nervously from her water bottle.

They're pretty sure they are on the right road. It is winding down the hill into the Bilati valley and they can now see the river far away in the bottom, a fast-flowing upland torrent.

They come down onto a flat saddle of land where another road joins theirs before dipping down into the valley. All around is lush green grassland but up ahead Nicolas spots a checkpoint, a striped pole across the road next to a dilapidated single-storey building.

'Hmm,' says Natalie in annoyance. 'That's not on the map.'

'Bugger,' mutters Sophie.

Yet more hassle. She has spent a lot of time getting the paperwork in place for the journey. Government officials demand documents for everything: they are rarely paid and make their living from bribes. She pulls her document wallet out of the glove box and flicks through it again. The key document, their blue *permit à voyager* issued by the Chief of Traffic Police in Goma, is on the top, pristine and triple-stamped.

Sophie is keyed up now. One last barrier and they can get there just in time. Several hundred kids live healthier lives – how can you argue with that?

As they drive up towards the barrier they can see government FARDC soldiers standing inside sandbagged positions on either side of it. This is the last outpost of their control before the militia-dominated land beyond and they are very nervy, assault rifles held across their chests and fingers on triggers. They are questioning the driver of a battered Daihatsu minivan, ordering his passengers out and poking around in their woven plastic sacks stuffed with vegetables and bananas.

As they wait in line Sophie asks Nicolas in French, 'What brigade are they?'

Nicolas peers at their shoulder flashes.

'Orange is 17th Brigade.'

'Is that good or bad?' She knows that the different units have different temperaments depending on which militia they come from and which colonel runs them.

Nicolas replies quietly, 'Well, they used to be CNDP. They were a good army – Tutsi like me, and they defeated the FARDC whenever they fought them. But then they did a deal with the government and became the 17th Brigade with Congolese officers. After six months they shot up a UN base in protest because their officers had stolen their wages,' he pauses and then finishes with a shrug and, '*c'est la magie du Congo*.'

Sophie frowns. 'Great.'

'Just take it easy, remember the training,' Natalie says cautiously from the backseat. 'Don't make eye contact, keep your voice down, just be sweet. Maybe we'll have to pay a bribe to get through.'

'OK, all right!' Sophie holds up a hand to cut her off. Natalie is really getting on her nerves. 'We don't pay for access, it's our policy.'

Natalie falls silent, the soldiers wave the minivan through and they drive up to the barrier.

Gabriel makes his way past the soldiers and heads down the hillside to Pangi market.

He is torn between turning round and getting out of there immediately and his belief that he can make a killing and return to Eve with a stack of cash. He could use it to try and fix up her hut or buy her something for the baby or maybe get her that sewing machine she wants.

Pangi is a typical Kivu village, a group of palm-leaf and wooden huts in the bottom of a steep valley strung out along the banks of a small, fast-flowing river. All around are rugged hills topped with bright green forest, spotted with patches of white mist; it's cold and overcast. Meadows and small fields of maize, beans and cassava cut into the woods on the lower slopes.

As he pushes the *tshkudu* onto the flat ground he keeps his head down but his eyes flick back and forth taking in little details, gauging the atmosphere. It's ten o'clock and the market is busy, people have been cut off by the FDLR troops for months and have come in from the bush to stock up on food and consumer items. He will have to move fast to find a pitch and set out his wares. All his money is invested in his stock and he has got to get it out in front of his customers quickly before they spend the tiny reserves of cash they have.

A crowd of a couple of hundred people are milling around in a grassy area in the middle of the village, women in their brightly patterned *pagne* and men in an assortment of jackets and tee shirts, cast-offs from the West. Around the edge of the area women squat behind their goods, carefully laid out on banana leaves on the ground: piles of bush fruits, mangoes, blood oranges, cassava tubers, chickens tied up by the legs and silently awaiting their fate, lumps of bush meat covered in fur and some monkey flesh with little black hands sticking out. Protein is scarce as all the cattle and goats have been killed or driven off by the FDLR. People pick over the goods and pay for it warily with filthy Congolese franc notes.

Gabriel is worried, his eyes and ears taking in danger signals. The scene is unusually quiet, there is none of the usual chatter of a market and there are no children around – normally a village is teeming with them. People's body language is tense and fearful; no one makes eye contact with each other. Heads constantly flick about looking for trouble, shooting sullen glances at the soldiers. The FDLR may have been driven off but the government FARDC troops are no better. The soldiers swagger around in groups with their rifles, occasionally taking some goods without paying and eyeing up women. The people live in patches like this between outbursts of fighting and flights into the forest. They are angry about their lives but powerless. The atmosphere is one of suppressed violence, like petrol vapour hanging in the air.

Gabriel scans the crowd; the grey sacks hang off his *tshkudu*, bulging with wares. A pair of soldiers stand at the side of the market with their rifle butts resting on their hips, heads flicking around in a predatory manner.

He is looking for an empty patch of ground to set up his stall. He spent a lot of time making a lightweight folding table from bamboo that he can display his goods on, rather than having them on the ground. He is sure this will draw the customers in.

As he scans around he accidentally catches the eye of one of the soldiers. He ducks his head immediately but the man has seen him and thrusts his jaw forwards aggressively, drawing his finger across his throat in a slitting gesture. Gabriel turns his head and moves away towards the other side of the market.

The soldier follows him and shouts, 'Hey you! Where is your permit to trade?'

Gabriel freezes, turns and hurriedly goes into his most placatory mode, ducking his head into his shoulders and keeping his eyes averted. 'Pardon, Monsieur Le Directeur, would you be interested in this small box of cigarettes?' He holds out the packet.

This is bad; people are turning round and looking at them.

'I said, where is your permit to trade? Are you deaf?'

The soldier snatches the cigarettes and stuffs them in the front of his combat jacket, his eyes dancing greedily over Gabriel's sacks.

'Ah, Monsieur Le Directeur . . .'

'Hey, you sound Hunde! Are you Hunde?'

'Err, no, I . . .'

'Hey, he's Hunde!' the man calls to the other soldiers in the market and they start moving towards them. A crowd is forming around them, a sea of angry faces straining for an outlet for their misery.

The soldier is right up close to him – he's big and his face is dark with anger. He shoves Gabriel in the chest. 'You are Hunde and you come into *my* market with no permit to trade!'

The crowd gives an angry growl; they are mainly Shi people like the soldier.

'We are confiscating your property!' He grabs the handlebars of the *tshkudu*.

'Hey! That's mine!' This can't be happening, it's all his worldly wealth.

The crowd closes around Gabriel, sensing his weakness. A hand shoots out and grabs a sack.

'Hey, get off, that's mine!'

Gabriel's face is contorted in desperation and fear. He is surrounded; he tries to pull the handlebars back from the soldier and pushes a woman grabbing at his goods at the same time. She shrieks and slaps him across the face.

The petrol vapour ignites in a flashover.

The crowd roars and a frenzy breaks out. The soldier brings up the butt of his rifle and smashes it into his face. His nose breaks and blood gushes down his front. He falls backwards and the crowd punch and kick him.

His scooter falls over and there is a mad scramble as people yank open sacks and clamber on top of each other to get at the goods on the ground, shouting, screaming and clawing. Combs, batteries, cigarettes, condoms scatter everywhere. His bamboo display table is smashed to pieces.

Gabriel curls up in a ball on the ground, his arms over his head. He's in the middle of a tornado, a mad whirl of screaming, kicking, spitting mayhem. Blows rain down on his arms, head, back and legs. Every part of his body is being battered.

Through it all the pain is still mind-shattering, it feels like his face has been smashed into the back of his head.

This is it . . . I'm going to die.

And then it stops.

The fire burns out as quickly as it started. The mob vent their anger, tear him down to their level of misery and then just as quickly lose interest in him and drift back to looking at the piles of bananas and tomatoes.

One of soldiers puts his heavy black boot on the side of his head and presses it down into the earth. He tastes the mud in his mouth mixed with the metallic tang of his own blood.

'That will teach you to come into an authorised area without a permit from the Person Responsible! You have learned your lesson today!'

The soldiers pick over the remains of his stock but everything has either been stolen or smashed – someone has even wheeled the *tshkudu* away. The troops look at Gabriel's inert body lying in the mud, laugh and wander off, lighting up some of his cigarettes.

He lies still for ten minutes, dazed and winded with broken fingers, busted lips, cracked ribs and a broken nose. People walk past him and carry on chatting. He doesn't exist. They don't see weakness: after decades of fighting and lawlessness there is no pity left in Kivu.

Slowly he pulls his hands away from his head and looks out. One eye is closed from a kick and his whole face is swelling from the rifle butt. He sits up, sways and looks around. Painfully, he eases himself up onto one hand and then gets his legs underneath him and creaks upright, his back bent from a kick in the kidneys.

He keeps his eyes down on the ground and shuffles away from Pangi market towards the trail he came in on, his clothes ripped and covered in blood and dirt. It is going to be a long and painful walk back to the refugee camp.

What will he say to Eve when he gets there? He has lost everything. What will she think of him now?

As he shuffles past the soldiers sitting on the log one of them is trying to make his transistor radio work but it has been trodden on. He gives up, throws it on the ground, smashes the casing with the butt of his rifle, pulls the batteries out and pockets them.

They don't even look at him as he staggers past.

Chapter Five

'You stink of piss.'

Eve's older sister, Beatrice, looks at her askance and waves the flies aside that are buzzing around them.

Eve's *pagne* is soaked in urine and the wetness has spread up through the cloth and into the waist of her tee shirt. She has no more clean clothes to wear; she has gone through all the ones given to her by her family in the two weeks since the rape. She feels dirty and uncomfortable, she is wet when she lies down to sleep at night and she is wet when she wakes up in the morning. The smell of sour piss is the constant companion in her life now.

Her rape was violent, involving four men and the barrel of a rifle; the metal foresight cut her deeply. It is part of the practice of warfare in Kivu province, an attempt to destroy women and smash the society they traditionally hold together. It has left her with a fistula, a tear in the wall of her vagina into her bladder so that urine constantly seeps out.

Her family look after her but their patience is finite – many victims of rape are rejected by their husbands and thrown out of their houses. She feels lucky that her family has not done that. She is broken and ruined and knows that it is her fault. Eve's head sinks lower and she shuffles away from Beatrice.

Where is my baby?

The thought recurs in her mind at least once a minute.

The two women are squatting on the ground on a low rise overlooking the refugee camp, rows and rows of palm-leaf shelters, covered in white plastic sheeting in a sea of dark brown mud. It is morning, with a cold, grey overcast sky, there is dew on the ground and people's breath smokes. They hear the chopping of wood, a babble of voices, the hawking and spitting of old men. It smells of mud, shit and wood smoke from the cooking fires.

People are packed into the view everywhere, clothed in a clashing kaleidoscope of patterns: red, yellow, blue, green, tartans, stripes, every possible combination of brash local styles and Western cast-offs.

Women wash naked children as they stand in battered metal bowls, making them blow their noses into their fingers and then deftly flicking away the snot. Older people stand around in groups with their arms folded and talk quietly, the men dressed in tattered old suit jackets to try to maintain some dignity. They look gloomily at what their lives have become: forced by the endemic warfare from their home villages into the camps, they cannot work and have no control over their destiny.

Everywhere there are kids, running around the shacks, playing, laughing and chattering. For them this is normal life, it's what they have grown up with. They are dressed in rags, adult tee shirts that are stained and ripped and drag in the mud. All are barefoot, their feet and ankles covered in purple ulcers from cuts that weep pus. It is a noisy, hectic, dirty place to live.

Worst of all though is the fear. They have food from the UNHCR and other NGOs but they have no law and order and the constant uncertainty is etched in deep worry lines on people's faces. Militia groups can wander in from the bush at any time, just as the Kudu Noir did with Eve.

They have no protection from them. The Congolese army, the FARDC, all are as bad as the militias, which is what they were before they were put into another uniform and then not paid by the central government. As former President Mobutu famously said to those generals who asked him for salaries: 'You have rifles, why are you asking me for money?'

Rape is another one of the FARDC's specialities. As for the police, the PNC, they don't get out this far into the bush; they stay in the towns and anyway are just unpaid bandits who live on bribes.

When the Kudu Noir had finished with her, Eve couldn't walk. She crawled under the piece of corrugated iron that had been her front door to hide. It did then provide some protection for her; to cover their tracks the Kudu Noir fired a white phosphorous mortar over where they had been – the airburst shell split the night with a white flash and showered burning pieces of felt soaked in the chemical. The ground around her was covered in an impossibly bright light that spewed white smoke. Wherever the pieces touched huts they burst into flame. Peering out from under the metal sheet she could see figures running around lit by orange flames and the banana palm leaves on the edge of the camp twisting in the heat.

Her hut was burnt to cinders and with it all her possessions: a short-handled hoe for tilling her vegetable patch, a plastic basin for washing, a metal cooking pot, two pieces of *pagne* cloth, a comb, a small piece of soap, some dried cassava, three cooking utensils, a candle stub, a tee shirt. That was it, that was her life.

Eve gets up and moves painfully away from her sister. She thinks about her boyfriend Gabriel: what will he say when he gets back from his trading trip? Will he reject her like her husband?

She rubs her forehead as if she has a terrible headache.

Where is my baby?

Fang stops shouting into his BlackBerry, hangs up and returns to his armchair, facing Alex as if nothing has happened.

He shakes his head. 'I have a steel shipment on a freighter getting into Port Sudan and the harbour master is a pain in the ass. We pay him too much already and he wants more – we go to Mombasa if he don't like it.'

Alex feels slightly bemused by this but doesn't show it. 'You were saying about the Rwandan involvement in the project?'

'Yes, it's delicate because they carried out massacres in Kivu when they invaded it in the main war between 1997 and 2003. So the people there hate them and they can't send troops back in on a permanent basis. That was a big part of the international treaty at the end of the main war, that all the eight countries involved would get their troops out of Congo.' He shrugs. 'There are no good guys in Kivu. So now they have to try this.'

'So what is "this"?'

'Well, they have agreed to provide logistical support for the military operation from Rwanda. Because of the international pressure they have been under in the past and their activities in Kivu, the Congolese would not accept them just sending troops into Kivu on a long-term basis. They have been very clear about this in our negotiations.

'We are envisaging a large Battlegroup operation that cannot just appear in Kivu – it will have to be established in secret in Rwanda first and have a supply chain running through there to the Kenyan ports.'

Alex nods. His military mind is attracted by the idea; it sounds feasible. Suddenly he stops himself.

What the hell are you doing? This is not something you are going to get involved in.

He throws out more objections to try to rubbish the plan.

'OK, but what about the UN? I mean, they have substantial forces in Kivu and they are not just going to say OK to this sort of deal. It is unprecedented in modern times; the US will go mad on the Security Council. They can't just let China grab a chunk of the middle of Africa.'

He looks at Fang in exasperation, sure that he has found a way to stop the flow of smooth certainty.

Fang nods to acknowledge the point but continues undaunted.

'Yes, you are right, there are about five thousand UN troops there but the Congolese government won't tell the UN in advance of the deal. In terms of the UN troops, they are allowed into a country only at the invitation of that country's government, they don't invade places. The Congolese president will simply withdraw their invitation as part of the lease agreement and they will be confined to base and then have to leave. It will just be presented as a *fait accompli* and there is nothing that the UN or the US will be able to do about it. If a sovereign state decides to lease some of its territory then it can do it.

'You are right though – they won't like it. But China and Russia will veto any action that the US want to take through the Security Council. The Americans don't have any troops anywhere near the area; there is nothing they can do about it. The Congolese President will issue a decree and sign the province over to us and then it is Year Zero for the Republic of Kivu. We'll have free range to start again and build a new country.' He shrugs. 'Although we may keep some UN troops on to continue policing work – we will see how it goes because they could be useful. No one in Kivu is very keen on them. They have been there since 2003 and they haven't stopped the fighting. They stop it blowing up into an inter-national war but they have been pretty ineffectual at bringing law and order. The province is just a series of fiefdoms run by different local groups.'

At this point Alex gets annoyed. 'Well OK, but *what about* the local people? I mean, have you consulted them about this?'

Fang makes a *moue* but continues, 'Well, the project is being developed with local political partners, the whole government will be run by them. We have found a local politician without links to any of the militias and he has agreed to be our front man.' He looks at Alex pointedly and then adds, 'I mean, you have to be realistic here, Mr Devereux – there really is very little government in Kivu. That's the problem. There is some control in the areas around the main towns but outside that it is anarchy. There are thousands of rapes there every year. For most people government just doesn't exist. This operation will establish law and order and give them the hope of a bright economic future.'

Alex sighs: he isn't getting very far with puncturing the plan. He holds up his hands in acceptance of this.

'All right, all right, I accept all that. But why does China want to be there in the first place? I mean, if it's so awful?'

'Ah, well. You see, you have a very Western view on Africa. Your media portrays it only as a basket case, a land of poverty and starvation or, even worse, a place full of smiley people who dance a lot.'

Alex has to nod ruefully; the shallow and patronising

nature of most Western media coverage of African issues is a bugbear for him.

'But in China, we see Africa as a long-term investment opportunity. The main thing we want in Kivu are minerals. The trade in tin, gold and coltan is worth about two hundred million dollars a year at the moment because it is all artisanal mining, just guys with hammers and spades. But once we get in there and mechanise it, it will be worth billions.

'The main mineral we want is coltan: columbite-tantalum. We need the tantalum for pinhead capacitors in things like mobile phones, laptops and game consoles.'

Fang grins, thinking about the future. 'When we get going, the profit margins will be immense! But apart from that, we have big plans to develop the agriculture export trade in Kivu. It's very fertile and has a great climate. We want to use Goma airport as an export hub for cut flowers, fruit and veg to the Middle East and Europe. We'll come to rival Kenya pretty quickly and the return on capital will be very attractive.

'The other big draw for us is that we are building the Chinese corridor from Tanzania to Sudan, up through the middle of Africa to open the whole continent up to trade, and we can't put the railway through Kivu at the moment because of the fighting so we need to pacify the province first.' He grins and points at Alex. 'That's your job, Mr Devereux.'

Joseph has just raped a woman.

He has never had sex before and is not sure what he thinks about it. His confusion is not helped by the fact that he is drunk on home-brewed beer. He staggers back across the bumpy ground following Lieutenant Karuta towards the firelight. It is dark and the FDLR troops have made a big campfire in the centre of the village to accompany their ongoing celebrations. He can see figures around it silhouetted in the firelight and hear them singing and shouting.

Everyone in the platoon is drunk, they have been eating and drinking all afternoon, stuffing themselves after months hiding out in the deep bush in western Kivu province.

Joseph stumbles along, doing up his trousers. Lieutenant Karuta regards what has just happened as a rite of passage for an FDLR soldier and led the initiation on the woman that he had hamstrung in the maize field in the morning. She had only crawled a few hundred yards by the time they got to her in the evening and it was easy to follow the marks on the ground and the bloodstains smeared on the maize stems. More men are finishing their business behind them.

They rejoin the main group and the men leer and wink at Joseph. He's the youngest in the platoon and a new recruit. He's a rather gormless-looking boy, heavily built and with shaggy hair from months in the bush. They giggle and pass him a gourd; he sits down on a log looking dazed, drinks deep and then stares into the bonfire.

After a while, the initiation continues – they blindfold him and make him walk around the fire. The soldiers have fun shouting and pushing him about and he feels scared.

'Now you do target practice, boy!'

'What?'

He feels Lieutenant Karuta's hot, sweaty arm around his shoulder and his beery breath in his face. 'Come on, you fought well today but you need to learn how to fight better.'

He leads Joseph away from the fire and then a rifle is shoved into his hands. He fumbles around, gets hold of it properly and slips his finger onto the trigger.

'Whoa, whoa! Careful!'

Men around him laugh.

'I can't see.'

'Doesn't matter, just point the gun here.'

Karuta's rough hands guide his so that the rifle is pointing slightly downwards.

'Now select automatic.'

He clicks the small lever on the casing downward, proud that he can do it blindfold.

'OK, now give it the magazine.'

Joseph pulls the trigger and thirty bullets blast out.

A howl of laughter goes up around him and Karuta claps him on the back.

'Heh! Well done, Hutu boy!'

Joseph grins, not sure what he has done, and tentatively pushes up the blindfold.

Sitting on the ground in front of him with her back propped up against a log, her hands tied behind her and a rag stuffed in her mouth is the woman from the maize field. Her body is riddled with bullet holes, her face looks ridiculous with the mouth wedged open with rags but there is an expression of terror frozen in her eyes.

Joseph stares at her aghast.

Karuta carries on laughing. 'You see how easy it is to kill someone! Come on!' He throws his arm around him again and wheels him back to the fire where there is another huge cheer as he stumbles in.

Joseph is numb.

'Hey, come on!' Karuta shakes him and starts singing a war song to get him over it. He jabs his rifle in the air and shouts at the men to get on their feet. They all jump up, grab their rifles and start jogging on the spot, shaking their rifles in time. Their black faces gleam silver with sweat in the firelight as they sing the words over and over again.

> Hutu boy, why are you sitting down?
> Kill your enemy!
> *Kwa! Kwa! Kwa!*

They make machete gestures with their free hands.

> Hutu boy, why are you sitting down?
> Kill your enemy!
> *Kwa! Kwa! Kwa!*

Chapter Six

Sophie's car pulls up to the barrier and the soldier steps towards her window. He is heavy-set with a fuzz of stubble and a sergeant's stripes on his uniform.

She winds down her window and he leans his rifle on the ledge.

'Your papers! Where is your accreditation?' he says in the aggressive, officious tones of Congolese officials. She smells beer on his breath. As he leans in to take the documents his wrist stretches from his sleeve and she sees he is wearing three gold watches.

Six other soldiers stand around the car. Their faces are impassive but their eyes flick back and forth watching everything, rifles held across their chests, fingers on their triggers.

Usually white NGO workers are regarded as neutral in the multi-sided conflict in the province and only get minor hassle for bribes rather than serious assaults. They float around in white Land Cruisers like some magic tribe with 'No weapons' stickers on the windshield (an AK-47 with a red cross over it) proclaiming their neutrality, but Sophie still feels nervous. The edge of the manila folder in her grasp is damp with sweat.

She opens it to show the sergeant. 'All our papers are in

order and we have our *permit à voyager* here.' She shows him the document on the top of the stack in the folder.

He grunts in reply and takes it from her.

'You are in a security zone, this is a military installation here!' He points at the cement block building with a rusting corrugated iron roof and ochre paint that is flaking off like a skin disease. Bullet holes are dotted across the front of it and there is a larger one where an RPG exploded. Piles of rubbish and plastic bags are caught in the grass and bushes around it. The ground on either side has been used as a latrine by the soldiers and drivers. 'You must park over there, switch off the engine and deposit the key with the security manager for safekeeping.' He points to a teenager with a rifle. 'I will confirm your accreditation with the captain.'

He snatches the folder away from her and marches into the building.

She glances nervously across at Nicolas who calmly reverses the vehicle and parks off the road where the teenager is pointing. He then reluctantly hands over the keys and they sit and wait in tense silence. Sophie gets out and paces up and down, glancing at her watch and the building. Nicolas leans against the jeep and lights a cigarette.

Five minutes later the sergeant comes marching back out with the folder and strides up to her.

'There is a problem with your documents. You must come and see the captain.'

'What?'

'Your *permit à voyager* is not present, you must see the captain to explain yourself!'

Sophie is incredulous and stares at him. 'My *permit à voyager*?'

'Yes.'

51

'It was on the top of the folder.'

'There is no permit.'

'It was on the top of the folder.' She raises her voice and gestures at him in exasperation, trying to think how he could have missed it. She is tired, hungry, frazzled and desperate to get to the clinic. Her frustration boils over. 'It was right there! I showed it to you!' She snatches the folder from his hand, opens it and shows him the place where the blue document had been.

The sergeant stiffens and glares at her angrily.

Nicolas is suddenly at her side. 'Ah, Monsieur le Directeur, can I offer you a cigarette?'

The sergeant brushes him aside and grabs the folder back from Sophie, jabbing his finger at her and shouting, 'You are in contravention of regulations on a military installation! You must see the captain immediately!'

Four other soldiers run over and stand around him.

Sophie glares back at him, refusing to be intimidated. 'We have vaccines – humanitarian aid – in the Land Cruiser that will go off in an hour's time if we don't get it to the clinic! This is for the children of the Congo! Your children! OK, fine, let's go and see the captain!'

She marches off towards the building and the sergeant and the four soldiers hurry after her. He pushes in front of her as she gets to the door and then halts outside a chipped and scratched inner door. He knocks and then opens it and walks in, Sophie follows; she is so angry she is not afraid.

The room is bare with grey breeze block walls and a hurricane lamp hanging from the ceiling. The captain sits behind an old plywood desk which is empty except for an old IBM PC and keyboard with a power lead but no plug. He stares up angrily at the commotion of their entry; both the sergeant and Sophie's faces are flushed with anger.

They both start talking at the same time.

'Here is the illegal traveller!'

'The *permit à voyager* was on the top of the folder! I showed it to him when he took it off me, you know you have it! I have vaccines to deliver in an hour or they will be ruined!'

The captain sits and looks at her insolently from his chair, head on one side.

'We can issue you with an emergency *permit à voyager* for a thousand dollars.'

'A thousand dollars! Jesus Christ!' She looks at him as if he is an idiot. 'We don't pay bribes. Where do you think I am going to get that kind of money!' She turns and points angrily at the sergeant next to her. 'You had it! This is ridiculous! Can we stop playing . . .'

The captain bangs the table and is on his feet in one fluid move. He switches from angry insolence to rage in the blink of an eye. He moves round the desk to stand in front of her and pulls his pistol out of his holster at the same time. The gun suddenly looks very large and solid as he points it at her.

'You are an alien travelling without the correct documentation! You are coming in here and making accusations against my men! You come in to my office and you do not salute me! Why do you not salute me?'

He slaps her across the face with his left hand.

Sophie is stunned. No one has ever hit her before or threatened her with a gun.

Her indignation suddenly turns to helpless terror and a feeling of total powerlessness. She has overstepped the magic line that surrounds white NGO workers, pushed her luck too far and broken the spell. She is in a small room with five large men. She now knows what it is like to be a local Congolese, totally at the mercy of the men with guns.

There is nothing she can do, no clever argument, no grand family connections, no degree from Oxford, no right or law that she can wave at them to stop them doing whatever they want to her.

Chapter Seven

The megaphone crackles and squawks, 'Move up!' and Eve dutifully shuffles forward in the line of refugees.

The local Red Cross worker at the head of the line wears a fluorescent yellow waistcoat over his white Red Cross tee shirt. He wears the megaphone on a strap over his shoulder, holding a clipboard in one hand and the microphone and a pen in the other. He looks harassed as he tries to tick people off his list and keep the food distribution session under control. It's only a small refugee camp, at Ikozi in south Kivu, just off the road from Bukavu out to Shabunda, but it still has five thousand people and is chaotic.

A former headmaster who lives in the camp helps him by measuring out the rice from sacks piled on the ground into the battered bowls and tatty sacks that people have brought with them.

Eve never wanted this passive life and it still feels alien to her. She was used to the hard work of village life: cooking, washing, tending the family vegetable patch. She is just an average girl with average dreams: she hopes one day to get the money to buy a hand-cranked sewing machine so she can set up as a seamstress and repair and make clothes.

Life has been pretty hard to her so far though. Her first husband, Bertrand, left her when she gave birth to an albino baby, regarding it as unclean. Eve's own mother had shrieked with fear when the baby had emerged and run out of the hut. Bertrand left to return to his home village and she hasn't heard from him since.

Some people do want albinos though. Hundreds are kidnapped and murdered in East Africa every year, their body parts dried and used as charms: tied to fishermen's nets in Lake Kivu to attract a good catch, ground into powder and sprinkled by miners on the sides of their pits to draw precious metals to the surface, strapped to the front of traders' trucks to bring them good fortune on journeys.

Where is my baby?

The thought of little Marie cut up and used in one of those scenarios is too much to bear.

Gabriel is the only piece of good news in her life. He met her when he was travelling through her village and was fascinated by her calm manner. The other girls teased Eve about him because he was so ugly. He wouldn't have been Eve's first pick but, as one of her friends said, love is a choice as well and in her circumstances she had to be realistic.

Gabriel is certainly ugly and he scares her sometimes with his intensity but he does also make her laugh. He is always so intent on impressing her, going on about his grand plans, angry in his desire to make money. He talks about his schemes for hours, using terms he has learned and that she doesn't understand: brand value, profit margins, return on investment. She just sits and looks blank as he rants at her.

After a while though, he eases up and starts talking about people he has met on his travels. She has never travelled outside her village, but he has been all over the province, to the main towns of Goma, Bukavu and Uvira in the south and even as far as Beni in the goldfields in the far north. When he relaxes he can make her laugh with his stories about scrapes he has got into and deals he has done. That's when she likes him, when his big jaw opens in a wide white grin and his prominent stomach shakes with laughter. They used to sit on the bench outside her hut and laugh and chat.

She hasn't heard from him in a while though; he is overdue from his latest journey. She wonders what has happened to him – will he reject her because of the rape?

'Move up!'

She shuffles forward and the headmaster bustles around, directing people to fill up their sacks and watching carefully that they don't take too much. She hands over the chit for her family and then heaves the sack onto her back and walks away slowly and painfully.

Alex is showing Fang back out to his chauffeur-driven car parked on the gravel drive in front of the house. The April shower has passed and they make small talk about the weather and the best route back to London.

Alex is relieved that the meeting is over; he isn't going to take the mission but he feels strangely disconcerted and cannot work out why.

As he gets to the car Fang turns and shakes his hand. The two tall men stand facing each other.

'I realise that Operation Tiananmen is very large scale and takes a while to get used to but I am confident that once you have had time to think about it you will want to be involved. It would be the largest operation you could ever command.'

Alex smiles politely. 'Well, thank you very much for your

time in coming here today to explain it to me.' He shakes the man's hand.

He waves the car off as it moves away into the distance down the mile-long drive through the parkland until it passes the beech copse and is lost. He turns and looks at the dogs sitting at the top of the stone steps – his father's two black labs, Bert and Audrey, that he inherited along with the title and estate when Sir Nicholas died a little while back.

The dogs miss the old man but Alex doesn't. His father had been another Blues and Royals officer, a cantankerous alcoholic who had beaten his wife and whose influence had blighted Alex's career in the regiment. He refused to let Alex go to university, which in the army, effectively barred him from promotion to colonel. Apart from which, in the small and snobbish world of the Household Cavalry, the reputation of drunkenness attached to the Devereux name had always made it hard for Alex to prove himself in the regiment.

His father's final summation of his career had come in an argument over the phone during which he had shouted, 'If you hadn't been such a fucking failure, the family wouldn't be in the mess it is!' Alex had been struggling to disprove this assessment ever since.

Although Alex bears a grudge against his father and the British upper class, he isn't going to bear one against the dogs. They need a walk, having been locked up in the kitchen during the meeting.

'Come on!' he says and walks off briskly round the corner of the house to the rose gardens in front of the Regency façade. The shower has blown over a trellis and he fossicks about, tutting and putting it back up. After that he spends a while throwing an old tennis ball for the dogs and they tangle with each other on the lawn.

He looks out over the parkland and then walks back round, entering the house from the other end through the door on the terrace into the library that he uses as his study in the red-brick Tudor section of the house. His desk is surrounded with piles of old copies of the *Economist* and periodicals from Chatham House, Royal United Services Institute, International Crisis Group and other defence think-tanks. The dogs jostle after him, puffing and grinning and wagging their tails. Now he has got his meeting out of the way he wonders what he will do today.

Life proceeds at a pretty slow pace. The repairs on the house are nearing completion, paid for with the money from his last big operation in Russia. It had fallen into disrepair as a result of his father's drinking but has now been restored to something like its former glory: the roof has been redone, the dry rot sorted out and the gardens replanted. He's got a final meeting in Hereford with the English Heritage surveyor but that's not until next week.

Alex stops and realises he really is feeling unsettled by the meeting with Fang. He was supposed to be the Englishman at home in his castle, lord of all he surveys, and yet on a personal level he feels unnerved.

It was like sitting in a room with a global business droid looking at him through the narrow metal vision slits of his titanium glasses. He was a commercial chameleon, with a different name for every market he operated in, a multi-tasking, open-sourcing, integrated business platform capable of working simultaneously in multiple time zones. The guy was ten years younger than him but he was the one driving the meeting, the man in a hurry who wasn't taking any prisoners. If Alex didn't accept the project he would just find another way – like his steel delivery in Port Sudan.

Alex wondered where did the business stop and the person start? The answer was nowhere. Fang was a money-making organism, unimpeded by morality or etiquette. He ate, slept and breathed money.

It wasn't just the personality though. It's the scale and audacity of the vision he presented that makes Alex feel old and out of date. He was talking about infrastructure projects to open up an entire continent. There was a tone of disdain in the way Fang talked about the Western view of Africa and how his was the new vision for the future.

And maybe he was right? Alex had done his best to trip him up but he hadn't managed to even make him stumble; the businessman had it all covered.

But the idea was bonkers.

It was all very well being young and enthusiastic and having visions about new world orders, but Iraq and Afghanistan had shown very well how the law of unintended consequences came into play when you started naively messing around with other people's countries.

Where was the exit strategy?

What the hell *would* the US and the UN say to it all?

The road to hell is paved with good intentions.

Alex pauses in thought and then turns and makes his way through the oak-panelled library, the dogs following him. He goes into the medieval hall and then walks across its huge stone flags and into the large archway that leads up into the fortified tower. This is the original part of the house from the time when the area was the lawless Welsh Marches, prone to invasions and cattle rustling from Welsh bandits across the border.

The eighty-foot-high tower has thick stone walls and he walks up the spiral staircase, stepping in the groove worn into the stone by generations of his ancestors' feet. He is feeling disconcerted and defensive and somehow the tower feels the right place to be.

He walks up to the top, opens the narrow wooden door and stands at the battlements. The dogs accompany him and sit smiling up at him uncertainly. The various roofs of the house are below him with their pointed gables and gargoyles, the gardens, parklands and outhouses all clearly visible.

But Alex stares out over them at the magnificent green hills beyond.

The captain glares at Sophie, his eyes wide and angry; white spittle flecks his upper lip. She stares at the black hole of his pistol muzzle. It's 9mm across but looks much larger.

The soldier behind her pushes her in the back with his rifle and she stumbles forward onto her knees in front of him.

Sophie is terrified and starts babbling, 'I'm sorry, terribly sorry, Captain. It's all a mistake, a terrible mistake. Forgive me please!'

The door behind her opens and Nicolas slips into the room, speaking quietly and with a large fan of twenty-dollar bills in his outstretched hand. He has hurriedly fished them out of the emergency stock that he carries wrapped in a plastic bag in the petrol tank of the Land Cruiser.

'Ah, Monsieur le Directeur, here is the payment for the *permit à voyager*, our sincere apologies for forgetting to buy one before we set out.'

He proffers them towards the captain, keeping his eyes and head down. The captain looks down at him. The intrusion has broken the violent tension in the room and the money is what he really wants. Somewhere in the back of his head he also knows that killing or injuring a white NGO worker would cause a fuss and could get him into trouble.

His ego has been assuaged by the grovelling of the woman on her knees in front of him; she looks pathetic. Nicolas is also in a suitably fawning posture and he takes the offer of a ladder to climb down. He grabs the money from his hand. 'Get out of my office! Your paperwork will be issued in due course, when we are ready. Wait in your vehicle.'

Nicolas hustles Sophie out of the office and hurries her over to the Land Cruiser with his arm around her. Natalie is sitting on the backseat looking anxious.

'What happened?'

Sophie gets into the backseat next to her, white as a sheet and shaking. The American goes to put her arm around her.

'I'm fine!' Sophie pushes her away, forcing herself to get a grip. 'I'm fine! We just had some issues, that's all, they're sorting it out. We just have to wait a while.'

With that she shifts away from Natalie and stares out of the window. Natalie looks stunned and gazes out of the opposite window. Nicolas sits in the driver's seat and waits patiently. The soldiers have their keys so they can't go anywhere. Time is running out for the vaccines but there is nothing they can do. No one can even bring themselves to look at the building, they are too scared of it.

After ten minutes of strained silence Sophie says, 'I'm just getting some air,' slips out, walks away from the car and stands looking at the view, feeling the gentle breeze blow over her.

She stays like that for an age, in a numb trance of her own thoughts. Time ticks on and the sun suddenly drops out of the sky; they're on the equator and there is only a short sunset. It gets chilly straightaway at six thousand feet and she goes back to the car to get her brightly coloured Kenyan shawl.

Eventually at seven o'clock the captain has judged that

he has inconvenienced them enough and the sergeant walks back over to the car with their permit tucked back in its original place on the top of the folder. He hands the keys wordlessly back to Nicolas who accepts them with profuse gratitude.

They drive away from the shabby little station and some of the tension drains from them. Natalie mutters, 'Thank the Lord,' but otherwise they don't talk – Nicolas because he is comfortable driving in silence, Natalie because she is afraid of Sophie and is now crying quietly on the backseat, and Sophie because she is shocked but also because she is furious.

She is furious at the soldiers for their pigheaded, money-grubbing wickedness and contempt for the people of their own country. The journey has been a complete waste, the vaccines are lukewarm and she will have to explain to the local field workers that she has wasted their time and effort and made them look stupid in front of the desperate people who are crying out for their help.

However, she is most furious with herself. She can hear a recording of her voice playing in her head pleading with the captain: 'I'm sorry, terribly sorry, Captain. It's all a mistake, a terrible mistake. Forgive me please!'

Pathetic! Utterly pathetic!

She rages at herself, staring into the night as the car headlights swing back and forth following the road down to the clinic at Tshabura. The indignity of it; Cecil-Blacks were not born to grovel. It goes against every fibre of her being. Her family would be ashamed of her if they knew. She is ashamed of herself.

Yet she did it. The memory of what happened in the grubby little office will stay locked up with her never to be revealed to anyone.

They finally arrive at the clinic at eight o'clock. The local workers run out anxiously holding up lanterns to greet them. Sophie immediately switches back into professional mode, addressing the circle. 'I'm sorry we are late; we were stopped at a checkpoint. I'm sorry, the vaccines are . . .' She shakes her head and looks round at the deflated faces in the lamplight.

She tries to be upbeat. 'Look, we can try again next month, I'll get onto the UN and we'll do it by helicopter next time.'

But they remain downcast; to her their expressions seem to say, 'Hoping for anything in Kivu always brings disappointment. This place will never improve.' She feels awful.

They drive the car through the high metal gates of the compound. Like any NGO facility it has items of value that could be stolen so it's surrounded by rolls of barbed wire and there are two watchmen with old shotguns and machetes.

They have a brief meal of *foufou*, tomato paste and beer and then they are shown to their rooms. As project manager, Sophie gets the luxury of a room to herself across the other side of the compound, a bare, cement-floored place with a camp bed and a candle on a chipped plate.

She sits on the bed in the dim candlelight. Now that she is finally alone her deepest reaction to the turmoil finally comes storming out of her. It's not that her pride and dignity have been offended – though they have – it's the memory of her utter helplessness and loss of control that makes her shake with rage. She bends forwards and clenches her fists in front of her face until the knuckles go white. In her mind's eye she can see the faces of the captain and the sergeant.

'*Bastards!*' she mutters through clenched teeth.

She is a humanitarian charity worker who has made sacrifices and striven hard to get where she is and is passionately committed to her work. She knows that if she had a gun and those men were in front of her now she would calmly shoot each one of them in the head and enjoy doing it.

Chapter Eight

Alex taps the end of a wedge into a log with a sledge-hammer and then pounds away at it, swinging the hammer high and smashing down blows repeatedly with all his might.

He is splitting logs out on the estate. The wood divides neatly and the two halves fall over and rock back and forth on the ground until they are still. Alex stands frozen for a long time, looking down at them with the hammer still held in his hands, its head resting on the ground.

That evening he finds he can't sit still in the drawing room by the fire and starts wandering around the huge, silent house. He opens doors into long-forgotten rooms and stands looking at the dustsheets covering the furniture, remembering scenes from his childhood.

Some of them are happy but a lot are uncomfortable: the noise of angry shouting and blows from his parents' room, his father passed out drunk on the dining room floor with the dogs settled around him for company.

He walks around the main hall with its large portraits of Devereuxs hung between the high stained-glass windows. He stares up at the pictures: an Elizabethan knight with his head held rigid by a huge lace collar worn over a breastplate, a fleshy Georgian reclining in front of a bucolic scene on the estate, a pompous Victorian in a black uniform with his sword held stiffly at his side.

Communing with his ancestors, that's what he's doing. Reliving the sense of what it means to be a Devereux. Throughout the ages they were soldiers – hardly any merchants or lawyers and certainly no priests or artists. Active, restless, aggressive men who had served the Crown all over the world, commanding troops and smiting its enemies with sword and shot. The house is littered with relics from their campaigns, shields and spears from Asia and Africa.

His father might have been an ineffectual aberration but with Alex the genes are back on track. From his army schooling at Wellington (motto 'Sons of Heroes') to his professional career, he is an aggressive and successful commander of men. It's what he does.

He looks at the dark doorway into the tower and crosses over to it, not turning on the light, he knows the distances. As he walks up the stone stairs each step becomes slower than the last until he pauses on a landing by a suit of armour and walks down a narrow, low corridor.

He used to play a game here with his sister, Georgina, when they were children, daring each other to come to this place. His hand finds the light switch and clicks it on. A weak bulb illuminates the short passageway.

Staring at him from the wall at the end of the corridor is a small picture, a foot high with a small title under it: Sir Henry Devereux, 1294–1356.

When Sir Henry had inherited the Devereux lands and title, they had fallen into decay and were under threat from the lawlessness of the times. He had immediately set about the problem by visiting every village in his lands and those just across the border from his and making a point of hanging a man in every one. From then on he was known as Black Hal and is still regarded as a bogeyman in the family.

The head and shoulders painting is by an itinerant Italian painter, with the crude flattened perspective of the day. It looks very formulaic and he is dressed in his armour in a very stiff pose. Even so, the artist has captured something about the man – there is a cold look in his eyes that warned of cruel violence if he was crossed.

Alex stands and looks at him for a while before switching out the light and returning down the darkened tower.

Eve's father, Laurent, looks round the circle of men.

'So, what are we going to do?'

He is fifty but looks seventy; his face is worn and creased like an old shoe. His eyes are rheumy and his voice rasps. He wears a tattered brown suit jacket, jeans and a grubby blue baseball cap and is sitting on a three-legged stool outside his shack in the refugee camp.

Sitting on logs and beer crates around him are the men of his extended family and in a half circle in front of him are the men of Gabriel's family. Some older women sit on the ground behind them. A week has passed since Gabriel staggered back in from his disaster at Pangi market. He sits to one side of the circle, his face still horribly swollen, his body covered in cuts and bruises.

The two families have come together to discuss what to do with him and Eve. She is squatting behind the shack with her two sisters as her fate is decided.

Laurent scans the ring of fourteen older men around him looking gloomy and awkward, holding their chins in their hands. Their faces are lined with fear from the perpetual uncertainty that they live with and their skin is grey rather than black from lack of food. Kivu has rich soils and high rainfall but no one can grow any proper crops because they never know when the militias will come and steal them, so they subsist on cassava – easy to grow but nutritionally poor.

No one wants to respond to Laurent's question but Gabriel's uncle Alphonse is famously tactless. 'Well, it doesn't look good for her. I mean, first she produces a *muzunga* and then she gets raped. I think she's cursed. Why else did the Kudu Noir come for her? Evil attracts evil, that's what I say. Besides she stinks of piss.'

There is outraged murmuring and head-shaking from Eve's family but none actively disagree with him: he has said what they are all thinking. She is a burden on them with her wound.

Gabriel clears his throat. Since he heard the news about her rape, he has been thinking about something and knows he has to come out with it now.

'Well, I want to get married to her.'

'What!' There is an outburst from his family.

His father, Bertrand, turns and looks at him. 'What do you mean, you stupid child? She's been raped, she's probably got HIV! She leaks piss the whole time. How can you marry a girl like that?'

Gabriel knows it is a ridiculous idea but since he saw her after it happened he has been mixed up with conflicting emotions. He feels a failure for losing all his money but he feels that he can still give her love to make up for the wrong that has been inflicted on her. He is young and strong, he will make it work. Someone will show compassion in this country.

He has been thinking it through and has some answers for his father. 'We can send her to Panzi hospital.'

'What?'

'It's that place in Bukavu where they stitch up rape victims.

They can test her for HIV and if they can stitch her up then we can get married.'

'Oh, and how much is that going to cost? You haven't got any money, if you hadn't noticed!' The loss has had to be shared by Gabriel's family who are very angry about it.

Eve's father senses he is onto something here though. Normally they would have to pay a dowry to marry her off anyway, and they know she is damaged goods, so this might be a way out of the problem.

'Well, we can give some money,' he suggests. He looks round at his male relatives. They look unenthusiastic but they don't disagree.

'Yes!' Gabriel is encouraged. 'We could split it – if they give half then I'll get the other half.'

'And how are you going to get that? You haven't got any stock left.' His father is always hard on him. But his father is also right, his capital has been wiped out.

However, Gabriel has been thinking of something else radical whilst he's been lying in his hut recovering.

'I'll go to the mines! I'll make a packet there!'

There's an intake of breath around the circle.

His father looks at him. 'Don't be ridiculous, people die in the mines the whole time! The militia will just steal your money.'

'Well, it's dangerous everywhere, isn't it!' Gabriel glares back at him and jabs a hand towards his bruised and cut face.

Bertrand grumbles and looks down.

Alex wakes up in the morning after his evening of communing with his ancestors and knows that he will make the decision to call Fang.

As soon as he heard the idea of the mission, a certainty

70

arose in his mind that he shouldn't do it and yet in exactly the same instant another feeling arose in his heart that he would do it. It was really just a matter of time until his rational side came up with a series of arguments to justify the decision.

Who was he trying to kid that he would be happy living the rest of his life as a provincial gentleman, fossicking around in the rose garden pinning up trellises?

Sure he has all the money he needs now but that hasn't proved to be the point. His dream of domestic contentment is eluding him like smoke: the more he frantically tries to grasp it, the more it dissipates.

Instead, what he finds is that whenever he sits still his cloud of personal demons settles on him like horseflies, biting and goading him to move on. Is this some curse of the Devereuxs? The restlessness that drove his father to drink?

He remembers a line from Latin lessons at school. In *The Aeneid* it is said of Achilles: 'His fame and his doom went hand in hand.'

Is that him? Driven on by an aggressive nature, an illustrious history and a need to compensate for the failings of his father, into ever-greater acts of daring that will eventually undo him?

He lies in bed and thinks, 'Am I afraid of peace? Why must I always be at war?'

In the end he is just like Black Hal, an aggressive character with a need to offset his internal conflicts by imposing control on external anarchy. Kivu will be a brave new world and his personal salvation all rolled into one.

Alex gets up, goes for his run and thinks about the problem as he slogs up a hill.

What was it that Camus said? 'All great ideas have absurd beginnings.' They all sound ridiculous when you first hear them because they are so radically different from what has been before. But after the idea has been implemented it becomes the orthodoxy and no one can think of doing it any other way. Maybe Fang's vision is the new world order for developing countries.

He could call Yamba or Col and just discuss it? They are his two partners in Team Devereux, the mainstays of his military operations. Both are in their late forties so in their company it is Alex who is the young challenger. Yamba Douala is a tall, severe-looking Angolan who fought for the legendary South African 32 Battalion in the long bush war in his country. He is a thinker, he wanted to be a surgeon when he was a boy and is currently using his money from their last operation to set up a health clinic back in his home province in Angola.

Colin Thwaites is a short, aggressive Northerner, formerly a sergeant major in the Parachute Regiment's elite Pathfinder unit. He is currently using his money from their last operation to get drunk in a large house he has bought for himself outside Blackburn where he grew up.

As Alex comes back down the hill towards the house, he finally resorts to the lowest common denominator approach to the problem.

'If the Chinese don't recruit me they will just get someone else to do it. The project is going to happen, so it might as well be me.' It is not actually a logical argument but in his suggestible state of mind it works for him.

He showers, has breakfast and sits down at his large desk in his study. He picks up the phone and thinks whom he will call first.

Advice is what we ask for when we know the decision we are going to take but are not yet ready to take it.

Of the two men, Yamba is the more prone to hypothetical

discussions. Col's blunt nature means he needs to make a black and white decision on an issue in a maximum of three seconds and is usually pretty scathing about it when he does.

Alex dials a number in Angola and waits as it rings.

Chapter Nine

'Hello, hello, welcome to Panzi hospital! My name is Mama Riziki and this is Mama Jeanne and Mama Lumo!'

The head counsellor, Mama Riziki, is cheerfully upbeat, an ample middle-aged woman in a multi-coloured dress and matching headcloth with a fake Louis Vuitton handbag hooked over her shoulder. She points to two similarly smiling women standing next to her. They are both brightly dressed ladies from the town of Bukavu up the road, unlike the four peasant girls that have come in to the hospital from the bush. Mama Riziki has been doing this job for years and knows that she has to cheer up these poor traumatised rape victims. One is only eleven.

'So, ladies, we are here to make sure that you enjoy your stay at Panzi and you go home healed and well. Some people are here for over a year and we will all become a big happy family.'

Mama Lumo butts in, 'Yes, and when you go home they won't recognise you, because we will feed you lots of rice and you will get big and fat like me.'

The induction session is happening on one side of the main hallway of the single-storey hospital building. A woman patient who is leaning against the wall chips in, 'Yes, look at my hair. My husband won't recognise me when I get back.

Mama Jeanne did it for me.' She touches her elaborately plaited hair and they both giggle with glee.

Eve is sitting on a bench with three other girls who also arrived that day. They all have the smell of stale urine hanging around them and one of them is pregnant. Eve has been feeling very nervous and awkward and so far has only talked quietly to one girl called Miriam, but the typical Congolese banter is beginning to cheer her up and she smiles nervously.

It's just what Eve needs to get her out of her shell-shocked, stigmatised mood. The taxi driver who brought her to Bukavu initially didn't want her in his minivan and demanded extra payment because she was unlucky. He made a big fuss about getting plastic sacks put on the seat so she didn't leak urine on it and no one sat next to her the whole journey.

But when the security guard shut the hospital gate behind her and she was inside the compound, Eve suddenly felt safe. It is the first time in years that she has had the feeling of being protected from the men with guns.

Mama Riziki is pleased with the girls' smiles and beams back at them.

'OK, so when you are under the care of your Mamas here you will do lots of things. You will help with cooking and cleaning in the hospital and we will keep you busy, oh very busy, with lots of courses. You can do bookkeeping or tailoring . . .'

'Yes, and cooking with me . . .'

'And I'll do medicine and hygiene.'

The courses help to keep the women busy and heal the psychological wounds of the rape as the surgeons stitch up the tears and gunshot wounds in their genito-urinary tracts to stop them urinating and defecating uncontrollably.

'We will always make sure you leave here healed and ready

to go back to your families. Sometimes it does take one or two or maybe three operations before the tears heal but we will always be with you. Praise God for your arrival here today!' Panzi is a Pentecostal-funded hospital and Mama Riziki prays over them.

Eve bows her head and prays hard. She knows her family doesn't have the money to let her stay for more than one operation.

'Yamba, hi, it's Alex.'

A guffaw of delighted laughter comes down the line.

'What?'

The cackling continues in such an infectious way that Alex starts laughing as well. Eventually, they both draw breath.

'Alex Devereux,' Yamba says his name and hoots again.

Alex grins and waits.

'It's good to hear from you.'

'It's good to hear you too.'

There was a pause as they both absorbed the pleasure of hearing an old friend's voice after a long time. They have had only sporadic email contact since the end of the last mission.

Yamba is someone Alex feels at home with. It is an odd combination – public school cavalry officers aren't often seen with Angolan mercenaries – but the two of them have been through a lot together. More important than shared experience are their shared values: a fierce, self-reliant professionalism offset by a black sense of humour.

'How are you, man?' Alex asks.

'Yees, OK . . .' Yamba says, smiling and nodding thoughtfully. 'How are you?'

'Yeah, OK.'

'How is your hut?'

'My hut? Oh, yeah, it's good, thanks,' Alex says, looking around at his house. 'It's got a new roof.'

'Oh? Like a thatched roof or maybe some tin, yes?'

Alex laughs again. 'Yeah, that's right, I got a piece of tin from the market, fits really well.'

'And have you got yourself a wife yet?'

Alex guffaws. 'No.'

'Ah, you are behind the curve,' Yamba says with relish; he loves using new idioms that he has picked up.

'I know, I haven't even got divorced yet. What about you, have you got a bird?'

'No,' Yamba laughs. 'I have taken up cooking and most African women think I am gay when I tell them I cook,' he cackles. 'But I have a little lady friend who I visit in Luanda every now and then.'

'A la-dy . . .' Alex says in a ridiculously suggestive tone.

Yamba laughs.

'And how are the poor and sick of Angola?'

'Oh, they keep dying on me.'

'Oh . . .'

'Yes, I shout at them and tell them not to but they just don't listen to me.'

Yamba is known as a strict disciplinarian with the soldiers he commands. He joined 32 Battalion as a teenager after his family had been killed by the communists and rose to the rank of sergeant major in a vicious bush war. He always wanted to be a surgeon.

He was educated at a Jesuit school as a boy – was head boy in fact – and the religious order's disciplined morality has stayed with him. He admired Father Joao's tough asceticism and still has him in his mind as the epitome of what a real man should be. It all shows in his appearance: six feet two, lean, shaven-headed. His face is as daunting as a dark cliff with lines like rivulets worn into it by exercise, self-denial and hardship.

'How's the clinic going?'

'Oh, OK, you know. I bribe the right people in the Ministry of Health, I argue with the right people in the Ministry of Health and sometimes we get supplies and sometimes we don't. We're not going to save Africa but I am racking up God points big time.'

Alex laughs. 'Good works.'

'Yes, good works. Isn't Catholic guilt a marvellous thing?'

'Hmmm.'

The laughter eases out of Alex's voice as he gets to the point of the call. 'Well, I have a good work in mind.'

'Oh, dear.' Yamba sounds amused.

'Hmm, this is quite a big good work actually.'

'Oh no, what are we doing this time? Haven't we interfered with enough governments? You're not on that again, are you?'

Alex's voice begins to sound more serious. 'Well, this time we're going to set up a new country.'

Yamba stops laughing.

Smoke drifts across the forest glade, catching in a shaft of lemony morning sunshine. Otherwise everything is still and silent.

It's just after dawn and the raucous chorus of birds has died down. The glade is surrounded by high trees and thick undergrowth, wet with dew. Two large mounds covered in earth, ten feet in diameter, burn gently and little streams of smoke emerge from cracks at the top like snakes and, in the absence of any wind, slide away down the slopes.

The charcoal burner stirs from under his shelter of white

78

plastic sheeting and pokes a long stick into the bottom of one of the piles, checking if it is ready. He is of indeterminate age – he is so black and wizened by his trade he could be middle- or old-aged. He reeks of smoke and his eyes are red and rheumy. His body is streaked with smears of sweat-congealed black charcoal powder.

He's been up all night tending to his two kilns. He has to heat the bundles of wood cut from the forest just enough to drive off the excess water – too much and it will turn to ash, too little and it produces unsaleable smoked wood. What he wants is that light, brittle residue that the women of Kivu use to fuel their cooking fires. The trade is worth thirty million dollars a year, wood in the deep bush is free and all he needs to do is to live in this isolated spot cutting trees and tending his kilns.

Charcoal burning is not a job for every man. The skills are jealously guarded and kept within a secret community; he learned the trade from his father along with many other secrets about how to communicate with the spirits of the trees and the animals that live in the forest and how to make charms for all of life's requirements.

He picks up a spade and starts shovelling earth over the vents at the bottom of the heap to cut off the flow of air. The combustion inside the mound gradually dies off and the streamers of smoke emanating from it fade to wisps and then stop. He makes himself a cup of black sweet tea, finds a sunny spot and settles back to wait for one of the traders he supplies.

He dozes off but about midday a call from the bush on the slopes below him wakes him up and he hears the sound of a man breathing hard and the thud of his feet on the mud.

A bare-chested man emerges through the bush heaving

his *tshkudu* uphill. The lean fibres of his chest muscles stand out as he pushes on the handlebars.

'Ah, Antoine, good to see you,' the charcoal burner says quietly and offers him a drink from his yellow plastic jerrycan of water.

Antoine smiles, takes grateful glugs, and then splashes his body and wipes off the sweat. He accepts a cup of tea and the burner asks, 'So what's going on in the world?'

'Oh, did you hear about that riot up in Butembo?'

'No.'

'Oh, Socozaki was playing Nyuki System. Nyuki were losing two–nil and so their goalkeeper walks up the pitch and tries to cast a spell on the other goal. So all the Nyuki players go mad and have a brawl on the pitch and when a policeman comes on to stop them he is pelted with stones by the spectators.'

Antoine shakes his head. 'So then the police fire tear gas and the crowd stampedes. Eleven people were crushed to death. What can you do?'

'Eh,' the burner agrees, 'the goalkeeper should have been more crafty.'

'Hmm. So how much for the bags?' Antoine jerks his head towards the pile of grubby sacks.

The burner names his price and Antoine looks disappointed. Then he pauses and a sly look creeps onto his face. 'Ah, but I have a present for you from the Kudu Noir.'

The charcoal burner sits up. 'Show me.'

The trader gets up and pulls a bundle out of a plastic sack on his *tshkudu*; it's about a foot long and carefully wrapped up. 'Have a look, it's the real thing.'

The burner opens it, looks inside and smiles slyly. 'A girl?'

'Yes.'

The burner nods with satisfaction. 'That's good, female

spirits are more powerful. I'll make the powder; the Kudus will be pleased with this. OK, so now we can trade.' He also gets up, goes over to his shelter and pulls out a small packet of grey powder in a clear plastic bag.

The trader looks at it with bright eyes. 'The real thing?'

'Yes. It's pure albino bone. Sprinkle it in a mine and the gold will come rushing to you.'

He rubs his jaw. 'OK, what's your price?'

Chapter Ten

'You are joking, Devereux! You are *joking*! You've lost it, mate . . . Oh my God.' Col rubs his forehead and draws his hand down the side of his face in disbelief. 'Who d'ya think we are, the UN? We're mercenaries, mate, not . . . whatever . . . nation builders or summat, you know the Red Cross, like.'

Alex looks back at him with a raised eyebrow. 'Col, I'm not asking you to put on a nurse's uniform.'

Col and Yamba are both in the drawing room at Akerley. Alex didn't tell Col the plan beforehand: he knew this would be his response and is prepared to ride out the storm.

Col is five foot six and balding with his remaining hair shaved down to grey bristles. He has grim eyes, a small moustache stained with nicotine and tattoos of the Parachute Regiment on one forearm and Blackburn Rovers on the other.

Alex sits in the armchair and waits for the tide of scorn to abate; his expression is as calm and patient as Fang's was the week before.

Col eventually sees this. 'You're not joking, are you? Oh Jesus.' He rubs his face before trying again. 'It'll be just the same as when they went into Iraq and Afghanistan. You just don't know what chain reaction you are going to set off. Better to leave well alone, let 'em stew in their own juice. If they want to fooking kill each other and run shitty countries then let 'em. People get the governments they deserve. All Africans are fooking mad, you know that!'

He looks at Yamba who keeps his face pointedly blank. This is a favourite topic of Col's for riling him and he is not going to rise to the bait that easily.

Despite appearances, the three of them actually get on well together because they are all exiles from their social backgrounds, united by their sense of professionalism and dedication to each other. Alex's troubled upbringing makes him loathe the rigid mental straitjacket of county society. Yamba was forced out of his homeland as a boy and has only been grudgingly let back in recently. Col should just be a Northern hard man but his quick mind was bored rigid by its staid culture and he sought escape in the army. He speaks good French (with a strong Lancashire accent) and travels widely in Africa to see his favourite bands. Despite his attempts to appear to the contrary, he is actually a book lover. He only learned to read when he joined the army aged seventeen, but since then he has devoured books. As a ferociously self-reliant man he likes the fact that he is never alone with one.

He points at Alex. 'Mixing soldiers and civilians is bad news. You and I have both been in Northern Ireland and you remember what a bag a shite that was.'

Alex thinks back to his days as a junior officer on foot patrol with his men, slogging round council estates with bored youths taunting them and throwing bottles and bricks.

'It takes very disciplined troops to do that work and I'm not sure we could get them in a mercenary unit. And you look at what happens when it goes wrong – Bloody Sunday, My Lai, Haditha where those marines raped that girl and shot her.'

Alex responds calmly. 'We're not going to be doing patrols in urban areas, it will be proper war fighting against the FDLR in the bush.'

'Well, the UN is going to hate us; you know what they think about white mercenaries. They'll get the ICC onto us or summat.'

'We will be legitimate employees of the new state. Besides, we won't be on show – the whole thing will be fronted by local politicians.'

Yamba sits and watches the exchange; he is wary of the scheme but open to discussing the issues. He is passionate about African politics and can see that the idea could improve Kivu and set up a new model for developing countries. However, what he is worried about is the look in Alex's eye. He has seen that slightly fanatical gleam before – a cocksure, knowing look that concerns him. He sometimes wonders what makes Alex such a compelling commander, what gives him the mystical charisma that makes men follow him into battle. He's not sure what it is but it works.

He looks at Alex now and asks cautiously, 'Are you sure this isn't so much about establishing the Republic of Kivu as the Republic of Devereux?'

'You mean, is this just a monumental egotistical folly?'

'Yes, is this just a toy country to play with, to set up a perfect world, the one we are always talking about?'

Alex looks away for a moment. 'I know what you mean and we should be wary of that, but on a practical level I think it is actually a lot more doable than it first looks and I think it would benefit the people. Executive Outcomes ended the war in Angola as did the Paras in Sierra Leone; I think we can do the same.'

Yamba nods. Executive Outcomes was a small South-African-led mercenary army that had a huge impact in ending the long-running war in his homeland simply by being very professional and imposing order on anarchy.

Alex continues. 'The UN has shown it can't impose order in Kivu and the world community likes to talk about it but doesn't actually do anything. They let five million people die in the main Congo war and no one really noticed.'

Col looks at the two of them and can see that Yamba is warming to the idea. What he hasn't told either of them is that last week he was horrified to find himself opening a can of beer at breakfast. After his large payoff he has found himself living the life of luxury he always dreamed of, sinking into sloth sitting on the sofa in front of his huge home cinema screen, drinking Thwaites Original.

When he realised what he was doing he threw the beer can out of the window, ran upstairs, got on his running kit and went for a ten miler out on the moors.

He can see now that Alex has got 'that look' in his eyes and is committed to the plan; he doesn't want to hear whatever objections Col has to it.

Col drops the scornful tone and slumps back on the sofa. 'Look – I'll do it, course I will, you know I'll back you, lad. I just think we need to be careful, that's all I'm saying.'

Joseph stands to attention and thrusts out his chest.

He is carrying a short-handled digging hoe in one hand and rests it on his shoulder in what he thinks is a military fashion. He is wearing shorts and is covered in mud and ash from burning and clearing a new field that morning.

His platoon is drawn up in three ranks of ten men in the centre of the village; they have just come back in from the fields and look a mess.

His platoon commander, Lieutenant Karuta, has also been working and stands in his wellies and shorts and a tee shirt in front of them. He paces around, looking annoyed, and thinking hard.

The soldiers stand to attention and eye him nervously; when he's in a bad mood he can be a right bastard.

He turns to them and shouts in his most commanding voice, 'I have had an urgent message from FDLR High Command.'

He takes hold of the bulky satellite phone on a strap over his shoulder and holds it in the air to emphasise the importance of the message. He's worried about the order he has to give and is trying to emphasise that it hasn't come from him.

'We have been instructed to pack up and fall back to base in the Lubonga valley.'

A groan goes through the ranks of the thirty men. Karuta had told them that they would be staying in Lolo for months and they were looking forward to some easy times. They have spent the last week clearing and burning the bush to make fields and hoeing the land ready to plant extra crops. It's been backbreaking work and now it seems it was all for nothing.

'Hey, shut up!' Lieutenant Karuta snaps and glares at them. They all drop their eyes. 'I'm not asking your opinion! We have been given an order – *a direct order*! By High Command! We will obey!'

He was perturbed by the order as well – they had been told to scatter into the bush to avoid the UN forces but now they are being told to concentrate again. He was talking to another platoon commander on the phone who had had the same order.

The soldiers look glum but don't say anything.

'You will pack up your kit and be ready to leave in an hour; we will take the women as bearers. Corporal Habiyakare, go and get them ready!'

The corporal goes off with three men to where some women are tied up in a hut.

The lieutenant continues. 'We have a journey of forty kilometres to get to Utiti.' He points north. 'We must wait there and they will send transport to collect us.'

One of the older men in the platoon asks from the back rank, 'Lieutenant, why are we going?'

Karuta looks awkward. He hasn't been told anything but doesn't like showing that he is not in the command loop, so he just shrugs. 'I don't know, but there is a rumour from the government in Kinshasa that it will ask the UN to leave the province soon so I think the FDLR High Command want to concentrate our forces.'

He shrugs again and turns away.

The group of five men coming through arrivals at Kigali airport in Rwanda are an unlikely crowd.

There's a tall, dark-haired man with a stern face, a serious-looking black man, a short balding man with a moustache and grim eyes, and a lanky Chinese businessman with a laptop case. The fifth man is middle aged and heavily built with a crewcut and a chunky gold necklace. He is pale-skinned and Slavic in appearance.

Arkady Voloshin is the other mainstay of Team Devereux. Formerly in the Russian Air Force he moved on to work for Victor Bout's air transport company in the 1990s, running guns, diamonds, booze, cigarettes, TVs and hookers in and out of Africa. He is an experienced pilot of both fixed wing and rotary aircraft and has good contacts in the world of international arms dealers and aircraft leasing companies.

Since his last mission with the team he has bought himself a red Ferrari and been touring the south of France with some Serbian arms dealer friends. He spent a lot of time and money in Monte Carlo casinos where he took up with a French-Senegalese prostitute called Celeste who looks a bit like Naomi Campbell. She then 'accidentally' became pregnant and he now finds himself both married, a French citizen and a father of a baby girl called Anastasia. He's not quite sure how it all happened but he does know that Celeste wants to remain in their nice apartment in Cannes and that she spends a lot of money.

Although the group in the airport look disparate, they are very at ease with each other and switched on, eyes scanning around the crowded arrivals area as they claim their luggage and move through the doorway into the large entrance hall in the 1970s airport.

It's early May, a month after Alex's initial meeting with Fang, and Team Devereux have spent the last two weeks holed up in Akerley brainstorming, planning the operation and writing their logistics wish list. They are here to see Rwandan staff officers to discuss this before heading over the border into Kivu to meet the local politician who will front the whole operation.

Alex spots a man holding a sign saying 'Mr Jones' in the line of people crowding along the rail awaiting the Sabena flight from Brussels and heads over towards him. He is a gloomy, dutiful-looking Rwandan in his mid-thirties, wearing casual trousers with a white shirt neatly belted in.

'Good morning, Mr Devereux,' he says in English and offers a soft handshake. He has a quiet voice with a heavy Rwandan accent and keeps his face still as he speaks. His eyes watch everyone very carefully as he shakes hands with the group.

'I am Major Zacheus Bizimani of the Directorate of Military Intelligence; I will be your liaison officer for your visit. Please come this way.'

Like Congo, Rwanda is a former Belgian colony and

French used to be the language of its educated classes. However, because of French support for the Hutus during the genocide, President Kagame cut diplomatic links with France, joined the Commonwealth and made English the alternative national language. All the signs in the airport are pointedly in English.

They push their luggage trolleys through and load into two unmarked minivans waiting outside with plain-clothes drivers. Any observer would say that they look like a group of businessmen arriving for a meeting.

As they drive into Kigali, the team scan around with interest trying to get a feel of the country that they will be working for. It is mid-morning and the sun is already high in the bright blue sky, the fierce light washing out the colour in the red soil of the hills around them, each one capped with a little white cloud. As with the whole Rift Valley, the area is at five thousand feet so the temperature is in the mid-twenties with a pleasantly fresh feel to the air.

'All looks very neat, don't it?' Col says to Alex.

Major Bizimani is keen to reassure them that Rwanda is an organised country that will be able to cope with a complex military logistical operation and leans back from the front passenger seat. 'Plastic bags are banned in Rwanda and every citizen has to do compulsory community work each week. President Kagame is following the Singapore model of development. It is all part of our Vision 2020 development plan for the country.'

'Right ho,' Col nods, looking impressed.

The road weaves between the crowded hills of the city and they arrive at the Top Tower Hotel with its ultra-modern entrance foyer and efficient red-suited staff. Yamba nods at a sign as they walk into the foyer and chuckles. 'Five star. Better than we usually get in Africa, eh?'

They check into their five rooms, all on the top floor with views out over the golf course on the hill opposite, before getting out their laptops and briefcases and heading up to the Ministry of Defence building on a hill on the other side of the hotel.

Zacheus checks the vans through the heavily fortified gatehouse at the bottom of the hill and points to a soldier on guard with his rifle held rigidly in front of him. He indicates the soldier's rifle.

'You see the stencilled number there?' Alex looks at the yellow lettering. 'We know the number and location of every rifle in Rwanda. In Congo they don't even know how many soldiers they have in the army. The government estimates between one hundred and one hundred and sixty thousand.'

The vans park in two reserved places in the car park at the top of the hill and the major then leads them through the manicured gardens and into the large complex of low-rise offices. Everything has an understated air of quiet efficiency and smartly dressed officers and suited civil servants move about purposefully.

Zacheus continues his propaganda. 'President Kagame is the only African leader to have a Diploma of Management from the Open University in Britain. He is very opposed to corruption and it is punished very severely. All government employees must be at their desks ready to start work by seven o'clock in the morning.'

He shows them into a large meeting room and directs them to one side of a table; they settle in and get their laptops out. A minute later and seven Rwandan staff officers walk into the room; they are all middle-aged, reserved and wear crisply ironed dress uniforms.

Their leader, an austere man in his late forties, introduces himself in perfect English. 'My name is Colonel Rutaremara and this is my Directorate of Logistics planning team.'

Colonel Rutaremara and his men take their time opening their briefcases on the table, carefully setting out laptops and piles of notes and aligning them squarely. Team Devereux sit and watch this slow process with interest.

The colonel eventually moves to stand in front of the large screen at the head of the table and fusses about with his laptop getting the PowerPoint slides correct. Finally he looks up and clears his throat.

'My team and I began logistics work in the DRC during our first invasion of Congo in 1997 when we marched an army through fourteen hundred miles of bush, right the way across the continent and took Kinshasa, ending Mobutu's twenty-seven years of rule. We believe we are practised in supplying armies in the field in Congo.'

Alex and his men nod appreciatively: it was one of the greatest feats of arms ever achieved in African history.

'We then occupied Kivu for six years from 1997 to 2003 and have been engaged in military operations there since then. Our Directorate of Military Intelligence have maintained an excellent secret intelligence network in the province. A lot of this is using agents that are part of the charcoal trading network that crosses the forests along the border.'

Chapter Eleven

Eve is lying on her back on a gynaecological examination bench with her legs up in the air in stirrups.

Dr Bangana is sitting on a stool between her legs doing a preliminary examination. There is a cloth screen between him and her but she can see the top of his head over it. His short curly hair is speckled with pepper and salt. He trained as a gynaecologist in Paris, building up a healthy practice there and learning a lot. But he had to come back to his homeland because he also learned that he had a conscience. Now his voice is grave from years of dealing with terrible damage like that inflicted on Eve.

'So, I know this is difficult but did they use an object?'

Eve can't bring herself to reply and just sniffs but Miriam, her new friend who is holding her hand, whispers, 'A gun.'

Dr Bangana nods and sighs, he wishes he could get the yobs that do this and make them come and see the results of their 'fun'. But he knows he has no power to do so and that no one else in Kivu does either so he just forces himself to focus on repairing some of the consequences of the problem. He can do nothing to affect its causes. He continues examining her and Eve flinches as she feels the cold instruments poking around inside her.

Eventually he sits back and looks up at her. 'OK, your wounds are stable for the moment; I will put you on the waiting list for a procedure. I'm afraid it could take weeks – we have a lot of casualties coming in every day from all over South Kivu and some of them require emergency treatment. The wall of the bladder is a very thin membrane and after the operation it will take a couple of weeks to see if the sutures hold and the tissue is able to heal.'

Eve and Miriam go out into the courtyard between some of the low hospital blocks and sit on the grass in the sun. Miriam gets out her knitting – they sit around a lot killing time – and they talk quietly.

'So have you heard from Gabriel?'

'Hmm, he passed a message through the watermelon seller at the gate.'

'What did he say?'

'He says he is leaving soon for the mines and hopes to make good money and that he will come and see me when he has paid off his family.'

'Do you think he loves you?'

Eve pauses. Panzi is a wonderful peaceful environment to live in and she loves all the Mamas and Miriam but her other experiences have taught her to be circumspect about anything positive.

She shrugs. 'He says he does. I don't know if he will come, I'll just have to see.'

A week after the meeting in Kigali, two Land Cruisers pull up in a meadow and Alex and the others get out. The jeep doors slam shut in quick succession and he is conscious that there is then absolutely no noise.

The group wander away from the cars stretching their legs and getting the feeling of carsickness out of their heads.

It's been a long drive up here from Goma – six hours to cover thirty miles as the crow flies.

Everyone stands still staring at their surroundings. They are in a sea of grass with an almost luminous green glow in the sunshine and everywhere they look beyond that are lines of rugged hills stretching away into the distance, each one more muted than the previous, all under a perfect blue sky, polka-dotted with white clouds.

Col wanders over to him. 'It's beautiful, reminds me of the Lakes in the summer,' he says wistfully.

Zacheus says, 'I'll go and check they are ready for us,' and walks off through the thick wet grass towards a hut by the stream.

They are in phase two of their reconnaissance mission in Kivu, and about to meet the local politician they will be working with in setting up the new state, although Fang has stayed in Kigali for more meetings. They have had a week of intense discussions. The Rwandans really do start work at 7am and seem to think it was normal that their partners should as well. They have made a lot of progress planning weapons, ammunition, supply bases next to the border, recruitment and training and getting the latest Rwandan intelligence on the distribution of the FDLR forces and the best way to tackle them. Evenings have been spent in team meetings in their hotel rooms preparing for the next day's schedule and emailing contacts to get plans rolling around the world.

So it came as a relief when they could pack a rucksack and drive three hours west to the border with Kivu. The roads were all brand new and smooth; Zacheus pointed out the British Department for International Development signs on the roadside with his usual pride.

They went over the border into the Democratic Republic

of Congo on tourist visas with Zacheus posing as their local Congolese guide. He dealt very efficiently in Swahili with the border police, bribing them only a part of what they were asking and quietly talking his way through the rest of their obstreperousness.

Going into the DRC was certainly a big change; from the land of dour but efficient Rwandans to the lively freewheeling chaos of Goma. 'There is a lot of money in Goma but not much law and order,' was Zacheus's disdainful comment. 'I was actually born in Kivu, I am Banyamulenge – that's a Tutsi living in Kivu – but I think I prefer Rwanda,' he said, with the first inkling of a smile they had seen all week.

The centre of Goma was scruffy and packed with rubbish and traffic, mainly motorbike taxis and flashy SUVs belonging to *comptoirs*, the middlemen who process and export the minerals. They threaded their way through the town and out along the shore of Lake Kivu, gleaming a glorious blue in the afternoon sunshine. They drove past many *comptoir* villas along the lake, swanky places with swimming pools and satellite TV dishes, shut away behind high security gates, until they came to the total tranquillity of Hotel Bruxelles, a large, elegant colonial era building newly renovated and with grounds overlooking the lake.

It was late afternoon when they checked in and only then did Zacheus finally tell them the name of the politician they would be seeing the following day. An intelligence agent by nature, he was under strict orders from Fang not to reveal the information until the last minute. 'Dieudonné Rukuba.' He said the name quietly. None of them had heard of the man.

In a quick meeting after dinner Alex issued a terse order. 'Have a look on the net, make any calls you can tonight to contacts, get anything you can on his background. If we are going to build a country with this guy we have got to find out if he's trustworthy. The British government thought Idi Amin was just the sort of chap they needed to sort out Uganda when they put him in power and we don't want to repeat that cockup.'

In the morning, they left early and headed down the N2 main road, south along the western shore of Lake Kivu. That was the easy bit. It started getting tricky when they turned west off the road and headed up a track into the steep hills. After that it was up hill and down dale. Their two drivers, both Directorate of Military Intelligence agents living in Kivu, threaded their way expertly along the narrow muddy lane twisting through upland meadows and woods.

Having gone up over six thousand feet, they came down into a valley with a fast-flowing stream and drove through the village of Mukungu, a primitive and rustic place with wooden huts and cowsheds. The residents stared at the jeeps and white men as they passed; none had ever been seen before in such a remote rural location.

After the village they turned up another small valley into a plateau area of lush meadows where brown cattle grazed quietly.

Now, standing in the meadow, Alex knows they haven't got long before Zacheus returns. 'Anybody find out anything last night?' he asks.

Yamba shrugs. 'Only that he is a local Kivuan and runs a political party called the Kivu People's Party.'

'Ah well, I'm one up on you there,' says Col knowingly. 'While you were all tapping away on t'internet, I were in the bar and had a beer with this South African bloke. He were a Parabat and saw me tatt when I were leaning on the bar, see? Crap tatts, can't beat 'em.' He holds up his forearm with his Parachute Regiment tattoo to Yamba, who rolls his eyes. Parabat is the South African army's Parachute Battalion, originally founded from the British army Parachute Regiment.

'He's been doing security work for a *comptoir* in Goma for the last few years, so we gets chatting and I says who's this Rukuba bloke then? Turns out he's quite a well-known figure in the province but no real power. Runs a sorta non-militia-based mutual aid society or summat. Does a lot a music with church groups. This bloke says he's a good politician and seems to get on with most people, which sounds like an achievement in Kivu. Although he said he thinks he's a slimy bastard and he doesn't trust 'im. Apparently there's some rumour that he was involved with something called the Kudu Noir when he started out in politics.'

Alex looks at him askance. 'What the hell is that?'

'Don't know, some sorta bush cult, animist whatever, to do with the spirit of the land in Kivu. You know, all that usual bollocks.'

Zacheus was heading back towards them, taking long steps over the grass. Alex looks round his men guardedly. 'Well, let's see what's he like.'

Gabriel squats down next to the broken moped at the side of the road. He's on his way to the mines and met its owner while he was walking along.

'Have you tried the fuel line?'

'No, where's that?'

'It's here, look.' Gabriel pulls the clear plastic tube off the engine of the battered blue 49cc Peugeot Mobylette and sucks the petrol out of it; he's always been good at fixing things.

He spits out the fuel and tastes some grit in his mouth.

He tinkers with the carburettor and then says, 'It's just grit in the fuel, should be OK now. Give it another go.'

'It needs a push.'

'OK.'

The man gets on the bike and Gabriel puts his hands on the back of his denim jacket and pushes him down the road. The moped splutters and then coughs into life.

The man brakes and revs the engine. He twists around in the saddle and flashes a warm smile. He's in his early twenties and has a kind, open face. 'You want a lift? Where are you going?'

'Sure. Thanks.' Gabriel jumps onto the seat behind him. 'I'm going to Lugushwa, to the gold mines.' An uncle of his recommended it as the best place to earn good money. Gabriel has never thought much of the man's opinion but he hasn't got any better information.

'No, don't go there. Come to Mabala, it's coltan and you get better rates because it's underground not opencast. My cousin Vernon runs a tunnel and needs guys. Come on.'

That sounds like sense and Gabriel doesn't need much persuading.

'OK. I'm Gabriel.'

'I'm Marcel.'

They shake hands over Marcel's shoulder and then he revs up and the moped putters away slowly.

'Why are you going to the mines?' Gabriel shouts into his ear over the whine of the engine.

'I'm a teacher but I haven't been paid in six months.' He shrugs. 'You've got to eat and what other jobs are there? What about you?'

Gabriel is reluctant to talk about Eve and what happened to her. 'Oh, I just need the money; like you say, what other jobs are there? Where's Mabala?'

'It's in the mountains above Shabunda. It's run by the FDLR.'

'Is that OK?'

'Yeah, it's fine. They're all the same, they all take pretty much the same cut.'

Chapter Twelve

Alex and his men walk up the hill towards their meeting with the politician who will lead their new country.

They cross a small stream at the foot of the hill and nod at an old man with a machete who stands guard outside a hut. He smiles uncertainly back at them.

They follow a muddy track as it curves up a large grassy hill. After winding around it comes out at the top into a farmyard of two large wooden barns and two cowsheds. A few farm workers stare at them, resting on their pitchforks. They cross over the muddy ground in the middle and walk towards the farmstead, a single-storey plank building with a wide veranda and lawn overlooking the valley they drove up. A hammock is slung between two trees on the lawn.

As they near the house Alex suddenly stops and listens. It is completely silent on the hilltop but he can hear the faint sound of a piano from inside; delicate, sparing notes that form a haunting tune.

'That's a Chopin nocturne?' He looks at Arkady quizzically.

'I don't know, I'm Russian not Polish.'

Col shrugs. 'I'll take yer word for it.'

As they walk on towards the house, the music cuts off abruptly and a group of ten young children, scruffily-clad boys and girls, come scampering out of a door and run away, giggling and shouting '*Muzungu!*' at them.

The men smile and Col calls back in Swahili, '*Habari za mchana.*' They all know a little of the East African lingua franca and are used to having 'Whiteman' shouted at them in remote locations.

A tall, slim man in his mid-thirties comes out onto the veranda wearing traditional dress – a long white gown and white pointed leather slippers. He is smiling broadly and has a sensitive, fine-boned face.

'I am sorry about the kids,' he says in accented English. 'I was just entertaining them a bit as we were waiting for you to arrive.'

He walks towards Alex with a dazzling white smile and shakes his hand firmly. Alex notes how his sharp facial features contrast with a shaved head and high forehead. He has long, fine fingers and his movements are neat and quick.

He shakes everyone's hand warmly and says laughing, 'Welcome to my humble abode. As you can see, I am just a simple farmer. Please come in.'

He shows them into a large low room with plank flooring and an old upright piano in one corner. They settle down around a white plastic garden table with white plastic chairs.

Rukuba sits at the head of the table and looks around at them, beaming. 'Gentlemen, it is so exciting for me to meet you here today, I am so glad that you have come.' There is an earnest pleasure in his voice and he sweeps his hand around as if he is speaking on behalf of the whole of Kivu.

'Let me tell you about myself. Well, in the beginning I am a Kivuan, I am one of the people of Kivu. I am half Tutsi and half Nande, so I feel I represent both the Banyamulenge and the *originaires.*' He presses his long-fingered hands to his chest and pauses for a moment.

101

His hands sweep outwards again and he continues with enthusiasm, 'Our political organisation is the Kivu People's Party. Unlike the militias and their political fronts we are deliberately non-ethnically aligned. We are a broad-based political group with a programme of pragmatic community activities, like building bridges or digging village fishponds, and we focus on raising awareness of issues such as sexual violence against women and livestock improvement. In so many ways we struggle to make the lives of the people of Kivu better.

'But I am not judgemental; I talk to the leaders of all the main militias, I know the commanders of the FDLR very well. They are always giving me shopping tips for the best tailors in Paris – they tell me I should stop wearing these.' He holds up his traditional robes and smiles at Alex's surprised look. 'The top commanders are very wealthy from their mines and they come and go to Europe a lot.

'So, when I am not talking to them, I publicise our work through my radio broadcasts on UN Radio Okapi and through my music. I am so blessed by God to have a good voice and I love to play for the people in the churches – Catholic, Pentecostal, the bush cults, I don't mind who. I play to bring the people of Kivu together, to try to heal our wounds and to bring peace at last to this land of such great beauty and yet such great pain.'

Alex finds himself being entranced by the man, his voice rising and falling, his hands sweeping back and forth like a magician's and his face so sincere and expressive. He glances at the others and they are all staring at him.

He continues, 'So, you will say, Dieudonné, all this sounds good, but you are not getting very far are you, my friend?' He flashes his big smile at them. 'Yes, I say, I regret that you are right. We have supporters throughout the country, I have good contacts with the charcoal traders, we know a lot of what is happening in Kivu, we have moral authority, we have soft power – but we have no real power, no hard power.'

He suddenly switches from a light tone to a fervent one and a vein begins to stand out on his temple. 'So, as you can see, I live a simple life here in the heart of my country. Yet every day I feel its pain. When I travel around and I see the thugs manning the roadblocks, when I speak to so many women who tell me how they are dragged off and raped every day on the way to their fields, when I see the FDLR and the army brigades continue to grow rich on the mineral wealth of our land, oh my heart cries out! I long for something else . . . something else.' A bright light of sincerity and conviction shines in his eyes as he looks round at them. 'And that, gentlemen, is where you come in. That is why we are so grateful to you and my dear friend, Monsieur Wu, because together I believe that we have found a way at last, after long years of struggle, to solve the problems of Kivu.'

He looks at them with such searching honesty that Alex for the first time really understands the pain of the people of Kivu. Up to now it has been a challenge for him, a fascinating experiment in international relations, a reassertion of the Devereuxs' role in the world, but he hasn't really connected to the six million people who will be affected by what he is going to do.

Cousin Vernon is an intelligent, weary-looking man in his forties with a neat moustache, short hair and a chewed yellow Bic biro tucked behind his right ear. He's wearing a mudstained tracksuit and anorak.

'OK, I need two more guys! Come on, good rates, I pay three dollars a kilo!' he shouts to the crowd of men milling around. It's 7 a.m. and he is recruiting for the morning shift in his tunnel, which he has named Versailles in a bid to attract labour.

The miners range in age from teens to thirties. They stand around dozily on the muddy track leading from the *manoir*, the village where they sleep, up the hillside to the Mabala mine. The *manoir* is at four thousand feet so it's cold and misty.

Gabriel can feel a light rain begin to patter on the hood of his cheap nylon anorak. He shivers, wraps his arms tighter around himself and shuffles his feet in his Wellingtons. Next to him, Marcel does likewise; it's their first day at work.

Other tunnel bosses are hawking for labour for the day, shouting rates and proclaiming the virtues of the different seams that they are chasing deeper into the mountainside.

On the edge of the crowd are some FDLR troops in dark green rain capes that reach down to their wellies at the front and back. They are part of the Gorilla Brigade under Colonel Etienne and several hundred of them live in a base on a hill overlooking the *manoir*.

One of the soldiers hears Vernon's rate and discusses it quickly with a friend. They unhitch their rifles off their shoulders, hand them to another soldier and stroll down to Vernon. 'OK, boss.' Soldiers need extra cash like anyone else.

Vernon nods. 'Names?' He whips his biro out from behind his ear.

'Robert.'

'Patrice.'

'OK.' He scribbles down their names in a little pocket book that he pulls out of his anorak. 'You got your own tools?'

They both nod and each pulls three bits of equipment out from under their rain slickers: a short-handled masonry hammer, chisel and torch with a rubber strap attached.

Vernon writes a symbol next to their names and points. 'Over there.'

The soldiers come to stand with Gabriel and Marcel and the other six men. They grunt a greeting and then Vernon comes over and they follow him and trudge up the hillside.

The Mabala mine is a huge hill of red mud that looks like it has been attacked by an army of termites. The green forest all over it has been chopped down and the hillside is littered with tree trunks and uprooted stumps. In between the patches of mist and drifting rain Gabriel can see the small entrances to many tunnels: Fort Knox, ATM, Golden Goose. Outside each one is a cluster of men; the night shift is coming out and their produce is being weighed and bagged up.

Vernon leads his new team half a mile round the side of the hill to Versailles. His nightshift manager is wearily bagging up the produce and they talk briefly before Vernon takes tools and torches off some of the workers and gives them to Gabriel and Marcel. Two small portable pumps attached to hosepipes leading into the tunnel whirr noisily next to the entrance.

Gabriel eyes the men nervously. They are covered in mud that has dried to a light ochre colour. As one of them wipes his forehead with the back of his rain-wet hand, he cleans a streak of dark brown skin in it.

Vernon gives them new batteries for the torches – 'I'll charge you for those' – and issues each of them with a plastic sack stained brown with mud. Gabriel pulls the strip of black tyre rubber attached to it round his head so that the torch sits above his left ear.

Clutching their sacks with their tools in them, the men duck down and follow Vernon into the narrow entrance. The tunnel is about four feet high so they have to stoop and proceed in an awkward slouching walk for fifty metres. It

105

slopes down, water drips on Gabriel's head and it gets very cold.

Vernon leads the way and the others follow the wobbling circle of his head torch as it illuminates the wet brown rock. He stops just as the tunnel turns a sharp right. 'OK, this is the tricky bit. To get to the seam we have to go under this outcrop of hard rock.' He thumps the rock with his hand. 'The passage is very small but it's worth it when you get to the other side, the ore is very high grade. OK, Pierre will lead the way, come up.'

They flatten themselves against the side and Pierre squeezes past to the front. Vernon then crabs along to the back, and checks his watch. 'OK, I'll see you at eight o'clock tonight. *Bonne chance.*'

Gabriel watches the white circle of light retreat back down the tunnel and glances at Marcel who has switched on his headlamp so that it silhouettes the side of his face. He sees him shrug.

'OK, follow me. This is scary but it's OK,' Pierre says in an unreassuring way. He crawls over to a muddy hole in the floor just wide enough for a man to fit into. 'You have to put your sack in front of you, push it forwards and then wriggle on a bit. It's about six metres to the gallery and the tunnel bends a bit under the outcrop. There's a kind of sump at the bottom where the water accumulates but don't shit yourself – it's fine. Just keep going.'

Chapter Thirteen

Rukuba finishes his speech to Team Devereux and a strange feeling like a spell hangs in the air for a moment.

Col shifts uncomfortably in his seat and eventually Alex breaks the silence. 'What sort of system of government do you envisage for the new republic of Kivu?'

'A democracy,' Rukuba shoots back without hesitation. 'You see, Mr Devereux – can I call you Alex?' Alex nods. 'You see, Alex, we have a lot of democracy in Africa anyway, but it is direct democracy, not representational democracy. Every village headman and tribal chief mediates a discussion about power. We are not as backwards as you might think in Africa . . .' He flicks his cheeky smile on again and giggles with pleasure. 'You see, my degree was in politics, I studied it at Kigali University in Rwanda.' He nods at Zacheus, who looks back at him blank faced. 'If you want to talk about politics, I can do it, ah . . .' he remembers an idiom and is delighted with it '. . . until the cows come home!' He claps his hands with laughter and points over at the cowsheds, rocking in his chair with laughter.

Everyone laughs and even Zacheus manages a smile now.

Rukuba continues. 'But of course we must be realists. The FDLR and the other militia groups are not just going to stop killing people and give up their arms like that. I mean, the

107

FDLR is supposed to be the Democratic Forces for the Liberation of Rwanda but they have not shown much sign of being democratic yet!'

Alex nods in agreement, thinking hard. 'Yes, I suppose "Genocidal Maniacs for the Promotion of Hutu Power" doesn't have quite the same ring to it, does it?'

The two of them laugh heartily before Rukuba continues. 'There will have to be more blood spilt on this precious land, but at least this will be a cleansing blood. At least from it a transitional administration will arise and then, after a period of stabilisation, democratic elections can be held.'

Alex wants to be sure on this. 'Do you think you can persuade the UN and the US to back the new state? I don't think they are going to like a Chinese-backed entity appearing in the middle of Africa – it will set a dangerous precedent.'

Rukuba looks at him straight. 'You're right, it is controversial, but I am sure that I can persuade the American Secretary of State to accept it on a pragmatic basis. It's the only way out of this mess. She is a woman and I will charm her.' He grins.

'What about the Chinese, though?'

'Well, Monsieur Wu has assured me that their interest is purely commercial. Obviously there will be a discussion to be had but I believe that I can steer a middle way between the conflicting interests.'

Alex nods, some of his fears assuaged.

Rukuba claps his hands. 'Come on, I must show you my farm; we can talk more as we walk. My family has owned this land for hundreds of years, we have been here for many generations and I am very proud of my cows, we produce the best cheese! Come!'

He leads them out of the room along a passageway into

the middle of the house and then down a flight of steps into a cellar. 'Mind your heads.'

He lights a hurricane lamp and shows them a large room filled with shelves of round cheeses with a yellowy rind. Rukuba hauls one off a shelf, cuts slices and hands them out. The cheese is medium hard and very tasty.

'Hm, that's good that,' says Col appreciatively.

'Lovely bit of cheese, Gromit,' Yamba says quietly behind his back in a bad Yorkshire accent. He is a Wallace and Gromit fan and likes taking the mick out of Col for being Northern.

Rukuba hears him and laughs. 'Ah, you like Gromit! I love him, so good.'

They troop up the stairs out of the cellar and the tall Kivuan leads them onto the veranda and then pauses, hitches up his flowing white robe to his knees and belts it tight so that he can change his slippers to a pair of black Wellington boots. He takes a staff leaning up against the doorframe and they set off around the farmyard.

At the cowshed he pauses and points out a large cow chewing the cud. 'This is my prize heifer, Madeleine, and these are my two best bulls, Rousseau and Talleyrand.' He points the staff at two huge animals in stalls, drooling gently and staring.

'Rousseau is a hero of mine; I did my thesis on him. The father of liberalism. Have you read Rousseau, Alex?'

'No, but I sort of know his ideas, I think.'

'Well, he based his ideas of democracy on the direct democracy of small Swiss cantons. This landscape is often described as the Switzerland of Africa so why not try them here?' he says, addressing the bull and scratching its massive forehead, 'Heh?' He pats it again and then heads off once more. 'I will show you my dairy.'

109

They go into a large low shed, where women are busy churning milk and straining curds in big vats. They look up and smile nervously as he comes in with the strangers.

He smiles and waves and cracks a joke in Nande that has them all shrieking with embarrassed laughter and covering their faces with their hands.

They continue on around the farm. Rukuba shows them the cows in the fields and strides through the thick lush grass with his staff and robe like an Old Testament prophet. They stand on a knoll looking out over the meadow where the cars are parked. From there they can see the village of Mukungu further back down the brown mud road.

They chat more about plans and make arrangements to communicate by email. Rukaba has a satellite uplink, the dish sticking incongruously up from the roof of the farm.

Rukuba then waves them off with his huge white smile and they wander back down the hill to the cars.

Alex, Col and Yamba get into one jeep and Zacheus and Arkady into the other. As they drive away over the bumpy meadow, Alex says, 'Well, he seemed very charismatic. He'll make a good front man. What did you think?'

'Hmm,' Col shrugs. 'Seems very eager to please. Smiles a lot.' As if that were nasty habit.

Alex looks at him in exasperation. 'Oh, come on! Smiling is not a sin. Just because he's not a grumpy old sod like you. He seemed very well-read on political theory. I liked his bit about Rousseau and democracy; he sounds very liberal-minded to me.'

Yamba is also being cautious. 'Hmm, yes, but remember Talleyrand was a famous political chameleon and Rousseau is also the foundation of fascism; his idea of the general will can also be twisted into the idea of a supreme leader who interprets it . . .'

Col butts in. 'Jacques Rousseau? I'n't 'e the bloke with the aqualung?'

Alex looks at him nonplussed and then guffaws loudly.

Yamba is momentarily puzzled and then his jaw tightens in irritation and he turns his head away and looks out of the window.

'Oh, sorry, Professor Douala, I seem to have interrupted your lecture, do please continue.'

Yamba tries to get going again but Alex is still laughing and he gives up.

Alex eventually manages to say. 'Look, he isn't a nutter, he isn't a warlord and he doesn't have multiple human rights abuses on his hands. That's about as good as we're going to get for a front man in Kivu.'

'OK, we have a problem.'

Fang looks at Alex, Yamba, Col and Arkady sitting round the table in the centre of the planning room in their government villa in Kigali. It's early June, a month after their initial reconnaissance of Kivu, the table is covered in maps and they each have a desk in one corner of the room.

Fang has just returned from one of their many meetings at the Ministry of Defence across the valley from the villa. The Rwandans have a large staff team working on the project as well. Fang speaks slowly, choosing his words carefully.

'There is a partner who is not conforming to the business plan. We need to restructure his involvement in it.'

Alex is baffled by the business jargon. 'What does that mean?'

'Our negotiators report that there has been a problem in the discussions between the government in Kinshasa and the local Congolese army commander in Goma.'

This doesn't sound good; the mercenaries look at him with tense faces.

Alex frowns. 'Hang on, I thought the whole leasing deal was supposed to be secret and now you're saying that they have been discussing it with the Congolese army in Kivu? What about mission security?'

There are angry nods around the table; they are all very touchy about this. If news of the mission leaks then the whole project could collapse or lose them the element of surprise that they are relying on to make up for the huge difference in size between their force and the troops opposing them.

Fang holds up his hand. 'Some discussions are necessary with the senior Congolese commanders in the area to get their commitment to the plan. But they have been with only two people – Brigadier General Sylveste Sabiti, commander of the 8th Military District in North Kivu, and Brigadier General Mutombo Oloba, commander of the 10th Military District in South Kivu.'

He levels with them. 'We have to do it. Otherwise we might end up fighting the Congolese army as well as the FDLR and we cannot do both.'

There are reluctant nods around the table.

Alex continues cautiously. 'OK, so what's the problem?'

'Brigadier General Sabiti fears that he will lose control of his mining assets if he agrees to the deal. Rukuba has assured him that he will keep the mines that his brigades control but he is not confident. He doesn't like Rukuba, says he doesn't trust him. He has a very nice set-up at the moment and doesn't want to lose it.'

The team absorb the news. It's easy to see it happening – just like the various militia groups, the different Congolese army brigades control different mines and, in the absence of any salaries, fund themselves with the money from them.

Alex thinks he can see what sort of restructuring Fang is thinking of.

'Is this a Unit 17 job?'

Fang nods slowly.

Unit 17 is the reconnaissance and black ops unit they have set up under Major Zacheus Bizimani. It combines agents from the Rwandan Directorate of Military Intelligence, Rwandan Special Forces soldiers and members of the Kivu People's Party who provide ground-level intelligence from inside Kivu through their party branches and the charcoal trader network.

Alex thinks for a moment. He knew this was coming, but it's still difficult to face it. Did he really think he was going to set up a new country in one of the most violent and chaotic parts of the world without shedding blood?

Fang looks at him hard. 'Now that Brigadier General Sabiti knows about the deal and is resisting agreeing to it, he is a liability to the business plan. He would be replaced by Brigadier General Oloba, who has indicated that he would be willing to take on the role of joint commander of the 8th and 10th Military Districts in a new combined, all-Kivu command.'

Fang's circumlocutions make the assassination sound like an opportunity for an act of generosity.

Alex takes a deep breath.

There are six million people living in Kivu, most in a permanent state of fear, hundreds of thousands in refugee camps, thousands raped and killed every year. Nothing about their circumstances will change for decades unless the operation goes ahead.

He looks at Fang and nods.

The road to hell . . .

Chapter Fourteen

Gabriel watches the bare legs of Patrice, the FDLR soldier, disappear down the burrow that leads out from the gallery in the mine.

His friend Marcel watches him as well and says, 'I think our position in life has become that of human maggots.' He used to be a French literature teacher.

'Maybe you should write a poem about it.' Gabriel grins. His torch is fading after their twelve-hour shift but he can still see Marcel's face streaked with ochre mud.

Marcel smiles, obviously taken with the idea. 'Maybe I could do something like *Metamorphosis*.'

'What's that?'

'Come on, hurry up!' Robert, the other FDLR soldier, shouts from the back of the gallery. He has been on the shift with them and tends to boss them around.

'OK. OK, I'm going.'

Gabriel drags his sack of ore in front of him, stuffs his hammer and chisel in it and shoves it down the hole. He wriggles in after it, his body sliding along the wet mud.

He's been working in the Versailles tunnel for a while now and the money is OK. He's building up his pot of cash to pay off Eve's treatment. He gets messages about her passed on from a friend of her family in the *manoir* who has a mobile phone. He knows she has got a date for the operation and prays it goes well. It's nearly killing him scraping the cash together. But once she is fixed up they can get married and the thought of it warms him and keeps him going.

By now he's used to the feeling of being in an enclosed space with thousands of tons of rock over his head and has taken on the friendly, macho attitude of the other miners. In the evenings the *manoir* stinks of dope and the lads get together and sing songs noisily. Marcel plays an old guitar and has a good voice.

The work is very hard though – twelve hours a day of bashing at the rocks with a hammer and chisel. At night Gabriel dreams of chips of rock, scrabbling through them to sort out the coltan ore. His right elbow is sore from the heavy blows he rains down all day and the loud *tink, tink, tink* of hammers on chisels stabs at his eardrums. The gallery where the ten men work is cold, dank and stuffy through lack of air: there's one rubber hosepipe pumping air in and one sucking it out but the system doesn't work very well. They also have to piss at the back of the gallery and with all the water around they just end up sitting in it all day.

At the end of each shift, when the maggots emerge from their burrows, Vernon is there to check their sacks, rummaging through them and pulling out handfuls of chippings, carefully assessing that the ore is good and not just rubbish that they have put in to make up weight. After that he hangs each sack under a portable scale, notes the weight in his little book. He deducts his half share from the overall value and then charges extra for torch batteries and tools.

After that he accompanies them as they trudge wearily down the hill to see the negotiants on the track outside the *manoir*. Vernon has certain guys he works with but there's always a market going on with men standing next to their *tshkudus* shouting their transport rates. Vernon haggles and then does a deal and they all go over and tip their sacks into the negotiant's. The FDLR soldiers then impose their tax on him by weight of the sacks. Finally he wheels the ore down the mountain to the main road ten miles away to give it to a *comptoir* in a big truck who will take it back to Bukavu for sorting and grading before it gets shipped on to Rwanda and then out to the Kenyan ports and on to China for putting into mobile phones.

Gabriel has got used to the process. He is thinking about getting back to their hut in the *manoir*, having a bath in a metal tub and crashing out.

He gets onto his hands and knees, takes the torch off his head and puts it in the sack before stuffing it down the tube, sticking his head in and crawling forward. It's pitch black; the mud is cold and soaks through his thin clothes. His elbows and knees scrape along the floor and the stink of wet clay is in his nostrils.

He comes to the sump in the tunnel; he hates this bit. He has to hold his breath and squeeze through the muddy water that fills the tube. He takes a deep breath, shoves his sack into the water and wriggles after it, closing his eyes and feeling the cold water enter his nose and ears. He shoves again and moves on a few feet. He's completely submerged now, eyes tightly shut.

That's when the ground moves all around him – one of the many earthquakes in the Rift Valley area. The whole tunnel compresses and then moves sideways a few inches.

His eyes fly open but he sees only blackness.

Alex Devereux is sitting at one end of a table in a small, dimly lit back room in the Rwandan Ministry of Defence in Kigali. The red epaulettes on his green uniform jacket are for a colonel in the Kivu Defence Force, the new army he is in the process of creating, if this presentation works.

It's mid-June, two weeks after Fang reported the problem with Brigadier General Sabiti and Alex has already issued orders for Zacheus Bizimani's Unit 17 operation to 'restructure his involvement in the business plan'.

In front of him are the five people who will make the final decision on whether to go ahead with his grand plan for a new country. At the other end of the table is the tall, gangly figure of the Rwandan president in a suit, with his military Chief of Staff next to him in his full dress uniform. Both are sitting back, staring intently at Alex with their arms folded.

On his left sit Fang and Mr Cheng, the head of the Kivu Investment Corporation, a tubby sixty-year-old man in a plain suit and tie. His hands are folded on the table and his expression is patient but critical. He speaks fluent English and has years of experience of African politics; he is not about to buy any plan that doesn't make sense.

On Alex's right is Dieudonné Rukuba. He looks magnificent in his traditional white robes but he hunches forward nervously over the table, anxious for the plan to be approved by the Chinese and the Rwandans. It is his only hope of bringing a solution to the ongoing problems of his homeland. His dark eyes glitter as they dart round the faces at the table.

Alex is feeling nervous but confident at the same time. He glances to his left and sees his team, Yamba, Col and Arkady, all sitting at the side of the room with various map boards and supplementary notes ready to bring them to his aid if he hits any problems in the Q&A at the end.

He is proud of them and the amount of work that they have put in over the last two months of solid effort to get the plan together. They have worked closely with the

117

Rwandan staff team and Rukuba and his network of supporters throughout Kivu to come up with a credible strategy. For their part, his team sit on the sidelines and will their boss on to do the presentation of his life.

Time to get on with it.

'Good morning, gentlemen, thank you for taking the time to come here today.' Alex's voice is deep and authoritative.

'Before I discuss the details of the plan, I'd like to start by outlining the theory behind Operation Tiananmen, our views on failed states and what we think is the best way to fix them.

'We think that failed states like Afghanistan, Somalia, Yemen and Kivu fail, not because their insurgencies are strong but because the central authorities are weak. They do not have the mandate of heaven, the power to govern. The insurgencies succeed because their central governments are corrupt. Like the Afghan government, their forces are so ineffectual and oppressive that the population will support any force that opposes it, even the Taliban. In Afghanistan the West is effectively trying to prop up a drunk.

'Similarly, in Kivu representatives from all of the militia groups have twice signed up to peace deals in the Nairobi Communiqué and the Goma Accords but none of them followed through on these promises and disarmed because the Congolese army cannot force them to do so. In fact the army actively contributes to the problem of lawlessness and rape.

'Now, attempts to fix these weak states in the past have failed because large outside forces intervening in a country create a nationalist backlash against them, such as the Taliban and the Iraqi insurgency. At the same time an overload of aid agencies spending billions of dollars of hard cash crowds out local civilian effort by creating a parallel government.

Ultimately the solutions to these problems has to be local. So why start out by trying to replace all local effort?

He is building up to a key point here, so he slows his voice and leans forward. 'The question is, how can you intervene in a country just enough to give the central authority the credible force to deal with the insurgency but without at the same time replacing it and provoking a nationalist uprising?'

It's nine o'clock at night and dark out on Lake Kivu.

The lights of Goma twinkle in the distance and beyond them the red glow from the volcano Mount Nyiragonga reflects eerily on the underside of the low clouds.

A large tourist pleasure cruiser is stationary a kilometre offshore from Goma, just inside Rwandan territorial waters. The boat is called *La Joie de Gisenyi*, after the Rwandan port town next to Goma where it is based. Fixed to its side are boards listing prices for day trips.

It is odd for pleasure craft to be out on the lake at night as there is nothing for tourists to see. There is also a larger than usual cluster of communications aerials and satellite dishes above the bridge. The ship is blacked out but below decks there is a packed operations room. There soldiers monitor dimly lit radio sets and Major Zacheus Bizimani is hunched over a map table, his face as expressionless as ever.

Behind him, on the bench seats usually occupied by sightseers, sits a group of heavily armed Unit 17 commandos with black balaclavas rolled up on top of their heads. Two rigid-hulled speedboats are towed astern.

In an opulent villa on the lakeshore, Brigadier General Sylveste Sabiti, commander of the 8th Military District in North Kivu, finishes his excellent dinner on the terrace overlooking the lake, cooked by his personal chef. A refreshing breeze blows in and Claudine, his young wife, pulls her YSL cashmere shawl tighter around her shoulders. She looks very like Beyoncé with her hair coiffed up on top of her head, large doe eyes and an impassive manner. She wears a white silk blouse, pencil skirt, diamond clasp earrings and gold eye make-up.

Sabiti is a bulky man with a fold of fat sticking over the back of the collar of his shirt, worn with a pink tie and well-cut tweed jacket. He crumples his linen napkin, chucks it on the table and strolls round to the front of the house with his wife. Servants hold open the doors to his black BMW jeep.

They drive out of the gates of his heavily guarded villa and turn right towards Goma. Two Congolese army Peugeot jeeps are waiting. They are open-topped, full of armed soldiers and move into positions in front of and behind the BMW.

Two hundred metres behind them a battered Mitsubishi minivan with tinted windows pulls out of a stand of roadside bamboo and follows at a distance.

The convoy drives two miles towards Goma, passing along the lakeshore at certain points. There is still some traffic on the roads but not as bad as it gets at rush hour. The jeeps enter Goma and drive slowly through the busy streets of the town. Groups of young men are heading out on the town and motorcycle taxis jostle and beep around the cars. Harsh electric light spills out from fluorescent tubes in shop fronts onto pavements strewn with rubbish.

They steer around Rond Pont de l'Independence and head south along the wide Boulevard Kanyamuhanga, the main clubbing street. The sides of the roads are lined with white Land Cruisers belonging to all the NGO workers out on the town. Prostitutes call out to white men in Russian, assuming they are aircrew. They leave the NGO workers alone; they are no good for business.

Soldiers have reserved a space on the kerbside for the Brigadier-General and he and his wife slip out of their jeep and cross the road towards Chez Doga. The single-storey club is sandwiched between a Mobylette dealership and a Lebanese *chwarma* shop with a kerbside rotisserie; the smell of roasting chicken drifts towards them across the street.

As they enter, two men in casual suits get up from the table at a roadside kiosk and follow them into the club.

Inside is a wide low room with tables and chairs. It's already getting busy with diners tucking into excellent Lebanese kebabs, fatush, falafel, and hummus. Two chubby Lebanese businessmen, smoking cigars and fiddling with their worry beads, look up as the army chief passes. He nods to them and they smile back nervously.

The commander sits at a reserved table near the back of the room and people begin coming up to him offering to buy him drinks and chatting. He drinks a Primus beer from a long glass and talks and laughs with various local businessmen and Lebanese *comptoirs*. The white NGO workers eye him nervously.

His wife drinks cocktails and goes for a dance with some friends; the music is a mix of Congolese and Western.

At one o'clock the commander and his wife leave the club and get back into their BMW. The two men in casual suits follow them out and one speaks quietly into his jacket lapel in the shadows. A passer-by neatly hands the other man a small rucksack and walks on down the pavement without any comment. Both men then get onto a motorbike and follow the convoy as it pulls out from the kerb.

The two jeeps and the BMW make their way back out of

town; there is no traffic now, security concerns keep most people at home at night.

The Mitsubishi minivan pulls in in front of the convoy as it leaves Goma and heads out onto the deserted road by the lake.

Chapter Fifteen

Alex continues his talk to the Chinese, Rwandan and Kivuan audience in the small room in Kigali.

'So what is the solution to the problem? How can we intervene successfully in a state to end an insurgency without at the same time undermining its government and provoking an uprising? We need to do a better job than in Somalia, Iraq and Afghanistan.

'We believe that the solution to the problem lies in a strategy that we call partnership intervention. What this means is that rather than just being an invasion and a complete replacement of the existing institutions the military effort will simply support the existing power structures.

'We have to be realistic in this operation; we are not a superpower and will not have many men. But we will have enough to give the new government the threat of credible force that it needs to make the insurgents come to the negotiating table, sign a peace deal and actually disarm. To use an African proverb, the new state will talk quietly and carry a big stick. The Kivu Defence Force will be that stick.

'So how will this work in practice? There are around thirty different militia groups in Kivu but the biggest and best organised is the FDLR. They are the key to solving all the problems of the region because most of the other groups say they exist simply to defend against their destabilising presence. If we can demonstrate to these groups that we have destroyed the FDLR then their *raison d'être* will disappear and it will also be a very powerful military signal to them that we mean business and can easily take them out if they don't disarm.

'Although all the militias together have around forty thousand soldiers against our force of a thousand, they are fragmented and their troops are poor quality. Also, we will be prepared to work alongside the Congolese army and the UN troops. With the granting of sovereign powers to President Rukuba the Congolese army should obey him and the UN will at least remain in base even if they do not actively cooperate with us. The situation will be fluid and we will respond as it demands.'

Alex knows that is the understatement of the century.

'The military phase of the operation will be an aggressive air assault campaign of the speed and scale that the UN has not been able to mount. It will begin with a surprise attack to seek a decisive break-in battle with the FDLR to decapitate their leadership. We will maintain the advantage of surprise, hitting the enemy hard and keeping them on the run until we have destroyed their command and control networks.

'The attacks have to be swift because in the past the FDLR's response has been to fragment into small groups, disperse into the bush and wreak revenge on the civilian population.

'After we have broken the back of the FDLR we will move to the second, non-military, stabilisation phase. This hearts and minds operation will focus on negotiations with and demilitarisation of the remaining militias. It will also require cooperation with UN and civilian NGOs to get former fighters into civilian jobs.

'In terms of timing, kinetic operations will commence in a year's time next May, at the start of the dry season to allow three months of clearer weather for intensive helicopter operations. The standard mercenary contract is for six months, so by next November we envisage a substantial draw down of the Kivu Defence Force foreign troops and a handover to the former Congolese army soldiers under the command of the Transitional Authority.'

Alex deliberately left out any discussion of what the exact nature of the Transitional Authority would be: democratic or some sort of managed capitalist dictatorship. The Chinese have been very cagey on the subject – they are aware of Western and UN sensibilities on the subject of democracy but at the same time this is their state that they are paying a lot of money for and they have their own way of doing things.

Alex felt that Rukuba seemed prodemocratic but he had not been party to any discussions between him and the Chinese. Ultimately it isn't his job to run the political system. He is a soldier and has enough to think about in winning the war.

He moves on quickly to wrap up. 'This will be a tough and rapid operation but I believe that at the end of it we will have established a new country with the mandate of heaven.'

The driver of the Mitsubishi minivan is careful to keep well ahead of the jeep full of armed soldiers. The motorcycle with two men on it following the convoy of three vehicles also keeps its distance.

As Brigadier General Sabiti's BMW approaches a section of road running along the lakeshore the minivan slows and the motorcycle speeds up, sandwiching the general's convoy between them.

The minivan slews violently across the road right in front of the lead jeep, which brakes hard to avoid it and swerves into the drainage channel at the side of the road.

The BMW and the other jeep manage to brake in time and screech to a halt. The soldiers in the back of the jeep are thrown around and drop their weapons.

The motorbike pulls up alongside the rear jeep. It is open-topped and the man riding pillion leans across and shoots the five soldiers with careful double shots from a silenced submachine gun.

The sliding door of the minivan whips open and four men dressed in civilian clothing and black balaclavas jump out and spray the lead jeep with silenced gunfire. The windshield shatters and the soldiers are riddled with bullets.

At the same time a group of black-clad Unit 17 commandos wearing balaclavas rise from the drainage ditch by the lake and fire on the lead jeep and the army commander's car. The tinted side windows of the BMW spiderweb with the impacts.

Two pairs of commandos run forward, assault rifles aimed at the car. One pair pull open the front door and shoot the wounded driver dead. The other pair pull open the rear door.

Mrs Sabiti has taken the brunt of the gunfire. Her neat hairdo is askew from bullet wounds in her head and her white silk blouse is soaked red from shots to the body and neck.

Her husband has been winged by a bullet across the forehead and blood pours over his face. He cannot see and his hands scrabble frantically for the door handle.

A burst of bullets hit him in the back of the head and he slumps into the door.

The commandos check that all the occupants of the three

vehicles are dead, pull the drivers out of their seats and hurriedly restart their engines.

The drivers of the minivan and the motorbike start up, load their passengers and drive away from Goma. A petrol tanker passes them on the other side of the road, its diesel gurgling and grinding in the quiet of the night. It pulls up fifty yards in front of the scene.

A commando quickly restarts the first jeep and backs it up out of the drainage ditch. The BMW is also restarted and straightened up on the road so that it faces the tanker, the handbrake is put on and the other jeep is driven up behind it and braked. While this happens other men swiftly check around the scene of the shooting to collect empty cartridge cases.

When they are ready, a quick radio order is given and the tanker driver accelerates forward and crashes into the BMW, crushing its bonnet under the front of the cab. He jumps down and the first jeep is driven up alongside the huge petrol tank.

A commando sets a device under it and the whole group then race back down the beach towards the two waiting speedboats.

As they head off into the darkened lake a flash of light and a huge blast behind them rips the night apart.

The head of the Chinese delegation, Mr Cheng, the Rwandan president and his chief of staff all applaud and nod appreciatively as Alex finishes the Q&A session.

There were a lot of tough technical questions from the Rwandans about timings, weapon systems and numbers of troops and helicopters. Mr Cheng was much more focused on the money: how much was it all going to cost, what were his budgetary assumptions and what was his contingency planning? Would the Kivu Investment Corporation get the return on capital required?

With the aid of his team Alex fielded the questions successfully. Arkady was authoritative, and surprisingly diplomatic in explaining the helicopter leasing deal. Yamba covered recruitment and training of the officers, NCOs and men, and Col did weapon systems and air assault tactics.

The meeting has gone well and all sides are satisfied with the plan. The five men in the audience stand up and start chatting to Team Devereux or moving forward to have a closer look at the various maps and charts on easels at the front of the room. Alex is now in full diplomatic mode, circulating, shaking hands and chatting with his employers. He has got to know the Rwandan Chief of Staff well and they have a strong mutual professional respect. The Chinese team have kept more distant and he has clashed repeatedly with Fang over budgets. Alex wants more helicopters but Fang thinks he has enough already.

After a certain amount of confused simultaneous bowing, back-slapping and handshaking, the meeting breaks up and Team Devereux head off back to their hotel. Alex nips back into the meeting room, past the armed guard on the door, to get his laptop.

He stands and looks at the charts and plans pinned up around him. He is coming down from the adrenaline high of the presentation and feeling tired after long hours of staff work in the months leading up to it. It was a bravura performance; he can hear his voice in the room, he sounded so authoritative and confident. But now the tension of the presentation has gone, the room feels empty and the animus of his ideas is absent. The maps and charts proudly proclaiming his grand plan look flat and insignificant, just bits of paper. He stands and looks at them and thinks, 'Have I got this right?'

He glibly castigated the British and American commanders for the mistakes they made in Iraq and Afghanistan, but is he guilty of the same? There are so many variables that are just way beyond his control, things that are completely off the radar, out there in the darkness, areas he knows nothing about.

Could operational security on a project of this scale really be maintained? Kinshasa's elite are notoriously fickle – could they be counted on to keep their mouths shut? At least they had played their part after the assassination of Sabiti, proclaiming it a tragic accident and appointing the more compliant Brigadier General Oloba to control the whole of Kivu.

But will he really be able to recruit a thousand good-quality soldiers from many different countries and train them into an effective, highly disciplined fighting force in the space of a few months?

And what will happen when they actually go over the border and begin combat operations? Despite what he said in the presentation it is going to be a messy, bloody battle. The FDLR has six thousand men based in difficult terrain and has been fighting in the province for nearly twenty years. They are not going to go quietly.

Finally, he knows that it is easier to start a war than to finish it. What is going to happen in the peace? Will the UN and US accept it? Will he be able to get the civilian NGOs to cooperate and help in the demilitarisation of the FDLR and other militia soldiers? Can he really trust Rukuba? He likes the man but really knows nothing about his past and the extent of his rumoured links to the Kudu Noir.

He collects his laptop and stands for a moment longer in the silent room.

Will this work?

Will it?

Chapter Sixteen

Gabriel is stuck in the narrow tunnel, underwater and in darkness.

He can't see anything, he can't breathe and he can't move. The earthquake has compressed the tunnel on top of him.

He panics.

He thrashes around, pushing the sack of ore out of the way in front of him, trying to work his way forward.

His air is going, he can feel his lungs shrivelling inside him, gripping the remaining oxygen until they scream with pain.

Two hard hands grab his forearms and pull him forward. He twists his head sideways and it squeezes under the obstruction. Cold mud scrapes into his ears.

Another powerful pull from the hands and he pops up above the sump like a tight cork being pulled out of a bottle. It's pitch black and he whoops in air. It's foul and cold but tastes sweet to him.

'You OK?' says a face right in front of him.

He coughs mud, spits and grunts.

It's Patrice, the FDLR soldier who went down the tube before him. In the Rift Valley area there is a lot of volcanic activity and Patrice is used to small tremors so when it hit and he felt the tunnel compress, he didn't panic but managed to get out the other end, then turned round and dived back in to grab the person coming after him. He grips Gabriel's arms and the men behind him holding his feet give another big heave and drag the two of them further out.

That night Gabriel lies in his rough wooden bunk in a hut in the *manoir* and tries not to think about the horror of the tunnel. But he can feel the cold clammy embrace of the mud squeezing his body.

He pulls his little stack of cash out from the slit in his thin mattress and counts the tatty dollar bills. He still hasn't got enough yet to pay his family back for Eve's treatment. He thinks about her and wonders how she is getting on after her operation. The last message he had from her family's friend in the *manoir* said they won't know for a while if the sutures have held.

He thinks about his narrow escape in the tunnel today and rolls the notes into a bundle and secures it with a rubber band. He says to himself, 'There has got to be an easier way of making money than this.'

Sophie Cecil-Black puts down her mobile phone and turns to Natalie, her American colleague sitting behind her across the office. They are in the Hope Street headquarters at their youth training facility outside Goma.

'That's the third person I've talked to today who thinks something is up.'

Natalie is engrossed in typing a tricky bit on a Gantt chart to organise a community action project and ignores her for a moment until she has finished it.

'Uh-huh.' She swivels her chair round to face Sophie. 'Something like what?'

'Well, no one believes that Sabiti died in a tanker accident. I know Kinshasa says that but it's just too convenient that

Sabiti and all his bodyguards could die in one go with no witnesses.'

It's been two days since Sabiti was killed and the province is buzzing with fearful rumours about what might be happening. People have seen many outbursts of violence in the past and they fear this might herald another one.

Natalie shrugs. 'OK, but why would the government want to kill its top soldier in North Kivu?'

Sophie shakes her head, 'I don't know . . . but that was Félicien on the phone from Shabunda outstation and he says that all the government troops are very edgy and that FDLR soldiers have been on the move in the area.'

'Well, what's new about that? This is Kivu.'

'Hmm.' Sophie scratches the back of her head, gets up and walks over to the window. She stares at the view up into the hills for a moment. 'I just sometimes wonder if we actually know anything about what makes this place tick.'

Natalie picks up her coffee cup and comes to stand next to her.

Sophie continues angsting. 'What I'm trying to say is, do we know what really makes things happen here? Nothing is as it seems in the Congo. You always know that someone is bullshitting you about something and I don't think we ever really get a grip on what the dynamics are behind the scenes.'

Natalie sips her coffee thoughtfully. 'Just the way it is.'

Sophie rounds on her in exasperation. 'But that's just not good enough! I mean, there were a lot of rumours in Rwanda before the genocide that something big was going to happen but none of the expats bothered to find out what was really happening! They did nothing!'

Natalie knows the anger isn't directed at her, it's just Sophie's way. She shrugs. 'Yeah, but come on, nothing like that is going to happen now in Kivu. The UN's here and besides no one really gives a shit about Kivu. It'll just moulder away for decades like the Palestinians, nothing's gonna change that.'

Alex is sitting in a meeting room in a cheap furnished office, rented by the day, near Heathrow.

Yamba dishes out copies of a brief summary he has typed up of the next candidate they will interview in the session. They started at eight o'clock and it's now mid afternoon. It has been a packed day so far and they still have eleven more people to see.

The candidates for the company and platoon commander posts in the Kivu Defence Force are all from personal contacts and have been coming in from all over the UK, Europe and North America. They need to get their officers in place quickly before they can then recruit their NCO cadre. It's July, three months after Alex's first meeting with Fang, but they still need to get on with it in order to allow enough time to get the troops selected and the whole unit trained up together in Rwanda to an operational level for the assault next May.

For secrecy reasons candidates are not being told where the operation will take place or its precise nature, only that it will involve proper war fighting, not just security work.

The hope is that by the time they get the guys out to Rwanda and working together they will be less likely to leave when they hear the actual details of what they are going to do. Alex knows that most mercenaries are men of action, not that bothered about the finer points of international law, and thinks he can persuade any doubters to stay on by saying that the mission will create a much better world. It's not perfect but what else can he do?

Col's interest is waning. 'So who's this bloke?'

'Will you please read the paperwork when I give it to you?' Yamba looks at him in despair.

'I hate paperwork.'

Yamba rolls his eyes.

Alex reads out the details. 'He's Jean-Baptiste Delacroix, been a captain in the French Foreign Legion . . .'

'Oh, what! He's a Frog! Bludy 'ell!' Col chucks the papers on the table.

Yamba looked at him incredulously. 'What's wrong with the Frogs?'

'Don't get me started, don't get me started. I hate the French.'

'But you speak French.'

'That's different.'

'But Alex has a French name.'

'It's Norman, actually,' says Alex rather too quickly. 'Big difference. Anyway, look, this chap's good, the Foreign Legion doesn't muck about, Col.' He reads from Yamba's notes, 'Experience in Chad, CAR and West Africa, tours in Afghanistan. Definitely knows what he's on about.'

Col suddenly becomes positive. 'OK, that's great; I am really pleased to have this opportunity to work with our valued European partners. Let's give him a fair chance and then tell him to fook off.'

He grins at the others.

Alex ignores him. 'Right, let's get him in, shall we?' He heads down to fetch him from reception.

Jean-Baptiste Delacroix is a short, muscular Frenchman full of intense energy. He is in his mid-thirties with a neat beard, light brown curly hair, a pugnacious stance and a ferociously hard handshake. His bright hazel eyes dart around as he meets the team, assessing everything about them.

They settle into their seats and Alex is his usual urbane self. Although his French is good enough to conduct the interview, the main language of command for the unit will be English, so he needs to test the man's ability.

'Well, Captain Delacroix, thank you very much for coming here today to see us. Can I start by asking you about your time in the Legion? It has a very good military reputation. What do think you would bring from it to another unit?'

Jean-Baptiste looks at him for a moment. In that instant his mind rushes through his fifteen years of memories and he wonders how he could explain the Legion to an outsider.

'Well, the Legion is a very different unit,' he says quietly. 'It is a state within a state, more like a monastic order. Once you join you are not allowed any personal possessions, no bank account, no civilian clothes. No contact with the outside world for the first stages of training and you cannot marry until you have served five years. So it is very intense but this produces a ferocious professionalism that I believe I would carry over into any other unit.'

Should he talk about his selection course as a private on the 'Farm', their isolated training camp in the high snows of the Pyrenees? Two hours of sleep in three days of constant hard physical activity, culminating in an all-night march. They only got through it by working in pairs, one man walking and holding the hand of the other man who slept as he stumbled along behind. Giving up was not an option in a unit whose unofficial motto was 'March or Die'.

Or should he mention the hand-to-hand combat training that followed for days and nights afterwards? Attacked repeatedly as they slept, bombarded with shouts of 'Alert! Alert! Alert!' and then the rain of blows from their instructors. He got used to sleeping with his fists clenched.

Alex nods. He is intrigued: he knows about the Legion's

136

ferocious training and cannot work out why such an intelligent, sensitive man would have gone through such a process.

'And can I ask why you decided to join the Legion?'

'In the Legion you do not ask.'

Jean-Baptiste says it in a completely neutral tone of voice, just a statement of fact.

Alex meets his eye for a moment. They both know that recruits effectively disappear inside the French state when they join, protected from the police and their home countries. After five years' service they can opt to be allocated a new name and identity. After World War Two the Legion sheltered many Waffen SS soldiers fleeing justice in their homelands.

This is the problem with mercenary recruitment. How can he tell why the men have left their units and what they have been doing? They are asked to bring a full service record but sometimes you have to read between the lines. When he gets round to recruiting nearly a thousand squaddies from all over the world he just won't have the time to do full background checks.

Will the men be competent at their jobs, will they be inept? Will they have criminal records? Assault on an officer, drug taking, rape, theft – squaddies are not saints, especially those who have left the army.

Alex decides not to push it in this case. Jean-Baptiste's gaze is straight and unflinching.

'OK, well, can you tell me what you have been doing since you left?'

The Frenchman is happy to move on. 'For eighteen months I have been in Paris doing what I originally meant to be. I am a sculptor.'

Alex nods in surprise and Jean-Baptiste smiles. 'Yes, the Legion was not the natural place for an artist but . . .' He gives a genuine Gallic shrug.

137

Somehow he managed to preserve his humanity in the midst of the fascism. Any disobedience was met with savage beatings – he looked at his corporal wrong on the parade ground once and that night three large NCOs got him in the washrooms and punched his head so hard it banged back against the wall, then shoved it down the toilet, pissed on him and flushed it.

'. . . But I am not that commercially successful, so I have come back to my other metier.'

Alex moves the interview on to his time in Afghanistan and the intense combat that he encountered there. Then they give him maps and instructions in English for a difficult company-level operational scenario and five minutes to understand it and come up with a solution.

Jean-Baptiste comes alive, leaning forward over the table, his head flicking back and forth rapidly between the maps as he assesses the situation. His answers are quick, decisive and correct.

When he has left Alex looks at the others. 'What did you think?'

Yamba nods, impressed. 'He's good, he has an excellent service record and he handled the scenario well. He's definitely someone we could work with.'

Col has spent most of the interview with his arms folded and his eyes narrowed.

Alex looks at him.

'Well, he's still a Frog but I suppose he'll do.'

Chapter Seventeen

Matt Hooper is a newly commissioned sergeant in the Kivu Defence Force but is currently wearing civilian clothing and standing in the arrivals hall of Kigali airport in Rwanda. He is awaiting the arrival of his platoon of men on the flight from Brussels. It's March, eleven months after Alex's first meeting with Fang in April, and the plans for the assault and invasion are coming together.

He's holding a tour rep's clipboard with a fictitious company logo, Adventure Training and Development Partnership, on the back. All his men are flying in on tourist visas and are down to do adventure training and volunteer development work in rural Rwanda.

Matt taps the barrier in front of him nervously with his biro and his head flicks round as the first passenger comes out of the door from customs. It's a middle-aged woman and he looks away again.

Matt is twenty-eight and from Norfolk, a real Fenlander, born and brought up amidst mile upon mile of flat industrial farmland. A bit of a lad, he joined the Royal Anglians aged seventeen as a squaddie to get out, did two heavy tours in Afghanistan and got promoted to sergeant. His Norfolk accent makes his speech slow but his eyes have that calm look that shows he's no fool.

He left the army two years ago, got a girlfriend, Danielle, a job selling high-end German kitchens, and then got bored. Now he wants to make a decent whack of money to start his own business.

He spots two likely lads coming through the doors pushing their luggage trolleys. Both have buzzcut hair, tattooed fore-arms and wear shellsuits.

'Over 'ere, lads!' He holds up the clipboard and waves them over to him.

Sean Potts and Jason Hall are both ex-squaddies bored with their lives as South London painters and decorators. Sean is Irish Catholic, has ginger hair and is built like a brick shithouse. Jason is from Deptford and, following in the Marlowe tradition, got involved in a stabbing before deciding to join the army to avoid further trouble. He is now looking to earn three years' money in six months in order to buy himself a Subaru Impreza, at which point he knows his life will be complete.

Matt gives them his big smile. 'Come round 'ere.'

He directs them round the barrier to where he wants to corral his platoon of new recruits in a corner of the arrivals hall.

When the last of his twenty-five blokes come through, he ticks them off on his list and checks them over. Big men in their twenties and thirties with thick necks, shaved heads and biceps bulging out of tight tee shirts.

He's been impressed how the recruitment process has weeded out the unfit and undesirable. He attended a selec-tion day at a paintballing site in the countryside near Heathrow. There were a hundred guys on the day who seemed to have come from all over the world, both NCOs and soldiers. Some looked past it, with potbellies and creaking backs; they hadn't lasted long on the fitness test and the assault course. The platoon-level exercises with paintball guns had also showed up who could and couldn't command a platoon in the field. Others on the course were obviously bullshitters and fantasists, walking around in combat jackets with badges sown on that proclaimed they had been in the 82nd Airborne and the Royal Marines.

He hadn't seen any of that type since he had got to Rwanda two weeks ago. He had been swiftly inducted into the training base in the Virunga Mountains on the border with Congo and had been impressed by how everything had been run like clockwork. Mission security was tight but Regimental Sergeant Major Thwaites had had a quiet word with him and let it be known that the objective was as part of a mission in Southern Sudan to support the newly installed government there.

Matt isn't that bothered really. The money was great, tax-free as well, and he is doing the job he loved. He is engaged to Danielle now, she wanted a commitment from him before he went off for six months and he was glad to give it. He misses her – there's no contact until after the op has started in a month's time, phones and laptops have been confiscated – but all the lads understand that OpSec is important. It is their lives on the line if word gets out.

He looks at his new recruits. He's got English, Dutch, Romanian, American, Canadian, Danish and Polish soldiers so language is going to be tricky to start with but they have a month of hard training in the mountains before they go on the op so he reckons he can get it worked out.

'Right, lads, we're in the two minibuses out the front. So stick your bags in the trailers and let's get going.'

Jason and Sean look at Matt, sizing him up. His Norfolk accent sounds a bit 'oo arr' to their South London ears but he's on the ball and seems a good bloke, got a big smile.

They drive three hours west to Ruhengiri near the border with Congo. The roads are good but the country is obviously dirt-poor, hardly any traffic around but loads of families trudging along the roadside or up and down the many hills with huge loads of firewood, water and vegetables bundled on top of their heads.

Jason and Sean have both been in Afghanistan and they are experiencing the same feeling of being strangers in a strange land again. Jason is squeezed into a seat next to a large soldier from Romania with very limited English. Normally Jason would take the piss out of him for this but he knows that if they go into combat then this bloke could be the man next to him in the firing line who keeps him alive. The fear of approaching combat focuses his mind and he instead spends the time teaching him words like 'rifle', 'casualty' and 'cease fire'. Sean leans over between the seats and they also teach him 'fuck', 'cock', 'birds' and 'shag'.

Matt is sitting at the front of the bus with a guy that no one else wanted to sit next to. He is a brute of a man, six foot two of muscle, bone and stubble with a spider's web tattoo on each side of his massive neck. The dome of his shaved head forms a single unit with his shoulders and his arms stick out from his body because of the size of his chest.

'Stein,' he says in a humourless German accent and shakes Matt's hand; it feels like a lump of concrete.

'So what unit were you in then?'

'Kar Ess Kar.'

Matt looks at him blankly. Stein spells the letters out with a finger.

'Oh right, KSK.'

'Shit,' he thinks, 'I've got a psychopath here.' The Kommando Spezialkräfte is the German equivalent of the

SAS. He's met other Special Forces guys like him – totally brutalised by the harshness of their training.

'Ya, I am in Afghan but then I want a break. I leave, I go to America for six months, I go to California, I drink, I fuck girls. I come back and now I want to fight again.'

He looks at Matt fiercely. His eyes are deep-set under heavy brows and there's a dangerous gleam in them.

Matt nods and thinks, 'I'll need to watch this one.'

They skirt round the edge of Ruhengiri town and bump down off the tarmac onto a dirt road. It starts heading up into the Virunga Mountains, a chain of eight volcanoes along the border with peaks just under fifteen thousand feet that are home to mountain gorillas. The sky clouds over and the bush presses in around them. Sean does a bad American accent for his new mate, Specialist Daz Vitriano from San Diego: 'In the jungle, man!'

Daz grins and shakes his head.

They climb the eastern slopes of the extinct volcano Mount Karisimbi and drive past a small rusty sign saying 'Interdit' marked with a Rwandan army logo. The border is a closed area with a lot of army bases against possible incursion from the FDLR. Jason is now too involved in a conversation with Daz to notice. They are talking about why a Subaru Impreza is a better pulling car than the Mustang that Daz is going to buy when he gets back home with his money.

The conversation cuts off when the bus stops at a small dirt road turning off yet higher into the jungle-covered mountains. A convoy of ten dark green Rwandan army trucks is turning in there, slowly grinding up the gradient and they have to wait. All chat stops and the lads peer anxiously out of the windows. They can see that the trucks are laden with artillery ammunition boxes.

They follow in the dust haze from the trucks and soon stop again at a barrier next to a guardhouse manned by Rwandan soldiers. They get on the bus and carefully check Matt's roster against the men's passports. Jason thinks their sergeant looks switched on and dangerous as he glares at each soldier checking his face against his passport photo.

They drive past a sign saying 'Camp Purgatory'. The road flattens out into a valley floor and passes an area with helicopters, gunships and troop carriers being worked on by mechanics. Jason glances nervously round at Sean. They are back on planet military.

As they drive on, all around are wooden barracks huts up the sides of the valley and a parade square in the bottom of it. Men in camouflage uniforms are moving around quickly and with a sense of purpose, unloading the ammunition trucks. They can hear the sound of a helicopter swirling around in the hills and nearby is the regular crack of small arms fire from a firing range.

The buses pull up in a line on the parade square in front of an HQ building. There's a flagstaff with a unit insignia flying next to it, a large red '1' on a green shield.

Matt Hooper pulls open the door of their bus and yells, 'Right, get out! Get your kit, fall in here! Let's go!' He's not smiling now.

Jason and Sean can see why. Standing on the veranda of the HQ building with his hands on his hips, watching everything very closely, is a classic British army hardman type. He is small with shaved hair, moustache, neat uniform and an RSM's badge of office on a broad leather strap on his left wrist.

Behind him is a tall, stern-looking white officer and a scary-looking black bloke. They were introduced on their

144

selection course as Mr Hughes and Mr Jones and are watching them closely now.

Matt gets them sorted into rough ranks and the small figure struts over to address them. His voice booms out in a harsh Lancashire accent and the men flinch at the volume.

'Right, my name is Regimental Sergeant Major Thwaites, and *you* are now in *my regiment*! S'arnt Hooper will get you sorted out with your mess and your scoff tonight and you will commence training tomorrow morning.'

Col watches their eyes switch their gaze internally as the message sinks in. This is not going to be a fun adventure holiday; they are back in the bullshit.

'The commanding officer of the regiment, Colonel Devereux, will now address you. Two Platoon! Atten-*tion*!'

The response to the drill command would not be acceptable in the Guards but even with the language difficulties the men can work out what is going on and they stand rigidly to attention and eye their new boss carefully for clues to what their new life will be like. Is he taking things seriously? Will this be some sort of slack-arsed, wild and crazy mercenary unit?

Alex steps up, his hands on his hips, leaning forward to address them. His combats are smartly pressed and his maroon beret is worn at the right angle. His voice is loud and deep.

'Gentlemen, you have made it through the selection process and now have the honour of serving in the First Regiment, Kivu Defence Force.'

Jason and Sean recognise the accent as classic British officer class, fiercely proper and correct, but with the whip-crack of command in it.

'Myself, S'arnt Major Thwaites and my 2IC, your Training Officer, Major Douala, are all looking forward to our training as a unit. It will be robust and challenging and will commence tomorrow morning. Reveille is O five hundred.'

Fang squeezes the trigger, the gun bucks slightly and a wide area of the plywood target explodes.

He shouts an expletive in Chinese and looks round at Col who is grinning back at him.

'Gleaming, eh? Right, put it on auto.'

He reaches over and clicks the selector lever down.

'Right, give it a full mag now.'

Fang grins, tucks the butt into his shoulder and squeezes the trigger again. There is a steady roar as the gun blasts away and twenty-nine big, fat, red, twelve-gauge shotgun shells stream out of the ejection point in seconds.

Fang screams and sprays the target area in buckshot. The steel ball bearings make the plastic target bottles dance on the ground and completely shred the plywood screen behind them.

The mag clicks empty and he laughs and hands the Barrett AA-12 machine shotgun back to Col. 'Awesome!'

'Yer, I saw it demoed in the States and just thought, I've gotta have that.' He handles the large matt-black rifle with love; it looks like a bulky M16 with a fat drum magazine under it. They are out on the firing range showing Fang and Rukuba around the base. 'The Yanks developed it for use in Iraq for close quarter combat so it'll come in handy when we're in the jungle, you know – you can't see the enemy in a bush but if you put a few rounds of this into it you'll flush 'em out sharpish like. They've also got a mini-grenade round that's quite a lotta fun as well. They're not cheap though so we've only got one per section but it'll work well with these.' He picks up one of the three assault rifles lying on the table. 'This will be the regiment's standard infantry rifle. It's basically just a Chinese version of an AK-74, so it's dead robust and very easy to train the lads on it.' He shrugs. 'Not a very sophisticated rifle but it'll do the job.'

He turns round and looks at Rukuba. 'You wanna have a go?'

The politician holds up his hands in polite refusal. 'Oh, no thank you, I am not a man of violence.'

'OK, suit yerself.'

Alex steps in at this point. The unit is now at full complement and they have got a lot to see on the tour.

'Right, let's go and see the air wing, shall we?'

They turn and walk back down the valley to the flatter land where the helicopters and drones are based.

Alex is now colonel in charge of eleven hundred combat soldiers. Most are light infantry to be moved around rapidly in helicopters for airmobile strike warfare. But apart from these six rifle companies he also has platoons of specialists: heavy machine guns, mortars, antitank, recce, snipers, signallers, medics, a large electronic warfare team and several batteries of 105mm light guns.

The number of men he needed to recruit from the mercenary market was so large that he has ended up with soldiers from a total of fifteen different countries – British, South African, Angolan, American and Canadian troops are the largest groups but he also has Germans, Belgians, French, Dutch and Italians. The NATO deployment to Afghanistan means that nearly all of them have recent war fighting experience. The French and Swahili speakers have been split up so that there is at least one in each platoon, meaning they can communicate with most of the locals in Kivu if they need to. But at the end of the day Alex needs guys with military experience who are fit and can fire a rifle. Basic infantry vocabulary is a few hundred words – they can make it work. The selection days that they ran in different countries have weeded out the dross and now it is just down to good leadership and training. They can hear that going on all around the valley now: shouting and screaming as NCOs beast their platoons over assault courses.

They have settled the men in well, issuing them webbing, boots, packs, sleeping bags, flak jackets, camelbacks, hats and helmets. The green camouflage uniforms have got variously coloured epaulettes for the different rifle companies.

They have also done the grim stuff: issuing dog tags, thin grey metal rectangles just over an inch long on a chain. Name and number, blood group and religion are stamped on them. The only time they will come off the men now will be the end of the tour or if they are dead.

Equally daunting for the men was signing off their insurance arrangements. The grisly business of enumerating the money owed for the loss of fingers and toes, maiming, facial mutilation, blinding, paralysis – paraplegic and quadriplegic – and death. A thousand and one reasons not to do the job. Most of them didn't even read it but just glanced at it and signed. If you thought about that stuff too much you wouldn't do the job.

The group walks down onto the flightline and Arkady struts over to them in blue oil-streaked overalls, proud of the fleet of aircraft he has assembled. He has also recruited the pilots, loadmasters, mechanics and airgunners to fly and service them.

Fang and Rukuba have met him in Rwanda and stand and listen politely to his briefing, although Rukuba is keeping his distance from the detail, rather than boyishly hoovering it up like Fang.

'So these are the troopships.' Arkady points to five large dumpy-looking transport helicopters. 'They are the

Chinese-built Mi-171C, the version of the Russian Mi-17; we have leased all ten. I get three of these for price of one Blackhawk and Blackhawks only take thirteen men – these take twenty-five or thirty fully loaded infantry.' He looks at them for acknowledgement of his acumen and they nod appreciatively.

'Over there are Beyoncé and Shakira.' He points to the two Mil Mi-24s. 'They're great performers,' he says and grins broadly, showing a gold tooth at the side of his mouth.

The two big gunships look like evil dragons. They have a double bulge of armoured cockpits at the front with a lumpy chin turret for a twin-barrelled 23mm cannon. Short stubby wings and rocket pods add to the overall ugliness of the machines.

He finishes off with less enthusiasm by pointing past the two helicopters, 'Those things are the drones.' Like a lot of pilots he still doesn't like the weird-looking pilotless reconnaissance aircraft being worked on by their Israeli support crews.

The day finishes off with tea in the HQ block; Alex has declared the base dry.

'Overall, I'm very pleased with the way it is all coming together,' Alex explains, standing in front of Fang and Rukuba as Col and Yamba watch; he's getting worked up now, leaning forward.

'You see, the problem we have here is how do we create a coherent unit from so many guys in such a short space of time? But it is possible. You see, if you look at other unorthodox units like Colonel Mike Hoare's 5 Commando in the Congo in the sixties or Executive Outcomes in the nineties, they all had limited resources and no formal military structure to rely on and *yet* they created units that completely outperformed in tough conditions. So the real question is, how do we get the guys to love adversity?'

The guests wait to be enlightened.

'Well, basically soldiers love a challenge and want to be heroes and with good leadership and training they can be. I mean, here we have *nothing* in terms of set military tradition or hierarchy; it's all down to us to make it happen. We have to pull First Regiment together and make our own legend.' He laughs. 'That's what we're going to be – legends!'

Chapter Eighteen

A huge explosion comes from his right and Jason Hall ducks down with a terse, 'Shit!'

Bullets start zipping through the bush overhead and leaves and branches shower down over them.

'Where are they?' Sergeant Hooper's bellow comes from the other side of a clump of bamboo at the front of his section's diamond formation and the men's heads swivel around awkwardly as they crouch.

Sean spots the muzzle flashes on the hillside overlooking them. 'One hundred metres, right of axis of advance! Muzzle flashes in treeline!'

'In the trees there!' a soldier shouts and now Matt can see them. The radio earpiece on his left ear crackles and Major Delacroix's voice barks, 'Hooper, you give fire support, I manoeuvre Three Platoon left flanking. Over.'

Matt repeats the order and Corporal Stein gets his sections into cover to give fire support. Apart from being deeply scary, Stein is actually trained to a higher standard than any of them so all the men jump to it when he is around.

Major Delacroix gives the command and Matt's men open up. Looking down through the trees he sees Three Platoon break cover, dash across the stream in the valley bottom and assault uphill against the enemy position. Loud bangs of grenades and gunfire echo across the valley.

Col, Alex and Yamba stand on a knoll up the valley and observe the training with their binoculars. Jean-Baptiste has done a good job of manoeuvring his men but the exercise isn't over yet.

This is Echo Company's first big twenty-four-hour exercise. The hundred and twenty men were dropped off by five helicopters in a clearing on the bend of a river two valleys away last night. Since then they have been lugging their full load of equipment and blank ammunition up and down the steep forested slopes whilst being attacked by Bravo Company.

Yamba's cold, hawk-like eyes flick up and down the valley assessing what is happening. He is a graduate from the South African Defence Force School of Infantry at Oudtshoorn and believes in doing things properly. Echo Company have had to practise their skills in bushcraft, night marches, river crossings and casevac, re-embarkation on the helicopters and then another assault into a hot LZ. And all of this at an altitude of seven thousand feet. The men are knackered.

They have got a way to go though. They must do a fighting retreat back down the valley before their final extraction by helicopter: the pilots and aircrew need the practice of working with the soldiers.

The exercise ends well; the men spill out of the back of the helicopters on the landing pads at Camp Purgatory in Rwanda, only miles from the border with Kivu. They are knackered but they know they have done a good job and there are big grins all round.

Alex comes over to congratulate Jean-Baptiste with a big smile on his face, 'Excellent job, Major Delacroix, very well done.' They shake hands.

The Frenchman is more than fulfilling Alex's expectations:

he's a dynamic commander, furiously intense but with a quick smile, and his men love him.

Jean-Baptiste's face is smeared in camouflage cream. He grins. 'Yes, it was good, we got stuck a bit in the ambush in the first valley.' He shrugs. 'Our spacing was not good but we can work on it.'

The men get cleaned up and, having passed their big test, the next morning have their formal swearing-in ceremony on the parade square.

Alex knows that the outward symbols of military belonging are important to the men and so they get the full works. Echo Company parades in front of him and the rest of the command element.

Jean-Baptiste stands front centre and bellows, 'Echo Company, all present and correct, awaiting your inspection, sir!'

Alex walks up and down the ranks of men, looking carefully at them, and rehearsing their names in his mind.

He makes a brief address in which he emphasises the importance of unit discipline. 'Some mercenary units got themselves a reputation for poor discipline.' They all know what he means – Congo had a dose of them when control in 6 Commando broke down in the late 1960s and troops ran amok attacking civilians. Given the nature of their task to bring law and order to an anarchic region, Alex is particularly sensitive about this.

'But you will not let me down! First Regiment is a disciplined unit that respects civilians and its Rules of Engagement.' He has been banging on about these Rules throughout their training. Invaders are never popular and he knows it would only take one incident of civilian collateral damage to ignite nationalist anger against foreign troops.

'Having completed your training, you will now be formally

153

inducted into the Regiment and be issued with one of these.' He holds up a small laminated card. 'This is the Ten Commandments of the First Regiment.'

It's a trick he has borrowed from Roger's Rangers, an unorthodox unit in the American War of Independence. It was reused by Mike Hoare in 5 Commando and now him. The list is an eclectic mix of rules for the troops, some practical and some ethical that sums up the tone of his command. Alex reads them out to the men. 'The first commandment is *Obey orders*. Then, *Attack hard* and *Defend hard*. Next, *Respect and defend civilians at all times.*

'The fifth commandment is, *Keep your rifle cleaned, oiled and to hand at all times. Check your ammunition, magazine springs and lips.* They are the basic tools of our job. Similarly, *Do not overload the helicopters.* We are an airmobile unit, without them we cannot function.

'Next, *Look after the men in your unit. Stay switched on – even in battle fatigue stay alert and notice what is going on around you. Shave every day.* And finally, *Conserve ammunition. Do not spray and pray.*'

The parade ends with the men taking an oath of allegiance to the flag as a unit and then coming up one by one to salute Alex, shake his hand and be issued with their copy of the Ten Commandments.

Alex looks each man in the eye as they come up and then scans the ranks as they stand awaiting his orders at the end. His heart swells with pride as he looks at them, thinking of the glory that they can win.

Glistening drops of sweat hang off the woman's nose and chin as she walks up the forest track. She doesn't notice them and walks with a blank look, her consciousness sunk somewhere deep inside her, concentrating on putting one bare foot in front of the other and keeping going up the muddy trail under her heavy load.

She has a huge bundle of food, cooking equipment and plastic sheeting piled up in a wicker basket on her back so that it comes up above her head. Her hands hold a bark strap that runs from it around her forehead to keep the basket from toppling backwards.

Joseph walks behind her. He doesn't have a pack, just his rifle balanced on his shoulder with one hand holding the muzzle. The path goes up and downhill winding through thickets of bamboo, sugar cane and elephant grass. His Wellingtons slide in the mud and on the way down one hill he slips and lands painfully on his coccyx.

The FDLR soldiers are walking through the bush en route to their new base in the Lubonga valley wearing their ragtag uniforms of green combats mixed with tee shirts and jeans. Joseph is at the back of the column standing guard on the nine women that they have pressed into service as bearers. He cuts himself a walking stick and uses it to balance as they cross a fast-flowing stream in a valley.

Heavy rain starts but they trudge on regardless. He can feel the cold water running out of his hair, down his cheeks and down the back of his neck. The mud begins to work its way up the instep of his boots and onto his trousers. He keeps his head down and soon all he can see and think about are the bare feet of the woman in front of him slapping along in the mud.

At five o'clock, Lieutenant Karuta calls a halt and they make camp whilst it is still light. The women are tied to a tree and the soldiers make rough shelters out of branches and sheeting. They are all exhausted and for once no one bothers raping the women. Joseph's coccyx hurts too much to even think about it. In the morning they awake cold and stiff and after a breakfast of water and bananas they set off again.

Midmorning and a burst of gunfire up ahead wakes Joseph from his daze.

'Get down! Take cover!'

The men scatter, plunging into the bushes at the sides of the trail.

They poke their heads back out, guns at the ready. 'What's up? What's happening?'

From where he is at the back of the column he can't see the head of it because ten feet in front of him the track curves round some bushes. Urgent whispers dart back and forth up the line.

'Shut up! Keep quiet!'

They all stare intently at the bushes as if they are able to tell them what is happening. He can hear a voice shouting from further up the hill but can't make out the words. There's a pause and then another voice shouts back. Silence follows and they all wait for five minutes.

Finally Corporal Habiyakare ambles back down the track.

'OK, get up! Come on, let's go!'

'What happened?'

'We ran into another FDLR platoon but Benois was on point and he wasn't sure who they were so he fired. The lieutenant sorted it out though, no one was hurt. They're going to the same rendezvous point as us. Come on!'

There are smiles of relief all round and they heave the packs back on the women and get going again.

They reach Utiti that evening and crash out in a hut by the dirt road.

The following morning four battered trucks stop at the roadside. The soldiers climb in and pass their bags up. There's a lot of chatter and laughter, it's exciting to feel

156

that they are going somewhere different; life in the bush is boring.

Joseph hasn't been on a truck for years and the speed and movement is fun, though as a junior soldier he gets the worst place at the back, where the fierce sun dries out the dirt road and the slipstream whips up the red dust from the wheels. The soldiers wrap their tee shirts round their heads but their hair, long and bushy after so long in the forest, gets coated in red dust like a group of clowns. The dust gets in Joseph's mouth and mixes with saliva to form red mud on his teeth.

They flash through scruffy roadside villages of wooden huts. The inhabitants run at the sight of them.

In one village they slow down as they pass through the centre of it and some Congolese army soldiers come out and stare at them. The platoon stare back as they drive past. Sometimes they fight each other and sometimes they cooperate, it all depends on individual commanders and the ebb and flow of local politics. They don't have an axe to grind with each other now and are obviously just passing through, so the FARDC troops just watch them go by.

The trucks drive on and slow again to climb over a high ridge, the gears grind and they swing back and forth up the switchbacks before finally swooping down the other side in a series of sickening turns. Joseph begins to feel very ill – at times the back of the truck is hanging over a steep drop. He throws up over it and huddles down with his head inside his tee shirt.

Finally the turns stop and he sticks his head out, they are driving over a fast-flowing river on a bridge of metal girders. He looks up ahead and sees that they are entering a steep-sided valley – Lubonga, the main FDLR base.

The aircraft has no pilot but it manoeuvres adroitly on the dirt airstrip, lining up to take off.

The Israeli-made Heron unmanned aerial vehicle is the size of a sleek, dark grey Cessna but with only a bulge where the cockpit should be. The rudders on its twin tail boom waggle and the wing flaps adjust. The rear-facing propeller between the two tailfins revs and it speeds down the runway.

Alex watches it anxiously; they only have one Heron and the runway is short and surrounded by hills. They do have one other drone, called a Ranger, that can be catapulted off a ramp on the back of a lorry, but they will use it more when they are over the border and don't have a runway for takeoffs.

Like its namesake, the Heron is an ungainly flyer; it lumbers off the ground and then jerks up into a steep climb to clear the ridge in front of it. It is sunset and he watches it disappear over the hills into the rapidly rising gloom.

He turns and looks at Major Mordechai Eisenberg. 'Looks OK?'

Mordechai nods. 'Yes, it always takes off like a brick.'

He is the head of the Intelligence, Surveillance, Target Acquisition and Reconnaissance unit, or ISTAR for short. He and his team are part of an Israeli company called Angel Systems who are now working for the Kivu Defence Force. Mordechai is forty, tall, lean and tanned, with a large hawkish nose and a permanently grim expression. After years of experience with the Israeli Defence Force and Mossad, fighting the PLO, Hamas and Hezbollah, he tends to assume the worst in life.

More recently he helped the Sri Lankan government win its campaign against the Tamil Tigers. Alex hired him because he has battle-tested intelligence gathering systems and an experienced team of analysts used to operating in a tropical environment. They not only gather the intelligence but also process it to track insurgents and produce a real-time target set for counterinsurgency strikes.

The Heron is off on its first mission over the border into Kivu to recce their main target. It's April, a month after the regiment came together and started training at their base in Rwanda. The invasion will start in a few weeks time in May at the beginning of the dry season.

'OK, let's get back to base and see what it comes up with.'

They walk over to a jeep, climb in alongside a few technicians and drive off up the valley back to headquarters.

At the drone control desk, on one side of the operations room, two technicians are sitting side by side at a computer console. The first is flying the plane with a joystick; in front of both of them are two screens, one on top of the other. The top one shows a map of where the plane is, with a vertical readout of its altitude and flight data. The lower screen shows what the various sensors in the large pod underneath the drone can see.

The second man has a larger-scale map up on his screen and taps it with a pen. 'The Lubonga base is here, it's about fifty miles, so at . . .' he checks the speed readout '. . . about ninety miles an hour we will be over the target in half an hour.'

The Lubonga valley is the place where their political contacts in Kinshasa and Unit 17 have indicated that the FDLR is concentrating its forces.

The Congolese government has always maintained covert links with the FDLR; they fought together for six years against the Rwandans during the main Congo war. They have now duped the FDLR into concentrating their troops by telling them that the Congolese President will demand that UN troops leave Kivu shortly as part of a drive to take more control of the country for himself. This has encouraged the FDLR commanders to bring their troops in out of the bush and into the Lubonga valley.

Alex knows that if he is to hit the FDLR hard in a surprise attack he will have to strike them here, so the drone is going to recce the layout of the base and its defences.

He nods, leaves the Israelis to get on with flying the machine and turns to the operations room. Yamba, Col, Arkady, his six rifle company commanders and other senior officers are all sitting on chairs in a semicircle in front of two large plasma screens on a wall.

They alone in the regiment know that the mission objective is Kivu and not southern Sudan. Alex didn't want some scrounging squaddie with a hidden mobile phone to try to leak the story to the press for a few quid. Uppermost in his mind has been the fake pictures given to the *Mirror* for a few grand by some soldiers purporting to show the beating of Iraqi prisoners. Piers Morgan might have lost his job over it for being sloppy but *he* isn't going to take the risk with his men's lives, or his own. He is planning to be in the helicopters going in to attack Lubonga.

All that is showing on one screen at the moment is a ghostly black and white silent image from the drone's infrared camera as it looks down over the mountains. The image drifts gently across the terrain of valleys and forest. It's not a Hollywood blockbuster but everyone is watching it carefully, getting a feel for the difficult terrain that they will be operating in. All the officers have pens and pads on their knees poised for when they get over the target.

It's going to be a long session, though; the drone can stay airborne for fifty hours. It lumbers on through the night, its specially silenced engine producing only a low whirring noise. Eventually the second technician looks at his on-screen map and taps it with a special pen to set up a box search pattern and locks the drone into it. The small satellite dish inside the dome on the top of the drone tilts to stay locked

160

onto its satellite uplink. It receives the information; the onboard computers process it and the plane banks into the surveillance pattern.

A sensor pod, the size and shape of a football, is suspended from metal brackets under it in a gimbals mount. It twists as the drone moves and its all-seeing infrared eye sends back its images.

Alex looks at the grey pictures with crosshairs in the centre of the screen and data readouts ranged around the edge. He can see the sides of the valley and a road along the bottom of it, then the image drifts over huts and he can see people moving about. To them it's pitch dark and they have no idea that an angel of death is drifting overhead. Alex has a weird cold-blooded feeling; watching people go about their normal life and planning how to kill them.

The surveillance continues over the course of the next day and they get a detailed picture of the layout of the valley and the camp: barracks, dining halls, ammunition dumps, trench systems and gun emplacements.

They also observe the routines of the men there and find what they think is the main command area. The unblinking eye locks onto it and they watch a column of four trucks come across the bridge over a river at the bottom of the valley and drive up into the main base. The men jump down and can be seen being greeted and then taken off to their barracks.

All this is taped and noted by the commanders planning how they will take these men on in battle and defeat them.

The Promised Land

Chapter Nineteen

The two undercover Unit 17 men have been hanging around the mobile phone relay station for several days now, selling beers, Coke and Fanta from a portable kiosk with a tatty parasol over it. They haven't had much business; the relay station is on the edge of town, but no one pays them any attention.

It's early May and the initial operations to support the invasion have begun.

The men have been watching the station very carefully, making a note of when the staff arrive and leave and getting to know the security guard who comes on in the evening to guard the gate in the barbed wire fence around the big telephone mast. They split some beers with him each night before they wheel their kiosk back into town.

Mobile phones are big in Kivu. They are an easy source of revenue for the many new providers: all pay-as-you-go, cash up front, with no landline infrastructure. They have a high penetration in the province and every village clubs together to get one. This mast is the main relay station for signals from masts on the hills west from there out towards Mount Bitoy and Walikale.

The two men watch the staff leave at the end of the day and the local boss of the station locks up and hands the keys over to the security guard with his tatty uniform, shotgun and machete.

It gets dark quickly and a pickup truck with four Unit 17 men in it stops down the street. The men get out; one is carrying a holdall. They circle around to an alley at the back of the station and slip black balaclavas over their heads.

The two vendors pack up their stall and wheel it over to the guard. 'Ah, brother!' they call out cheerfully holding up a cool Primus.

'Ah, brother!' he laughs as he takes the beer and the two men move in close to him.

Major Zacheus Bizimani sits on top of the old lorry as it grinds forward in the queue at the border crossing into Goma.

Around him are twenty men, women and children all clinging on to the top of a load of sacks full of charcoal. They are all Rwandans going to visit relatives across the border in Kivu and have brought chicken coops, goats, mattresses and huge bundles of belongings tied up in brightly patterned cloths.

Zacheus is wearing a grubby tracksuit top and some old shorts with large rips in them. He looks down past his flip-flops and watches the border police as they haggle with the driver. The lorry looks decrepit, a large crack running across its windscreen and rusty body panels.

The old gap-toothed driver grumbles but pays the bribes and they let him pass. The truck pulls slowly away and drives on through Goma and then out and up the road into the hills to Masisi.

'Hey, this is my stop,' a woman shouts to Zacheus and he bangs on the roof of the cab to tell the driver to let her and her children off. Eventually all the passengers depart and Zacheus gets into the cab with the driver.

By late afternoon they are in the hills and forests and drive through the area of high ground that peaks in the cloud-wrapped mass of Mount Bitoy. They skirt the mountain to the north and begin to come south again into the Lowa river valley. The old man chews nuts and chuckles to himself as he steers the truck around the hairpins.

'Slow down, it's coming up.'

'Right,' the man says through a mouthful of nuts.

They stop at a steep track and the truck heaves itself up the slope into the woods. Zacheus takes out a GPS device from a compartment hidden under the floor by his feet and switches it on.

They bump along the track for a mile and then come into a small clearing. The GPS device chirrups as they emerge from under the thick cover of trees and it acquires a signal.

Zacheus checks a compass and gets the man to line the truck up on a bearing facing northwest. After manoeuvring to and fro the truck stops and the engine shuts off.

There is absolute silence.

Zacheus looks around the clearing and sees figures walking towards them through the trees. He jumps down from the cab and goes over and talks to the Unit 17 men dressed in civilian clothing.

The soldiers wheel five 125hp dirt bikes out of the bush into the clearing, strap sacks of goods to the front handlebars and stuff wicker panniers full of baggage before mounting up, two to a bike, and driving off down the trail. Five men remain behind with the old man and the lorry.

It gets dark but the motorbike drivers pull night vision goggles from their bags, fit them on their heads and then continue on up the mountain trail. Eventually it becomes too steep and they wheel the bikes off the track and conceal them in a large clump of smilax bushes.

The men move about quickly and purposefully, pulling packs and webbing from their luggage panniers. They each quickly assemble and load a silenced MP5 submachine gun with a folding stock and pack grenades and knives into their webbing.

Zacheus checks the GPS again against his compass and looks up the slope. The men form up behind him and he leads off.

Sophie Cecil-Black holds up her hands. 'OK, everyone, can you just settle down and let's get started.'

The fifteen NGO workers and six local staff in her team are crammed into the living room of the charity's villa on the outskirts of Goma. It's hired from a local businessman and has been well used by generations of aid workers on their tours. The cane sofas are stained and sagging and the coffee table is marked with beer bottle rings and cigarette burns from late night boozing sessions.

It is 1st May, midmorning, and the aid workers sit on the floor, cram on the sofa and chairs or stand behind them, cradling mugs of coffee. Standing at the front, Sophie has great presence; she's tall and carries her head high. She looks over them – bright, young, committed men and women from all over the world dressed like her in jeans and tee shirts.

'OK, so I have got us all together to discuss the security situation. As you know the UN have raised the alert level to Condition Charlie earlier this week because of an unspecified threat. We are supposed to stay at our duty stations and all nonessential travel is banned.'

Along with the other charities in Goma she has pulled her field workers in from outlying areas in the hills, hence the overcrowded villa. There is a lot of fear in local communities and the aid workers are all on edge. Sophie cares about her team and takes their security very seriously.

'A lot of the current tension started with the death of General Sabiti last summer. Has anyone picked up any word of what might actually be happening?'

'Well, no one believes the petrol tanker crash story, that's a given.' As usual Natalie is the first to open her mouth. She's sitting on the floor with her iPad on her knees, taking the chance to use the house's connection to the internet landline.

'Yeah, that's just bullshit, man,' says Dirk from Holland. 'I don't know if Kinshasa was thinking people would actually believe that it was an accident. I mean, him and his entire group of ten bodyguards all killed, with no witnesses – come on.'

He looks round the room and there are nods from everyone.

Sophie agrees. 'OK, so there's all sorts of rumours going around: Sabiti fell out with Kinshasa, he fell out with Oloba, the Rwandans are behind it and are going to invade again.'

Mariana, a Spanish worker, chips in. 'I've heard a lot of stories about FDLR troops on the move from our people up country,' she says. 'I don't know where they are going but they have been attacking villages in Walikale district and then moving on.' She shrugs and looks around; again there are nods of agreement and other people tell stories they have heard of FDLR troop movements.

Charlie, an English public school type who has recently been making moves on Sophie that she has haughtily ignored, adds, 'Well, I've been trying to get through to my team in Walikale but all the mobile phone networks went dead last night, haven't heard a peep from them since then.'

Concerned conversations start up around the room.

Sophie calls them back together. 'OK, OK. So no one seems to know what . . .'

'Hey!' Natalie looks up from her iPad and interrupts her in a shrill tone. 'My internet connection cut off just like that. What the hell is going on?'

Chapter Twenty

Alex is standing in front of another group of people. He also looks tall and commanding.

'Right, gentlemen, this is the battleplan for Operation Wrath, which is an assault on the Lubonga valley, the break-in battle for our campaign in Kivu in two days' time on 4th May.'

He pauses and grins wryly. 'Not Sudan, as I am afraid some of you might have thought.'

He looks round the thirty officers and senior NCOs present. These are the captains, lieutenants and sergeants who will be in charge of the platoons going into the assault.

Sergeant Matt Hooper looks back at him with fierce concentration. This man holds his life in his hands and if the plan is bad then he and a lot of the men in this room will die. Matt absorbs the deception and thinks, 'Fair enough.' Colonel Devereux has already shown in the recruitment and training of the regiment that he is a switched-on commander and it's reassuring to know he takes operational security seriously.

Alex looks back at the large-scale model of the Lubonga valley made out of sand on the floor of the briefing room. The men are hunched in around three sides of it and Alex stands at the top of the valley with a PowerPoint screen behind him.

171

'The FDLR have chosen this valley as their main base for good reason. It is a very strong defensive position.'

He starts pointing out features with a long cane.

'The valley runs northwest off the slopes of Mount Bitoy. That's off the model here, so have a look at the first aerial shot.' They glance at the colour printouts in their hands and can see a high-altitude picture of a ragged peak rising up over eight thousand feet.

'The mountain is covered in dense forest and we cannot find any landing zones on it anywhere.

'Now, carved into the side of it are a series of steep river valleys. This one has the river Lubonga running down it for just over three miles.' He indicates the blue piece of string down the middle of the model. 'At the foot of the valley it flows out into the larger river Oso. This is the only road into the valley via a bridge over the Oso.

'We've had a drone up over the valley and have a good idea of where the main concentration of enemy barracks, headquarters and ammunition dumps are. We estimate that they have about two thousand men and a similar number of family members.' He points to little flags with symbols on them dotted along the floor of the valley. 'They have also cleared some areas for fields and we will use these for landing zones later on in the assault.

'However, our main problem is getting into the valley in the first place. The entrance to it is heavily guarded. The ridges along the sides are about a thousand feet of very steep wooded slope so an infantry assault up them just isn't an option.

'They have also got themselves covered from an aerial assault with these four anti-aircraft gun positions up on the ridge on the western side of the valley – the top of the ridge on the eastern side is too narrow for anything to fit on it.

There are two positions near the mouth of the valley but the most important are these two at the top of the valley, which have been designated Objectives Jericho and Babylon. Have a look at the next shot in your pack.'

The men flip on to aerial photos of the gun positions.

'They each mount two twin-barrelled ZU 23mm anti-aircraft guns.' The men look at the magnified images of the double barrels pointing up out of sandbagged emplacements.

'These have a range of two and a half kilometres so between the four of them they create an interlocking field of fire that effectively shields the whole valley from any helicopter landing. We considered a frontal attack by the gunships to destroy them but it just wasn't feasible – we cannot afford to lose either of them at the start of the campaign.'

Alex glances round at his men as they look back up at him. Their faces are tense; they can see that this looks like a tough assault. He keeps his expression controlled and ensures that his voice has the crisp crack of command as he explains his ideas for getting through the air defences. It is a complicated plan with several moving parts and he has to keep confident and inspire them to believe that it will work.

'Now, as you can see, the top of the western ridge is clear of forest but it is sharp, only ten feet wide in places. However, at certain points it is blunter, about thirty feet wide where these gun positions are. They are the only sites available for helicopter landing zones.

'The first landing will be at Objective Jericho. It is a mile along the ridge from Babylon but is out of line of sight from it because of this area of higher ground in the ridge between them which will shelter us when we land.

'Jericho itself is only wide enough to take two helicopters

at a time and that will be tight. They won't be able to actually land, so the lads will have to jump off the tailgate.

'The assault will start with six helicopters in the first wave carrying Echo Company.' He nods towards Jean-Baptiste, with Matt and his other platoon commanders crouched around him.

'They will land in three waves of two aircraft. I will be in the third wave with Tac so I can direct things from the air as the assault starts.'

Tac is his Tactical Headquarters, consisting of him, Col, his signallers, Forward Observation and ISTAR officers.

'That is the start of the assault, gentlemen. Can I take any questions from you on it now?'

He looks at the men as they study the model, thinking hard. They are all experienced soldiers and know that the battlefield is an inherently chaotic place where no plan survives first contact with reality. They are staring at the thin ridgeline, envisaging the hell that will be unleashed on it.

The FDLR soldier chucks a pair of heavy black army boots caked in red mud onto the floor in front of Joseph and walks on past his dugout.

'Hey, small boy, clean my boots.'

Joseph sullenly picks them up and glances over at Corporal Habiyakare. He wishes he would stick up for the men of the platoon against the other FDLR soldiers but Habiyakare understands their place as new arrivals in the pecking order of the base and ignores him.

It's the 3rd May and they have been posted to an anti-aircraft gun position on one of the high ridges that ring the Lubonga valley like the sides of a bathtub.

Up here they are at seven thousand feet and it is cold and damp. Cloud often boils under the ridgeline as the air is

174

pushed up over it, producing a damp misty draught through the dugout.

Joseph wants to have a go on one of the twin-barrelled 23mm guns but the gunners won't let him. A few times a day men are sent out along the ridge to patrol – hence cleaning the muddy boots – but one look down the steep thousand-foot drop tells you that no one would ever bother trying to get up there.

Still it's not all bad. They get good rations of fish and rice and can warm up in the main hut in the evening and watch videos on a TV powered by a car battery. Mainly Nigerian zombie horror films badly dubbed into French but some Chuck Norris and Rambo ones as well, which he loves.

He doesn't like the horror films; they contribute to the bad dreams he has. He sees the events of the attack on the village play out again in his head. He dreams in vivid colour of forests, gunfire, screaming faces, the rape and then the face of the woman that he shot with the rags in her mouth and her stupid terrified expression. All the events are chaotic and he has got clumps of blood-red mud stuck all over his clothes that he can't get off. He scrabbles angrily at it and shouts at the people in the dream but they don't listen to him.

That night he lies awake in the barracks hut. In the hills below the ridge he can hear a distant gun battle going on between militias. There's a *thock-thock-thock* of heavy machine-gun fire, then a pause before a faint popping of rifles answers it.

The sound takes his mind off the events of the day and he drifts off to sleep thinking, 'I wonder who's firing?'

Jason Hall nervously pulls the magazine off his rifle for the third time and checks that the rounds are sitting snug in the top of it and that the lips aren't dented. He clicks it back into the port and looks at Sean Potts. His lips are pressed together and he is rocking back and forth slightly as they sit on the ground.

Sean looks back at him, mutters, 'Come on, for fuck's sake,' and looks over with irritation at the command tent set up at the side of the helicopter landing pads. They and the rest of Echo Company are waiting to load into the six big Mi-17s that are sitting on the pads with their engines running and rotors turning. Their exhausts glow red-hot and the caustic smell of avtur fuel is in the air.

The choppers are painted white and have 'UN' written on each side of them in big black letters. UN Mi-17 helicopters are frequently seen over Kivu so Alex hopes it will deceive anyone who sees their approach to the target. With the sabotage of the mobile phone stations and the Rwandans cutting off the internet connection to Kivu, claiming a technical fault, he hopes they can create a news blackout in the area for a few days to allow him to get his troops in and fight the main battle without a huge international reaction blowing up and getting in his way.

It's nine o'clock in the morning of the 4th May and the men have been grouped in chalks waiting to load for an hour now.

Jason agrees with Sean's obvious irritation. He grins and has to shout over the hiss of the helicopter turbines, 'Fucking head shed, sort it out mate.' Colonel Devereux is in there with Major Delacroix, RSM Thwaites and the rest of Tac, waiting for God knows what.

Yesterday was a very sombre day in the camp as everyone had to do their last-minute preps before the assault, stripping and cleaning weapons, readying medical packs but also writing their letters home: 'To be posted in the event of my death.'

176

Jason's been through it before but it gets him every time. His letter read:

Dear Mum and Dad
If you are reading this I am afraid it is bad news, I have been killed in action. I want you to know before I go that I am so proud of you and I wanted to say thank you for all that you have done for me, so please stop crying.

I'm sorry I wasn't a better son. But this is the job I love doing and it has its downsides – I suppose you could say that I had a really bad day at work.

I love you both very much
Jase

A lot of the lads were pretty emotional, some walking off to the base perimeter, smoking and staring off into the distance with their thoughts. There's no privacy in the barracks blocks to hide the tears so Jason just had to sit on his bunk, sniff and write through them.

Sean shouts to Matt Hooper, 'Sarge, I'm going for a piss,' and clambers to his feet under the load of his equipment, heading off to the edge of the landing pads; a stream of men is coming and going to the makeshift latrine as the tension builds.

They all have a full load of combat gear, flak jackets, rifles, spare magazines and grenades, belts of link ammunition wrapped round them to feed the squad machine guns and two 81mm mortar bombs in their backpacks to supply the mortar crews. They have been briefed on the mission and there's a feeling of fear but also excitement. Sean shares a grin with Daz Vitriano as he walks back past him.

Matt Hooper stands and looks over his men. They are ready to go, the tough training has shaken out the wrinkles

177

and bonded them together. He looks at Corporal Stein, who is even bigger than normal with all his equipment on, and sees that he is smiling quietly at the anticipation of violence; the bloke's a nutter. He is usually stony-faced, spending most of his time doing pull-ups and bench presses with the weights they have made out of old ammo boxes filled with gravel. Now that combat is approaching he looks like a kid expecting Christmas.

Matt's gut twists with fear. They all know it is going to be a tough assault up on that high ridgeline and Two Platoon will be in the first wave of helicopters to land.

The only thing that keeps them all from running off is the grim determination not to show their fear and weakness in front of each other. He touches the pocket on his thigh again and checks that his morphine injection pack is in there.

Colonel Devereux walks out of the command tent with Major Delacroix, looking grim-faced.

At least he's coming with us, though; he must believe in the plan.

All the men's eyes are on Alex, waiting for the first order in a complex chain of events.

The noise from the turbines makes any verbal orders impossible.

Alex's hand jabs forward decisively towards the helicopters and he mouths, 'Load up.'

Chapter Twenty-One

While the troops wait by the helicopters, Zacheus is lying in a bush, freezing cold, soaked in dew and shivering. He clamps his mouth shut so his teeth don't chatter. He is barely twenty feet away from the enemy.

He and his team of nine Unit 17 men climbed the steep forested slope up to the ridgeline in the dark, pulling themselves up hand over hand using tree trunks and branches. It's 9 a.m. and they have been waiting in the bushes just down the slope from Objective Jericho since 4 a.m. They are at seven thousand feet and the temperature is not far above freezing.

Dense morning mist hangs around them but Zacheus can hear the men in the anti-aircraft gun emplacements coughing, spitting and urinating off the edge of the ridge. They talk a bit and someone bangs around getting a cooking fire going.

Zacheus's hand shakes as he checks his radio in his backpack and adjusts the earpiece on his head. He feels the comforting weight of the submachine gun slung on his back. He hopes he will warm up and stop shaking soon; they don't have long till the assault is due to start. He looks around at the man lying next to him, who is also shivering.

Three hundred metres east along the ridgeline from him, away from Objectives Jericho and Babylon, another team of two men have slipped over the ridge in the night and are laid up in the bushes further down the slope inside the valley.

They have tied an aerial to a bush above them. One man sits with a pair of headphones on, monitoring a small computer linked to the aerial. The other man operates an encrypted UHF radio tucked into the uphill side of a tree trunk next to him.

Ten miles away from Lubonga the old truck sits in the remote clearing in the forest. The team of five men Zacheus left with it are getting busy.

As dawn comes up they climb onto the truck and start undoing bolts and pulling off the wooden supports on its sides. Once these are stripped away, they unload the sacks of charcoal from the top. Although the truck looks as if it is piled high with them there is actually only a single layer. They dump the sacks off the side and clear away a tarpaulin, exposing a wide block of three-metre-long metal tubes like drainpipes.

The truck engine starts and its hydraulics whine. Stabilisers expand out from under the rusty body panels that have been fixed to it and plant themselves firmly in the ground. The end of the tubes nearest the cab rise up into the air, showing that there are in fact forty tubes all packed together in a box shape. The end of the box swings round to point the forty barrels of the BM-21, 122mm multiple launch rocket system towards the Lubonga valley.

Rukuba is oozing warmth and bonhomie into a satellite phone as he talks to the leader of the FDLR.

'Ah, General Musoni, how are you?'

He is sitting in the ops room in the headquarters building

in Camp Purgatory talking into a phone in Swahili with the whole of the ops room staff gathered around staring at him.

There's a pause as the general replies and then Rukuba sparks up again. 'Yes, very good, thank you. And how was your wife's surgery in Paris? . . . She's OK, uh huh.' He nods sympathetically as he listens to the FDLR commander describe his wife's varicose vein operation at a clinic in Paris.

Rukuba continues as if he is alone in his sitting room having a chat with an old friend. He leans his head over to one side and lays his thin fingers along his cheekbone.

'Oh well, I'm very glad that that has been sorted out. Well yes, I'm OK, my cows are doing very well.' He laughs; both of them are big cattlemen. He continues talking about his breeding programme and how he is improving his meadow.

Yamba looks at him in astonishment. He cannot believe how cool he is being about the whole thing.

The two technicians manning the drone desk are staring hard at their screens as Rukuba talks next to them. The tall Israeli intelligence officer, Major Mordechai Eisenberg, peers over their shoulders monitoring the Heron and Ranger drones carefully.

He looks round at Yamba and whispers, 'Heron has a fix.'

Yamba mutters into the throat mike he is wearing to communicate with Col down on the landing pads.

'Heron is fixed.'

Alex turns away from the troops as they file into the helicopters and walks back into the command tent.

Col looks up from the small radio he is monitoring with an earpiece strapped to his head. 'Right, the Heron has got a fix.'

Alex nods. 'OK, good, now we just need the other two.'

He slept fitfully the night before. He dozed off and then

181

the thought of action sent a flood of adrenaline through his system that rinsed the sleep out of him like a cold shower. He finally slept in the early hours only to have the ugly noise of his alarm bust into his head at 5.30 a.m.

He hates the waiting.

They've checked everything important a hundred times. This morning is the culmination of thirteen months of careful planning and preparation. Until they actually get going he can only fret pointlessly. All the usual worries about personal injuries and death come flooding back.

But what's his greatest secret fear?

That his men won't obey his orders.

Then he starts thinking of the men who did obey his orders in the past and died as a result of it.

Cut it out!

The men are all volunteers and they know the risks. If they didn't want to be mercenary soldiers then they should have stayed at home and been traffic wardens instead.

Rukuba continues chatting. 'Ah yes, of course, I could send Rousseau over to you. He's the best bull I have, yes, he has got a lot of spunk!' He laughs conspiratorially with the general.

'Ranger is fixed.'

The second drone has locked on.

Yamba now looks at the radio operator with the UHF set next to him. His face is even more severe than usual.

The radio operator turns and nods, scribbling down some coordinates on a pad as he does so.

Yamba mutters into the microphone, 'DF team has fix.'

There is a pause as the three bearings are combined and the target's coordinates fixed.

'Transmitting coordinates to Beelzebub now.'

Another pause as Beelzebub's targeting computing works out its trajectories.

'Beelzebub is locked on and ready to fire.'

Alex looks at Col relaying the orders to him on the radio. 'The Ranger has got a fix as well now.'

Alex nods. 'Good. Now we just need the DF team. Come on, boys.' He grins and looks at Jean-Baptiste who grins back; the guy is a fighter. You can see he just wants to get stuck in.

'OK, DF team has a fix as well. We have triangulation on Jerusalem.'

There is a pause on the radio and Col receives a fire mission request from the multiple launch rocket system.

'Beelzebub requests permission to fire.'

Alex looks at Col with narrowed eyes and nods.

'Fire for effect.'

The radio operator in the ops room repeats what he is hearing on the command net to the men in the operations room. 'Permission to fire given.

'Beelzebub firing now. Shot twenty seconds.'

In his mind's eye Yamba sees the 122mm rockets screaming out of the barrels of the Russian BM-21 multiple launch rocket system, in sequence, two per second, each launched in a loud flash of propellant.

He's seen the impact of the weapon before – they used multiple launch rocket systems like it in the Angolan war. It is specially designed for this sort of artillery ambush, to dump several tons of high explosive onto an area within twenty seconds to catch the enemy in the open before they can take cover.

It is an apocalyptic weapon.

Yamba looks at Rukuba who is still chatting, immune to all the tension around him. The guy's ability to dissemble is phenomenal.

'Oh right, so you think that would be a good place to get some shirts? What's it called again? Boutique Oiseau? What's the address . . .'

He flinches and yanks the phone away from his head as a loud burst of static comes out of it and the line goes dead.

He looks at the phone for a second and then a slight smile spreads over his face.

Chapter Twenty-Two

Zacheus lies in the bush and waits for the rockets to come over him.

He pats the man next to him on the arm and gives a thumbs up. The signal is passed on down the line and all ten men pull black balaclavas on their heads, get their submachine guns off their backs and cock them.

The rockets are on a downward trajectory into the valley and skim just over the ridgeline. Being under them is like standing on the edge of a railway platform as an express train goes past. They smash the air aside and the pressure wave pushes down on the men who press their faces into the trembling earth.

The satanic screaming overhead goes on for twenty seconds but Zacheus forces himself up at the start of it and drags the man next to him up as well. The line of ten men scramble forward, grabbing onto bushes and tufts of grass to heave themselves up the last steep slope.

As his line of sight comes up over the curve of the ridge, Zacheus is tensed, expecting to see figures with rifles pointing down at him. Instead he sees three tatty wooden shacks with the two gun emplacements dug in front of them.

Some men are crouching down around them in terror at this sudden visitation from the devil, staring overhead at the rockets. Others are standing with their backs to him watching with horrified fascination as the first munitions explode over their headquarters buildings two miles down the valley. A rolling barrage of airbursts carpets the area and the distant crumps of the explosions echo off the valley sides. A large cloud of smoke and dust slowly mushrooms up into the air.

The Unit 17 men take their chance.

The ten submachine guns spit bullets and the soldiers are knocked off their feet. The men clear the gun emplacements first, shooting dead the crews, and then start on the shacks, chucking grenades in through the doors and then bursting in and finishing off survivors with gunfire.

A few men try to run off along the ridge and are shot down at longer range. Two men in a trench look up with terrified faces and hold their hands up to surrender but are shot dead.

In a little over a minute of intensive machine-gun fire and grenade bursts thirty-three enemy are killed.

Zacheus calmly changes the magazine on his weapon and keys the mike on the radio. 'Black Hal, this is Striker 1, Jericho is down. Repeat, Jericho is down.'

Alex acknowledges the signal and Zacheus then sets his men to stripping rifles and ammunition from the dead and gets them into defensive positions. Now he has to make sure he can hold onto the gun emplacement until the helicopters get here. The aircraft are fifty miles away and even at top speed it will take them twenty minutes. He glances anxiously along the ridge to the west towards Objective Babylon; the gun emplacement a mile away, hidden behind a knoll of higher ground halfway between them.

Zacheus then looks away from Babylon and turns towards the spectacular view from the ridge, rugged lines of green hills marching away into the distance. He ignores the aesthetics and prays to see the dots of the helicopters appearing in the blue sky.

In the Babylon gun position Joseph runs out of the kitchen shack at the sound of the rockets. The men are standing and staring at the explosions going off down below in the valley.

'What's happening?' he asks Lieutenant Karuta but the man ignores him and runs over to get on the radio to his counterpart in Jericho along the ridge.

Alex, Col, Jean-Baptiste and the rest of Tac run out of the command tent towards the waiting helicopters, which are winding up their engines to lift off.

They duck their heads down under the fierce rotor wash and keep clear of the exhaust being pumped out by the red-hot turbines. They run in under the high tail boom of the Mi-17 and up the ramp into the cargo bay packed with twenty-five pumped-up soldiers, all sitting on the floor facing the ramp with their feet around the person in front.

As soon as they are in, the loadmaster hits the hydraulics and the ramp rises up and locks, leaving a gap above it. Alex and Col scramble forward over the men to the front of the aircraft, Alex needs to plug into its radio to keep in touch with the other units.

He sticks his head through the open door into the cabin. The two Russian pilots are side by side surrounded by dials and switches on the dashboard and overhead. The copilot passes him a spare headphones and mike set and he is relieved to be back connected to the command net.

'Shakira, Beyoncé, all Demons, this is Black Hal, launch now.'

The engines overhead scream, the noise is deafening, rotors clawing at the thin high-altitude air to haul ten tons of dead weight vertically upwards. Alex feels the fuselage vibrating violently and pressure in his knees as the heavily laden machine waddles up off the ground.

All around them twelve helicopters rise up as one.

Demons 1 to 6 are the Mi-17 troopships carrying Echo Company tasked to land at Objective Jericho and then assault Objective Babylon. Demons 7, 8 and 9 carry half of Bravo Company to drop into the valley once the anti-aircraft guns are down. They will have limited fuel to loiter in the area so Alex knows they need to get the guns knocked out quickly.

Demon 10 is another Mi-17 with a cargo net slung under it full of long green wooden boxes contained rocket reloads for Beelzebub.

Arkady is flying with his gunner in Beyoncé, with the other Mi-24 gunship, Shakira, next to him. They will escort the assault force in to the target but will have to circle out of range of the guns at Babylon until the troops have captured it.

Alex feels a flush of fear as the force finally takes off. He adjusts his helmet and is glad of the reassuring weight of the assault rifle across his chest. He won't be firing it – if the commanding officer of the regiment ever fires his personal weapon then things have gone badly wrong – but it is an important symbol for the troops that he is coming with them and means business. He glances at Col next to him and draws encouragement from his expression of calm determination.

Their biggest mission yet. It's a complex operation with a lot of tight timings but it is the only way he can get a chink in the enemy's armour and then crowbar it open and get in at them.

At least the weather has been good. It's a sunny day with patchy white clouds; the benefit of starting the campaign in the dry season. He leans through the door into the cabin to look out of the bulbous front canopy. Ahead of them lies the massive bulk of Mount Karisimbi, its rugged sides covered in bright green jungle. Spread out in front of and below him are five white helicopters. At a distance and against the vast backdrop of the green mountain they look tiny and their spinning rotors make him think of delicate sycamore seeds twirling in the air. As he looks at them, the sun catches and flashes on their discs. In an odd moment he feels he has never seen anything so beautiful.

Up ahead in Demon One, Jean-Baptiste is also looking forwards out of the cockpit canopy; he is going in on the first wave with 2 Platoon. Whilst 3 Platoon secure the Jericho gun emplacement his men will run off along the ridge to seize Babylon a mile to the west. He is keyed up for the assault; he needs to get to the high ground between the two bases in order to be able to fire down on it and knock out the guns. He looks over the lines of seated troops in front of him and can see Volunteer Sean Potts sitting with his PKM light machine gun upright between his legs. They will need them and the mortar crews to suppress fire from the base.

The Russian copilot checks his maps and his GPS and keys the mike. 'Five minutes,' crackles through on Jean-Baptiste's earphones. He turns and shouts to Matt Hooper over the din of the rotors, 'Get them up!'

Matt nods and slaps the shoulder of the first man in front of him. It is repeated down the lines and the heavily laden troops struggle to their feet in the cramped cargo bay. Like all of them Sean hates being packed inside this flying box full of highly explosive fuel. He's tensed up and ready to burst off the ramp as soon as it bangs down on solid earth. He glances at the soldier next to him. His face is tense and his knuckles are white as he grips his rifle across his chest.

The hydraulics lower the ramp and they are staring out of the back of the aircraft at lines of forested hills whipping just below them, treetops thrashing in their wake.

The aircraft banks left to swing round and approach parallel to the ridge to keep them away from the Babylon guns. It forms up next to Demon 2 and they skim low over the hills at one hundred and fifty m.p.h., rising and falling with the terrain to avoid any anti-aircraft fire. They rise up to just under the ridgeline to make a fast approach assault landing. Jean-Baptiste grabs onto a strap on the forward bulkhead – he knows the Russian pilots can be cavalier, pushing the operating envelope of the airframe.

He takes a quick last glance through the front window and glimpses a tiny streamer of purple smoke on the huge bulk of the ridgeline; Zacheus has popped the smoke grenade, indicating they are clear to land.

The smooth whirr of the rotors slows to a rhythmic clatter – *whop, whop, whop* – as they slow down. The pilot flares hard, putting the nose up and using the underbelly as an airbrake. The packed lines of men lurch towards the front of the chopper and grab onto each other; it's a gut-wrenching ride.

With the last forward momentum, they bank right and pop up over the top of the ridge. The pilot swings the tail round so that they are facing out of the valley and Demon 2 does likewise next to them.

The copilot is hanging out of the side window shouting distance instructions over the intercom. They are only going to touch the ramp down, they don't want to be on the exposed ridge a second longer than necessary.

At last the ramp bangs down on the ground.

In ten seconds all twenty-five men bolt out of the back of it, throw themselves on their belt-buckles in an arrowhead formation and both choppers are taking off again. Engine notes scream and rotor wash blasts out mud and bits of grass as they lift away and then drop down the ridge to leave the LZ clear for the next wave.

The soldiers have their heads up over their rifle sights scanning for targets through their goggles.

Matt is up and shouting at them, 'Get up! That way!' His outstretched arm points west down the ridge towards Babylon.

Chapter Twenty-Three

Alex hangs on as Demon 6 flares and they decelerate hard.

The landings are going according to plan. The first two waves of two aircraft have each dropped their men on the ridge and slipped down away from it. The four platoons are forming up on the narrow flat area.

Demons 5 and 6 are coming in next to each other now.

The aircraft swings round hard and the men stagger. He glances out of the side door and sees Demon 5 next to him on his right touch down its ramp and the lads start running out. His own troops do the same.

Over the noise of the rotors he hears the sound of heavy calibre automatic gunfire. Demon 5 lurches sideways towards him. He can see explosions on the far side of it, it's hit and on fire. The blokes aren't all off yet and some are thrown off the ramp as it rises up to escape the threat.

His own pilot sees it and jerks the control column to the left; Alex and Col are thrown onto their knees.

Get out of this flying fuel can!

The pilot panics and starts taking off. Alex can see the last of his guys jump off the ramp as the aircraft lifts clear.

I am not going to be separated from my men.

'Go! Go! Go!'

He scrambles to his feet and he and Col both run towards the opening at the back of the aircraft as the chopper dips its nose and starts dropping off the ridge.

He sees the ground falling away under them; the gap is opening up.

They both hurl themselves off the ramp.

Alex lands on his chest with an explosive gasp. His flak jacket stops the rifle strapped across his chest from breaking his ribs but it digs in hard and smashes the air out of him. He can't breathe but his hands scrabble frantically to grab a bush to stop himself falling back down the slope.

Next to him Demon 5 takes a 23mm round in the gas tank and explodes. Its main rotor detaches and spins off into the void and the white body of the aircraft drops like a stone, tumbling in flames nose over tail down the ridge, bodies of the men inside thrown clear and smashing into trees.

Alex gasps for breath and pulls himself up. He's in agony from the blow to his chest but he is determined to get back to commanding his men.

Col crawls up the slope next to him and they stick their heads up to see what is happening.

Alex glances to his left and sees two streams of bright tracers flashing down at them from the high ground between Jericho and Babylon. Somehow the enemy has dragged the two anti-aircraft guns up on the hill and now has a perfect vantage point to fire down on them. The weapons roar out, each spitting sixteen hundred rounds a minute and the clattering bursts of fire roll down the valley and echo back and forth like metallic thunder.

He pushes himself up onto his knees and sees the rounds smashing into the camp, destroying the three shacks and setting them alight, shooting up the two Jericho guns. Their ammunition starts cooking off, banging and popping.

The men from the first waves and the Unit 17 troops have all thrown themselves over the blunt edge of the ridge and are lying flat on the ground with their heads just below the top. The guns turn on them and start chewing up the ground along the edge. Shells smash into it exploding and blasting out mud and steel shards over the men's helmets.

Two soldiers are hit by splinters and slide back down the ridge screaming. Mates grab them and stop them slipping off down the slope.

Someone is roaring over the sound of the explosions.

'Man down! Man down!'

'Who's hit?'

'Medic!'

Col jumps up and scrambles along the line over the backs of the men on the ground. As the senior soldier of the regiment it's his job to get the men organised. He spots the medical officer face down with his medical pack on his back. Col pulls him upright and they sprint bent double along the ridgeline in full view of the enemy towards the casualties.

'Where's the casualty!' Col roars.

'Over here!'

A hand goes up from under the rim of the ridge.

'Who's hit?'

'Volunteer Rodriguez, he's T4!'

Dead.

Shit.

The medic turns to the other man with facial wounds and makes a rapid assessment. He's alternately screaming with pain and sobbing through his hands; his face is covered in blood. The medic holds his hands out of the way so he can get a good look at him. He can't see any major arteries hit.

'Yer all right, mate!'

He's pulling open his pack and getting dressings out when two men stagger along the ridge, dragging a body, one holding him under the arms and one with his legs. The injured man looks completely out of it, head lolling back and eyes rolling up.

Col sees bloodstains on his chest.

Shit.

'Over 'ere!' Col shouts and the men dump him down.

The medic swaps over to him. 'Where's he hit?'

He checks his pulse – still there in his neck. 'He's still here, he's T3.'

There's a loud bang of a shell exploding overhead and they both flinch down.

The guy is lying still making a gurgling noise, hot spurts of blood coming out of his neck.

'Get his flak off!'

Joseph jumps into a trench up on the high ground and levels his rifle down at the attackers. He's excited, and shouts along to Corporal Habiyakare, 'I'm going to shoot these bastards!'

When the attack started Lieutenant Karuta quickly organised the thirty men in the base to drag the two weapons up out of their emplacements. They are light mobile field artillery and have two wheels that fold flat under them when they are in firing position. It took thirty seconds to lever them back into place and then a team of men dragged each one quickly up onto the high ground.

'Who are they?' someone yells between bursts of fire from the two anti-aircraft guns behind them – they fire at such a rate that clouds of exhaust gases swirl around the crew of two men who sit on low seats behind them.

195

Corporal Habiyakare shouts back, 'I don't know, they landed in UN helicopters but they've got green helmets not blue ones. Doesn't matter,' he laughs, 'let's just kill 'em!'

The men all shout and start firing their rifles. At half a mile range the fire is not accurate but it feels good.

Chapter Twenty-Four

Further back along the ridge Alex is collecting Tac, Zacheus and Jean-Baptiste together to coordinate a response. He sticks up his head over the lip of the ridge between bursts of fire frantically trying to see a way out of their predicament. Rifle rounds crack and zip overhead.

He feels a rising tide of panic in his chest and forces it back down. The assault has hit a lethal obstacle – half of the force is pinned down here on the ridge and the second wave of choppers with Bravo Company on board are in the air waiting to land in the valley once the two gun emplacements are down. They have limited loiter time and will eventually have to turn back to base, which will disrupt the whole momentum of the attack.

Apart from which he and his men are pinned down under heavy enemy fire on a high ridge with no way off and are gradually being shot to pieces. He thinks of his grandiose schemes for bringing control to Kivu and the irony is painful. The whole mandate of heaven is running into the ground of this blighted outcrop.

Just sort it out, Devereux.

A strange calm descends on him as the fury that he normally feels in his soul is suddenly matched by the intensity of events outside him and an equalisation of pressure occurs.

He has found a strange peace at last and starts to deal calmly with the problems.

Jean-Baptiste scrambles towards him along the line of men to him, his face full of intensity. 'I have four machine-gunners ready to fire.'

'Good.'

Alex rolls over onto his other side and grabs the radio-phone off the backpack of his signaller and gets on the net.

'S'arnt Hooper, this is Black Hal. 2 Platoon to advance along the ridge under cover from 3 Platoon and Fire Support Group.'

The problem is that there is a limited amount of space on the ridge so he can't bring his other men into play. Jean-Baptiste has got all their machine gunners together to act as a Fire Support Group. Rifle fire at this range won't be much use. The AA guns have got small armour plates in front to protect their gunners but their legs stick out under them so the machine gunners can try and hit them and it will at least put off their aim as 2 Platoon advances.

Alex sits up and yells to his left, 'Mortars ready?'

A team is balancing precariously on the slope, trying to dig the baseplate into the mud with entrenching tools. It needs to be firm or it will be useless when the mortar fires.

'Two minutes, sir!'

'Major Delacroix, get the mortar bombs passed back along the line!' Each man has two in his backpack.

Along the line to his left, Sergeant Matt Hooper lies on his front next to his signaller; the top of his radio aerial gets snipped off by a bullet and goes spinning away down the ridge. Rounds are cracking over them constantly.

He thinks about sticking his head up into that lot and the idea hits a brick wall.

They will have to crawl along on their stomachs under

whatever covering fire can be given. He turns and shouts back down the line, '2 Platoon, fix bayonets! Prepare grenades!'

Stein is screaming at the men, '*Sort it! We go!*'

Alex gets on the radio to organise a final tactic to cover the advance. 'Beyoncé and Shakira, this is Black Hal. I need a rocket strike from you.'

Arkady's voice crackles in his ear, 'Black Hal, this is Beyoncé, it will be extreme range and danger close.'

'Beyoncé, roger that, we don't have any choice.'

He knows that the gunships will have to stay a couple of clicks out from the ridge to keep away from the guns. One hit from a 23mm shell and their delicate flying machines will be toast. The rockets are unguided and at extreme range they could spray over 2 Platoon as well, who are on the outside of the ridge exposed to their fire. He prays Arkady's aim is good today and keys the mike again.

'S'arnt Hooper, this is Black Hal. Prepare for danger close airstrike and assault guns immediately after it!'

Up on the ridge, the waiting and the fear are getting to Matt. He rolls over onto his back and thinks, 'Jesus Christ – jump up over that line of earth and run into a wall of lead coming over it?'

He thinks about Danielle.

'I didn't sign up for this.' His face goes white.

Stein scrambles next to him, takes one look at his frozen face and goes mad. He grabs his webbing and pulls his head up close to him and screams at him.

'*You fucking pussy!* We wait rockets, we go! I lead!'

His pupils are dilated, his nostrils flared, his brutal face white with the cold fury of a man about to kill. The ferocity of it hits Matt like a punch.

Like fear, courage is contagious and Matt nods vigorously, snapping himself out of it.

Stein goes back to getting the platoon organised. '2 Section covering fire! Potts over there!' He directs Sean and the other machine gunner to the back of the line of men.

His absolute resolve galvanises them and they lock and load fresh mags, fit their bayonets and loosen pins in grenades.

'Smoke grenades!' Stein gets the men to hurl them forward as far as they can to give them some cover.

Then his heavy hand thumps down on Jason's webbing shoulder strap and drags him forward.

'Hall, you follow me!'

Sean readies his PKM machine gun. 'More link!'

A soldier slips an ammo belt wrapped around his waist from under his flak and passes it down the line. More belts are passed along and Sean slaps one into the feed tray and snaps the cover shut. He nestles down on his belly and gets the butt in tight against his shoulder ready to stick his head up.

Matt takes the radio telephone away from his ear and screams, 'Air thirty seconds, take cover!'

He rolls on his back and watches the two small dots far away in the sky and thinks, 'What cover?' as he turns and presses his face into the ridge.

In the lead gunship Arkady wheels into the strike. He keys the mike to his wingman. 'Shakira, this is Beyoncé, rockets, shooter, shooter, my lead, fire at 2km, me break left, you break right, target anti-aircraft guns on ridge.'

'Roger that, Beyoncé.'

His gunner squints into the sights on his heads-up display. The AA guns have spotted them coming in and start firing at him. He can see the bright stabs of muzzle flash. The red tracers seem to start out lazily at first and then speed up until they are ripping past his canopy with a noise like tearing metal.

He ignores them and keeps his eye on the two flashing

guns on the ridgeline. He squeezes the trigger on his joystick. The pod of 80mm rockets on the wing just down and to the right of him fires off in sequence, one rocket a split second after the other.

Twenty rockets screaming away downrange trailing angry orange propellant fire.

His wingman flows in behind him and does the same.

The first salvo of twenty rockets goes diagonally across the ridge, exploding in orange flame and bursts of bushes and mud. The last half overshoots the guns and goes screaming off into the air before dipping down to smash into the other side of the valley.

Shakira's salvo is better and runs straight along the top of the ridge, dotting it with explosions that stitch their way across the gun positions.

Jean-Baptiste is screaming at the Fire Support Group, 'Up! Up! Up!' They jump up from cover and run into the shot-up gun emplacements to give them a better angle of fire. Six light machine guns start pouring fire at the AA guns.

Matt hears the screaming of the rockets coming in and then a blast wave hits the left-hand side of his face that knocks his jaw sideways and rattles his teeth. Mud and debris whack into him. He clings to the ground and wishes he was inside it.

Sean wriggles forward, rests the end of the machine-gun barrel on its bipod, squints through the sights at the hill and squeezes the trigger. The gun jumps hard against his shoulder, the metal cartridge belt jerks and gets sucked through the chamber in seconds as he pours fire at the enemy. Expended cases pile up by the ejection port on the right-hand side with a metallic tinkling as he hoses down the trenchline.

'*Get some!*' he yells and then slaps a new belt in to give them another hundred.

Stein is up and screaming at the men.

Matt's ears are ringing and he can't hear what he is saying. He shoves himself up onto his knees and then runs forward over the edge.

Jason jumps up and with twenty other men of 2 Platoon they follow Stein and Sergeant Hooper in a race for their lives.

Stein leads the charge.

He sprints through the swirling purple smoke bent double with his rifle and bayonet out in front of him. He feels the heavy covering fire from the machine guns snapping through the air just over his head.

The men of 2 Platoon burst out of the smoke and they still have hundreds of metres of open ground to cover. They move like racing snakes, weaving and ducking, not stopping to fire but relying on the rest of the company to keep them alive.

Stein looks ahead and can see that one of the AA guns has been hit by a rocket and is lying on its side, smoke and dust from the strikes still swirling over the position. His legs are pumping and his lungs are bursting.

Enemy soldiers stick their heads up over the trenches and rifle shots chatter out. He feels bullets cracking past his face.

Close now, close enough.

He throws himself down on the ground, pulls a grenade out of his webbing, rips the pin out with his teeth and lets the lever ping off. The fuse is fizzing in his hand.

One second, two seconds. He glances ahead and carefully lobs it forward.

He watches the green ball sail up into the air and drop down neatly into the trench. There is a shout of fear and then a flat crack and a burst of red dust.

Other men drop to the ground around him and post their grenades.

He waits for the cracks and then he's up and screaming, 'Let's go!'

He has a mad magnetism and the men all jump up and charge forward to the trench line. They stand on the lip and shoot the survivors.

A communication trench runs back away from the front line. They're still taking fire so Stein jumps down into the forward trench and Jason follows him. The trench turns ninety degrees. They pause and post a grenade round the corner.

The blast covers them with dust and Stein sticks his head round and gives it full auto with his rifle and then charges forward screaming. The pair run on and the trench system widens out into an area packed with retreating enemy soldiers who can't get out of the trench because of the maelstrom of fire over their heads. They turn and look back in terror as Stein runs screaming into them.

He fires and his rifle clicks empty. He runs at them and plunges his bayonet into the nearest man's chest. Maddened with bloodlust, he twists and pulls it out again, stabbing right with his bayonet and then smashing left with the butt into a man's face.

Jason comes in behind him and shoots a man before he too clicks dry. He follows Stein into the mêlée with the wicked bright steel of his bayonet.

The two of them go at the enemy like savages, stabbing and yelling.

Alex stands and watches through his binoculars as the attack goes in. Jean-Baptiste and Zacheus do likewise next to him.

He sees the men scamper forward over the open ground, ducking and weaving.

'Come on lads, come on lads!'

One twists and goes down.

'*Merde!*'

Alex can see a large figure at the front. 'That's Stein! Look at him go!'

Puffs of dust from the grenades pop up out of the trenches and a second later the distant cracks drift back to them.

'That's it! They're in! *Yes!*' Alex clenches his fist in triumph. *Fantastic, they're out of the shit!*

They watch the rest of 2 Platoon close up and secure the trench system and the AA guns.

'Jesus Christ . . .' Jean-Baptiste takes his binoculars away from his face and rubs his eyes.

Alex nods and they share a look.

They both know it was a bloody close thing.

Col runs up, the front of his combat smock and webbing covered in blood. 'Jensen is . . .' He makes a cutting gesture across his throat.

Alex nods; right now he is too busy to do more. The assault is only just starting; they have got a lot more business to attend to. He needs to follow up the rocket strike on the headquarters in the valley and make sure he exploits this opportunity to deliver a crushing blow to the FDLR.

Chapter Twenty-Five

'He's so sweet.' Eve lets the fat baby boy get hold of her finger and stick it in his mouth. She is in the gardens of the grounds of Panzi hospital in Bukavu, sitting in the shade of a tree with Miriam and Adele, the boy's mother.

Paul, the boy, is a rape child and Adele has been in Panzi for six months now being cared for as she has the baby and her operation. She grins at him and he lies on his back and gurgles, lets go of Eve's finger, grabs his foot and sticks his big toe in his mouth.

'He's so fat,' says Miriam approvingly.

'Yes, maybe they'll accept him when I go home?' says Adele hopefully. Rape children are usually viewed as evil in the villages and cast out.

Eve looks at him and wonders about her lost baby. She hasn't been able to think about her for months; her mind has simply shut down on the subject. *Maybe it's a good sign that I can think about her again?*

'Do you want kids?' Miriam asks Eve.

'Hmm,' she says. 'Well, hopefully when down there is fixed and I can go back soon to see my family. I miss them so, so much.'

She had the operation a week ago and the flow of urine dripping out of the catheter has slowed to almost nothing.

Dr Bangana says he will take it out tonight and see if the sutures hold. The problem is that as the bladder heals and retains urine, the pressure on it builds up.

In their prayer sessions in the hospital's Pentecostal church, Eve has been praying that it will heal. Her money has all gone on the operation and she can't even afford the small amount charged for her board and lodging. It will be back to the life of a miserable outcast in the refugee camp if it doesn't work.

The women play with the baby and then Eve goes off to her bookkeeping class. She is enjoying the course and picking up the skills quickly; she is a very tidy-minded girl.

That night she wakes up in the hospital ward and her hand darts down between her legs. She gives a sob of pain. She is soaked in urine again.

Alex crosses over to the edge of the ridge and looks down at the mortar crew, who are still trying to dig in.

'Right, lads, you can stop mucking about down there. Get up here, dig in and give it some welly.'

He and the rest of Tac then spend a few minutes surveying the valley. Zacheus and his Unit 17 men stand at a distance, their job now over.

Alex checks the Tac laptop displaying the images being beamed down from the Heron and Ranger drones overhead.

After that he's on the radio to the remaining choppers. 'Demon 7, Demon 8 and Demon 9, this is Black Hal, you are cleared to land at LZ Sidon.'

'Beyoncé and Shakira, good shooting. I want you to cover second wave landing at Sidon.'

Now that they have a toehold on the ridge it has become their friend and not their enemy. They can get the mortars set up and fire on the enemy down the length of the valley, like shooting fish in a barrel.

Jean-Baptiste has already gone off with Echo Company along the ridge to attack the remaining two AA gun positions.

The battle has only just started though. Alex knows that he needs to get the first wave of five Demons back to base, refuelled and loaded with the second half of Bravo Company and half of Foxtrot. He can then get all of Bravo into the valley to sweep the enemy down it whilst Foxtrot is inserted just over the bridge at the bottom of the valley as a blocker detachment to crush the enemy between the two of them. He'll bring Alpha Company forward as well, put their mortars and machine guns on the ridge to act as a Fire Support Group and their rifles into the valley, as soon as the choppers are free.

This has to be a decisive victory. He knows that any enemy troops that escape will disperse into the bush and start murdering civilians; it's the FDLR's standard response to any attacks on it and has been very successful in preventing UN forces from attacking them.

He also wants to get into the enemy headquarters area as soon as possible and search it for information before anyone left alive down there can remove it. He needs the intelligence immediately to set up the next wave of strikes on the FDLR in order to keep them on the back foot. Mordechai Eisenberg's team, Unit 17 and the Rwandan intelligence officers are all fired up at Camp Purgatory ready to translate and process the information.

He looks up from an aerial photo of the valley and sees a group of soldiers approaching his command post. There are three enemy prisoners being escorted by four soldiers. The enemy troops look in poor shape after the assault; there's two boys carrying an older man between them. One of the boys has his shirt off and blood-soaked bandages wrapped around his chest. The other has a huge swelling on one side of his face that has closed his right eye.

The older man carried between them has a patchy beard and his trousers have been cut down to shorts in order to bandage up grenade splinters in his legs.

Col and the rest of Tac gather round behind Alex to look at them. The lead soldier salutes him and says in a heavy South London accent, 'Major Delacroix sends three prisoners from the assault, sir. Twenty-three dead and a few legged it. We got these ones though.'

Alex looks at him. The soldier has taken off his helmet and his hair is slicked flat with sweat, the front of his combat jacket soaked in drying blood and mud. He checks the name-tape written in black indelible ink on his chest, 'Thank you very much, Volunteer Hall, very good of him. I see you bashed this lot about a bit.' He is grinning broadly.

Jason grins back with pleasure. 'Yeah, me and Corporal Stein sir, 'e's a bloody legend, sir. Really got stuck in 'n' smacked 'em about like. I copped this lad round the 'ed wiv me rifle butt, went down like that.'

Jason is a good storyteller. Alex and the rest of Tac roar with laughter, letting off steam after the hideous tension of the landings.

Joseph is shaking with fear as the men gather round and look at him. He knows what happens to prisoners of war, he's seen these groups of men laughing and then beating prisoners to death. He flinches as the tall officer peers at his face. He has no idea who these strange soldiers are.

'Right, let's see what they know, we need some int on the HQ. Cuff them and let's split them up. I'll interrogate this lad. Col, you take this old chap.' He looks round and allocates another French speaker in Tac to the other boy.

They'll make use of the shock of capture to extract information through tactical questioning. Joseph starts shaking as his wrists are cuffed tight in front of him with black plastic zip ties.

'Bring him over here.' Alex pulls his large-scale aerial photo of the valley out of his combat jacket front and walks away.

Joseph squeals with fear and Jason shoves him forward with his rifle. Alex makes him sit down on the ground and lays the aerial photos in front of him. The kid is clearly in shock so he takes it slowly. 'We are here.' He points to the position and makes sure the kid understands.

'Where is headquarters?'

The boy peers at the map with his one good eye and eventually gestures to an area with his bound hands.

Alex nods.

Good, they hit the right target. He proceeds to confirm the location of ammunition dumps and barracks and then goes and cross-references the information with Col.

'He's a slimy old bastard that one.' Col jerks his head back at Lieutenant Karuta. 'Must be a *génocidaire*.'

They confirm the locations and Alex quickly calls over the mortar platoon sergeant and briefs him. He's now got his four 81mm tubes set up on firm, level ground and they quickly start banging bombs out down the valley.

Alex and Tac stand and watch the black dots as they curve gentle parabolas through the sky and then land with little cotton-wool bursts. Correcting aim is simple and they start pounding the enemy targets. One smashes into an ammo dump and sets off a huge explosion near a base further down the valley.

'*Shit!*' Alex says and the men give a huge cheer as the blast wave rolls over them like a slap in the face. They stand at the lip of the valley and laugh and applaud.

A grey-brown mushroom cloud of debris slowly forms and roils up into the clean air. Subsidiary explosions go off all around the area and up the sides of the valley as mortar bombs and rockets are hurled through the air.

Col is grinning from ear to ear and shaking his head. 'Fooking 'ell,' he mutters in disbelief looking down at the scale of the devastation.

The four helicopters with Bravo Company roar overhead and drop down to land in the valley and the men on the ridge jump up and down, wave and cheer them on their way.

Major McKinley is an understated Canadian in charge of Bravo and gets his men shaken out into extended line and sweeps forward. The valley starts to echo with crackling small arms fire and the pop of grenades as they find pockets of enemy and clear them out. The Alpha Company FSG sets up on the ridge and Alex sees little lines of machine-gun tracer zipping down into any pockets of resistance.

Echo Company take the next AA emplacement along the ridge and the two gunships are now free to operate in the upper reaches of the valley.

Arkady zooms in tight over the ridge and drops down into a shallow dive. He puts another pod of rockets into a cluster of buildings where the enemy is making a stand and obliterates it. Bravo Company sweep on and clear out the burning huts.

Jean-Baptiste takes a leaf out of the enemy's book and wheels two captured AA guns along the ridge and starts a duel with the last base. Bright bursts of tracer spit back and forth but the fight has gone out of the FDLR soldiers and they quickly abandon the base and scramble down the hillside. Jean-Baptiste orders the guns turned on them as they flee and along with the hundred rifles and machine guns of

Echo Company the enemy soldiers are chewed up in a huge burst of dust and explosions.

The FDLR units are losing coherence and ceasing to function in a coordinated manner. Alex guesses that their top commanders have been killed in the artillery ambush and against overwhelming airpower and the steady mortar and machine-gun fire from an elevated position there is nothing they can do. As soon as they stand and fight they get pummelled.

The valley is falling and the battle is moving down it and away from Alex so he calls in a chopper to lift him and Tac forwards. The mortars come with them and more ammunition is dropped in a cargo net. The pilots are working hard ferrying back and forth to base. Demon 7 has a winch attachment and gets to work on the grisly task of winching men down to recover the bodies of the three aircrew and four men who died when Demon 5 was shot down. Alex then gets it to stop off on the ridge and pick up the three prisoners and take them back to Purgatory.

Alex's aircraft lands in a maize field and they run out. Clouds of smoke are drifting across from the next-door field that has been set on fire by burning tracer.

He sets up his command post under a large tree.

The signaller calls him over. 'Cheesehead for you, sir!'

Alex keys the mike. 'Cheesehead, this is Black Hal, go ahead, over.'

He likes Major Jaap t'Hooft, a no-bullshit blond Dutchman, who takes his job, but not himself, seriously and has got Foxtrot Company in good working order.

His heavily accented voice crackles from the speaker on the radio, full of tension. 'Black Hal, we have . . . er, the issue here.' He looks up from his position on the far side of the Oso river looking up the Lubonga valley. 'A large enemy

211

force is trying to cross the river via the bridge and we can't hold them back much longer.' He ducks down as a burst of machine-gun fire rips overhead.

Alex hears it crackle in the background.

He keys the mike again. 'How many enemy do you estimate? Over.'

Jaap looks at the hundreds of enemy soldiers crowding onto the bank on the far side of the fast-flowing river. Some are trying to swim for it and being swept downstream. He can see an outstretched arm sticking up out of the water, moving fast.

'We have hundreds, I say maybe a thousand altogether, it's mainly soldiers but there are civilians mixed in as well. I can see more coming down the valley. I have sixty guys here and we can't get another chopper in under this fire. We are dug in but we can't stop them getting across, small groups are getting across the bridge. If they all rush it we can't stop them. Over.'

Alex looks grim and keys the mike. 'Roger that, Cheesehead, wait out.'

He needs time to think about his options. He looks up and sees Col is watching him with his lips pressed together.

'Shit,' he says quietly, 'they've got civvies mixed up in 'em.'

Alex nods. He can't call in the gunships to do a targeted airstrike and knock out the bridge; Arkady and his wingman have hit bingo fuel and had to return to base.

He shakes his head, 'We can't let them get away. Every one of them that gets away will be another bastard we have to hunt down in the bush. That means my men's lives and the FDLR will wreak havoc on the civvies in Kivu after this.' He jerks his head to the burning valley around them.

Col nods; he knows what they are both thinking. He looks at Alex closely. 'Beelzebub?'

Alex pauses and then speaks in a voice edged with a harsh metallic tone. 'It's like with Sabiti: it's difficult but it's for the good of the province as a whole. This is no time to get sentimental.'

Col nods silently.

It isn't going to be that easy though. Alex takes a deep breath and walks away from the command post. He's thinking about his Ten Commandment cards, the Fourth Commandment: respect civilians at all times. Should he now kill hundreds of them?

His briefing to the Chinese and Rwandans in Kigali also comes back to him. Will this be a massacre that sparks a nationalist backlash?

He stands with his hands on his hips and stares down the burning valley.

Chapter Twenty-Six

'Beelzebub, this is Black Hal, do you copy, over?'

'Copy you, Black Hal, go ahead.'

'Request artillery strike, forty rounds 122mm rockets.' Alex reads out the coordinates for the bridge. 'Advise when you have acquired target.'

'Roger that, Black Hal.' The Rwandan artillery officer in Unit 17 reads the fire control orders back to him, 'Ready to fire in one minute, out', and starts entering the data into the targeting computer.

Around the battered truck parked in the forest clearing, his men are just completing the reloading of the BM-21 launcher. It takes three men at a time to haul the six-foot-long white rockets out of their wooden boxes, hoist them up onto their shoulders and then stagger over to the launch tubes and slide them in.

Alex keys into the command net for Foxtrot Company overlooking the bridge. 'Cheesehead, this is Black Hal, stand by, danger close artillery strike in one minute on bridge, get your heads down. Over.'

'Roger that, Black Hal. Query – is this advisable? We have multiple civilians attempting to cross the bridge with soldiers. Over.'

Jaap peers up out of his foxhole and sees the panic-stricken crowd jamming the bridge, mainly soldiers but their wives and some children as well. They are carrying rifles and bundles of possessions, pushing, shoving and shouting. Some fall down and are trampled, others get pushed off the sides between the metal girders into the fast torrent and sweep downstream. The soldiers on the bank behind them are keeping up a steady covering fire on his men, bullets are thudding into the earth all around him and he ducks back down.

Alex doesn't want to hear his objections. He has taken the difficult decision to launch the strike; he knows he will kill innocent women and children. Does the Dutchman really think that he can sort out a place like Kivu without collateral damage?

He is the commander who sees the bigger picture – every FDLR soldier he kills here is another problem solved. They have been dishing out punishment to the civilians of Kivu for decades and now they have to take responsibility for their actions.

He keys the mike and says aggressively, 'Cheesehead, this is my decision, get your men in cover. Out.'

Jaap turns and yells, 'Artillery incoming! Take cover!' and his men abandon their attempts to return fire and hunker down in their shellscrapes. Jaap curls up in a ball in his foxhole, head down under his arms, helmet pressed against the earth side, mouth open so that over pressure won't blow his lungs out and prays that the gunners have got the targeting right.

'Black Hal, this is Beelzebub, we are ready to fire.'

Alex doesn't hesitate.

'Beelzebub, fire for effect.'

The artillery officer hits the electronic firing switch attached to a long wire running to the truck and the dreadful torrent commences. Two rockets per second scream out of their tubes, the truck jolts down on its suspension with each launch, exhaust flames and gases fill the forest clearing and the glowing procession of death arcs away into the blue sky.

In his foxhole, Jaap doesn't hear the rockets approach, they come in too fast, just the enormous bang of the first one as it bursts over the crowd sending a shockwave that jars his skull. Each blastwave pulls the air out of his lungs and sprays shrapnel over the valley side. A giant fist is pounding down on him twice a second for twenty seconds.

'Jesus, how long will this last? I'm going to die,' he thinks as the pummelling continues.

Suddenly it stops.

He slumps down and whoops air back into his body. His head is ringing with pain and he can't hear anything.

After a minute he uncurls and crawls to the lip of his foxhole and looks out over the valley and whispers.

'*Jee-sus Christ.*'

The big Mi-24 gunship roars low over Alex, its 23mm cannon clattering and sending shell casings tumbling down around him.

Alex ducks his head under the powerful downdraught and watches the brass casings glint in the sun as they fall like gold snow. He carries on running; they have got to hurry.

The gunships have refuelled and rearmed and are back on station overhead smashing any resistance. Mortars continue to rain down ahead of the First Regiment troops. They have fired hundreds of rounds over the day and the tubes are red hot now.

It's midafternoon and he needs to get to the main base, extract actionable intelligence and then get all the troops out of the valley before it gets dark at six. They have smashed the enemy and killed a lot but many have scattered into the woods and fields along the sides of the valley and it only takes one bloke with an RPG to take out a chopper.

Alex is running along with the one hundred and twenty troops of Bravo Company. They stop to fire occasionally at enemy troops but they are scattering down the valley in the face of the gunships and mortars.

Everyone has heard the hammering booms of the rocket strike as they rolled back up the valley from the bridge. Alex has shut it out of his mind and is concentrating on gathering the intelligence, getting it back to base and planning the next wave of strikes.

After a mile they come to the main headquarters area of single-storey wooden buildings that took the first rocket strike in the morning.

The base is a shambles. Roofs smashed in by a giant aerial fist, trees knocked over, cars and trucks beaten down onto their axles and burnt out. It's silent and they walk through carefully, their feet scraping on broken glass from blown-out windows. Soldiers scuttle ahead from one piece of cover to another in teams, kicking in doors that lean drunkenly in broken frames and clearing buildings.

There is no one left alive. Alex looks at the bodies scattered around him, either shredded into pieces by shrapnel, or externally intact but with internal organs pulped by the blast waves, dried blood trails running from their noses and ears. They died in the morning and the dogs and crows have been at them since then. Pools of blood are everywhere, the flies are drunk on it, wriggling and drowning in the congealing mess. There are so many clouds of them buzzing about that they get into his mouth and he spits them out in disgust.

The dogs have gone feral with bloodlust, lapping it up. They growl and bare their teeth at the soldiers as they approach the corpses. Some have to be shot at to drive them off.

The men locate the main HQ building and, after troops have swept it, Alex walks in, ducking under a caved-in roof beam and stepping over a severed head.

'In here, sir.' He walks through into an office and looks at the broken body of General Musoni lying on the floor where he was knocked backwards off his executive chair. Dried blood trails run from his ears and his satellite phone lies in a corner of the room after his fatal conversation with Rukuba.

Alex looks around the office. Pink floral print curtains flap in the broken windows and there's a spiderplant pot smashed on the floor. He goes over to the cheap veneer wood desk where a French copy of *The Purpose Driven Life* is lying in an open drawer.

The soldiers are sombre as they look around.

Alex knows they don't have the time to be.

'Right, get everything that looks like intelligence: I want laptops, any mobiles or satphones, maps, those filing cabinets! I want Musoni's body and any other high value officers you can find. Come on, let's crack on! Just bung it all in the chopper and let's go!'

The men get cracking and Demon 3 settles down in a cloud of dust next to the base. Relays of men run out of buildings lugging bundles of files and equipment up the ramp and dump it inside. Mordechai and the Unit 17 intelligence people will sort it out back at base. The bodies of senior officers are taken in order to prove they have been killed when they start the media war later on in the campaign.

As RSM, Col is responsible for making sure that all the men get off the battlefield and back to base safely. He is busy on the radio coordinating with the pilots to organise the extraction. Jean-Baptiste with Echo Company and the Alpha Company FSG all need picking up off the ridge but Foxtrot is in the most exposed position across the Oso river at the bottom of the valley.

Col shouts to Alex as he walks past lugging a computer hard-drive. 'Colonel, do you want a lift down to the bridge? I've got cabs coming over in a minute.'

Alex pauses and looks at him. He knows he should go and face up to the consequence of his decision. He nods and hurries on to the chopper.

Demon 2 lands and he boards with the four men of his close protection team. They man the machine guns at the side and rear door, scanning the valley as they skim along it – it's their job to keep the boss alive. Two other aircraft follow them in line astern.

As they come towards the bridge, Alex keys the mike on his headphones. 'Hover here, I want to see it from the air.'

He looks down out of the side door at the devastation. Each aerial blast has scattered bodies under it like corn into a sunburst. The strike was accurate and carpeted the area up the valley from the bridge as well as the structure itself. The heavy metal girders have been blown off its sides and one half of the road surface has been smashed into the river.

The field of death covers the approach to the bridge, fanning out from the riverbank. There must be nearly a thousand people dead down there. Brown bodies with their clothes blown off by the blasts and red blood, all lying with the careless abandon of death. He can't tell soldiers from civilians, they've all been pulped by the blast waves.

The slaughter of the innocents?

No, most of them were combat soldiers, so don't get soft now. You've been through this already. This is war, this is your job, just get on with it.

His close protection team are standing at the tailgate staring out at the destruction. One of them glances back at Alex's face as he surveys the scene. His stare is intense and severe. What's he thinking about?

Horror, guilt and war crimes.

'His fame and his doom went hand in hand.'

Is this my doom?

Alex keys the mike on the intercom to the Ukrainian pilot. 'How much fuel have you got?'

'Full load, sir, we just refuel, it's only fifty mile here. We got enough for six hundred miles.'

'Is there an emergency venting system?' He knows full well there is one to ditch fuel in the event of a crash; he's worked with Mi-17s for years.

'Er, yes sir.'

'Good, I want you to fly slowly over the site and bleed off as much fuel as you can spare.'

He keys the mike to the other two aircraft and orders them to do the same so that the whole site is covered. They move slowly over the carnage, and thousands of gallons of clear avtur gushes out of a vent in the bottom of the aircraft and is dispersed by the strong downdraught like a sprinkler system.

The other two aircraft repeat the trick and then all three of them land on the far side of the bridge.

Major Jaap t'Hooft has got his men drawn up in three chalks ready to board. They are all shaken up by the bombardment and they trudge wearily into the choppers, glad to get away from the appalling sight in front of them.

He walks over to Alex who is standing with his arms folded over his chest looking across the river. Jaap's face still looks shocked from the blasts. He stands next to Alex, trying to think of something to say but it all just sounds trite so he keeps his mouth shut.

Alex turns and looks at him. 'We had to do it,' he says with finality. ' Come on, let's get out of here.'

They walk back over to a chopper packed with men bristling with weapons. Alex goes to the little sliding hatch in the window on the pilot's side and shouts up for something that they pass out to him.

He walks back round to the ramp, and squeezes in next to his men at the back.

The choppers take off and then pass over the carnage. The others fly ahead but Alex's pauses for a moment.

A figure leans out of the back of it over the raised ramp and a single bright red flare arcs down into the field of bodies. The avtur erupts and flames sweep across the field.

As the helicopters clatter away up the valley, the orange light from the flames washes over them and a pall of stinking black smoke spreads across the land.

Chapter Twenty-Seven

The slight, middle-aged man wears a cheap suit and an anxious expression. He stands at the gate at Panzi hospital and says to Mama Riziki, 'Well, if I could just come in to talk to you about it?'

He glances nervously around him at the crowd of food sellers who have set up their goods on patches of newspaper to sell to people coming in and out.

'Well, tell me what it is about?'

The man looks pained. 'It's a private matter.'

'Oh, OK, let him in.' She gestures to the security guard and ambles back to the main buildings. 'We can talk in my office.'

They sit down and she looks at him. 'So?'

'Well, I am here to make a donation to a woman. God has given me a word and told me to give the money to someone who really needs it.' He unfolds a roll of crisp dollar bills.

Mama Riziki looks at it and raises her eyebrows. 'Well, he must have had a big word with you. If you want to donate to the hospital then that would be very kind, we are always very grateful for the support of our . . .'

'No, God has told me to give this money to one woman, someone who is destitute and has no other means.'

'Hmm.' She pauses. 'Who are you?'

'My name is Mr Nguy, I live in Bukavu.'

'OK, well, I do have someone in mind. She has run out of money and needs another operation but she can't afford even to stay on in the hospital any more so we would have to send her back to her village. If you could pay for another operation then that would be a miracle for her.'

Mr Nguy beams. 'God is good, yes. Can I meet her first?'

Eve is lying in her bed, curled up in a ball. The sheets are soaked with urine but she doesn't care any more. All the other girls are outside in the gardens but she is so depressed she can't even get out of bed.

Mama Riziki walks over, strokes her head, sees she has tears in her eyes and croons over her and kisses her cheek.

'Hey, baby, there is a man here who wants to speak to you. He has some good news.'

Eve raises her head and looks at Mr Nguy standing at the end of the ward smiling nervously at her.

'Who is he? I've never seen him in my life. What does he want with me?'

The last helicopters touch down that night on the landing pads under harsh arc lights and wind down their engines for the first time that day.

The soldiers pour off the ramps, tired but elated. Echo, Alpha and Bravo Companies are in high spirits; Alex stands and watches the guys' faces as they walk back up the hill to base. They know that First Regiment took casualties but victory is a great painkiller. They're relieved to be through the battle and alive, they know they did a good job and the enemy took a pummelling. Some of the guys grin at Alex as he welcomes them back and flash victory signs. 'Got 'em, sir!'

Alex feels weak and shaky but straightens his shoulders, grins and gives a thumbs up. He is still in command mode;

he will process the emotions later. He knows he has to whip the wheel at this point to prevent the blues setting in. They've all had a very long day and burnt up huge reserves of energy – the firefight on the ridge felt like a normal year's worth of adrenaline packed into a few minutes.

The soldiers from Foxtrot Company, though, are looking shaken up both from the bombardment and the massacre. The men's morale is a delicate thing and Alex knows he's got to nip any malaise in the bud. He calls Col over. 'Let's have a word with them later on.'

Col nods; as RSM he's the one who will do the rounds of the barracks that evening, visiting the men as they sit on their bunks cleaning their weapons, chatting to them and taking soundings of their mood.

'Right, I'll let 'em get cleaned up and then we can see them later.'

The sixty men from the blocker group all cram into one long hut. They're sitting on the top of the double bunks and on the floor to see Alex.

He stands front centre, flanked by Col and Major Jaap t'Hooft to present a united front. It's an intimate meeting so they know that the CO cares about them, and they stare at him expectantly.

Alex is in a forthright, robust mood, standing with his hands on his hips and his feet apart. He gets straight to the point.

'Gentlemen, what you have seen today is an appalling sight. It was an intense bombardment and the enemy took heavy casualties, some of them civilians. That is something we all regret and it is a terrible thing to witness.'

He pauses and scans their faces.

'However, I will make two clear points. First, it was my decision as commanding officer to call in the artillery strike and I take full responsibility for it. Tactically and strategically I had no other choice.

'Second, it is important to emphasise that Operation Wrath and the battle of Lubonga valley that you have just fought was a military victory and not a moral defeat.'

Another pause and a look round.

'We have to be realistic. We cannot fight this war and delude ourselves that innocents are not going to die. There was no way that we could separate out the civilians and if we had let the soldiers escape then the damage they would have inflicted on other civilians would have been immense.

'Kivu has been suffering lawlessness since 1997; thousands die unnecessarily every year and thousands of women are raped every year, a lot of them by FDLR forces. This situation will continue for decades because no one in the international community has got the guts to do anything that will actually solve the problem. The UN mission here is just a figleaf to cover their consciences.'

He scans the faces, still in rapt attention.

'Well, gentlemen, today, we in the First Regiment of the Kivu Defence Force have taken the first major step to changing that situation. Through your bravery you have inflicted a crushing defeat on a group that is a listed terrorist organisation both in America and the EU.

'We have captured a goldmine of information that our intelligence analysts are going through now.' He points behind them to the large hut set aside for the purpose up the hill where Zacheus, Mordechai and the Unit 17 team are hard at work.

'This will enable us to draw up a target list for raids that will mean that we can finally destroy the network behind this organisation. We can then disarm the other militia groups and finally restore civil society to Kivu.'

'Gentlemen, you did a good day's work today. It was tough but in years to come a lot of people will look back on what you did and thank God for your efforts.'

Col stands in front of the entire regiment of a thousand men and reads out a list of the dead.

He's on the raised area in front of the headquarters building. The men are drawn up in front of him on the parade ground in ranks, bareheaded and clasping their berets in two hands in front of them. Some are looking up at Col thoughtfully but most just stare down at the ground.

Twenty-one bodies are zipped into grey bodybags laid out on planks on trestles in front of him, each covered with a piece of camouflage netting. A makeshift cross has been made out of spent 105mm brass shell casings and stands behind them all. It's rough and ready but heartfelt.

It's 5th May, the morning after the battle, and Col's huge voice booms out in the chill morning air. 'Flight Officer Karpenko. Flight Officer Pankratov. Aircrewman Zablotny. Volunteer Jensen. Volunteer Rodriguez, Corporal Parker . . .'

The names roll on and the men listen in silence. It could be theirs next time.

Combat soldiers are irreverent yet profound. Most of the time they are crass and insensitive, cheering their mates' misfortunes and celebrating enemy suffering. However, in honouring their dead they demand that due ceremony is observed.

Alex stands next to Yamba and Col and scans along the ranks. Some guys look blank-faced, others sombre, others have tears streaking their cheeks. He glimpses Corporal Stein's brutal face staring at Col with laserlike intensity.

Alex thinks about the speech he is just about to give. He has to articulate the collective emotion of this new military

226

family as it comes together to grieve and he's got to get the tone right.

Col finishes the list, pauses and then says, 'The commanding officer will now address the regiment.' He calls them to attention and then stands them at ease again. It's all part of the ceremony.

Alex's voice comes from deep within and is big enough to carry right to the back of the formation. However, it is softer-edged and has lost some of the harshness from his speech the night before and he pauses frequently.

'Gentlemen, this is a very solemn day. We have come together as the First Regiment to mourn the deaths of our comrades. They were soldiers and airmen and they died carrying out their jobs with bravery and distinction. We all feel their loss keenly.

'However, these men have not died in vain. Yesterday we inflicted a crushing defeat on the enemy that will allow us to continue the campaign and lead to our eventual victory and a better world for the six million people of Kivu.

'You all performed superbly in the battle of Lubonga valley. That and these men's sacrifice has bonded us together as a unit and sealed it with blood. Being part of First Regiment now means a huge amount more to us all. We are a young unit and we face overwhelming odds but what you and these men did yesterday showed that we are brave, that we can fight and that we will win!'

After his speech a Russian, Danish, Spanish and English soldier come onto the platform and, led by Col, the regiment mumbles its way through the Lord's Prayer in their various tongues. A lot of the men don't know the words but the slow rumbling rhythm of a thousand voices has enough of a sense of the divine to speak to their souls.

As the ceremony draws to a close they observe a

two-minute silence and the men look down, lost in their thoughts.

Alex stands at attention and keeps his face straight. He does feel what is happening but he has an old-school, dutiful way of dealing with it, channelling the feeling into making sure he does his job as CO well. He is there to voice the men's emotions not to feel them.

Six men who were close to each of the dead then come forward from the front ranks and lift the planks bearing the bodies onto their shoulders. Jean-Baptiste is solemn as he helps carry one of his men; Echo Company lost twelve soldiers in all in Demon 5 and on the ridge. Major McKinley carries one of Bravo Company's dead from the fighting in the valley. Arkady is among the Russian pilots and ground-crew who carry their own comrades.

The drill is awkward and unrehearsed but they slowly make their way over to a Mi-17 sitting on the parade ground with its rear ramp down, waiting to take the bodies to Kigali from where they will be repatriated. Each party enters the cargo bay and leaves a body before the next one goes in.

The men turn and watch as the engine starts, the ramp closes slowly, and the blades begin to turn. Dust blows back over them and they shield their eyes as it lifts off. The pilot slowly rotates in the air so that the helicopter faces the regiment and dips its rotors to them.

It turns and rises upwards; the men watch until the dot is lost in the bright blue morning sky.

Chapter Twenty-Eight

A heavy explosion shakes Gabriel awake at two a.m.

He sits upright in his bunk. Another massive bang rattles the wooden shutters of the hut and makes the empty beer bottles on the floor clink together.

'What's that?' Marcel's frightened voice comes from the bunk above him. They listen and another explosion comes from the hill across the valley from their *manoir*.

Shouts start in the huts down the muddy street from them and they pull on their trousers, wellies and anoraks and run outside. Crowds of miners are standing and staring across the valley half a mile away at the FDLR base on the hill overlooking them. It's cloudy and freezing cold and everyone's breath steams in the dim lights from the open hut doors.

A brilliant orange flash in the air over the base destroys Gabriel's night vision and the thump of the explosion knocks the air out of his lungs. More explosions pound the base.

The artillery fire stops and the noise of helicopters swirls in from the darkness. The beating of heavy rotors slows over the FDLR base but the aircraft are completely blacked out so he can't actually see them. It feels creepy just trying to sense their location by sound.

'What the hell's going on?' someone shouts to no one in particular.

'It's the UN.'

'Don't be stupid, they wouldn't take on the Gorilla Brigade.'

Gabriel and Marcel stand and stare with open mouths.

'What about Robert and Patrice?' Gabriel finally mutters, wondering if the soldiers they sometimes work with are OK.

There are four helicopters now landing on the hill, dropping troops and then lifting off immediately. They hear orders being shouted, intense bursts of machine-gun fire and the flat cracks of grenades echo back and forth across the valley. Windows smash and doors crash open. They hear more shouting of orders and screaming of men in fear.

A building catches fire, flames licking up from a lower-floor window.

'That's Colonel Etienne's villa,' Marcel mutters. They have often looked up at the white clapboard house, envying the power he has over them and the wealth he creams off from their labour. It feels disconcerting to see it attacked in the middle of the night so swiftly and so violently.

The raid continues and they can see the bright flashes of tracer fire spreading down the hill into the barracks. Some of the buildings are already on fire from the shells at the start of the raid. A cluster of muzzle flashes in the dark shows where some resistance is beginning to take hold against the assault.

Alex is watching the raid on the plasma screen in the ops room, the infrared images relayed to him by the drone circling high above it all. Col, Yamba and other senior officers are also crowded round. Kill TV they call it. It's 5th May, the night after the Lubonga battle and Alex is already using the intelligence from the material they seized from FDLR headquarters. He needs to keep the element of surprise and hit the enemy in their bases before they realise what is happening. He is using fresh men from the rifle companies not involved in the Lubonga battle, which all helps to keep the regiment focused on its ongoing mission.

'Good, they're in,' Alex mutters. The landing is a delicate part of the op but there is a lot more to come.

'Artillery was spot on,' Yamba murmurs approvingly. Two 105mm light guns were dropped by helicopter into a clearing on a hill ten miles away earlier in the day and a temporary firebase established. They will use the two guns as fire support for two other raids that night happening in a twenty-mile radius area around the firebase and then pull the guns out the next day.

Alex always feels odd watching the silent black and white movie of his men in action but it is also very convenient from a commander's perspective. He keys the mike on the radio net. 'Beyoncé, this is Black Hal. Can you neutralise the pocket of resistance behind Barrack Four on the north side of the target?'

'Black Hal, this is Beyoncé. Roger that.'

Arkady's gunner, Boris, uses the magnified image from his infrared targeting sight displayed in a monocle that drops down from his helmet over his right eye. He can see the FDLR soldiers crouching behind a line of outdoor cement-wash troughs, using them as cover to fire back at the men of Golf Company. He thumbs the targeting crosshairs over them, the long twin-barrelled cannon in the chin turret under his feet swivels round and he presses the fire button on his joystick.

Gabriel hears the clatter of rotors move in again overhead and bright flashes of heavy-calibre automatic gunfire stab down from the black sky. Wherever the lines of light touch the earth, orange explosions and sparks shoot up illuminating bodies being blown to pieces.

Resistance breaks and the FDLR troops start running away down the road into the valley between the base and the *manoir*.

Gabriel and the others can't see them in the pitch black but the dark of the bottom of the valley is suddenly split open by two bright white flashes and loud bangs that roll back up the hill to them.

After the Claymore mines go off, spraying hundreds of ball bearings across the road, multiple bursts of machine-gun fire open up on the troops from higher up the *manoir* side of the hill.

Corporal Stein can see the men below him in the green underwater vision of his night vision goggles and steers the line of tracer from his PKM machine gun onto them. Using his Special Forces skills he has infiltrated an eight-man blocker detachment into the ambush site from ten miles out and laid up in the forest waiting for the start of the raid. The FDLR soldiers are caught in the trap and shot to pieces in the valley.

After the barracks are cleared of men on the hill, phosphorous grenades are lobbed inside, the bright white flashes illuminating the night, and the buildings start burning fiercely.

The four big helicopters clatter back in to the site and in the light of the flames Gabriel can see men running out from the headquarters building carrying bundles of documents and even a filing cabinet. Handcuffed and hooded prisoners can also be seen being shoved along with rifles into the choppers.

Shouts call the assault troops back in and they start re-embarking on the helicopters. The gunship overhead lands on the road in the bottom of the valley and the blocker detachment slide the side doors open and scramble into the troop compartment. As they lift off a few rifle rounds hit the titanium armour and ping off harmlessly.

All five helicopters disappear back into the night and the crowd in the street listen to the sound of them fading into the darkness. The buildings on the hill are burning furiously and light up the whole valley with orange and yellow flames.

Gabriel and Marcel look at each other open-mouthed. It is fifteen minutes since the first shell woke them up.

Chapter Twenty-Nine

Dieudonné Rukuba stands in front of a large audience seated in neat rows. 'Ladies and gentlemen, welcome to this press conference to announce the foundation of the new Republic of Kivu.

'I would especially like to welcome our distinguished guests from the United Nations, African Union, European Union and United States.' Rukuba gestures to the people sitting in the front row, staring at him with guarded expressions, wary of having any connection with this strange, new and unknown quantity.

Rukuba's hand sweeps on and around the room. 'Also to our esteemed NGO workers from Kivu and our valued colleagues from the Kivu People's Party and the Kivu Defence Force, welcome one and all.'

Rukuba's French is impeccable and he speaks in a calm soft voice. He is in no hurry, adjusts the microphone, pauses and coughs slightly before beginning his main speech.

It's 7th May, only three days after the opening battle of the campaign in Lubonga. He is standing at a podium on a raised platform at the front of the large dining room in Hotel Bruxelles on the lakeshore five miles outside Goma; they judged the city itself too volatile to hold the meeting, as crowds have been out on the streets. The room is from the

1950s colonial heyday of Kivu and has elegant curving arches along both sides. The audience of two hundred people eyes him warily and stewards from the Kivu People's Party in cheap suits hover nervously at the edges checking everything is set up right.

Press photographers crab around in front of the podium trying to be unobtrusive whilst getting the right angle for their shots. TV cameras on tripods poke out of the arches on either side of the room and are packed in at the back behind the chairs, their operators hunched over their viewfinders. All the big networks, news agencies and papers have scrambled their correspondents to fly out to Goma: BBC, Al Jazeera, CNN, France Press, Reuters, AP, *New York Times*, *The Times*, *The Telegraph*, *Le Monde*.

Rukuba is wearing his traditional white robes and looks very tall, serene and statesmanlike, a blaze of bright light set off against a large green flag of the Republic of Kivu behind him. It is based on the Congolese flag but instead of a sky-blue field divided diagonally by a red stripe it has a bright green background with a red stripe across it.

'Ladies and gentlemen, my name is Mr Dieudonné Rukuba and I am the President of the Transitional Administration that now governs the new Republic of Kivu. I will give a short speech and then take questions from the floor.

'You will have heard the statement from the President of the Democratic Republic of Congo yesterday announcing the establishment of the new state on a ninety-nine-year lease and giving it his blessing.

'We are profoundly grateful to the President for his help and support in the establishment of this exciting new venture, which we believe will at last bring peace to the region as well as economic development and prosperity.'

He pauses and takes a sip from his water glass.

At the back of the room, standing to one side watching through the arches are Alex, Col and Yamba, out of their army fatigues for the first time in months and dressed in chinos and casual shirts. They all have their arms folded across their chests, watching intently.

Sophie Cecil-Black is squeezed into the middle of one of the rows of chairs. She wishes they were further apart; her long legs have to twist to one side uncomfortably. However, like the rest of the people in the room, she is rapt with attention. She cannot believe what she is hearing. She has met Rukuba before through some work he was doing with the Kivu People's Party. He came for a tour round Hope Street's big rehabilitation and training facility for street kids outside Goma and was charming, but she is still sure that there is something very fishy about the deal. Nothing in the Congo is as it seems.

'So what is my vision for Kivu? My vision is for a strong and peaceful country. As part of the establishment of that I would like to introduce Monsieur Fang Wu, the representative of the Kivu Investment Fund.' He gestures to Fang who is sitting at a table on the platform next to him. Fang gets up and bows low to the audience and sits down again; Sophie is surprised at how tall he is.

'With the aid of a six-billion-dollar investment programme from our Chinese partners, we will be able to establish a new network of tarmac roads and proper bridges in Kivu. This will be followed by a large programme of agricultural investment to produce dairy products, fruit and fresh flowers for the EU and Middle Eastern markets as part of the East African Trade Federation, which we have been allowed to join, whilst Congo as a whole has not.

'At the same time all of the mines will be taken into nationalised ownership and, with a large investment in mechanisation, will be able to produce many times more than they currently do. We estimate revenues of a billion dollars a year for the new state. As you can see, ladies and gentlemen, we have big plans.'

Rukuba pauses and looks out over the audience. They are staring at him, either not able to take in what he is saying or not trusting him. Either way he is prepared for a rough ride at the Q&A session.

'Obviously you will be wondering how all this can be achieved given the poor security situation in the province. Well, I can tell you now that the newly established Kivu Defence Force has already struck very severe blows against the FDLR, the most intransigent of the militias, who for decades have terrorised the people of the province. After our brave servicemen have eliminated this organisation in a few weeks time we will offer a two-week period for the remaining militias to consider whether they want to disarm and join in a peace conference. Former militia soldiers will be disarmed, retrained for civilian jobs and given work in the reconstruction of the country.'

His voice drops almost to a whisper. 'However, I can also tell you now, ladies and gentlemen, that those who do not surrender will meet with the same ruthless response that my men have given to the FDLR. I am determined to crush once and for all the lawlessness of Kivu province.'

Alex studies him hard as he says this and feels a slight shiver run up his spine. There is something menacingly intense about how Rukuba says such hard words in such a quiet way.

He thinks about the raids going out tonight: he will helicopter back to base as soon as this session is finished, in order to be in the Ops Room to command them. Mordechai and Unit 17 studied the mountain of information they retrieved from Lubonga and quickly put together an entire order of battle for the FDLR with locations and details of defences.

For the three nights since then all the men of First Regiment have been hard at work on helicopter raids across the province. The main inhabited area of Kivu is a semicircle two hundred miles in diameter, well within Mi-17 range, so they have been able to hit key FDLR installations across the whole area. Ammunition dumps, barracks and command centres have all been smashed in the middle of the night using their advantages of night vision capability, speed, surprise and heavy artillery.

The enemy hasn't known what has hit them and every raid they carry out yields more intelligence that feeds into Mordechai's analysis system to generate more targets for the next night. They have also sent details of *comptoir* links to the Rwandans who are busy shutting down the group's mineral trading network and passing their bank account details to the EU and American authorities to freeze their assets. The FDLR and its support network is being dismantled from all sides.

Rukuba continues, 'So, that is a very brief summary of our plans and what we have achieved so far. Now I am sure that you will all have many questions that I am willing to answer.'

He looks at the audience who just stare back at him, still unable to comprehend the scale of what they have just heard.

Chapter Thirty

Joseph squats on the ground and looks up as eleven more prisoners are brought into the razor-wire cage.

It's early afternoon and these are the ones captured in last night's raids. They look shell-shocked, eyes staring, deep circles of exhaustion under them. He shuffles up to the men squatting on the earth next to him to make room. There are over a hundred guys in the prison already and more come in every night.

Like him they were attacked by surprise with great speed and violence, their comrades slaughtered around them and then yanked out of the life they knew. They have come from the low shed next to the helipads where they have been photographed, fingerprinted and had biometric data taken with a simple swab of the inside of their cheeks as soon as they touch down. Once they have been documented, they are interrogated, pumped for information by Rwandan interrogators using the shock of capture, threats and lots of screaming and shouting.

Joseph hears it every night. With that and the constant thudding of the helicopters taking off and landing, the bright arc light illuminating him at night and columns of troops marching back and forth to the helicopters, he hasn't slept much since he was captured.

He looks up at the white soldier patrolling outside the wire, his rifle held across his chest ready to shoot him. He still has no idea who these men are. Despite an aggressive interrogation he hasn't actually been hurt and a medic has dressed the swelling wound on the side of his face. He's been told that Lieutenant Karuta is in the hospital block up the hill having the grenade splinters taken out of his legs but he can't be sure that is true. Whoever the soldiers are they seem more interested in the old *génocidaires* like Karuta: all the guys put into the razor-wire prison are young men in their teens and twenties, too young to have participated in the Rwandan genocide.

The new prisoners slump on the ground as soon as there is space and stare ahead of them in shock. Joseph and the others are too depressed to say anything; he hugs his knees and wonders what the hell is going to happen to him.

Rukuba continues the press conference.

'Ladies and gentlemen, I am now willing to take questions from the floor. I am happy to take them in French or English.'

He says this to get some response from his audience, who are still trying to think through the inconsistencies and ramifications of his brief speech. Slowly journalists start putting up their hands.

'Yes, over there.' He gestures to a veteran hack who stands up.

'Bill Jakowski, *New York Times*. Er, Mr Rukuba, you will know that the United Nations Security Council is still debating the extraordinary announcement from Kinshasa in a closed session at this moment in time. What do you anticipate will be their response to the Kinshasa announcement and to the plans that you have just unveiled for this new . . .' he stumbles over his words as he tries to think how to encapsulate them '. . . commercial, market, state, entity . . .' Uncharacteristically he dries up and sits down.

Rukuba doesn't miss a beat. The delivery continues as smoothly and calmly as before but this time in perfect English.

'Well, thank you for your very pertinent question, Mr Jakowski, I always read your work on Africa with interest. My response is to say that this is primarily a domestic internal issue for Congo rather than one of international relations and therefore I do not think that the United Nations will need to become involved.

'If the legitimate government of a sovereign state decides to subdivide and lease a part of that state then that is entirely within their power to do so. UN troops in Kivu have been instructed to return to base for the moment but my Transitional Administration may continue to call on their services depending on how the security situation evolves.

'The government of Congo was elected in a UN-sponsored and approved election. Do you think that the government of the Democratic Republic of Congo has the right to decide what happens in its own country, Mr Jakowski?'

Bill Jakowski has written at length on the corrupt nature of the DRC government but suddenly this doesn't seem the right forum to air his views so he keeps quiet.

'Yes, please.' Rukuba gestures generously to a woman near the front.

She stands and another American accent sounds in the room. 'Sarah Hollands, Associated Press. I think Bill had it right there when he wasn't sure how to define this new entity that we are talking about. Could you talk a little more to what exactly is going to be the nature of this new government and, more specifically, will it be democratic?'

'Thank you, Sarah. Yes, what we are proposing is a world-first. I agree it is confusing but it will function in effect as a sovereign state. As President of the Transitional Administration I have suspended the previous constitution of Kivu and declared a state of emergency that will last until the security situation is resolved. After that there will be a period of consultation with the people of Kivu on the new constitution and then some form of elections will be held.'

She cuts right back at him. 'Mr Rukuba, "some form of elections" doesn't sound very convincing to the international community.'

Rukuba is unfazed. 'As I say, there will be a period of consultation with the people of Kivu and it is not for me to judge the will of the people.' He smiles charmingly and takes the next question.

'Sophie Cecil-Black, Hope Street – we're an NGO in Kivu as I believe you know?' Rukuba smiles and nods. 'I am sure everyone in this room is very glad that you are tackling the issue of the FDLR but I wonder how you have been able to do it when UN forces and the Congolese army have been trying and failing since 2003?'

At the back of the room Alex, Col and Yamba all exchange looks. Alex knew the issue of the Kivu Defence Force was bound to come up at some point; white mercenaries have a bad reputation in Africa. He is used to being regarded by diplomats and NGO workers as a life form somewhere between rodents and jackals. He watches the tall, striking-looking girl in the green tee shirt carefully. Something about her name rings a bell in his head.

Rukuba continues his smooth rebuttals. 'Well, I am sure that you would not expect me to be able to comment on such a sensitive security issue at a time when our forces are engaged in active . . .'

'Are white mercenaries involved? I have heard reports of sightings from my field workers upcountry.'

Rukuba is for once forced to give ground. 'Some security consultants have been hired but I cannot go into more details now. Yes, next question please.'

The Q&A goes on and the general air of suspicion and hostility continues from the press. The diplomats from the UN, EU, AU and USA don't ask any questions at this stage, letting the journos and NGO people do the spadework as they try and work Rukuba out.

He continues to be charming and generally holds his own but has to be downright evasive on a number of points. Alex thinks he is doing a good job in a hostile atmosphere. He likes and admires Rukuba; he can scarcely believe that the vision of a new world for Kivu that the two of them set out to achieve is actually coming to fruition. He is standing here listening to this wonderfully charismatic man announce the new state that they have both worked hard for a long time to set up. Deep inside him the insecurity that drove him here eases a little: 'See, look at what I have created!' he says to it.

Eventually Rukuba holds up his elegant hand and says, 'Well, ladies and gentlemen, I think we have covered most of the main areas. In a minute I will invite you to attend an off-the-record buffet lunch on the terrace overlooking our delightful Lake Kivu, which will give me a chance to meet more of you in person. However, first I think it is important that we hear from one more speaker.'

The audience looks baffled by this new addition to the programme.

'We have all been debating the fascinating points of international law and development policy. However, I think that it is important that we do not get ahead of ourselves here and forget what the purpose of this new state is – to build a better, more secure world for the ordinary people of Kivu. The ordinary people that the international community has so far failed to protect.

'So, to refocus our minds on this subject, I think it is important that we hear from the authentic voice of Kivu.'

He nods towards the back of the room and one of the Kivu People's Party attendants pushes a small figure forward down the central aisle. As she shuffles along, the correspondents and diplomats turn round and crane their necks to see who it is. She is short, stocky and barefoot and wears the simple, grubby *pagne* worn by the peasants in the province. As she moves past them people notice that she has a wet stain down the back of her dress.

Rukuba leaves the platform, comes down the steps and walks up to meet her. He smiles, puts his arm around her and escorts her up the steps to the podium.

Eve's head can only just be seen over the wooden stand and Rukuba adjusts the microphone down to her mouth. She wonders how on earth she is going to get through this.

Chapter Thirty-One

Eve looks out over the elegant hotel dining room packed with diplomats, journalists and TV cameras focusing on her; she cannot comprehend them.

They are from a world utterly alien to her upbringing in a small village of two hundred people, hours from the nearest road, and her recent existence in a shack made of twigs in a squalid refugee camp.

She has to do the speech though to repay the kind man who has paid for her second operation and she just focuses on that and reads from the French text that Rukuba has written for her and that she has rehearsed until she knows it by rote. Her voice is picked up clearly by the microphone but it is a whisper and the audience of jaded hacks, NGO workers and career diplomats all sit forward on their seats straining their ears to hear her.

'Ladies and gentlemen, my name is Eve Mapendo. I am eighteen years old and I come from the village of Kato in Mukurawa Commune in South Kivu, although this village was attacked by militias and abandoned and my family and I all now live in an IDP camp called Ikozi.'

The contrast between the formal, factual tone of the speech and her humble origins emphasises them and the audience will her on through the painful process.

'A few months ago our camp was attacked by a militia called the Kudu Noir and my young baby was stolen and killed. I was raped by a gang of four men and they also used the barrel of a rifle on me. Apart from the trauma of the rape I also suffered a vaginal fistula and leak urine constantly. Like many rape victims I was stigmatised by the event and have experienced rejection from many members of my community.

'As you can see I have suffered much because of the chronic political instability that affects my homeland. But far more important than my personal story is the bigger picture of what is happening now to Kivu. As you know, the region suffers thousands of rapes and deaths every year because of political violence and lawlessness. The United Nations and the Congolese government have struggled valiantly since 2003 to end this but their efforts have not been effective.

'I have come here today to say that I fully support and endorse the actions of our new President Dieudonné Rukuba as he takes a stand against this endemic violence, and of the brave soldiers of the Kivu Defence Force. As I speak, they are on active operations to bring the conflict to an end and their actions have already dealt greater blows to the FDLR than years of effort by previous forces.

'I will shortly have another operation that I hope will heal me for good. In the same way, I hope and pray for the healing work that President Rukuba is doing, that it will establish the mandate of heaven and bring law and order. We hope this will lead to lasting peace and prosperity for our beautiful but tragic land.

'Ladies and gentlemen, thank you for coming to the first press conference of the new government of the Republic of Kivu today. God bless the Republic of Kivu and God bless you, President Rukuba.'

As she ends the speech, Mr Nguy is so overwhelmed with emotion that he jumps up from his seat at the side of the hall and shouts, '*Dieu-donn-é!*'

The other KPP workers around the hall were equally ecstatic and yell the response to his chant, '*Don de dieu!*'

Rukuba smiles at their enthusiasm and rises from his seat at the table next to the podium, crossing over to Eve and putting his arm around her. She is still in a numb state as she is led away by her friend Miriam and the KPP stewards.

Rukuba steps up to the microphone, smiling quietly as he pulls it back up to his height. 'Ladies and gentlemen, can we give Eve a round of applause for her brave speech? Then I invite you to join me for a buffet lunch on the terrace.'

The audience of experienced foreign policy workers claps in a loud but reflective way, devoid of the enthusiasm of the KPP workers. They are thinking about how they have just had an object lesson in learning that what is foreign policy for them is very domestic policy for Eve.

Lake Kivu sparkles a delightful blue under a sky spotted with small white clouds. The guests spill out of the high doors from the dining room onto the terrace and the lawn running down to the lake.

The manager of the hotel trained in Brussels and takes his catering very seriously. He is used to doing big wedding receptions for *comptoirs* and local businessmen and has pulled out all the stops: waiters in bow ties circulate with champagne and canapés and the guests tuck in, feeling in need of something after Eve's understated but powerful speech. Stewards from the KPP politely ask TV crews and press photographers not to bring their cameras out: 'Private lunch please.'

Rukuba and Fang are standing in the middle of the terrace

247

with KPP party workers around them as well as Major Zacheus Bizimani and two other Unit 17 soldiers in suits and wraparound shades who scrutinise the crowd constantly.

Both the politicians have champagne glasses and are laughing and chatting with journalists, enjoying their charm offensive. It is as vital a part of the process of building the new country as the military campaign that is going on alongside it. Despite his rhetoric Rukuba knows he will need help from the UN and other big donors like USAID and DfID. Fang is equally adept in this diplomatic milieu, chatting away happily with a Ugandan diplomat about trade relations.

Alex, Col and Yamba keep a low profile, standing on the lawn at the edge of the crowd, sipping their drinks and surveying the scene as Rukuba holds court on the terrace. Alex was wary of coming to the event but Rukuba insisted. They have agreed that he and the other mercenaries will keep out of sight as much as possible or they will get into problems both with the politically correct donor community and African leaders still banging the anti-imperialist drum.

'I thought that went OK?' Alex looks at Col and Yamba and they nod. 'That Sophie Cecil-Black character' – where has he heard that name before – 'gave him a hard time about the identity of the Kivu Defence Force but I think otherwise he got through it pretty well.'

'Yes, I think he will have them eating out of his hand soon, you know.' Yamba nods towards Rukuba.

'Yer, they're all a bit wary like now but I think they'll warm up,' Col agrees.

Alex nods. 'Yes, it's been a long old road but it feels bloody good to be here, doesn't it?'

He smiles hopefully and the others do likewise. It's about as optimistic as they ever see Alex getting. He's feeling pleased with where they have got to but is always looking for the next obstacle to overcome. 'Will I ever be at peace?' he wonders.

He drains his glass and waves to a passing waiter for another. 'I needed that, been far too long. Think we might relax the dry rule on base.'

They chat on, savouring the sunshine and the chance to relax for an hour, with no one in uniform and no life or death decisions to make for a while. That can wait for the raids going out tonight.

'I'm gonna get a beer, can't stand champagne,' Col says. 'You want one?'

'No, I'm OK.'

Col walks back up onto the terrace and sees the tall NGO girl who asked the question about mercs. After a couple of drinks he can't resist going over and taking the piss.

'Oh no . . .' Yamba sees him talking to her and nudges Alex, who groans and closes his eyes.

The exchange looks awkward: they can see that Col is being overly friendly in a facetious manner and that she is looking down at him disdainfully and doesn't seem to know why he is talking to her.

After a while the short mercenary cheerfully says goodbye, gets himself a beer and saunters back over to them with a smirk on his face.

Alex looks at him in exasperation. 'Did you have to do that?'

Col carries on grinning.

Yamba asks, 'What's she like then?'

Col shakes his head. 'Nah, no tits.'

His reputation as a tit-man is well established.

'Anything else to report?' says Yamba, his eyes sparkling with suppressed humour.

'Well, she's a bit like a cross between a giraffe and rhino really, you need a step-ladder to get near her . . .'

'You would.'

'Yer, but did you see her bloody nose, like this.'

'Well, sounds like a nice girl,' Yamba says.

'Gotta fooking great rod up her arse, I tell ya.' Col continues. 'Took one look at me and stuck her nose in the air.'

Yamba shrugs, as if to say that that is not an unreasonable course of action.

Alex watches the exchange sceptically with his arms folded but says nothing.

Zacheus slips through the crowd and walks over to them. Alex smiles and says, 'Major Bizimani, very good to see you.' He's been impressed with the man's military professionalism and the way that he is running Unit 17 with very little need for supervision. The intelligence network that he has established is excellent with contacts all over the province.

'Very good to see you too, Colonel Devereux.' As ever he keeps his eyes down and speaks quietly. 'President Rukuba would like you to come over and see him, please.'

'Sure.'

They thread through the crowd and up the steps. As they get nearer to the gaggle around the President, Alex sees that he is in animated discussion with Sophie.

'Ah!' Rukuba looks up in joyful surprise as Zacheus taps his arm. 'Yes, this is the person that I wanted you meet, Colonel Devereux.'

Alex takes in the tall striking woman in front of him. Despite the jeans and tee shirt there's something about the erect posture of her head and her rather beaky nose that gives her an unmistakably aristocratic look.

He pushes aside the recent discussion of her and switches

into professional mode, straightening his shoulders and putting out a hand. 'Hi, Alex Devereux, pleased to meet you.'

Sophie looks at the tall dark-haired man; he has a good-looking but serious face and radiates an air of disciplined efficiency. His voice has the unmistakably deep patrician timbre of the British ruling class. It is the tone used by generals, cabinet ministers and bishops throughout the ages. It speaks of politeness, respectability and authority. It is everything she has come to Africa to get away from. Involuntarily her neck stiffens and she draws up her head.

However, she is also a product of that class and by conditioned reflex she extends her hand to shake. His is large and the grip crushing. His eyes look to make contact with hers but she averts them, acknowledging his presence but not his person.

'Sophie Cecil-Black, pleased to meet you,' she says in a tone that implies she is anything but.

A flicker of recognition goes across Alex's face; he holds her hand for a moment longer then frowns. 'Do you have family in Shropshire?'

'Yes, cousins, why?' she says defensively.

'Oh, we used to shoot with them. They're . . .' he tries to think how to put it diplomatically '. . . slightly eccentric but great people when you get to know them.'

His father used to describe them as 'mad as a bag of badgers'.

Sophie nods, acknowledging what they both know. 'Sorry, I didn't catch your name?'

'Alex Devereux.'

'Hmm.' She cringes internally, not wanting to have anything to do with her background. 'Yes, I thought I knew the name,' she says in a distant way and a polite shutter goes down over her often animated face.

Rukuba misses the strained social nuances. 'Oh, well, that is great. Colonel Devereux, I want you to start working with Miss Cecil-Black. We have just been discussing her large training facility for street children near here and I am interested in funding it further for reintegrating former militia soldiers. What do you think?'

Alex recovers from the awkwardness and nods. 'Yes, that would be tremendous.' He's aware he already has a lot of prisoners building up in a makeshift detention facility and he wants to get them off his hands. 'We'll definitely make arrangements to do that.'

Gabriel and Eve hold hands at arm's length and she cries quietly, sometimes wiping her eyes with the flat of her hand. It's 8th May, the day after the press conference announcing the new state.

He just sits and gazes at her. Traditional Kivu village society is very conservative so they don't embrace or kiss even though they are alone in the gardens at Panzi.

'He has done marvellous things,' she sobs again. 'He is an amazing man,'

Gabriel nods, 'He has done marvellous things in our sight.'

Neither of them can believe how good President Rukuba has been to them.

Gabriel has seen the Kivu Defence Force at work at first hand. The assault on the Gorilla Brigade was brutal but it was also impressive to see them tear down the FDLR barracks in fifteen minutes, that symbol of authority that had hung over his head.

He bought a new radio when he was at the mine and listened with awe to Rukuba's first big speech on Radio Okapi. It was in Swahili, the language of the common people of the east, rather than French, the traditional language of the educated classes. In villages, streets and crowded bars all across the province, people hunched around their sets to hear this man who said he was their new President and that they now lived in a new country – they felt confused and fearful.

However, it was another masterpiece of communication from Rukuba. He was calm and spoke with a deep, authoritative voice, listing the problems of lawlessness and poverty that they all knew so well and asking when would it ever get sorted out with the current methods?

When he told them that his forces had already killed General Musoni, the leader of the FDLR, there were sharp intakes of breath and nods of assent. The man obviously meant business. Film of the general's broken body was released on YouTube to prove it and posters distributed to villages by KPP workers. He also repeated his offer of a two-week period for other militia groups to decide to enter peace talks before being targeted as well.

When he told them that he had big plans for investment in the province to create new jobs, there were smiles of hope. When he said that they would all soon be wealthy enough to be able to buy TVs and even cars, there were broad grins.

He ended by saying, 'People of Kivu, I will speak to you at the same time every week. I will be your guiding father and I will hold your hand in this time of uncertainty. I will keep you updated with news of developments as we ensure security throughout the province. Contact representatives of the Kivu People's Party with any information of militia movements and together we will build a peaceful and prosperous Kivu.

'Good night and God bless you all. I remain your faithful President, Dieudonné Rukuba.'

'He really cares about us.' Gabriel nods, unused to having

a politician who took the time to do regular broadcasts to the ordinary people and not only that, one who seemed to be able to deliver real change after so many years of war.

'I can't believe he paid for my operation. This time it's holding.' She glances down at herself and Gabriel nods; he came to Panzi with the stack of cash he had earned but found that all her bills had been paid.

'Well, we will get married soon,' he says with a pragmatic certainty, and she bows her head.

He gets out a wodge of dollar bills. 'Go back to Ikozi and make the arrangements. There is something I have to do first and I will join you in a week.'

Chapter Thirty-Two

Sophie points Alex towards the large grass field just inside the perimeter fence.

'We've got a big football tournament on today. We use it as an outreach technique to bring the kids onto the site and reassure them that we're OK.'

It's two days after the press conference on 9th May and her team of local NGO workers wearing fluorescent Hope Street waistcoats are trying to sort out a crowd of a hundred barefoot and ragged street children from Goma that they have bussed onto their site two miles outside the town.

'I'm afraid you won't be able to bring those in here.' She points to the assault rifles held by the four soldiers of Alex's close protection team, and then points to the large 'no weapons' sign by the gate through the fence.

'Right.' Alex considers the problem for a moment. The situation in the province is still very much a war zone and his troops are on active operations that day. However, they are near Goma where the situation is stable and he is now able openly to wear his KDF uniform with his colonel's shoulder tabs on his shirt and a beret.

They arrived by Mi-17 and he can always get his bodyguards to him quickly and get out if any trouble kicks off.

'I'll take the radio,' Col says helpfully.

'OK, you two stay with the chopper and the rifles and you two come with us.' Alex also unbuckles his gunbelt and hands over his 9mm Glock to the soldiers.

'Right, I think we're ready.' He faces Sophie and smiles; despite their slightly awkward start he is determined to be professional and pleasant. He didn't really mind her disdainful manner when they first met although he did comment unfavourably to Col on the fact that she has a tattoo in the small of her back – he'd spotted it poking out from under her short tee shirt when she had turned round and left.

'And what's wrong with tattoos?'

'Squaddies have tattoos, not birds.' Despite his difficulties with his own class Alex still has straightforward views on women's appearance.

Col has come along today to help him make an assessment of the facility and to see if they think they can release any prisoners to Sophie's organisation. Yamba is holding the fort back at their new base, Camp Heaven; they have been shipping troops and equipment across Lake Kivu from Camp Purgatory for the last week. Now that the news blackout is over and the project has gone public, they need to be seen to be operating from a base inside Kivu in order to distance themselves publicly from Rwandan support.

The group walks through the gate towards the football pitches. 'So are you a footie fan then, ma'am?' Col asks politely. He's also decided he will be thoroughly professional today and realises he has some ground to make up after his initially facetious manner at the press conference.

She looks at him cautiously but knows they have all got to get on. Despite her initial reserve about Rukuba she was impressed by his speech. She realises that he offers the best hope for the province and he has been talking about a huge injection of funding for her work.

'Umm, not really, netball was more my thing. But all the kids want to be Didier Drogba or Michael Essien and play for Chelsea or something.'

Col sucks his teeth in disgust. 'Oh dear.'

Alex rolls his eyes; Col's hatred of Chelsea is well established.

'They should play for a proper football team like Blackburn.' He bares his forearm tattoo to Sophie, who nods politely.

They walk over to the pitches where the local workers and foreign staff are sorting the kids by size; the boys often don't know their own age. They wear torn shorts and tee shirts and are skinny, with scabby knees, snotty noses and bright quick smiles.

Sophie explains, 'Most of their families have been killed in the fighting and they live rough on the streets in Goma. They mainly survive by begging but they also start mugging people when they get big enough.'

The workers shout, blow whistles and organise queues to dribble between little cones and then shoot at small five-a-side goals across the pitch. The kids love it, charging around and smashing the ball with gusto and then running to the back of the line.

Col and Alex watch with genuine interest.

'I quite fancy having ago meself actually,' Col jokes and walks off down the touchline. 'Come on, lad!'

Alex turns to Sophie and says genuinely, 'It's great to be out here, makes a very nice change from running a war. You've obviously got a good setup.' He nods across at the classroom blocks over the field. 'It would be great to be able to hand over some of the younger prisoners we capture to you.'

'What, those you don't kill first, you mean?'

She isn't being deliberately unpleasant; her acerbic nature just came up with the remark on automatic.

Alex drops his gaze and his expression becomes very grave. He looks up at her and she sees a terrible sadness in his eyes. He looks away at the young boys running around on the pitch.

She suddenly feels very awkward. 'Well, anyway, let's go and have a look at the training facilities.'

She leads the group over and they tour round the class-rooms and the workshops for carpentry, mechanics and building.

At the end of the morning they watch the final of the five-a-side tournament and loudly applaud the winning team as they jump around proudly waving their plastic medals on ribbons.

Sophie leads them back to the gate and Alex and Col and their bodyguards collect their weapons from the team by the helicopter. The mood is a lot more settled than it was at the start. Sophie is actually sincerely polite for once.

'Thank you for all you have done, Colonel Devereux, we need the security you provide before we can get Kivu going.'

'No, my pleasure, it's been great to come here and see some peace for once. This is exactly what we are working for and I will try to end this war as soon as possible.'

He shakes hands with Sophie and they exchange a calm, level look before he turns and walks back to the helicopter.

On the morning of the same day a female Congolese jour-nalist from Radio Okapi looks at Gerald Kaumba, sitting across his desk from her in his office; he's the mayor of the small town of Lubero in North Kivu.

'That's quite a strong statement, sir,' she says.

Unlike the politicians in the main towns he is being a lot

258

more unguarded in his comments. He's a big, heavy-set man wearing a loud orange print shirt and belligerently repeats his accusation into the microphone attached to her laptop that sits on the table between them.

'I don't care! I am a Congolese patriot and I will not accept this new president that has been shoved on us by Kinshasa! We've had enough of other powers ruling us in Congo.' He starts angrily counting them off on his fingers. 'First we have Belgians, then the Americans support Mobutu, then the Rwandans put Kabila Senior in power and then the mining companies keep his son there! I don't trust General Oloba to take over the government forces and I don't want this Rukuba!'

The journalist is happy for him to rant on; she knows it will make good copy for the news programme that they are putting together on reactions to the takeover.

She goads him a bit more. 'But will anyone notice that the Kinshasa government doesn't rule us any more? It's not like they were here much, only when they wanted something from the mines.'

'I don't care! If we start chopping up the country, where will it end? What else will the Chinese want to buy? Our mothers? And I don't trust Rukuba; he's a slimy bastard! He's always been mixed up with the Kudu Noir – how can a man like that rule the country?'

The journalist lets him continue and when the interview is over she goes out to her car, edits the report on her laptop and transmits it by satellite to her editor in the main Radio Okapi office in Goma. He gets the report and adds it to a package of coverage that goes out that lunchtime – some people welcoming the change and saying it will be good for investment, but others scared about what will happen next. Gerald Kaumba's rant features heavily in this section.

Late that afternoon the mayor gets into his Land Cruiser and his bodyguard drives him the short distance along the single main street in Lubero, up the hill to his compound overlooking the scruffy town.

In his office at one end of his bungalow, he talks on his mobile phone to friends and contacts and tries to rally some support to oppose the takeover. Everyone is being very cautious, sitting on the fence and saying they want to see more of what Rukuba does and negotiate rather than take any action.

Kaumba is in a foul mood by the time he sits down with his wife and family of five children in their large kitchen. He sits at the head of the table and shovels *fufu* into his mouth with his fingers, sullenly glaring into space. His wife and mother-in-law know better than to say anything and quietly manage the children and then clear away.

The mayor goes back into his study and continues making telephone calls late into the night as his family quietly go to bed and the three night watchmen take up their positions around the barbed wire fence ringing his house and large garden. They heft their AK-47s nervously and stare out into the darkness. The whole town is unsettled and they can hear shouting and arguments going on down the hill in the shacks and bars along the roadside.

A car engine revs loudly on the road that winds past the house out of town into the bush. It is coming down the hill fast, the driver weaving quickly around the loops in the road; his lights swing back and forth across the roof of the house.

The guards look away from the town and stare up at the dark hillside. Who is coming in from the bush at this time of night? They walk away from their posts over-looking the town and stand in a loose group on the lawn looking towards the truck.

A long burst of machine-gun fire erupts from a stand of bushes across the road from them. It scythes over the three of them, throwing their bodies onto the ground and smashing windows across the ground floor of the house.

The pickup truck rounds the last corner; on the back of it are six men with black cloth hoods over their heads and machine guns slung over their backs. They are clinging on to the sides of the truck with both hands as the driver veers off the road, bumps across the grass verge and smashes into the chain-link fence, flattening a metal post and careering to a halt on the lawn in front of the house.

The six men jump out and start howling and baying as they run to surround the house, their rifles held up in front of them. The mayor bursts out of his study door with a handgun and runs to the hallway to defend his wife and kids but two men burst through the front door as he does so and a man crashes into him. They fall onto the floor in a scrabbling, punching mess and then the mayor gets a kick in the head from the other attacker. He slumps on the floor stunned and is dragged outside. His wife and kids are all screaming from further inside the house.

The two Kudu Noir soldiers throw him face down on the lawn and the others set about him with machetes. He screams and curls up into a ball but the blades bite down on him repeatedly, severing a hand and then hacking away at his neck and head.

A Kudu runs forward and throws a phosphorous grenade into the front door. The burst of white-hot sparks sets fire to the hallway and others are thrown in through the windows. Flames begin licking up the side of the house and over the guttering.

The men then run back to the truck, which has turned round. They spend a moment working on something on the ground and then jump into the back again and roar off, bouncing over the verge and down the road into the town.

The outburst of gunfire has silenced the arguments in the town and people have retreated nervously back inside. The pickup truck careers down the single main street with the men standing up in the back and firing long bursts of machine-gun fire over the roofs of the single-storey buildings and howling their bloodcurdling screams. The truck screeches to a halt outside the mayor's office, the men jump out and one quickly bangs a stake into the ground and puts something on it before they get in again and drive off out of town.

No one dares move from their houses for the rest of that night.

In the morning some of the fear dispensed by the Kudu Noir is washed away by the sunlight and the first men creep along the road to see what is outside the mayor's office.

His head is on the stake with two twisted kudu horns driven into the top of it.

The End of Days

Chapter Thirty-Three

The United States Assistant Secretary of State for African Affairs, John R. Ciacola, is a pleasant and reasonable looking man, as one would expect of a career diplomat.

He has neatly trimmed grey hair and wears a beige tropical suit and a sensible tie and glasses, which he adjusts with one hand as he looks up at Alex.

Alex doesn't know him but he does know that he holds the third most senior rank in the State Department and that he has been sent straight from Washington rather than the ambassador in Kinshasa coming out to Kivu. Whatever he is going to say comes straight from the top.

It's 10th May, the day after the football event, and he's flown into Goma airport and then down to First Regiment's new base, Camp Heaven, in a UN helicopter. They are sitting in what passes for Alex's office, a screened-off area to one side of the main operations room which is buzzing with orders and the crackle and squawk of radios as the military campaign continues, raids being both planned and executed.

Alex is in his uniform with his colonel's insignia on his shoulder flashes. Ciacola seems to feel he is very much on Alex's turf and looks a little nervous. He had to leave his three-man close protection team outside the ops room as Alex didn't want them poking around. Ever since his previous involvements with America's intelligence services he has been very wary of them.

Alex isn't sure what the diplomat wants but decides to be positive. 'So, Mr Ciacola, thank you for coming to see me. How can I help?'

Ciacola clears his throat and speaks in a clipped East coast accent, 'Well, thank you, Colonel Devereux, it is very good of you to see me. As you can imagine the United States has been following developments here in Kivu very closely over the last few days. I have been instructed by Secretary of State Patricia Johnson to pass on her very great concern about the events.'

'Concern in what way?'

'Well, as you know, Secretary of State Johnson takes a close interest in the issue of sexual violence against women in Kivu and was instrumental in the passing of the three UN resolutions against it.'

Alex nods.

'But aside from that, as you can imagine, we are very concerned for the safety of the two hundred forty-three United States citizens in the province. We do not have any forces within easy reach of this area and, now that the role of UN has been reduced, we are looking to you for security. What guarantees can you give that they will be protected?'

'I can assure you that the KDF will do everything in its power to protect the lives of US citizens and those of all nationalities in this new state. As you can hear,' Alex gestures towards the ops room, 'combat operations are continuing and will do for some time . . .'

'How long?'

'Mr Ciacola, I am not going to give a timeline for operational security reasons but it is obviously in our interests to win this war as quickly as we can and with minimum casualties.'

'My apologies, Colonel Devereux, I'm sounding hostile. The American government fully supports your efforts to root out and destroy the FDLR, it is on our terrorist list. But we are also monitoring the situation because we expect the highest ethical standards of behaviour and concrete progress towards democracy.'

He looks at Alex quizzically.

'Well, I hear what you say, Mr Ciacola, but that is something that you will have to discuss with President Rukuba when you see him later on today. I support a move to democracy but my role here is primarily military; I am a paid servant of political masters.'

Ciacola isn't going to be put off that easily. 'It is something I will raise with the President but I think we both know that you have a very significant leverage on events at the moment.'

Alex looks back at him without agreement and thinks, this is my operation and the last thing I want is to have you come into my office and tell me what to do.

Ciacola can see the hostility in his eyes. 'Colonel Devereux, I think there is a wider point that you are missing here. You seem to be winning the war but the question now is, who will win the peace?'

'What do you mean?'

'What I mean is that that there is a much bigger game being played out here than just the conflict with the FDLR. Colonel Devereux, I need to be candid with you about this.' He pauses.

Alex narrows his eyes; this sounds worrying.

'Are you a student of history, Colonel Devereux?'

Alex doesn't want to walk into any traps so he just nods noncommittally.

'OK, well, it is a given that great powers rise and fall. The Greeks, the Romans, the Soviet empire – dare I say it

– the British empire . . . they all come and go. Nothing stays the same forever.

'Now, in the international relations community it is increasingly being argued that America has had its day, that empires take a lot longer to fall than to rise, and that we are on a downward trajectory.'

'This is all very interesting . . .'

'OK, well, the point is this. Some people perceive that the American empire, if you will, has arisen very quickly in the twentieth century and is now in its long slow downward phase as China rises . . .'

'Well, they do own most of your debt.'

'Correct, you are absolutely right, the United States in many ways is an unsustainable model of consumerism that is built on debt and the President has made it very clear that he is working on ways to address this . . .'

'Not getting very far, is he?'

'No, but,' Ciacola holds up his hands, 'that is another issue. The point for your activities here is that there is a clash of social models in the world at the moment between the Western democratic, free society and the much more directed, managed capitalist society of China. The clash of civilisations that actually matters right now is not between the West and radical Islam, it is between us and the Chinese.'

Alex stops interrupting as he begins to see where this is going. It is sounding dangerous.

'China is the emergent world power, we all know that and there is nothing that we can do about it. The US will no longer be the sole superpower in the world; we are going to have to get used to working in a multi-polar world. And we are ready for that. But the big question is, can a great power like China rise without there being a war?

'China has up to now kept quite a low profile

268

internationally, following its policy of harmonious living. It is, however, just too big to maintain this passive posture and it's looking for a way to assert its huge economic power. But because of their own experience of being colonised by the West they are uncomfortable with outright colonisation of other states.'

'Apart from Tibet.'

'Correct, but by and large they don't want to start a shooting war with anyone because China is the world's largest exporter and it would destroy its economic growth. So we believe that their government is using this project in Kivu as a test-bed to see if they can launch a new way of asserting themselves on the world stage.'

He looks knowingly at Alex. 'Nothing happens in China without the government's approval, particularly not a project of this scale and audacity.

'So this whole long preamble is really just a way of saying that we in the States see this as a conflict between rival systems of government. A lot of developing countries are already modelling themselves on China and many countries around the world will be watching closely to see what happens.'

'Well, that will depend on what President Rukuba decides to do after his period of consultation with the people of Kivu.'

'Well, precisely. That's what we're worried about.'

'Meaning?'

'President Rukuba has given some vague assurances about consultations but we don't see any comments about electoral timings.'

'This is the Congo – things don't happen on a four-year electoral cycle here.'

Ciacola sighs. 'Colonel Devereux, we are both men of the

world, we both know that there is a long and depressing history of African strongmen coming to power promising elections and fairness to all and then beating the hell out of every opponent they can find and proclaiming themselves President for Life.'

Alex knows full well that he is right and keeps quiet.

Ciacola continues, 'The Chinese have already had a very malevolent effect around the world in supporting oppressive regimes with appalling human rights records like Sudan, Zimbabwe and Iran. We don't want this experiment in Kivu to bolster those who are calling for less democracy and good governance.

'At the moment we are prepared to be cautiously supportive of the new regime but if it were to become a dictatorship then we would not stand idly by. The United States does not have many military assets in the area and we are not contemplating that line of action but we could make life very uncomfortable for a new power by blocking any recognition in the UN and, most importantly for you, Colonel Devereux, by suspending the citizenship of any United States citizens involved in your armed force. I believe you have quite a few?'

Alex's eyes drop as he calculates what damage that could do. About twenty per cent of his men are American and many of them are in key roles. It would be a very significant blow to his efforts that he could do without right now.

Ciacola sees this and knows he has scored a direct hit. Alex looks at him questioningly. 'So what do you want me to do?'

'We want you to continue to resolve the security situation but we also want you to ensure that democratic elections do actually take place and that a Western, democratic model of government is established here. We do not want Kivu becoming a high-profile poster boy for the new Chinese way

270

of running the world with some sort of managed capitalist dictatorship.'

Alex looks back at him steadily, thinking hard. He doesn't want to seem to give in to Ciacola's threats but he can't afford to be arrogant about them either.

'Well, as I said, the reality is that those decisions are not within my remit. I am a paid employee of the coalition of interests and I do what I am told.'

He knows it sounds weak even as the words leave his mouth.

'Oh, come on, Colonel Devereux. We both know that you are the military power behind this project and that if you don't support what is happening then it won't happen.'

Alex doesn't answer for a moment and just looks at him. Finally, he says, 'Mr Ciacola, I respect the wishes of your government. I am a supporter of the democratic model of government and I will do what I can to see that it is implemented, but in the final analysis this may well be beyond my powers. I should also point out that there is a timing issue on all this.'

'Which is?'

'Which is that most of my force are on a standard six-month tour contract. Most of them began training for the op in March, so that means that by the end of August the bulk of the regiment will have rotated home and the leasing agreement on the helicopters will also expire.

'Now, renewal of both those factors is under review by President Rukuba and our Chinese partners in the Kivu Investment Corporation, depending on how events on the ground go but I can't say what they will decide. The Chinese want us stood down as soon as possible because we are expensive. It's the 10th May now so if they do decide to keep us then I need to get on with the renewal process fast.'

Ciacola rubs his chin and looks at Alex. 'Hmmm. Well, I think we have both stated our cases, Colonel Devereux. We will see how events unfold but you need to be mindful of American concerns or we will not hesitate to take robust action.'

The meeting ends and the two men shake hands warily. Alex reunites the diplomat with his anxious bodyguards and they leave.

Yamba comes up to Alex as he watches the UN helicopter lift away. 'How was that?'

Alex rubs his eyes wearily and looks back at the ops tent where another long day's work beckons; he's been hard at it for months now.

He shakes his head. 'I tell you; I could really do without this clash of superpowers crap right now.'

Chapter Thirty-Four

Gabriel heaves himself off the back of the old blue Peugeot Mobylette as Marcel cuts the engine. His groin and legs are painfully stiff from hanging on for hours as they bumped up the tracks to Rukuba's farm at Mukungu.

Gabriel grimaces as he bends his legs and straightens out the second-hand suit that he bought in Bukavu. His legs are splashed with mud and he tries brushing it off with a handful of lush grass from the verge.

Marcel also has on an old suit. He takes his teacher's briefcase from the basket on the handlebars and gives it to Gabriel. It's empty but Gabriel insists on looking the part.

'Do I look OK?' he asks.

'Hang on.' Marcel straightens his clip-on tie and stands back. 'OK.'

The two of them walk up the dirt road towards Rukuba's farmstead. It's heavily rutted with vehicle tracks and they walk past a small shantytown of tents and shacks put up by KPP supporters and other people who have flocked to their guru's rural retreat. It's 10th May, only a week after the invasion started, and Chinese work gangs are erecting temporary houses and installing a sewage system. People peer at them as they walk by.

Gabriel talks quietly to Marcel with his head lowered as

they walk past. 'I listened to the President's broadcast last week and he said that he would continue to live the life of a simple farmer, close to the soil of Kivu and its people and away from the corruption of the old political classes in Bukavu and Goma. The man is truly a saint.'

The lush grass of the meadow in front of the farmstead is now muddy and beaten down by vehicle tracks and feet. They step across it towards the small stream at the foot of the hill, which is now encircled by a barbed wire fence.

The old man with the machete has been replaced by three Unit 17 soldiers with flak jackets and rifles standing at a gate through the fence. They peer suspiciously at Gabriel through their wraparound shades. 'Where is your pass?'

'Er, good afternoon. My name is Mr Gabriel Mwamba, I am a businessman from Bukavu and this is my business partner Marcel.' He proffers a business card; he printed it off on ordinary paper in an internet café in Bukavu and cut it out with scissors.

The guard looks at it suspiciously. 'What do you want?'

'We would like to see President Rukuba in order to discuss new business opportunities with him.'

'Do you have an appointment?'

'No.'

The man grunts and goes back into a new wooden guard-room to make a call up the hill.

'You can go up but you will have to wait to see the President.'

They frisk both the men carefully and peer inside the empty briefcase before handing it back.

Marcel shoots a nervous look at Gabriel as they walk on up the hill.

'Don't worry, it'll be fine,' Gabriel reassures him. 'Remember adversity is spelt opportunity.'

The track twists round and they come up into the farm-yard. The cows have been moved out and the barns converted into offices now, half of them full of Chinese engineers and logistics staff and half with KPP officials. A large array of satellite dishes and telecoms equipment is set up in the orchard and a big generator is beating somewhere behind the cowsheds. There are no children around.

Zacheus emerges from the farm building as they approach. 'Mr Mwamba, you do not have an appointment with His Excellency? He is very busy.'

'No, I'm afraid I don't, but I have many business proposi-tions to put to him.'

'Hmm, OK . . . Well, wait here.'

They sit on the veranda outside the house and watch the busy scene in the old farmyard. People come and go and a helicopter clatters in and lands in the meadow. A delegation of Chinese businessmen is driven up the track in a new Land Cruiser and enter the farmhouse.

The two men sit and wait all afternoon. Eventually Zacheus comes out and says, 'The President has five minutes, he can see you now.'

They walk through the front room and see that it is a busy office with computers and printers manned by KPP staff.

They go through to the back of the house and out onto a lawn overlooking the view back down the valley. The President is stretched out in his hammock strung between two trees. Zacheus introduces them and they sit on white plastic chairs.

Rukuba is tired and distant. 'What do you want?' he asks quietly.

Gabriel begins hesitantly, 'Mr President, I am over-whelmed to be here, I want to thank you so much for paying for my fiancée Eve's operation. I have come to offer my services to your new government in whatever capacity I can help.'

Rukuba frowns and then sits up. He strokes his fine face with his long fingers and looks thoughtful. 'Well, Mr Mwamba, there is a lot of work to be done.'

Major Mordechai Eisenberg walks slowly across the operations room towards Alex holding a sheaf of computer printouts in his hand.

'Colonel, can I show you something?' With his craggy face and aquiline nose he looks perpetually gloomy, so initially Alex doesn't realise there is anything amiss.

It's lunchtime on 11th May, two days after Alex talked with Sophie at the football event and they are gearing up for the briefing for the night's helicopter raids. Alex is standing next to the birdtable; it is the focal point of the large operations tent, a big table covered with a map of the province under a clear plastic cover with different coloured marker pens showing areas controlled by the FDLR and other militias. Alex is staring at the targets for tonight and mulling over his decisions, making sure he has got them right.

All around him the large tent is crammed with thirty staff officers hunched over desks and laptops or talking quietly as they process intelligence from the drone control station at one side of the tent, check details for the raids and keep the Battlegroup running. The atmosphere is tense and stuffy; several radios crackle and squawk intermittently and a generator drones outside.

Alex turns from the table, still thinking about the raids and looks at the Israeli, 'Hi.'

'Something has come up on the nodal analysis computer.' Mordechai looks uncomfortable.

'OK?'

'We are processing the data that we requisitioned from the mobile phone companies and there is a lot of traffic from two phone numbers into the bush around Lubero on the afternoon before the mayor was killed there.'

'Do we know who the numbers belong to?'

'Well, that's the thing; the computer tracks all numbers on our database to see when they intersect with another target number. The phones that were calling Lubero were actually on our friendlies list.'

Alex looks at him warily, sensing a problem. 'Whose numbers?'

'They were listed as staff in the office of President Rukuba.'

Alex's eyes flick away from Mordechai as he thinks hard about what to do. An explanation occurs to him. 'Well, I'm not surprised they were calling contacts in the area after what he said on the radio, but that doesn't mean they were trying to kill him. I mean, we still don't know what the Kudu Noir are or whose side they are on. No, I think we'll leave that one; we've got enough on our plate with the FDLR. Let's just crack on with that.'

He's made his decision. He pushes the matter out of his mind and turns back to the birdtable.

Chapter Thirty-Five

'Well, welcome to Heaven,' Alex says, spreading his hands and smiling in a weak attempt at humour.

The setting is idyllic. Lake Kivu sparkles in the sun, dramatic green hills rise up from the lakeshore in front of him. But Sophie and Natalie both look back at him awkwardly; they don't particularly want to be here and are playing it very straight. They wish he'd just get on with the tour, allow them to make their assessment and leave.

Rukuba has persuaded the management board of Hope Street to accept a large funding injection in return for their cooperation with the process of reintegrating former militia soldiers into society. Sophie's job is to assess the new base for a permanent Hope Street presence and detail what facilities they want built. If this site works out then a network of reintegration centres will be established across the province. They are moving fast and it's now 12th May, three days after Alex inspected the training centre near Goma.

Alex gets the point and drops the bonhomie. 'OK, right, well. Can I introduce my second-in-command, Major Douala?' Sophie eyes the tall Angolan and shakes his hand warily, as does her colleague.

Yamba is more formal than Alex. 'Pleased to meet you,' he says to both of them.

Alex continues, 'And you've met Regimental Sergeant Major Thwaites.'

Col nods at Sophie awkwardly and mutters a gruff, 'Ma'am.' She smiles but without any warmth.

Although she doesn't like being associated with a mercenary operation, Sophie is a pragmatist and can see that the KDF looks like being the future of Kivu so she might as well cooperate with it.

As usual her mind is hunting for inconsistencies in what she sees, and as she looks along the coils of razor-wire fence either side of the gate to the base, she asks, 'Why did you decide to build the base on a peninsula?'

Alex is glad to get on to talking practicalities. 'Well, the site is strategically perfect – the peninsula is uninhabited and three miles long so we can put all our men in one base and we just have this one fence to guard.'

'Why's that such a good thing? I thought your men ought to be out there in Kivu like the UN are in lots of bases where they are close to the people?'

'Yes, that is one way of doing it but the problem of dissipating your forces across the region is that you end up using most of your blokes on force protection, i.e. guarding fences like this, so you can't use them for deliberate operations. The whole idea behind First Regiment is that we are an air-mobile strike force, we can cover the whole province from this base because it's in the middle of Kivu and we can get out and attack the enemy when and where we want to, so we dictate the time and pace of the battle not the enemy.'

'Hmm.' Sophie doesn't seem satisfied.

What Alex doesn't mention, because he is keen to play down the Rwandan connection to the operation, is that the peninsula also sticks out into Lake Kivu so that he can be supplied from Rwanda directly across the lake by boat. This is ideal because he doesn't want to have long overland lines of communication that could be attacked by militias.

'Well, why don't you put your men in Goma or Bukavu? They're the political centres.'

'Well, the theory behind our operation seems to be working so far – it's called partnership intervention.'

Sophie frowns.

'The idea is that we are the stick to back up the central authorities by giving it the threat of credible force, we're not here to replace the government. Also I don't want my blokes mixed up with civvies, it always causes problems.'

Sophie relents and nods.

Alex continues. 'Obviously as we move from military operations through the demilitarisation stage to policing work then we will have to get more involved but really we want to be handing over as much of that work as possible to civilian organisations like yours.'

Sophie appears less than comfortable acknowledging the continuity between their two areas of work.

'OK, let's have a look around anyway.'

Col leads the way through the razor-wire gate, nodding to the sentries in the sandbagged machine-gun posts on either side of it. The base is buzzing with activity; it's still in the construction phase. They stand to one side as three large civilian container lorries lumber past on the muddy main road.

'Where are those from? I've seen that logo before.' Sophie points to the Arabic insignia on their sides.

'They're from Fadoul Holdings. We've just signed a contract with Mr Fadoul to be our main supplier for food, he's Mr Supermarket in Kivu.' Again Alex doesn't mention the reduced Rwandan involvement that this allows.

Natalie chips in, 'Oh right, they have great falafel in their store in Goma,' and Alex smiles politely, glad that she is along and he won't just be getting the third degree from Sophie the whole time.

They carry on through the base and Alex shows them the lines of large green tents for the different companies of troops. As they walk through Echo Company's lines, Jean-Baptiste salutes, and his eyes then flash over the women with more than professional interest as he walks past. In the tents the men are either crashed out asleep on their camp beds or sitting around with their shirts off, stripping and cleaning weapons, waiting for their raid that night. Sophie eyes the shaven-headed, tattooed, muscular men warily.

Activity continues all around them with the noise of building work, quartermasters in-loading stores and the whirr of helicopters. This noise becomes gradually louder as they approach the flight line and Alex has to raise his voice. 'What we're doing here is building concrete landing pads so that the whole thing doesn't turn into a mud bath when the rains come.'

He points out three gangs of Chinese workers who are working frantically with bulldozers and cement mixer lorries to clear and concrete large circular helicopter pads. 'They're also digging a big fuel depot area over there behind those big earth berms. Fang will tell you more about it.'

He waves as the familiar gangly figure walks across from one of the groups of workers with an overseer.

'Good to see you, Mr Wu.' They shake hands and Alex introduces Sophie and Natalie, before continuing, 'We were just admiring your work.'

Fang smiles with delight. 'Yes, we work fast. We trucked the heavy equipment straight in from Kenya through Rwanda.'

Alex nods. The builders have an almost desperate air as they shout to a crane driver to position a tub of concrete correctly over a pad. He turns to the group. 'These guys work twelve-hour shifts seven days a week, I'm not kidding you. They are unbelievable, and they just love it, can't seem to get enough.'

They look at the workers; all are small, furiously active men in their early twenties, wearing jeans and cheap nylon tracksuits stained with red dust. They each have a canteen of water on each hip so that they need to take fewer breaks to refill.

Fang nods to the man next to him. 'This is the site foreman.' The man bows and Alex sees that the short hair on his head is slicked with sweat into little spikes that show white scalp between the strands.

Fang is full of pride and cannot resist a dig. 'This is Chinese industry, you will see, we will rebuild Africa. The West's time is over.'

Alex drops his expression of polite interest, his eyes zero in on Fang, and Sophie glares at him as well.

Chapter Thirty-Six

Joseph sits on the ground in the new detention facility in Camp Heaven and plucks idly at the chain manacling his feet together. It's the same day that Sophie is being shown round the base.

'What are they doing?' he mutters to Simon, the other young FDLR soldier captured with him.

'I don't know,' Simon shrugs. They were taken out of their newly built wooden cells and have been sitting on the ground in a wired-off section of the detention facility for half an hour now. The older *génocidaires* were kept in Camp Purgatory where the Rwandans are investigating their involvement in the 1994 massacres.

The Rwandans are not interested in the boys and young men, most of whom were not even born in 1994, and put them on ferries over the lake to the new camp. Many of them have committed rapes and murders in Kivu but the Rwandans aren't bothered about that; they committed enough of their own crimes in Kivu and don't want to even start raising that issue.

Since then, the numbers of prisoners in the cells have been increasing as more are flown in from the KDF raids every day. The older ones are sent straight on to Rwanda so the group of over three hundred currently sitting in rows on the floor are all young men.

'Hey, someone's coming.' Simon nudges him and Joseph stops playing with his manacles.

An armed guard from the KDF walks alongside the wire with a young-looking Congolese man in a new suit carrying a briefcase. Joseph and Simon scan his face for clues as to what might be about to happen to them. He is a squat, ugly-looking man but he has a friendly expression and Joseph feels less worried.

The man is let into the locked enclosure. He stands in front of them and begins talking in Swahili. 'Good morning, gentlemen, my name is Mr Gabriel Mwamba. I am a representative from the youth wing of the Kivu People's Party. I am here to talk to you today about the opportunities for training that this party can bring you as we all struggle to build a new Kivu.'

The tired faces look at Gabriel in confusion but he's enjoying his new role and wants to motivate the young men with the passion he feels about the new opportunity that Kivu has.

'All of you here have been in the FDLR. As you know, the new army of the republic of Kivu, the Kivu Defence Force, is fighting a successful war against the militias. You know this, or you would not be here otherwise.' Gabriel's tone is generally positive but he pauses to make sure the boys get the message about who is boss.

'Now, you are sitting on your backsides in this cage all day thinking what will happen to me? Will I be prosecuted for war crimes? Will they get the International Criminal Court on me? You all know the cases from the Congo like Jean-Pierre Bemba of the MLC and Thomas Lubanga of the UPC militias.

'Even if we do not decide to hand you over to these people then we could set up our own courts here in Kivu and try you. The great President Rukuba has said that he wants justice to reign in his new land!'

Gabriel holds up a finger and glares at them. 'You have all committed crimes and done terrible things!'

Joseph looks down. He knows he has – the dreams continue every night of the woman's screaming face and him covered in mud that he cannot remove.

Gabriel relents a little. 'Well, I can tell you that President Rukuba wants to see justice done but he also wants peace. So he will be more likely to overlook your cases if you are prepared to renounce your evil ways and show willing to help in establishing our great new country of Kivu.

'The President has signed an executive order and I am here to offer you the chance to join the new youth wing of the builder of this new country, the Kivu People's Party. If you join then I can get special preference for you in training and early release from this prison. Now who thinks that that sounds like a good idea?'

Alex managed to steer Sophie and the others round the rest of the base without further controversy. Col has been tactfully silent, and now they are sitting on folding chairs on a bright green grassy slope going down to a small cove. The lake is looking as pristine as ever, it's a balmy sunny morning, they are drinking tea from green army mugs and all appears well with the world.

However, Sophie does not share the relaxed mood.

With a first in politics from Oxford, an MSc from SOAS and a career in development, she is not going to let Fang get away with his throwaway comment.

She looks at him sitting across the semicircle of chairs from her. 'Mr Wu, what exactly did you mean by saying that the West has had its day and that only China can rebuild Africa?'

Alex groans internally but at the same time he wants to hear what is said. This is a big issue that is weighing on his mind at the moment.

Fang is pumped up on the success of his vision so far and barely pauses for breath. 'In China we do not see Africa as the West does, as an object of charity to feel sorry for. Africans are not victims. When I look at Africa I don't see starvation and wars, I see opportunity, I see money. We give investment not charity.

'Does anyone in the West have that vision? No. What can the West offer? Pop stars.' He laughs contemptuously. 'You organise a concert or send Bono along or maybe Madonna will adopt some more babies. It is a joke. I am offering managed capitalism and prosperity, not democracy.'

Sophie is glowering at him but he continues blithely. 'Western ideas about democracy just don't work in developing states. Democracy is about a lot more than voting. It works in rich societies but it doesn't work in poor countries.'

Sophie shoots back. 'But there are plenty of democracies in Africa now.'

'Yes, but most of them are sham democracies – the ruling parties just manipulate the results and the country divides along ethnic lines. Look at what happened in the Kenyan election in 2007, it nearly pulled the country apart.'

Fang leans forward in his chair towards her.

'Democracy is about a lot more than just voting. The West needs to understand this and then get the sequence of developing a nation right. Before democracy you need prosperity and before prosperity you need security. What is the point of actually working and producing wealth if a man with a gun just comes along and steals it? I mean, your organisation will be retraining the prisoners to give them jobs so they don't need to join the militias. But you can only do that because of the security that we are providing.' He gestures with satisfaction to Alex and the military base around them. 'We are establishing the mandate of heaven. That must be the first step in building a new state, not democracy.'

Sophie is not going to accept this lying down. 'Well, I think you are being very sweeping about the West's engagement with Africa. We do actually do a lot of good.'

Fang shrugs in a disinterested way. 'No one in the West actually bothers to think about the long-term causes of African poverty. Most of the poverty here is man-made because of poor African leadership. You have been giving aid money to Africa for fifty years and it is poorer in many areas than it was at independence fifty years ago. Why? Because it is so badly run.'

'Well, there is the legacy of dysfunctional colonial borders!'

'Yes, but that is only half of the equation, and it is the half you cannot change. What do you want, an African world war to redraw all the borders? The West must stop feeling guilty about the colonial legacy, it must stop using past failings to excuse present wrongs!'

Fang glares at Sophie, who cannot think of an answer and looks across for support at Yamba, who is sitting next to Fang. She assumes that as an African he will be on her side. He has been listening carefully to the discussion but keeps his expression neutral.

Unfortunately, she has picked the wrong person to be soft on poor performance.

Yamba clears his throat and nods gravely. 'Have you ever tried setting up a health clinic in rural Angola? The corruption and bureaucracy is unbelievable. Fang is right; Africa is undergoverned and over-bureaucratised. We should not be making excuses for that fifty years after independence. Southeast Asia was in a very similar state of development fifty years ago but they are much more advanced now than Africa. We have to stop blaming colonialism and start taking responsibility ourselves as Africans.'

Fang nods enthusiastically as Yamba says this and launches into another tirade.

'What Africa needs to get out of poverty is a sustainable capitalist revolution. Where will that come from? BandAid? No, Africa needs Chinese capital and skills to come in and build infrastructure before it can develop. A democratic political system is too divisive to do this but managed capitalism means that the resources of the state can be organised and directed to achieve this, just like you British developed India under a dictatorship. It is the only way forward.'

He bangs his fist repeatedly on his palm. 'No discussion! No talk! People want action! Action that will bring them peace and jobs!'

Alex is looking backwards and forwards between the two of them as the discussion goes on, thinking about Ciacola's demands for democracy and what it would do to the KDF if they are not met.

Fang seems to be getting the upper hand at the moment and concludes contemptuously. 'Most of the West's charitable efforts in Africa are more about making themselves feel better than really trying to do anything to solve the long-term structural problems.'

Sophie has been glowering at him as he speaks. She knows a lot of what he has said is true but is thinking hard how to counter it.

In the end she just comes out with a sour-sounding, 'Well, I think what you are talking about sounds like a licence for dictatorship and tyranny. I mean, who is going to make sure that the managers of this managed capitalist paradise behave themselves? Who guards the guardians?'

Fang just shrugs, ignores her comment and sips his tea.

Alex looks out across the water at the beautiful green hills of Kivu rising up steeply from the lakeshore.

Sophie glances across at him for support and sees he is thinking hard.

Chapter Thirty-Seven

Alex looks at Rukuba across the table from him.

'Right, so, we could put the Rwandans here then?'

'No, that's next to the FJPC, they hate each other.'

'OK, well . . .' He scans the map of the area around Rukuba's farm at Mukungu, looking at the camps that the Chinese have built for the delegates coming to the peace conference in early June. It's 28th May and over the last two weeks the different militia groups and national delegations have been accepting invitations to the talks. They are now moving little cards around the sites, trying to fit in all the various groups.

Fang butts in. 'We're building a big site here. They will have to go there – that way they will be isolated, they've got one of the biggest delegations.' He points out a hilltop half a mile away from Rukuba's farm. 'It's a big compound on a hill, they'll feel safe there.'

'Hmm,' Alex grunts agreement; he's very twitchy about security for the conference. Rukuba refused to have it in Goma or Bukavu and insisted it be held in his new village capital, which has advantages and disadvantages. On the upside it is away from the main towns and therefore any popular protests and the risk of troops getting involved in riot situations, but it does mean a huge amount of infrastructure has to be built.

Fang has his work gangs hard at it with road graders, cement lorries, diggers and bulldozers, digging drains, putting in water tanks, erecting tents and prefab buildings all over the area. A new network of roads winds through the previously pristine green upland meadows linking the sites together.

The war against the FDLR is still going on and some murderous attacks have been carried out on civilians. However, nearly thirty different militias have seen the pounding the FDLR has taken and agreed to come to the table, along with other interested parties like the UN, USA, EU, Rwanda, DRC, Uganda and Burundi. There are also a lot of local Kivu politicians: mayors, police chiefs, FARDC commanders, bishops and *comptoirs* who all want to have their say on what sort of new government structure will emerge from the talks. Sophie and other NGO groups will also be in attendance, helping to sort out the demilitarisation process. A media centre has been built to accommodate the many journalists covering the event.

Rukuba is hosting the talks and is very particular about who he wants where. 'Write them in for Site 18,' he says to Gabriel, who writes a card and puts it over the site. Gabriel has been working flat out with the KPP organisers to get all the logistics in place. He loves the work and is getting on well with Rukuba, whom he hero-worships.

Eventually they decide where to put everyone, allocating some of the most unpopular groups to stay in hotels outside Goma. They will be flown up every day by helicopters.

Alex looks at Rukuba and nods. 'Right, I think that is all in place then?' He has hardly seen the President since the start of the military campaign because they have both been frantically busy in separate locations. Alex is watching him closely now, trying to discern how power has affected him, but he retains his intrinsic trust in the man.

Rukuba looks carefully at the plan, nods and smiles. 'Yes, we are ready for them. The Republic of Kivu will be proud of me!'

On 1st June Alex watches delegates arrive at the farmstead on the first day of the peace conference. They go through a sandbagged security checkpoint at the bottom of the hill. He's hired a commercial event management firm from South Africa to do this bit, and smartly dressed black female staff greet guests with a smile and guide them through metal detectors before they are photographed and issued with security passes. They walk on through the gatehouse and up the tarmac road to the farm.

He's got two companies of soldiers on standby around the different sites in the area but they are kept out of sight as much as possible. As far as the press and the delegates are concerned, this is an event run by the new Republic of Kivu and the flag of the country flies proudly from a large flagstaff over his head on the lawn outside Rukuba's house. The Heron drone circles overhead scanning for any hostile forces approaching them and he has his two gunships on five-minute standby to scramble up here from Heaven if he needs them.

White Land Cruisers arrive from the outlying accommodation stations and park on the tarmac area that used to be the meadow. Alex nods to John Ciacola as he enters with his large US delegation and they shake hands cordially.

'Good to see you, Colonel.'

'And you.'

'This looks like a good setup you have here.'

A smile. 'We do our best.'

'The Secretary of State has asked me to give you her best

wishes; she is very pleased that peace seems to be coming to the region at last.'

'Well, that's very kind of her, I appreciate that. I'll see you in there later on.'

'You'll be at the table?'

'Yes, I'll be advising on the technicalities of the demilitarisation process, but . . .' he looks pointedly at Ciacola '. . . I do the military stuff and I don't have much sway over what sort of political framework will emerge after that.'

'Hmm.' Ciacola looks disappointed.

'You'll have to slog that out with Rukuba and the Chinese.'

The Americans go through into the secure conference area and Alex stands back and watches the different militia delegations come through the entrance. They are a mixed bag. Some are wealthy and sophisticated from the proceeds of the mines that they run, used to travelling to Europe and expensively dressed. They swagger through the security eyeing up the hostesses and revelling in getting to play the big power game. Others are the real bush *mai-mai* groups. They wear old, badly-fitting suits and tatty uniforms. Out of their home element and with no weapons, they are scared and glare around them with furious suspicion.

Alex eyes them with concern. How the hell are we going to get these guys to reach an agreement?

The conference drags on for a week. Groups come and go up the hill to the large tented village erected outside Rukuba's farmhouse. On the first day a brawl breaks out in the queue for lunch between members of two militia groups with a long-standing hatred of each other. Six men end up grappling and punching each other on the floor. KPP stewards and Unit 17 soldiers in suits rush in and separate the men, dragging them out of different sides of the tent complex to calm down. Order is restored, tables and chairs put upright again and the conference resumes.

Over the week a more settled atmosphere replaces the edginess of the first days. The delegates get used to each other and the idea of actually cooperating peacefully.

Rukuba plays his role masterfully, acting with great dignity and stature as if he had ruled Kivu for decades. Much of this is because he has the big stick of the KDF to wave at any groups that get above themselves and refuse to cooperate or hand over their weapons or control of their mines. There is a lot of grumbling and complaint but the Chinese and other big donors step in and smooth the process with inducements of cash for development projects in the areas controlled by groups.

Fang is hard at work with Sophie, other NGOs and his Chinese engineers and project managers working out how many of the forty thousand soldiers in the province are in need of work and how he can fit them into the infrastructure and agricultural projects that he is planning.

Gradually, through much arm-twisting and cajoling, a framework deal is thrashed out and one by one the different groups sign up to it. Rukuba closes the conference with aplomb at the end of the long final day; he stands on the stage at the front of the main tent packed with rows of weary delegates and members of the press.

'Ladies and gentlemen, thank you all for working so hard this week. We have all come on a great journey together for the good of this beautiful land.' He pauses and looks out through the open sides of the tent at the shadows slipping like a silk shawl across the shoulder of the nearby hill. 'It has been an extraordinary time for us all but I am sure that now through your efforts we will have peace in this land. From now on I will pursue a policy of Kivu nationalism to overcome the tribal and political differences that have kept us fighting each other for so long. From now on there will not be Hunde and Nande, there will not be Shi and Nyanga, *originaires* and Banyamulenge, there will only be Kivuans! And then I will have peace in Kivu . . . my Kivu!'

Chapter Thirty-Eight

Alex looks at Rukuba reclining in his hammock in front of the view down the valley. 'So you're pleased with the way it went, then?'

It's the 8th June, the day after the peace conference closed, and teams of Chinese workers are dismantling the tents behind the house. Alex can see trucks inching down the hill laden with gear and driving off across the empty car parks.

Rukuba looks absolutely exhausted and rubs his eyes. He's wearing a blue shellsuit and is distracted by his weariness.

'Hmm, it was good. We got what we wanted, heh?' He peers at Alex sitting next to him on a white plastic chair. Zacheus and Gabriel hover in the background on the veranda of the house but otherwise they are alone.

Alex nods and rubs his face; Rukuba's exhaustion is bringing out his own. 'Yes, I can't believe we have finally got here. God, I'm shattered, I think I need to take a day off, I can't even see straight sometimes.' He squints at the view.

Rukuba follows his gaze and then laughs. 'Yes, that's the problem with Kivu when you're tired, everything gets blurred after a while and one hill does begin to look like another. How did you think it went?'

'Good overall, considering. I mean, obviously the liberal press hate us intrinsically for being Chinese-backed mercenaries but as long as the deal brings peace then they seem to be prepared to hold off from damning us completely. Although did you see this?'

He pulls a printout of the front page of that morning's *New York Times* website and shows it to Rukuba who scans it, muttering as he goes. '"Kivu experiment brings peace but bodes ill for the future . . . Rukuba unknown entity . . . use of white mercenary thugs not to be encouraged."' He glances across at Alex who shrugs. '"Rumours of war crimes"?' He glances up with more concern.

'I think they must mean the battle of Lubonga valley but that was collateral damage. I don't know how they picked up on it if that *is* what they mean.'

Rukuba looks into the distance, thinking. 'You're right, as soon as the area was safe enough to go back to, I had KPP workers dump the remains into the river after they were burnt – on health grounds it was the only thing we could do. The press couldn't have got there ahead of them.'

Alex nods. The memory of the burning field of the dead still haunts him but he has got used to pushing it aside. He has rehearsed the collateral damage defence of his actions so many times in his head that he now doesn't acknowledge of any other view.

He moves on, nodding towards the article. 'I thought Ciacola went a bit heavy.'

Rukuba scans down a bit. '"The United States and United Nations expect a democratic outcome from the national consultation exercise and will be minded to act if it doesn't happen."'

Alex asks hesitantly, 'How's the plan for the consultation going?'

'Hmm?'

'The national consultation exercise on democratic

government or . . .' he pauses and tries to think of a neutral phrase '. . . other sorts.'

'Oh, well, I think we need to recover from the conference first and get the militias disarmed before I start on that. I am taking soundings at the moment through KPP and Unit 17 but I need to get the people of Kivu to take some pride in themselves first. I want to build up Kivuan nationalism, to get my people off their knees and thinking about us as a success story.'

He puts down the papers and suddenly swings round on the hammock so that he is facing Alex. 'There is so much we have to do. I have to name my cabinet, sort out the infrastructure projects and I have many great plans for my country, Alex. I will launch a competition to write our new national anthem and I will perform it on stage, Fang is building me a new stadium here. We will have a national football league and the final will be in a great new stadium in Goma.'

Alex just listens, slightly overwhelmed by Rukuba's burst of enthusiasm. He lets him rant on for a while and then asks cautiously, 'And what about the KDF contracts, have you thought any more about that? Fang was telling me he wants us kept on longer than August. I think we need to stay in order to stabilise the country, otherwise you'll be dependent on the old government troops and they aren't up to much. It's 8th June now and I'll need to start talking to the guys or recruiting new people soon if we want to make it happen.'

Rukuba looks irritated and grunts. 'Well, Fang has his own ideas. I think Kivu needs to stand on its own two feet.'

'Well, look, I need a decision from you, Fang is pushing me . . .'

'Look, I will make my decision in my own time!' Rukuba flashes a look of anger at Alex who bows his head and nods.

Chapter Thirty-Nine

The two helicopters wind up their engines on the new concrete landing pads and Col has to raise his voice to Sophie as she comes over to him. 'Here's a flak jacket and helmet, ma'am.'

'Thanks.' She takes them but doesn't put them on. It's her first trip out on a mission with the KDF but she wants to make the point that she is not part of the military. She's in her jeans and tee shirt as ever and apart from that is relying on her day-glo Hope Street waistcoat to distinguish her from the troops.

It's 14th June and she has been living in Camp Heaven for a month now in a wooden bungalow hastily built by the Chinese work gangs. A little group of houses has been made in a separate area in the base for the teams of NGO workers that are helping with the demilitarisation process of the militias. The Red Cross and other UN humanitarian agencies are coordinating with First Regiment as the military campaign moves over into policing work.

Alex hurries over to them carrying his flak jacket, helmet and rifle, bent down under the growing rotor wash. Although the mission is simply to go and talk to a village chief with links to a *mai-mai* militia he isn't taking any chances.

He pulls a map out of his flak jacket front pocket and

talks to Sophie. 'Right, the village is called Violo. It's ninety miles west out into the bush in the Biasi river valley, so it's beyond the range of any of our artillery firebases.'

A *mai-mai* militia group that has agreed to disarm at the peace conference controls the long forested valley. Now Alex needs to start working out the mechanics of actually implementing the disarmament process. Getting the men with guns to give them up after so many years of violence is a tricky process. A connection through Unit 17's intelligence network has found a local village chief who is willing to act as an intermediary between the KDF and the militia.

Although it is risky going out there, this is exactly the sort of first-hand contact that Alex is desperate to get in order to gauge the mood on the ground and work out a process for other handovers. He can only tell so much from sitting in his ops tent listening to intelligence briefs from Mordechai and Unit 17 people.

Sophie is coming with them to discuss arrangements for reintegrating the *mai-mai* troops into society. She has been hard at work for the last month getting the project going in Camp Heaven. Although she is wary of the military and wouldn't admit it, she is actually interested to be going off on a mission, having been watching the helicopters coming in and out for weeks.

Jean-Baptiste joins them, and after shouted introductions he points to the two chalks of soldiers drawn up next to the pads and nods to Alex. 'OK, let's load up.'

Jason and Sean scuttle forward and board the dark green Mi-17, Sean clutching his PKM machine gun. As they pass the colonel they glance at the tall girl with the NGO waistcoat and, once past, Jason winks at Sean.

Alex, Col, Sophie, Jean-Baptiste and the rest of Tac cram into the back of the aircraft, the ramp closes over half the view and the rear gunner loads a fresh belt into his machine gun and settles himself into position next to Sophie. She edges away from him. Because of the risk of the area they are going in with two platoons from Echo Company, totalling forty-five soldiers, and a mortar team as well.

The aircraft sways airborne and heads off west over the mountains fringing the lake. She peers over the edge of the ramp as the upland pastures begin to give way to rugged tree covered hills. What would have taken well over a day by road takes them a mere twenty-five minutes by air.

Alex squeezes up to the front of the aircraft and talks on the radio to a KPP worker in the village in French to guide them into it. They fly over a steep-sided valley with lines of fields and meadows cut out along the banks of the river in the bottom of it.

A purple smoke flare guides them in and the two big choppers slow and thump down on a meadow.

'Let's go!' shouts Sergeant Matt Hooper and the men are out and on their belt buckles, forming a perimeter and scanning the village and the hillsides for threats. The helicopters are airborne straightaway, hauling themselves back over the ridges out of the line of any fire.

No threats emerge from the trees around the edge of the village so the troops form up and Tac advances with them to the edge of it. The local headman walks out with a group of elders and Alex and Sophie and Tac settle down to the meeting in the shade of a large tree on the riverbank. Jean-Baptiste deploys both platoons of men in a defensive screen in case of any trouble.

The village headman is called Malike Kasongo. He is old with wiry white hair sticking up around his head like a ragged cloud and wears a tatty suit jacket and stained jeans. At one stage in Congo's many wars he was shot through the mouth as punishment for speaking out against a militia. The bullet smashed out his teeth and made a hole through both cheeks. No one had the plastic surgery skills to mend it, so his voice has a whistling sound.

He sits on the seat of honour, a roughly made three-legged stool, the wood old and stained brown with wear. A cluster of ten old men from the village sit around him on the grass in a semicircle and a gaggle of curious children stand at the edge of the village gawping at the new arrivals.

Alex sits and exchanges ritual pleasantries with the chief about his family's health and thanks him for allowing them to come into the area to see him. Sophie then presents gifts of three boxes of Ugandan Supermatch cigarettes and they wait while tea is brewed in a battered metal kettle. The strong brew is sweetened with local cane sugar that leaves a sticky residue on their teeth as they sip it and offer thanks.

The chief has to drink in sips, carefully holding the liquid in the front of his mouth and then knocking his head back. He passes the cigarettes round the group. Alex and Sophie politely refuse and the village elders all lick the side of their cigarettes to slow the burn rate and savour the flavour.

Alex feels very humbled to see the poverty of the area, the grey, malnourished faces of the people and how, despite all the years of suffering engraved on his face, the old man has preserved his decency and generosity.

He begins the discussion in French and they talk about arrangements for disarming the *mai-mai* group in the valley. 'They are just here to protect us,' says the old man. 'We don't mind them, they are our tribe. And no one else will protect us.'

The discussion continues and the sun rises up to midday, washing out the bright green of the foliage on the forested valley sides to a muted grey-green. All shadows disappear as it moves directly overhead.

After they agree an outline plan for handing over weapons, Sophie is curious to know more. 'What do you think will happen next in Kivu? Do you want a democracy here?'

The old men squatting on the ground grumble and the chief puffs air out through his cheeks. 'What's the point of an election? The government will just steal it. What good did democracy ever do us? I can't eat votes!' He gestures as if he were putting food in his ruined mouth.

'We don't want a democracy, we want a Kagame!' He jabs a finger east towards Rwanda's strongman ruler. 'We just want someone to come in and sort out this mess! We don't want to have a local militia, we just want peace!' There are furious nods of agreement from the circle of men.

Alex and Sophie exchange a quick look.

The discussion moves on and Alex tries out another new idea. 'I'd like to leave a satellite phone and some solar batteries with you so that you can call us if there is a security problem in the area and we can scramble a helicopter to come and sort it out. Or you can report any intelligence. Would that be acceptable?'

The chief discusses it with the elders in their local tribal language for a while and there are nods and shrugs.

'Yes, that would be acceptable.'

He receives the bulky satphone with a confused look and Sophie explains how to dial the stored numbers in it. It is a strategy that they have been working on as part of the demilitarisation process.

The meeting is beginning to come to an end when Jean-Baptiste slips in next to Alex and whispers something in his ear.

'Excuse me,' Alex says and ducks out of the circle to look at the laptop that Jean-Baptiste has brought with him. It shows an image from the small tactical drone they brought with them in the helicopter as it circles the valley scanning the forest with an infrared eye.

'There are groups advancing from upstream and from downstream on both sides of the valley, about fifty men in each of the four groups.'

Alex looks at the ghostly white forms with rifles and RPG launchers that he can see running through the woods. Two hundred enemy soldiers.

'How long till they are here?'

'Five minutes.'

'Do we know if they are *mai-mai*?'

Jean-Baptiste shrugs.

Alex looks away from the screen and his practiced eyes quickly scan up and down the valley assessing the tactical situation. The sides are steep and hard to climb; they are caught in a trap with forty-five soldiers against two hundred. They can't get the choppers in to extract them with that number of weapons in the trees either side of the valley.

'Right, I'll check with the chief that it isn't the local *mai-mai* but I think we are going to have to stand and fight and then work out how we can extract ourselves. Pull the men back in from the screen and get them up on that bluff there.' He points to a spur of high ground sticking out into the main valley between two small streams.

'We can't get stuck down in here in the valley being shot at from both sides. Get the mortars dug in and we'll ambush them as they come across the streams on either side of that bluff.'

He pauses and looks at the blurry black and white images as the drone tracks the incoming soldiers. 'What the hell has that guy got on his head? It looks like horns . . .'

* * *

Alex needs to be sure that the approaching soldiers are hostiles before he engages them. He doesn't want a friendly fire incident on the *mai-mai* just when he is trying to disarm them.

He takes the laptop back over to the chief in the gathering and shows him the image of the horned man running through the bush.

'Are these *mai-mai* troops?'

'No, they're all down the valley, I was there yesterday.' He peers at the image, 'A man with horns?' he says. 'That's the Kudu Noir.'

There is an outburst of muttering from the men around him.

'You must go.' The chief stands and picks up his stool and leaves quickly. The group disperses and the people hide in their huts in the village.

Sophie looks at Alex. 'What's happening?'

'We've got Kudu Noir forces approaching from up and down the valley. I think you might want to put that on.' He jerks his head towards her flak jacket and helmet on the ground as he scoops up his own and begins buckling them on with well-practised speed.

'Right, let's get up that hill!' Alex's voice has the crack of command in it that Sophie hasn't heard before as he points to the west side of the valley.

Jean-Baptiste is shouting at his troops, pulling them back in, and she sees men running across the fields towards the cover of the trees on the spur of high ground. They run after them and race up through the trees onto the bluff. She's properly scared now but there is a reassuring sense of purpose about the men's actions as an experienced war machine gears up.

Jean-Baptiste bellows, 'De Waal! I want the mortars dug in here!

Alex calls Tac together for a quick briefing. 'S'arnt Major Thwaites take One Platoon on the north side of the bluff, Sergeant Hooper take Two Platoon south, ambush the enemy as they cross the streams.'

Tac set up in a dip in the ground on the top of the bluff and the four men of Alex's close protection team get their entrenching tools out and start digging in like demons. Banks of earth begin to line the top of the dip and Sophie tries to keep out of the way.

Alex nestles into the side of it with his signaller next to him and gets on the radio. 'Heaven, this is Black Hal, request you scramble Shakira and two Mi-17s for extraction operation at Violo.' He reads out their grid reference. 'We are threatened by enemy infantry force, two groups of fifty men, one to north and one to south on both sides of the valley.'

'Roger that, Black Hal, will scramble Shakira and two Mi-17s. Advise will be approximately fifty minutes including flight time, Shakira has just returned from a contact and is bombing up.'

'Roger that, Heaven, ETA fifty minutes. Warn the crews the LZ will be hot. Repeat, LZ will be hot.'

Fifty minutes to fight to stay alive before they have any hope of extraction. A lot can happen in one minute on the battlefield.

Alex looks grim and glances around at the tall trees overhead. No breaks in them to allow a landing zone for a helicopter to get in so they will have to extract from the fields in the valley which will leave the choppers vulnerable to enemy fire. He's got to neutralise the enemy before they can land.

The men around him have fallen silent as they wait for the attackers to approach. Alex whispers instructions to a circle of his commanders crouched around him in the dip.

'Major Delacroix, take the drone laptop and direct mortar fire. The enemy will be too close to us to use it on this side of the valley but I want the fire over the other side to keep that group pinned down and stop them crossing the river.

'Corporal Baker, get ready to talk Shakira onto the target. We'll try and destroy them on this side in the trees but we'll need the gunship for across the valley.' Corporal Baker, the Forward Air Controller, nods and begins pulling out his map case and checking his GPS for grid references.

'Medics, I want the RAP set up over there.' The two men move off and unpack their rucksacks and set up the Regimental Aid Post in a sheltered area between the huge buttress roots of a tree.

Alex has a three-dimensional model of the battlefield in his head. His problem is having to split his force in three directions: the mortars and ten rifles are to engage the enemy east across the valley, the remaining thirty men are split into two groups of fifteen, each countering fifty men coming down from the north and fifty from the south.

'I want the PKMs in Fire Support Groups over there and there to cover each side of the bluff.'

In the trees just down the slope from Tac's position, Matt Hooper is getting Two Platoon sorted out. He is feeling nervous and conscious of the fact that he froze during their crucial assault on the Lubonga ridge. He glances across at where Corporal Stein is getting his section into cover behind trees and bushes where they can look down onto the stream. Matt wants to do better this time, both for himself and for his men. He forces thoughts of Danielle out of his head and just tries to get on with the job.

He positions his two men armed with the AA-12 machine shotguns down the slope so they are nearer the enemy, their bursts of buckshot will be lethal in this sort of close country where the enemy is hard to detect.

Major Delacroix's voice crackles in his platoon radio earpiece. It's as calm and controlled as ever. 'Enemy are one minute away.'

All is silent in the woods as they wait for the troops to appear. Jason is one of the men with an AA-12 and pulls the bulky rifle tight into his shoulder; he's hyped up and itching to use it.

He scans forward across the narrow valley watching the bushes fifty yards away carefully and waiting for the first man to emerge. The plan that has been whispered along the line to him is to wait until a decent number of the enemy are across the stream and then open up on them so they can be cut off and killed when they are trapped on the lower slopes.

He hears some sounds across the stream, the cracking of twigs breaking, heavy breathing and thudding feet as men run on the soft ground. A bush downhill from him twitches, its leaves shaking, and his eyes lock onto it immediately.

A head wearing a black cloth balaclava with ragged holes for eyes and mouth emerges. It looks inhuman, like something from a horror film. Jason holds his fire, finger on the trigger, tensed and waiting for more of the men to emerge and cross the stream.

A single rifle spits from the slope above him and the man ducks back into cover.

Fuck! Who fired? Fucking twat!

Jason fires a couple of rounds into the bush and the leaves blast off it in a five-foot wide circle as the buckshot hits home.

Matt Hooper knows he has spoilt the ambush by firing too early. The other men open up and long bursts of automatic fire rake across the other side of the valley, but the enemy can't be seen. The battle has broken out on both sides of the bluff now and he hears the two mortars at the top of it booming out as they lob shells over the other side of the main valley. He doesn't want another failure to dog him; they need to engage the enemy more closely.

'Two Platoon, follow me!' His voice booms out through the trees and he runs down the slope, yelling at the surprised men to follow him.

They jump up from cover behind trees and run after their platoon leader. Stein sees him go past but it's too late to stop him so he screams at his section, 'Give covering fire!'

Matt and his men dash across the stream splashing through the water. Bullets zip past them as the enemy rallies and fires back. A grenade sails out above him, plops into a patch of the mud and explodes with a ragged splash, directing its shrapnel up into the air. The mud crater smokes gently.

Jason splashes through the stream and runs into the gloom of the trees opposite. He's got tunnel vision; everything in the rest of creation has ceased to exist. His sight, hearing and smell are all sharpened. The blood thunders in his veins and the rifle feels alive and dangerous in his hands. Fire stabs out at him above and from the right. He swings the barrel round and squeezes the trigger; the weapon convulses smoothly in his hands and he pumps out three rounds at the man. Screams in the gloom indicate a hit.

Then he hears the shout through the trees to his left. 'Man down! Man down!'

Shit.

'Who's hit?'

Chapter Forty

Up on top of the bluff in Tac's position, Sophie cringes down in the dip. Mayhem is breaking out all around her. Enemy fire pours into the bluff from across the valley, bullets zip overhead and thunk into the tree trunks blowing off chunks of wood. RPG rockets scream in and explode in the tree canopy scattering shrapnel and branches on them.

On either side of her, the two PKM machine guns are clattering out long bursts supporting the troops lower down the slope. The two mortars next to her boom out again. White flame blossoms momentarily in the gloom illuminating the large tree trunks around them. The crews duck down their heads away from the blasts and the shells fire off over the other side of the valley. The violence is another order of magnitude of experience, above and beyond anything she's experienced in civilian life.

'Come west fifty metres!' Jean-Baptiste shouts over to the mortar crews as he watches the shell bursts on the other side of the valley.

Alex is next to him in the dugout. He is following the flow of the battle through the crackling radio traffic on the net and the noises all around him, the heavy thudding of the PKM machine guns, the lighter cracks of the assault rifles, the sharp explosions of grenades and the shouts and screams echoing through the trees. He feels alive and alert, all his senses switched on and pulsing with energy, the Devereux instinct flowing in him as he barks orders and conducts his hellish orchestra in the strange music of battle.

Hooper's rash attack across the stream has caused casualties.

Alex yells into the radio, 'Corporal Stein, I want you to cross the stream and get the casualties back over this side. I will get additional fire to cover you.'

He pulls the two PKMs off the north flank and all four machine guns pour fire down into the trees below them as Alex watches Stein lead his section across the stream. They disappear into the trees and emerge a few minutes later dragging three casualties.

His south flank is now disorganised and weakened. As Stein retreats back uphill black hooded figures slip across the stream and start approaching up the slope towards them, making weird animal screams that echo around the woods. Alex is unperturbed and gets on the net to Col to organise his response.

Sophie glimpses Stein as he races up the hill with an inert Matt Hooper on his back in a fireman's lift. He runs past Tac and dumps him down at the RAP and then turns back. He is puffing hard from the climb and his face and back are red and wet with Matt's blood. Another two groups of soldiers carry screaming casualties past her.

As the battle closes in, she glances across at Alex as he gives his orders. 'Right, you four, follow me, the rest of you stay here. Major Delacroix, you're in charge if I don't come back.'

He grabs his rifle with one hand and slips over the lip of their shelter, moving nimbly for a big man, a look of murderous calm on his face.

He leads his close protection squad down the slope towards the enemy. Confused firing and screaming is coming through the trees. His assault rifle is up in front of him, his face set hard over the sights, eyes narrowed and all senses focused along it. He signals to the men to fan out into a line and wait for the enemy to approach.

His senses speed up so that every movement slows down a hundred times. In the gloom he sees a ragged head shape emerge from behind a tree and run up towards him, howling as it comes. He puts the tip of the iron foresight of his rifle onto the figure's chest as it runs and squeezes the trigger twice. The rounds hit home and the figure flies backwards down the slope. The automatic action spits two smoking cases out of the ejection port onto the ground next to him.

His men open up with jagged bursts of fire and more come from their left as Col leads his squad in a flanking attack at the same time.

Caught between the two fires the enemy turn and flee back down the slope. As they run across the stream the four PKMs at last have clear targets and cut them down. The enemy are forced to turn back into the cover of the trees and Alex and Col's two squads and the rallied remainder of Two Platoon, Jason amongst them, all move down the slope and close in on the survivors. Grenades and murderous fire pour down at them but the men do not surrender and are all gradually pinned down and shot.

Next to Tac a shout from one of the two medics goes up from the cover of their tree root. 'Anyone free, give us a hand!'

Sophie forces herself out of the dugout and scuttles across to them. They have triaged the casualties. One is hit in the arm and bleeding heavily but not about to die so they are concentrating on the other two.

Matt Hooper was next to a tree when an RPG hit it. His left arm is severed at the elbow, he took a load of shrapnel in the guts and his face is half blown off. He's thrashing around on the ground delirious with pain and screaming. Sophie comes round the large root buttress and sees the horrific sight of his arm stump flailing around, the bone gleaming white and wet and spraying blood. The medic is struggling to get a tourniquet on him.

'Hold him still!' he shouts at her. She grabs his other arm and the medic gets to work on him as blood splatters over both of them.

'You're OK, mate, you're gonna make it! Just keep still!'

An RPG bangs overhead and they both duck down.

Alex runs back up the hill with his squad and jumps back into the dugout.

'Baker! Where's the air?'

'Just talking to them now, sir, they're wheels up and inbound.'

'Tell 'em we're going to need a danger close airstrike on the northern flank. We've just sorted out the southern side, but we can't dislodge that lot without air.'

'Yes, sir.'

Bullets are still snapping above them from the enemy east across the valley and from the northern flank.

In the middle of this mayhem, Baker has the radio telephone held tight against his ear, and is talking calmly and authoritatively to the Russian pilot of Shakira as he streaks in ahead of the two slower troopships, racing to get to them at two hundred miles an hour.

'Shakira, this is Widow Three Three, we need a danger close airstrike to clear troops opposite the north flank of our position. Suggest you circle and watch my tracers.'

The Russian pilot speaks calmly and with intense concentration so that he sounds almost bored. 'Roger that, Widow Three Three, we are inbound with full ordnance load of rockets and flechettes from east.'

The battle goes on for five minutes and then they hear the scouring sound of the big gunship overhead and the tree branches thrash about madly under its downdraught.

Baker pops a red smoke grenade and throws it forward through the trees away from Tac. The curls of smoke pour up out of the canopy as the Mi-24 circles overhead.

'Widow Three Three, I have eyes on your smoke. Can you indicate target?'

'Roger that, Shakira, firing red tracer now. Watch my tracer.'

Baker holds his thumbs up to Sean who fires a long burst across the hillside to the north across from them.

'Widow, that is very close, I will have to dive onto enemy position from above to minimise spread of flechettes.'

Baker confers with Alex. 'Happy with that, Shakira. Black Hal has given permission for danger close flechette strike on north flank of our position.'

'Roger that, Widow, gaining altitude now.'

Baker sticks his head up out of the dugout and screams to the men down the slope, 'Air thirty seconds! Take cover!'

The pilot hauls back on the cyclic and the two massive turbofans pull the aircraft vertically up at a stomach-churning rate. His eyes watch the altimeter and when he judges he has enough altitude he circles, leaning the cockpit over so that his gunner can get a clear view of the small puff of red smoke amidst the green forest down below them.

When they dive down at it, the gunner will have to laser the target for range, get the sights set on it and then fire the rockets in a couple of seconds before the pilot has to pull out of the dive or they will embed themselves in the hillside at over two hundred miles an hour.

The pilot leans the chopper over into a vertical dive; the small front window of his canopy completely fills with solid, green earth. As they plummet towards it, the gunner gets the sights on his heads-up display onto the tiny area of hillside a hundred metres away from Tac's position. He lases, sights, clicks the cover off his red firing button with his thumb and presses it.

Six large rockets blast away from the pods under the wings on each side of the aircraft. Bursting charges explode and each rocket breaks open sending out a cone-shaped spread of five-inch long tungsten darts with fins at one end, tapering down to a needle-sharp point.

Hundreds of darts strike the wooded area like a huge shotgun blast from above. A funnel of death saturates the side of the small valley and the whole target area convulses and jumps up into the air in a cloud of splintered white wood as if a giant chainsaw has suddenly chewed it up.

The darts are small but moving so fast their kinetic energy slashes through wood, metal and bone, slicing limbs and internal organs.

The pilot hauls back on the stick and the ten-tonne helicopter screams in protest as the huge forces pull at its main rotor. Blood drains from his head and his vision blurs.

Corporal Baker watches the strike go in from the dugout, stands up, punches the air and yells, 'Go on, yer brute!'

The massive gunship roars over his head at two hundred miles an hour and the downdraught smashes branches off the trees.

'Fucking 'ell!' someone in Tac squawks in high-pitched alarm.

Sean peers over his machine gun at the awesome display

315

of power he has just witnessed as bits of white wood and green leaves float back down to earth. He is ecstatic with relief and shouts contemptuously, 'See yer later, mate!'

Col's battlefield voice bellows from the woods below him, 'Get up! Go! Go! Go! *Move yerselves!*'

One Platoon shake off the shock and dash down the slope, across the stream and up into the jagged remains of the trees, stripped of their leaves. The enemy troops left alive are stunned, standing gawping around them or crouching down in terror. Bursts of fire cut them down, the slope is covered in bodies lying still or twisting on the ground in agony.

Col comes across one as it writhes making a wet gasping noise, and looks down at it in surprise over his rifle sights. It is the body of a man lying on his back with the large horned head of a kudu rising out of its shoulders.

'Hodges, cover me!' Col barks at a soldier who runs over and sights his rifle on the body as Col moves round to come at it from the head, out of Hodge's line of fire. He stares at the creature as he approaches cautiously; it is a conjunction of a man and an animal, as fascinating as it is appalling. His hand reaches out slowly towards one of the thick twisted horns.

He pulls slowly and the mask comes off the man. It is a heavy object with a wicker frame underneath the skin of the neck that holds it steady on his shoulders. Col can see what the man's injury is now – arterial blood is jetting out of the left side of his neck. A flechette has cut down through him, slashed his trachea and exited through his ribs on the right-hand side. He is drowning in his own blood.

The man gapes like a landed fish and his wide-open eyes stare at Col, the whites of them glaring in desperation.

Col knows there is no way they can treat a serious casualty like that now – even if they didn't have to pull out

316

immediately the bloke would be finished. He looks at him and thinks, do I let him suffocate slowly or do I do him a favour and finish him off?

'He's not gonna make it,' he mutters to Hodges.

He stands back and drags the mask away from the man, brings his rifle up to his shoulder and bangs two rounds out into the top of his head.

He can hear other shots and shouting as the men clear the hillside. He grabs the mask in one hand and takes it with him as he oversees the sweep and then pulls the troops back up onto the bluff.

Alex twists around in the dugout, looking away from the devastation across from them. The huge build-up of pressure has been released. He catches Sophie's eye and shakes his head and grins. 'Bloody hell,' he says, and starts laughing with relief.

The need to release the tension is so great that Sophie finds it weirdly hilarious as well and bends double with spasms of laughter, her ribs tensing in on her painfully. The shudders break up the solid block of fear in her stomach.

Everyone in Tac bursts into hoots of laughter. Jean-Baptiste is shaking his head, giggling and repeating, '*Merde, merde, merde.*'

Alex eventually collects himself. 'OK, Baker, now for the other side of the valley.'

A second airstrike is set up. Sean indicates the target area with more tracer along the treeline across the main valley from them.

Shakira radios back. 'Widow Three Three, target in treeline seen. I circle and launch strike from west over your heads.'

The sound of the chopper whirs away from them as he circles and comes back in a shallow dive on the target.

'Widow Three Three, commencing run-in, range good, two pods 80mm rockets, get head down! Firing now!'

The thunderous roar of the Mil is overhead and there is a scouring, ripping noise as the rockets fire off in a stream and smash into the valley side in a succession of violent red flashes. The treeline explodes in flame and dust, branches and chunks of wood, bits of bodies and guns are blown high into the air. Sharp secondary explosions start as RPG rockets explode.

More whoops and yells come from the troops all over the bluff. They are clear to go home.

Chapter Forty-One

Alex looks at Sophie.

'Are you going to be OK?'

'Yeah, I'm fine.'

She doesn't look it. Her face is pale and streaked with blood and dirt. She nods towards the white clapboard bungalow next to hers. 'I'll go and see Nats.'

It's late afternoon and they have just touched down on the helipads after the battle at Violo. Alex walked her back up the hill to the cluster of NGO workers' houses that look out over the lake on one side of the peninsula and they are standing on the little veranda outside her white plastic front door.

'Look, I'm sorry about what happened.'

'No, no, that's fine. It's not your fault.'

'It is really.' He looks annoyed at himself. 'We'll have an after-action review now and try to work out how it happened.'

He looks away. He doesn't want to discuss military details with her but he is thinking hard, wondering how the hell the Kudu Noir knew they were going to be in the valley at that time. They had obviously come in force determined to ambush and kill them. If it hadn't been for the tactical drone spotting them then they would have been caught between the different forces in the floor of the valley and shot to pieces. Someone in the village must have leaked the information but he can't think why. No one else outside of his headquarters knew they were coming. Maybe the militia didn't want to disarm and allied with the Kudu Noir?

'How do you feel?'

'I don't know.' She shakes her head, looks down and sees her watch. 'I can't believe it's only four o'clock, it feels like I've had another life. I just feel . . . numb really. But also part of it all . . .' She nods towards the helipads where the troops have disembarked, rushing the casualties over to the hospital tent.

'Is Sergeant Hooper . . .?'

Alex shakes his head. Hooper was lying next to him on the floor of the Mi-17 as the medics struggled to save him. They had the tourniquet on his arm and a drip in him but couldn't get at the abdominal bleed from the shrapnel and his lifeblood leaked away on the floor of the chopper.

'Kazcmarek should be OK though, they got a chest drain in him and stopped his lung collapsing so they should be able to stabilise him now. He's bought himself a ticket to Kigali though – it'll be a while till he's right.'

She shakes her head. 'I can't believe how they get through it.'

Alex nods in agreement. 'Hmm, Two Platoon is pretty shaken up about S'arnt Hooper but we've taken quite a few casualties now and we seem to be able to get over it. Adversity acts like a bond that pulls us all tighter together.'

Col has been typically robust about the whole thing, saying he is going to put the kudu head up over his desk in the ops room as a trophy.

Alex looks at her, trying to gauge how she will deal with the shock.

'Look, all the lads think you did a great job getting stuck

in and helping with the casualties. For your first firefight that was a bloody good effort, they're impressed. I'm impressed.'

She smiles. 'Thanks.'

Alex looks at her in a new light and thinks, 'I like you a lot more now than I did when I first met you.'

'OK, I better take those.'

'Oh yes.' She hands him her bloodstained flak jacket and helmet.

'Well done, see you.'

'Yeah, thanks, see you.'

He walks off and she goes next door. Natalie is out. She unlocks her front door, washes her face and curls up on her bed staring at the wall. Every ounce of energy has been burned out of her body by the adrenaline rush. She falls into a black pit of sleep.

'Come on! Come on! It's time!'

Simon jiggles his arm and Joseph pushes him away. 'OK, I'm doing it!'

'It's 93.5 FM.'

'I know.'

He tunes in the radio and the reception weaves through the static and eventually locks onto Radio Okapi, the old UN radio network that President Rukuba has taken over.

It's 15th June and they are desperate to hear the first semi-final of *Kivu Anthem Idol*. President Rukuba himself will host this two-hour show from eight o'clock and the whole province is glued to their radios. The competition has been running for the last month and has caught the national imagination. In bars, in the streets, in villages across the country, people are waiting to hear their favourite singers perform their newly written national anthems.

Posters of the President are everywhere, beaming down

from the roadside hoardings in his trademark white robes. He is smiling his electric smile and pointing outwards with the slogan 'Papa Rukuba wants you!' running over his head. In front of him is a stack of one million US dollars in prize money. Joseph stood and stared at the poster when he first saw it: he has hardly ever seen a dollar bill in his life, let alone that many of them in one place.

The final will be in two weeks' time on 30th June, Congo's old independence day from Belgium, except that President Rukuba has pronounced that from now on it will be Kivu's independence day from Congo.

Joseph and his new friend Simon took up Gabriel's offer of joining the KPP youth wing and got fast-tracked into the training and reintegration programme. Neither of them can read so they didn't get on any business courses but were given a *toleka* each, a heavy-framed, Chinese-made bicycle with a wide seat on a reinforced pannier at the back to use as a taxi. After a quick maintenance course they were released and taken to a new KPP youth wing accommodation block on the outskirts of Bukavu. The prefab building had only just been put up by Chinese work gangs.

They are both very happy with their new lives. They have a roof over their heads, they have the means of earning a living and spend their days cycling up and down Bukavu's hills lugging shoppers and their bags around the town.

They have just brought two women back from Supermarché la Beauté out on the main promontory into Lake Kivu. They pedalled hard and dropped them off on Avenue Lumumba where they parked their bikes and are now sitting on the kerbside with a second-hand radio that Joseph bought especially to listen to the show. Simon has bought an old mobile phone so they can vote by text. The kerb is strewn with bits of litter, half-eaten chicken legs and cola nut husks and their only light is what little spills out of shop fronts and the bar across the street.

The whole show is run by the Lebanese media company that organised the Arab Pop Idol competition that brought the Middle East to a standstill when it was on.

In this semi-final they are both rooting for a girl calling herself Diamante who sings a power ballad with trite lyrics entitled, 'I love you Kivu'. The other songs in this round are much more upbeat Congolese-style dance tunes but there's something about the plaintive, gentle nature of the girl's voice and the simple longing in the lyrics that makes Joseph cry every time he hears it.

All around them the city is falling silent. Cars park hurriedly, no one walks on the streets, the only people not inside are clustered around radios on the street like them. A group of ragged urchins sees them and gathers round to listen; Joseph glares at them and makes a quiet gesture but allows them to press in close.

The upbeat theme tune comes on, the announcer does a big build-up in Swahili and then says, 'And now, live from his humble farm at Mukungu in the hills of Kivu, we bring you, your very own Pres-i-deeent Rukuba!'

A huge cheer comes from the bar across the street and everyone in the group shouts, 'Rukuba!'

Joseph and Simon yell along with them and grin at each other.

'Hello, my people!'

'Hello, Papa Rukuba!' the live crowd up at Mukungu yell and Joseph's group and people all over the province join in. This is the sort of government you can enjoy.

'It's Friday night and what are we gonna do?'

'Have fun!'

They know the shouts by now.

'Yeah, let's have some fun, I'm gonna play you a favourite dance number of mine and guess who my special guests are this week?'

'Who? Who?'

'Yes, none other than System Wemba Wemba!'

'Oh my God!' Joseph screams; he cannot believe that the band are live on stage in Kivu with the President. How does this man do it?

They are the biggest dance band in Congo at the moment, notorious for their fast and raunchy *soukous ndombolo* songs. How has the man managed to bring them to such a backwater as Kivu? He is a genius.

Rukuba has a chat with the lead singer and they banter away. The President is good at this knockabout humour and has everyone laughing. The singer then takes his place on stage and adds, 'Joining us for our first number on keyboards and vocals will be President Rukuba,' and counts them in.

The whole street goes mad and Joseph dances a *soukous ndombolo* with a young street girl. His moves are fast and the two really blow everyone away. Dancing is free and it's one of the few things in his life he takes pride in.

The show rolls on with Rukuba skilfully building up the tempo to the first contestant's dance song and then slowing things down to do an interview with a woman from a village in north Kivu. His voice suddenly becomes sorrowful. 'So, my people, we know we are going through the process of building a new nation. We know that we have to confront the pain of our past.'

He talks the woman through her experience as she explains how she was attacked and raped by a militia. The street party stops and everyone stares at the radio crying openly along with the woman as she sobs on Rukuba's arm and he comforts her.

Joseph sits on the kerb wracked with tears, reliving his guilt as he listens to the woman. The girl he was dancing with cannot understand his emotion and puts her arm around him.

Rukuba lets the woman finish and then leads neatly into his point. 'So, my people, we must be strong now as we build up our new nation. We must learn to stand on our own two feet. For too long Kivu has lived on her knees but now Kivu has stood up!

'I think it's the right time to move on to our second contestant tonight. Please welcome onstage . . . Diamante.'

A warm but more muted reception greets the young singer as she walks on. Joseph sits up and wipes his eyes.

The lyrics are simple but in combination with her powerful and dignified voice they encapsulate the pain and the hope of the new nation. The group of grubby children standing on the dingy, rubbish-strewn kerbside in Bukavu all sing along to the chorus with tears in their eyes: 'I love you Kivu!'

Chapter Forty-Two

A week after the battle at Violo, on 21st June, Alex is again standing on the veranda of Sophie's bungalow, but this time the atmosphere is a great deal more positive.

He looks her up and down and cannot help but look impressed. 'OK. You look . . .' he fishes for the right word, trying not to sound like he is taking too personal an interest in her '. . . tremendous.'

She's pleased and grins mockingly. 'Standards, Devereux, standards. Even in the wilds of Africa one must have one's little black number at hand. Never know when it will come in handy.'

She is wearing a sheer black sleeveless dress, her hair coiled up behind her head. In her elegant heels she's nearly as tall as Alex. She looks leggy, slim and stunning.

'I think this must be the first time I've seen you not wearing jeans.'

'Well, I'm not *just* a sandal-wearing peacenik, you know.' She looks him up and down critically. 'Hmm . . . I think you should take your tie off; the Lebanese are never that smart. Come on.'

She clicks her fingers and waits as he undoes his tie and hands it over. 'Is that Guards?' She eyes the red and blue stripes.

'Well, Household Cav, yes. Same thing.'

'God, you really are *genuinely* pompous, aren't you? I cannot *believe* you are going out to a Lebanese party in Kivu in a pinstriped suit and a blooming Guards tie.'

'Well . . .' Alex laughs, 'I don't have any other suits.'

She chucks it inside her front door, locks it and says, 'Come along then, chop chop,' and sets off to the helipad.

Alex follows and they walk down the road to the flight line.

'So who is this Fadoul chap again?' Sophie asks.

'He's the guy who supplies all our food here – you know the trucks with the Arabic logo on them?'

'Oh yes, of course. Why on earth does he want *you* to come to a party?' she says disdainfully.

'I don't know really. Fang says he's been asking to meet me for ages. Apparently he's got some sort of big coming-of-age bash for one of his sons, he's having all the local Lebanese over and asked me to come with someone.'

'Oh, right. Well, it will make a nice change from all this war business, I suppose.' She continues with overdone enthusiasm, 'In fact, I think it will be *tremendous fun*. Come on, let's go, I haven't been to a party for *ages*!'

Alex hasn't seen the fun side of her character much before; he's had suspicions that it is there and is relieved to see that it does actually exist.

They walk down to the helipads where Col is waiting with a close protection squad of four men, who are dressed in their combat gear with flak jackets, rifles and a light machine gun.

'Evening, ma'am, evening, Colonel. Luvly evening for a jaunt down the lake, eh?'

Sophie is getting on better with Col these days. 'Hi, S'arnt Major.' But she looks at the soldiers in disbelief and turns to Alex. 'Oh for heaven's sake!'

Alex is forced on the defensive. 'Look, I can't take any chances. I am the commanding officer and there are a lot of people out there who don't like me. We have no idea how good this guy's security is. You know after all that Violo trouble we had . . .'

Sophie rolls her eyes and shrugs. 'OK, OK.'

'Look, don't worry, they'll stay with the helicopter – they're not coming on the dance floor.'

She laughs and they walk over towards where a camouflage-green Mi-24 gunship is winding up its engines, looking angry and spiky with rocket pods and cannon.

'Oo, me hair,' she says in a joke accent as they near the rotor wash, and pulls her cashmere shawl over her head.

Col slides back the door to the troop bay and they step up and settle into the line of four bucket seats back-to-back down the centre line of the aircraft. There are knowing glances between the four men sitting on the other side with their backs to them.

Sophie turns to Alex and laughs, 'This is the most ridicu-lous mode of transport ever. I cannot believe I am going to a party in a gunship.' He grins in response.

They take off and cruise the twenty-five miles north along Lake Kivu. The engine noise prevents any talk and Alex leaves the sliding door open so that they can both sit and stare at the spectacular view, framed like a cinema screen by the door, of rugged green hills plunging down to the lake, which shimmers in the low evening sun. The rays light the clouds from underneath making them burn like red flames in the sky.

They land on a large estate five miles outside Goma on the lakeside. As they come in they can see a high fence around the whole area with armed guards patrolling it. Alex is reassured to see that the man takes his security seriously.

The main villa is set in the middle of the grounds. It is a huge white affair with red tiled roofs and numerous verandas, balconies and terraces. Bougainvillea grows up the walls amidst palm trees and neatly manicured gardens. The large front driveway is packed with BMWs, Mercedes and Lexus SUVs.

They land on a wide lawn that slopes down to the lake. Two Mi-17s painted in the Fadoul company livery and three smaller executive helicopters are already there. They duck out of the troop bay, the engines wind down and Alex stands and issues instructions. 'Right, aircrew, stay here. S'arnt Major Thwaites and the squad will come with us up to the house and do a recce, we'll take it from there.'

Sophie listens to the briefing, then looks at the men, puts her hand on Alex's arm and says facetiously to him, 'Do try to relax, dear.'

Col and the other men burst out laughing. Alex realises he is overdoing it and laughs, points at her and says, 'Look, you will stay in the bloody helicopter if you don't behave.'

They set off up the slope to the house and hear the noise of a large, chattering crowd ahead on the main terrace; there's at least a hundred people there already. The smell of roasting lamb drifts down towards them and the terrace is decorated with fairy lights. A stage with a disco mirror ball over it is set up at one end. It's a family gathering of all ages, from toddlers to grandparents.

'Think we'll stay with the cab, sir, or we might spoil the atmosphere,' Col says.

Alex nods. 'I think you're right, looks like quite a party.' He glances at Sophie. 'Ready then, dear?'

She grins and waves at Col and the soldiers. 'See you later, S'arnt Major.'

'See you later, ma'am,' Col says with a grin, casting a glance over her svelte figure as she walks away. *Still not my cup of tea but not bad.*

They make their way up onto the terrace and through the crowd, which consists mainly of local Lebanese but also includes a few Congolese businessmen and their glossy wives. Everyone seems to know each other and greet with three kisses on the cheeks. People stand around in groups chatting happily; a few glances follow the tall European couple as they go past.

Alex and Sophie both use their height to peer around over the crowd to try and find Mr Fadoul. 'I think that looks like someone's holding court over there.' Sophie nods towards the back of the terrace and Alex spots a large table with lots of people gathered around it.

He leads the way, squeezing past Lebanese wives with big blonde hairdos, monster heels and spray-on dresses. Sophie notices a teenage daughter in a very short pink chiffon dress eye up Alex as he goes past.

They get to the table, which is surrounded by people. A girl of six in a white party frock is having a silver plastic tiara fixed in her hair by her mother, who is dressed in a black and gold leather dress.

Mr Fadoul glances at his wife and then sees them and jumps up, all smiles and bonhomie. He's fifty, short and bald on top with black hair round the side of his head; his thick-set shoulders crease the arms of his cream linen suit jacket.

He reaches out a hand to Alex and greets him effusively in French. 'Ah, Colonel Devereux, how good to see you. Yes, thank you for coming to my son's party, Hazem is sixteen.' He nods adoringly towards a gawky-looking boy standing next to the table with some friends, wearing an oversized black suit, white shirt, black string tie and trainers. He glances at Sophie. 'Ah, and you are?'

330

'Sophie Cecil-Black, pleased to meet you.'

'Bilal Fadoul, my pleasure.'

As he stretches out his hand to shake, she sees he has thick black hairs on his wrist with a chunky gold Rolex and a small string of ebony worry beads around it.

'Ah yes, the two of you are the right height for each other but not me, eh?' he says looking up at them and laughing. Alex and Sophie laugh politely as well, trying to ignore the assumption he has just made.

'Good, now let me get you a drink. Hazem! Get me a new bottle and two glasses.'

The cowed youth grabs a bottle of Jack Daniel's and two highball glasses full of ice and gives them to his father. Bilal cracks the cap on the JD with relish; half fills them and hands them over. 'I'll leave the water to you.'

Alex takes his drink and looks slightly confused. 'Thanks . . . I thought you were Muslim?'

Bilal laughs. 'Ah, no, not all Arabs are Muslims. We're Ishfaqi.' He gestures to the community of people around him. 'We live all over the Middle East, we're a sect, a bit like Druze and Alawites – you know, a mixture, a bit of Christianity, a bit of Islam, a bit of whatever. We like to think we take the best of all worlds.' He looks at his whiskey and grins, clinks glasses with theirs and knocks back a slug.

Sophie takes a large glug, coughs and laughs. 'Oh gosh.'

Alex shoves some water in his and offers the jug to her, grinning facetiously. 'Bit strong for you, dear?'

'Yes, I think I will, actually.'

Bilal licks his lips, savouring the booze. 'Yes, it's this, you see.' He pulls a chunky gold symbol on a chain out of the mat of black hair in his shirtfront. 'It's Ishfaqi in Arabic, you know I have it on my trucks? It means compassion.'

'Oh, yes, we've seen it.' Alex and Sophie both nod.

Bilal looks slyly at Alex. 'I think you have met Ishfaqi before, heh? Remember the Dark Heart Prophecy, eh?'

Alex's face freezes at the mention of a painful piece of his past but Bilal breezes on, 'Ishfaqi believe that God acts through certain people in this world, his saints. You are one of those people, Colonel.'

He finally registers Alex's guarded look and says apologetically, 'OK, never mind then. That's all history.' He flaps a hand.

Sophie's acute gaze flicks between the two of them but she doesn't say anything.

'OK, let's go and meet some people. Come on, this is my wife, Rashida. Darling, say hello to Colonel Devereux.'

The woman in the black and gold dress looks up, slightly flustered from doing her daughter's tiara, and smoothes her voluminous dyed blonde hair into place. 'Oh, yes, hello. My husband says you're the man who is making us all safe now.'

Alex looks embarrassed and Sophie helps things along with a cheery, 'Yes, he's such a hero, isn't he?' She rests a hand patronisingly on his arm and beams at them before turning to talk to Mrs Fadoul.

Bilal looks at him with a twinkle of humour in his eyes. 'OK, so come and meet people.' He looks around him and claps an arm around the shoulders of a man next to him. He's fifty, short and lean with a clipped moustache, grey hair and an erect posture.

'Ah, yes, another military man. Colonel Devereux, this is Captain Mahmood Bashoor, the head of my air force.' Bilal chuckles and winks. 'Mahmood was a captain in the Syrian air force but now he flies my helicopters for me, I usually keep them at my refinery in Goma.'

Alex smiles and chats to Mahmood about his experience

in Kivu. He's been there for ten years and knows a lot of useful things about flying helicopters in the province.

After a while, Alex moves on and sidles up to Sophie, muttering, 'I think the JD is beginning to get to me – can we get something to eat?'

'Yes, good idea.'

They head to the barbeque and fill up their plates with roast lamb, roast vegetables and couscous, then choose a table overlooking the party and sit down.

'So what's all this Dark Heart Prophecy stuff then, eh?' She narrows her eyes at him.

Alex puts down his fork and finishes his mouthful. 'Look, I don't want to sound like a complete dickhead but can we just not talk about that, please?'

'Oh, I suppose it's classified, is it?'

Alex just looks at her pleasantly before picking up his fork once more and gesturing at her plate. 'This lamb's good, isn't it?' He sticks another piece in his mouth and chews it with a satisfied look.

She rolls her eyes. 'Well, these Ishfaqi seem to think you're the bee's knees?'

Alex looks doubtful. 'Hmm, I really don't know much about them. If they want to think that I'm some sort of saint then I'm not going to disabuse them. I can do with all the help I can get in Kivu at the moment. Anyway, what the hell, they throw a good party.'

Bilal comes over to check they are OK and plonks himself down next to Sophie. He seems very taken with her and asks about her work so she explains about her football charity outreach activity and Bilal suddenly lights up and says, 'Ah! I've got some goalposts I can let you have. I've got a pile of them in a warehouse in Nairobi, they're good, proper size ones, and have really strong aluminium frames.'

'Oh, thank you very much.'

'What's your email address? I'll tell Mahmood to deliver them wherever you want by chopper.' He waves casually down the lawn at his two aircraft, clearly loving the chance to show them off.

Once everyone has had enough to eat, there is a crackling on a PA system and Bilal stands up on the stage under the disco glitter ball with a microphone and addresses everyone.

'OK, thank you, thank you. So now it's time for Hazem's ceremony. We have to do this in Arabic but don't worry, we'll start dancing soon.'

He hands the mike over to an old man with a long white beard who wears a black robe and headdress like an Orthodox priest. Hazem comes awkwardly onto the stage with his male family members and they say prayers over him in Arabic.

Alex and Sophie can't understand a word but they both sit and look around fascinated. Sophie leans over to him and says behind her hand, 'This is just *bizarre*. I can't believe we're in Congo, it feels like we're in Beirut.'

He meets her eye and nods. 'I know and I'm supposed to fighting a war, not having fun.'

The ceremony ends and a Lebanese band gets onto a platform at the back of the stage with small hand drums, reed clarinets and lutes and begins belting out dance numbers with a thudding beat, wailing pipes and vocals over the top.

Sophie grins and starts wobbling her head from side to side in a belly dancer imitation.

She pokes Alex. 'Come on, let's go!'

He holds his hands up defensively. 'Look, I just don't dance, OK?'

'Oh, come on!'

More cajoling has no effect so she mutters, 'God, you men are so *crap* sometimes,' and gets up and walks over to the stage. People join together in long chains with their arms around each other's shoulders and dance a *debke*, alternately sidestepping and then dipping down or kicking out their legs. The men get their worry beads out and whirl them around over their heads and the women ululate loudly.

Sophie looms over everyone in her heels but is welcomed into a line and makes a complete mess of the timing. Bilal's six-year-old daughter, Jamila, comes over in her white flouncy dress and tiara to help her and they stand at the side of the dance floor and practise.

Alex is enjoying himself on the terrace, eating baklava and sipping some excellent red wine when Jamila and Sophie grab him from behind. The six year old is not interested in excuses and two soft little hands get hold of his index fingers and pull hard. She says in French, 'Come on, mon Colonel, let's dance!'

He is dragged onto the dance floor and pushed into a line of dancers to much applause. After a while he actually gets the hang of it and can't help grinning from ear to ear. He is surrounded by people whirling worry beads over their heads, shouting out the lyrics to the song in Arabic with its heavy thudding rhythm and chaotic wail of pipes. His line passes Sophie's and he sees her head thrown back, her face flushed with laughter and alcohol, alternatively dipping down and kicking her long legs out with gusto.

Later that night, two very drunk, laughing guests wobble back down the lawn towards the helicopter, leaning on each other.

'What time d'ya call this then?' Col mutters coming out of the dark towards them.

Sophie is genuinely apologetic. 'Oh, S'arnt Major, thank you so much for staying up for us. You're such a sweetie,

335

we're so sorry.' She kisses him on the cheek and he can't maintain his anger any more but shrugs and looks at Alex.

'Sorry, matey, got a bit carried away in there. You know, business relationships . . .'

They clamber into the troop bay and Alex squeezes into a bucket seat next to Sophie, feeling her leg pressed against his.

Once they are back on the helipad Col rapidly dismisses the squad and hurries off to his barracks.

Alex walks Sophie back up to her bungalow and there is the obligatory awkward pause outside her front door.

'Oh, I've got your tie,' she remembers and unlocks her door. 'Come in.'

Chapter Forty-Three

Secretary of State Patricia Johnson has expensive blonde hair, shrewd eyes and a habit of holding her head high. She's in her mid-fifties but looks trim and energetic in her dark blue trouser suit.

Under Secretary of State John Ciacola looks at her across the huge desk in her office in the State Department building in Washington DC, hoping he's not going to get a grilling.

He doesn't subscribe to the usual male misogynist view of her as a ball-breaking, lesbian Communist – she may be a female Democrat but she's married to a former President and is always polite. However, he still can't get away from the feeling of sitting in his high school principal's office.

It's 22nd June and this is the first face-to-face meeting they've been able to have since the peace conference in Kivu finished on 7th June; they've both been travelling a lot. He knows that Johnson takes a very personal interest in Kivu because of the issue of sexual violence against women and has done a lot of work to secure the three UN resolutions against it. He also knows that things are not going according to plan in the province, but isn't sure how to break it to her.

Johnson has one hand resting on her desk and her large executive chair pushed back from it. She looks at him with her sharp blue eyes and says, 'So what's your feel for the guy, John?'

'Err, Rukuba is . . .' He takes a deep breath and sits back in his chair. 'It's hard to say really. He's very bright, he's very talented, speaks English, French, Swahili. He's very charismatic, a great performer – he played his role very well in the negotiations. He's just . . .'

'What?'

Ciacola pauses. 'He's just too clever, too charismatic. I can't put my finger on it, there's something about the way he can turn it on and off like a light. It's too controlled, too easy for him, almost like he's laughing at people.'

Johnson frowns. 'That sounds a little extreme, John.'

He shrugs. 'Yeah, you're right, maybe it is. I just don't know what makes this guy tick; I think that's what's bugging me. I mean, he has popped up out of nowhere, heading this Kivu People's Party which we know very little about. I've worked in a lot of failed states and the idea that you can have people in them who've been involved in politics for decades who are just squeaky-clean, apple-pie democrats is just naïve. I mean, look at Karzai.'

Her eyes narrow onto his. 'Our valued Afghan partner?'

'Well, yes, he talked a great show at the Berlin conference in 2001 when we went in, everybody loved him, spoke good English and was charming – but look what a corrupt scumbag he's turned out to be.'

She drops her eyes to her desk and refrains from passing comment on Ciacola's undiplomatic phrasing. She knows that he is right, Karzai has become a complete liability.

'The other guy Rukuba reminds me of is Karadzic.'

'Oh, come on, John, he's not a genocidal maniac.'

'No, but I worked with Karadzic in Yugoslavia. The guy was a blast, one of the funniest, most charismatic people I've ever met.'

'Hmm.'

Johnson looks out of the window at the neat green trees and lawns of the government district.

'OK, so that's the person – but what about his policies?'

'Well, that could go either way. Rukuba was careful to say all the right things to us about democracy but equally he didn't make any binding commitments. I mean, he has got the Chinese on his back the whole time and they sure as hell won't want to put that much money in and not have it directed by a one-party state.'

Johnson nods and Ciacola continues. 'He's got this policy of Kivuan nationalism that he says he wants to implement but again he didn't give any details.'

'I don't like the word nationalism.'

'No, neither do I, but maybe he just needs to build up a support base for himself against the Chinese so he can implement democracy against their wishes?'

'Maybe.'

'We'll just have to see how his national consultation exercise goes.'

'So what's your overall conclusion?'

'Well, I think I've been a bit too pessimistic really. To be fair, they have ended the FDLR reign of terror in the province and all armed groups have signed up to a peace deal that is actually working. So let's be positive about it – we have at last after decades of war got peace in the province.'

Johnson looks at him shrewdly. 'Just not the sort of peace that we want?'

Ciacola nods.

She folds her hands on the desk and looks at him fixedly. 'Well, John, it is up to us to make sure that we do get it.'

'Look, do you mind if I don't stay tonight? I just need to get some sleep.'

'No, that's fine, I know you're an old man.'

Sophie grins at Alex across the table. He's rubbing his eyes with one hand but manages to laugh.

It's 28th June and they have been seeing each other for a week now since Mr Fadoul's party. Sophie has just cooked dinner for them in her little bungalow. She looks at Alex across the remains of their dinner, lit by a candle stub in an old Primus beer bottle and thinks, 'God you look tired.' He has a greyish pallor and marks like bruises over his cheek-bones but somehow it is more attractive seeing him look vulnerable.

She gets up, pulls her chair round to his side of the table, puts her arm around him and rests her head on his shoulder. He leans his head on hers and they stay like that for a minute in silence.

He's been surprised at how affectionate she is; he's not very good at it himself but he likes it and enjoys her company. He always finds that women need to engage the gears of his mind before they turn his heart over and she has done that and mixed it up with a lot of irreverent humour. He's very fond of her and has a giddy feeling that a fun relationship is about to tip over into something more.

'I like your hands,' she says peering at them on the table. They are large but neatly proportioned with a sprinkling of black hair on the back.

'Hmm.'

'What did you do there?' She points at the little finger on his left hand, half of which is missing. He isn't going to tell her how he lost it in Russia and just mutters, 'DIY accident.'

Something in his voice doesn't sound right and she lifts her head from his shoulder and cranes round to look him in the eye. But he obviously doesn't want to talk about it and she is too tired to make an issue of it so she lets it go and puts her head back down.

'What are you doing tomorrow?' he asks after a while.

'Oh, those football goalposts that Mr Fadoul promised have arrived and I've got to get them sent out to the outstations.' She's working with Fang and other NGOs to set up a network of demilitarisation and training centres across the province. 'They'll be good for helping with outreach work, it all helps keeping the men out of trouble.'

As the militias are being disarmed the problem they are now facing is keeping the thousands of young men in the province occupied and getting them into jobs as fast as possible before they get into crime or start causing political trouble.

'What about you, what are you doing?'

'Um.' He has to think for a moment to remember; being with Sophie has become a delightful retreat from the pressures of his job.

'Urgh,' he groans as he remembers and then considers how much he ought to tell her. 'This is not for public distribution, OK?'

She nods her head on his shoulder.

'No, I'm serious.'

'Promise.'

He takes a deep breath and puffs his out cheeks. 'Well, we've got this stupid bloody argument going on between Fang and Rukuba at the moment and I'm in the middle of it.'

'What, about democracy?'

'No.' Alex shakes his head wearily. 'I think that that has fallen by the wayside.'

'Really?' She sits up and looks at him in alarm.

'Well, Rukuba says he's doing this national consultation exercise thing but when I asked him about it recently he basically said it was the national anthem competition . . .'

'Oh for God's sake.'

'Hmm, he says he's sort of communing with his people.'

'Oh, that's bollocks!'

Alex nods. 'Yes, I know, but what can I do about it? I'm not going to tell the blokes to go and arrest Rukuba, am I? And the Yanks are on my case again about it, Ciacola was on the phone today about Johnson's visit . . .'

'*She's coming here?* You didn't tell me!'

'Well,' Alex looks evasive, 'I did say this was not for public distribution. The American Secretary of State doesn't always like to advertise her movements around the world.'

'Hmm. When's she coming?'

'Sometime in mid-July . . .'

'What, in a couple of weeks?'

'Well, we're just trying to sort it out. The Yanks are being very tricky about security arrangements.'

'But the war's over, though?'

'Well, yes, we have pretty much finished the FDLR but we've still got a few remnants to mop up, plus the demil process and the Kudu Noir seem to be getting stronger for some reason.'

'And you still don't know who they are?'

Alex nods reluctantly. 'Hmm, Unit 17 doesn't seem to be able to tell me much about them.'

'What's Unit 17?'

Alex is forced into an evasion. 'They're a sort of

communication outfit that we have. All I can find out is that the Kudu Noir are some sort of cult cum criminal gang who go around kidnapping and killing albinos for magic powder.'

Sophie looks at him and pulls a face.

'Yeah, well, unfortunately now they seem to be expanding their operations. It's a bit like what happened in Iraq when criminal gangs took advantage of the lawlessness of the invasion to join up with Al Qaeda and start a huge kidnapping business. Most of the insurgency ended up being paid for by them.

'So now the Kudu Noir seem to be getting into political assassinations. We've had four incidents of them attacking and killing politicians across the province. Very messy business, they tortured and mutilated all of them before they died.'

He refrains from going into the details. KDF troops took crime scene photos of the bodies hanging from trees and they are images he has been trying to forget.

'Oh God,' she says, shocked, and then, 'Why did they do it? Were there any obvious connections between the victims?'

'Not really. A priest, a mayor, a local headman and a *comptoir*.' He shrugs. 'Mordechai can't see any pattern to it and neither can I. Someone must be ordering the hits, they're not random, but we don't know who or why.'

She strokes his hand for a while and then he pulls her gently onto his lap. She wraps her arms round him and strokes his hair whilst he rubs her back.

After a while she remembers where they started. 'So, what did you say about Fang and Rukuba arguing?'

'Well, I need to start renewing the contracts for the regiment or getting new guys in pretty soon. I mean, where are we now? Late June and we are due to expire in August. If we want to re-lease the choppers then Arkady needs to get on with it. If we don't have them we can't do anything – we can't move, we don't have any trucks, we're airmobile, that's the whole point of how we work.'

She nods. 'What does Fang say?'

'Well, they want to keep the regiment on because they don't trust the local Congolese troops to run the show but Rukuba is pushing his Kivu nationalism agenda, all that "Kivu has stood up" stuff.'

He stops rubbing her back and looks at her straight. 'So basically at the moment the fight is that we have the guns, the Chinese have the money, Rukuba has political authority and no one has a clue how it is going to work out.'

Chapter Forty-Four

Joseph and Simon are bursting with excitement as the bus winds up the road towards Rukuba's base at Mukungu.

'Look, KPP!' Simon shouts and the whole crowd of forty young men pack over to one side of the vehicle, slide back the windows and yell and wave at more young men on the roadside who jog on the spot and wave dark green and red Kivu flags as they pass.

The bus driver toots his horn repeatedly and Joseph sticks his head out of the window, waves a victory sign to them and yells 'Kivu for the Kivuans!' in Swahili. He nearly falls out but Simon drags him back by his belt.

It's Friday night and the 30th of June, which means two things: the final of Kivu National Anthem Idol and the declaration of their independence from Congo. They drive past more bands of young men and some women from the KPP youth wing as they come out of the accommodation tents and huts that were built for the peace conference.

Hundreds of people are streaming up the valley towards the farmstead, all wearing dark green and red KPP tee shirts and waving the Kivu flag over their heads. In the dark the lights of trucks and buses glare as they bring supporters in from across the province.

Gabriel is at the front of the coach. He's ecstatic at how

excited his newly released detainees have become about the whole event. It's great to see how the whole country is really pulling together.

The bus pulls over and parks in a newly made car park. They get out and Gabriel just manages to keep the group together as they push their way through the crowds on the road.

When they reach the area that used to be the meadow in front of the farm Gabriel simply stares at how it has been transformed. It is a natural amphitheatre and has terraces cut into its sides for people to stand on. The area down the hill from the farm has been turned into a stage with a massive lighting rig. The Lebanese company organising the show have thrown every special effect that they have at it and big searchlights are mounted on the hills all around the bowl, their beams crisscrossing and flashing overhead in the night sky.

Gabriel leads the group onto a terrace where they have a good view out over the scene. A huge sound system booms with the theme tune of the idol show and the whole crowd screams. The compère does an especially long build-up. 'Who do we want to see!'

'Papa Rukuba!'

'Yes! *Dieu-donn-é!*'

He holds his mike out to the crowd who scream the response, '*Don de dieu!*'

After a lot of hyping up the theme music builds and the lights suddenly cut out. The starry night sky is suddenly all that can be seen and a huge shout goes up from the crowd. There's a chill in the air because of the altitude and steam shows in the starlight, rising up off the crowd packed in front of the stage.

Joseph, Simon and Gabriel and the others all stare up at

the darkened hill above the stage. There is a pause and then a single powerful spotlight shoots out from behind them and picks out a figure in blazing white robes standing on the top of it holding two large tablets in his hands.

The crowd gasps and the figure strides down the hillside. As he comes, portentous music builds up until Rukuba finally strides onto the stage and the full light display bursts out flooding the amphitheatre.

Joseph and the crowd go mad, jumping up and down and shouting his name.

Twenty miles away in the operations room in Heaven, Alex, Sophie, Yamba, Col, Zacheus and Mordechai all look at the radio, alarmed at the amount of noise coming out of it.

'Bludy 'ell, what's going on there?' mutters Col.

Zacheus translates the Swahili for them and as ever keeps his face impassive but the heightened atmosphere is obvious.

Eventually the screaming dies down and Rukuba starts his usual smooth running of the show. He welcomes the four finalists, including Diamante, on stage, along with the special guest for the night, another big dance band, this time from Kenya. Each contestant walks up a big ramp with silver confetti blowers spewing on either side of them. KPP stewards and Unit 17 men strain to hold the crowds back.

Voting continues furiously by phone throughout the evening. Joseph and Simon both now have mobile phones and vote repeatedly after Diamante does her piece again.

Rukuba goes easy on the politics this time with no searing interviews of people whose lives have been transformed by his coming to power. He just lets the party build and the crowd dances and cheers as the evening nears its climax.

He is a master of oratory, changing the tone of his voice from a deep empathetic rumble to a high indignant squawk

347

as he needs to. He is in complete symbiosis with the crowd, using the call and response technique so his interaction with them becomes like a swaying back and forth of a couple in a dance.

Finally the contestants all line up, holding hands and looking tearful in front of the huge computer display screen. After a protracted build Rukuba announces that Diamante has won and Joseph nearly rips his vocal chords yelling for her.

She runs through another reprise of her song and the whole crowd joins in, swaying along to the lyrics, tears pouring down their cheeks.

Rukuba comes onto the stage and hugs her, holding both their hands up in the air before striding across the stage and taking his place at a large podium that rises up out of it for his speech to mark independence.

'People of Kivu! My people!' He quietens the crowd. 'On this day, we have come together to sing, to celebrate and to salute! To salute the new force in world politics, the new type of country that will lead the world to progress! We are that country – we are Kivu! No longer divided by our tribes but united in Kivu!'

A big cheer goes up from the crowd.

'Kivu is doing this, my brothers and sisters, Kivu is leading the world! I have been listening to you over the last weeks, I have been hearing your voices, hundreds of your voices.'

Zacheus translates rapidly and around the radio set Alex and the others share a worried look.

'And you have been telling me what you want.'

A lone voice right in front of him in the crowd shouts, 'Rukuba!' and he pauses and smiles indulgently.

'You have been telling me what sort of system of government you want for your new country *and that system of government is me!*'

A massive roar erupts across the stadium and is echoed throughout the province, with people cheering in the bars and streets.

Alex and the others just look grave.

'And so, I will lead your new government, I will announce them now!'

A steward brings him the large white tablets that he brought down the hill at the start of the evening and he reads off the names of his new cabinet. As he does so the ministers cross the stage and one by one shake his hand, then move to stand in a line behind his podium. The crowd cheers each one.

'Tonight is our independence night. For too long Kivu has lived on her knees, but now Kivu has stood up! It will stand on its own two feet and be a free and independent Kivu. Right now I am declaring our independence from Congo, not just for ninety-nine years but for ever!'

More cheering.

'I am ordering all remaining UN forces to leave the country immediately and all other foreign forces will follow shortly. Soon we will achieve full recognition in the United Nations as an independent and sovereign country, we will be masters of our own destiny! And so on this night, as the world sleeps, Kivu awakes!'

Again the crowd erupts and a huge burst of lights and fireworks explodes over them.

Chapter Forty-Five

The helicopter skims low over Lake Kivu. It disappears behind a grey curtain of drifting rain and then re-emerges.

Alex watches it alternately blur and then reappear as the windscreen wipers on his Peugeot jeep struggle to keep up with the downpour. Even in the dry season these storms blow up fast on the lake and create deluges across the province. The rain drums on the tarpaulin cover of the jeep. They got it off the local Congolese army – Fang won't pay for trucks for the regiment.

Fang radioed him urgently from a meeting he was having in Goma with the directors of the Kivu Investment Fund. It's 1st July, the day after Rukuba's big independence day announcement.

The green Mi-17 settles down on its pad next to the other nine Mi-17s and the two Mi-24s. All are grounded because of the weather and look forlorn with their drooping rotors tied down against the wind. Alex only agreed to let one go and pick up Fang because he sounded so worried on the radio. He's flying on to see Rukuba at Mukungu after this meeting with Alex.

The chopper waddles down onto its wheels and then sinks onto the pad. The ramp descends and Fang runs out and peers around him in the spray and rain. Alex flashes the jeep lights at him and he runs over and yanks open the passenger door. He crams his long legs into the front seat and slams the door, gasping and wiping the rain off his face. Streams of water run out of his hair and the windows steam up.

'So . . .' He shakes his head and collects himself, pushing his hair up off his forehead.

Alex turns in his seat and looks at him closely. It's the first time he has seen Fang look flustered. The overwhelming confidence in his great new vision for the world that so impressed Alex in Akerley has gone. There's a frightened edge in his voice.

'So, we have had a meeting of the fund board to discuss the President's announcement last night and the directors are not satisfied with the situation.'

That much was obvious already so Alex simply listens. After the broadcast last night ended, he and his senior commanders had a very tense conference about what might happen next.

Fang tries to keep his language diplomatic to preserve a semblance of control. 'The President has overstepped the terms of the contract in several ways. By scrapping the lease agreement – we have already had complaints from Kinshasa about that this morning – and by ordering all remaining UN forces to leave immediately. That timescale had not been agreed by the board.'

Alex agrees. 'Sure, but those are side issues, aren't they? It's the KDF that is the issue and he's ordered all foreign troops out shortly. What has he said to you about us?'

Fang cannot stay diplomatic and throws his hands up with an exasperated expletive in Chinese. He shakes his head. 'Nothing! He told us nothing!'

Alex takes a deep breath and thinks for a moment. 'OK, well, look, we just have to keep calm and work this one through. I think maybe he's got a bit overexcited with all the anthem hype and we just need to let the situation settle. Let's not do anything to up the ante.'

Fang is in no mood to be mollified. 'No! He needs to remember who is paying for this new country! It is not *his* country, it is *our* country! This is a joint project; we have not put *six billion dollars* into this to have him steal it!'

Alex nods, trying to allow Fang the opportunity to get his anger out of his system before he goes on to see Rukuba. This is developing into a nightmare.

'He has really fucked up! We had the UN on the phone all morning complaining, they say they have to go if he tells them to but they are not happy about it. And . . .' he remembers the worst bit '. . . Johnson's staff called and says that she is very concerned about the events and doesn't want to see the chance for peace slip away so she is bringing forward her visit to the province to see Rukuba in person and seek assurances from him.'

'*Bloody hell.*' Alex rests his forehead in his hand. 'When's she coming?'

'Next week, 7th July. They will be contacting you shortly about security.'

Alex takes a deep breath and thinks.

Eventually he says, 'OK, look, see Rukuba today and just settle things down. We have to present a calm front as far as the outside world is concerned. If we start telling people that the situation is out of control then Rukuba might do something rash and it *will* get out of control.

'We just need time to talk and all get back on the same page. Johnson can have her visit, Rukuba will be charming and she'll go away and we can get back to the job. He needs your money as much as you need him. I'm sure this will all blow over.'

Fang has one last outburst and jabs his finger at him. 'Yeah, and we need your guns and we pay your salary so you do what we say, OK!'

The President of the United States, Asani Jaafar, looks at his Secretary of State. 'Patricia, I am not saying you can't go, I am just saying that we need to think carefully about it.'

He always makes sure he uses her full name; he tried 'Patti' once when they were running against each other for the Democratic nomination and it didn't go down well. She's a determined character and that's why he invited her inside his government rather than have her causing trouble outside it.

He turns on some of his famous charm and smiles warmly at her. She doesn't look happy but presses her lips together and refrains from saying whatever it was she was about to say. It's 2nd July, two days after Rukuba's independence day speech and they are discussing US policy towards the new state.

The cause of her annoyance is sitting across the table from her in the Oval Office. Admiral Harry Kruger is the Chairman of the Joint Chiefs of Staff, the senior military officer in the United States. He has white hair, wears a black admiral's uniform and has a heavy-featured face with a belligerent look to it. He is super-smart, top in his year at Annapolis, and not very good at hiding it.

Kruger chips in. 'What I'm saying is, why can't we send John?'

He looks at John Ciacola who drops his gaze; he doesn't want to become the reason why his boss doesn't get to go on the trip that she has set her heart on.

Patricia Johnson slowly places her hand on the table and speaks in a very measured tone to the admiral. 'John has conducted the first phase of negotiations admirably, he has laid the groundwork very well for US relations with the Rukuba administration. But what we saw in Rukaba's independence day speech was a worrying shift in policy towards exactly the sort of government system that we don't want being advertised to the world.'

She is really sincere about this and drops some of the control in her voice and levels with him. 'Harry, if we look at this in terms of the long-term rise and fall of great powers, we know that the American democratic social model is under threat from Chinese managed capitalism. However, the situation at the moment in Kivu is very fluid; it is not a done deal. Rukuba is finding his feet and I believe that with a personal visit from me I can swing that balance.

'At the end of the day, I do *not* want Kivu to go down in history as the turning point when we went eyeball to eyeball with the Chinese way of doing things and blinked. Not on my watch!'

This rare display of passion from such a controlled person has an impact on Kruger and he actually stops himself from saying what he was about to say. He shuffles in his chair and clears his throat. 'OK, well, I am merely contending that I am not confident from a military standpoint that we should approve the visit because we can't cover you militarily. Our nearest fast air assets are with the Fifth Fleet in Bahrain, which is over two thousand miles away – i.e. they are ineffective. We have Combined Task Force 151 off the coast of Somalia but that is an anti-piracy operation and has only got helicopters. Otherwise I've got two Spectre gunships and some Rangers in Kenya but again that's eight hundred miles away. The only thing that I can get there real quick would be cruise missiles from the USS *Gettysburg* with CTF 151.'

Johnson looks at him firmly and says, 'Harry, we are not going to be conducting United States diplomacy in the Great Lakes region with cruise missiles.'

Kruger cannot resist getting in a fact. 'Well, a certain President fired them at a target in Sudan just north of that area in 1998.'

Johnson's blue eyes fix him with a piercing stare. 'Harry, my husband's actions are his own business. I am currently Secretary of State and I do not view cruise missiles as acceptable instruments of diplomacy.'

The President intervenes at this point. 'OK, folks, let's just keep our eye on the ball here. Harry, you have made your point very clearly and I thank you for that, I hear what you say. On balance I think Patricia is right. I think this is a key moment and that the personal touch could make all the difference. I accept that it is a volatile situation but, Patricia, I want to thank you for your courage in volunteering to go to Kivu.'

Chapter Forty-Six

Sophie turns and looks out of the rear window of the Land Cruiser.

'Quick, we've got to turn round!'

Her driver, Nicolas, checks his rear mirror. 'We can't, there's a truck behind us. Don't worry, it'll be fine, it's just people getting excited, it's not a bad atmosphere yet.' He is as calm and softly spoken as ever; he has lived through a great deal in Kivu and tends not to panic.

'But they're burning tyres!'

He doesn't reply, instead concentrating on steering the Land Cruiser round a barricade of broken lumps of concrete and branches that have been pulled off nearby trees.

It's 5th July and the Secretary of State is visiting the province in two days' time but for Sophie work goes on as normal. It's late afternoon and they're coming back from a trip down south to a remote outstation near Mwenga, driving back into Bukavu. They have to go through the town to get back to the N2 road along Lake Kivu.

The traffic has had to slow down, and with trucks in front of them and behind them they can't see who is causing the blockage, although they can see the smoke from burning tyres drifting over the shantytown shacks on the edge of town.

They inch along in the traffic jam and hear the sound of singing and shouting up ahead. They come onto the straight road that runs down the hill into the town and Sophie sees a large crowd on an area of waste ground next to the road. There are men and women all singing, jogging on the spot and waving Kivu and KPP flags. A makeshift stage has been put up and someone is standing up on it leading them in a song.

Sophie quickly locks her door and Nicolas does the same. The crowd is spilling across the road and she can see that there are a lot of young men in it stripped to the waist, their muscled torsos running with sweat as they jog and sing. Many have Kivu flags but she also sees machetes being brandished aloft, flashing in the sun. A lot of the men are drunk and wave plastic bottles of home-brewed beer. As they get nearer she sees that many of them are former Congolese army soldiers, their green shirts undone, brandishing their assault rifles over their heads. In the centre of the crowd she glimpses a group of men with black cloth hoods on their heads with eyeholes cut in them, dancing and singing with the others.

As they inch past, the crowd presses up against the car and a young man sees her, yells something, grins and starts banging on her window. His face is pressed up against the glass right next to her head and his eyes are bloodshot with booze. His friends all join in and start banging on the car windows and pulling at the door handles; they are happy and shouting but the effect is terrifying. The car is completely surrounded by the mob.

'Keep your head down, don't make eye contact,' Nicolas says tersely and Sophie forces her chin down onto her chest.

'Jesus, Jesus, Jesus,' she finds herself muttering in panic.

The mob starts rocking the car from side to side and

Sophie and Nicolas are thrown about. She clings onto her seat, her knuckles white at its edges.

Nicolas can't make any headway with the buffeting and the traffic stops dead. The large truck behind them suddenly sounds its powerful horn and the noise blasts through the car.

The young men all give a huge roar in response to the horn, let go of the car and rush behind them to the truck and start banging on that and climbing up onto it. One gets on the roof and waves a Kivu flag shouting '*Dieu-donn-é!*'

'*Don de dieu!*' comes the response from the crowd.

Nicolas takes his chance and drives away fast.

The American Special Forces major continues going through his tick list with Alex.

'OK, now let's talk about proximity to medical facilities and standards of care available. Where is the nearest facility to Mukungu, are there facilities on site?'

Alex groans internally: this list of questions has been going on for an hour now with no end in sight. He admires the American's professionalism but its humourless and unremitting nature is getting to him. It's 5th July and Patricia Johnson is arriving in two days' time.

He forces himself to give a professional response, keen to reassure the Americans that he is in control of the situation.

'OK, well, there is a first aid station at Mukungu and I can supply a combat medical emergency response team that can deal with any critical injuries and stabilise them. What we would do then is fly any casualties back to the medical centre here in Camp Heaven, where we can do major surgery in the field hospital.'

Major Frank Reilly makes a note on his clipboard and the

three Secret Service men around the ops room birdtable do likewise. Reilly is a Delta Force major whose lean face, neat grey hair and reserved expression are strangely at odds with the strong physical presence of his six-foot-two, muscle-bound physique. Like the Secret Service men he is wearing civilian clothes but exudes military precision.

He senses Alex's frustration, puts down the clipboard on the map table and looks at him calmly. 'Colonel Devereux, I apologise for all this bullshit but we have a job to do. It is our responsibility to ensure the Secretary of State's safe arrival and departure from this meeting. We may be the world's military superpower but in Africa our resources are pretty thin on the ground. We can't even find a country that will host Africom command centre so we need your cooperation.'

Alex nods and smiles, acknowledging his attempt to improve the atmosphere. 'Yes, running operations from a bunker in Germany isn't really going to help.'

'Well, exactly.' Reilly pauses. 'Colonel, can I level with you?'

'Sure.'

'I've done two tours in Iraq and two in Afghanistan and seen a lot of things. I have to say that my combat indicator lights are going red when I look at this scenario.'

'Well, I think you are being overly hasty there, Major. I know there have been some changes of plan but overall the situation is stable. The KDF is in complete military control of the province, the FDLR is finished, the militias are being disarmed, our choppers can get anywhere in a short space of time. I can assure you that the Secretary of State will be completely safe.'

'Hmm. OK, Colonel, I will take your word for that.'

The meeting goes on for another hour and finally Reilly sums up the plan. 'OK, so the Secretary flies into Goma airport on July 7th at 15.00 hours. Five KDF Mi-17s will rendezvous with her on the tarmac and take her and her security detail and entourage straight up to see President Rukuba at Mukungu. Unit 17 presidential bodyguards and KPP staff will ensure safety on site' – Rukuba has barred Alex from sending any First Regiment troops there – 'and you will maintain a First Regiment rapid reaction force here at Camp Heaven capable of deploying to Mukungu inside of ten minutes. You will keep your Heron surveillance drone overhead throughout the Secretary's visit to check for the approach of any outside hostile forces.'

Alex nods. 'Correct.'

'OK, so as we agreed we'll send in a beefed up Special Forces protection team with the Secretary but we are depending on you for the choppers and to guarantee overall theatre security.'

Alex folds his arms across his chest and looks back at him resolutely. 'Absolutely, Major, I give you my word.'

Later that day Alex sits on a chair talking to Rukuba in his hammock, where he seems to spend more and more time, looking out over the hills of Kivu and brooding.

'Mr President, I have to tell you that I am very concerned about the security situation now.' Alex has stopped calling him Dieudonné as he used to and only uses his title now.

Rukuba looks at him with lowered eyelids and a blank expression but says nothing.

Alex presses on. 'We have to make sure that the whole project continues to be a success for Kivu and for that we need to maintain the partnership that has worked so well this far.'

Again no response, just the distant look.

'In terms of First Regiment I have to balance my

responsibilities to you as head of state and to the Kivu Investment Fund as the financial backers behind the project.'

Alex takes a deep breath. 'In order to get the contracts paid for my men at the end of the tour I need to make sure that I maintain good relations with the fund, who have indicated that they want me to start to recruit men for a new tour after August. Now I realise that that puts me at odds with the statement you made in your address about the withdrawal of foreign forces . . .'

'*And my statement stands!*'

Rukuba whips his legs off the hammock, swings round and points a long finger at Alex in one flash. His eyes stare at the mercenary as he continues in a vicious tone, 'Don't come up to my farm, in my country and lecture me, Colonel! You and the fund might think that you can run this country without me but you cannot. I am Kivu!' He thumps his chest. 'Kivu is me! We are inseparable.'

Alex drops his gaze and doesn't try to say anything; he has made his point but the President is not in the mood to hear it.

'Mr President, I respect your wishes and I am sure that we can continue to make Kivu a success.'

He needs to get away from the whole issue of political control of the military. 'And with that in mind, I am continuing to make preparations for the visit of the Secretary of State in two days' time.'

Rukuba sits back in the hammock and stops glaring at him.

'I will ensure the safe arrival of the Secretary of State at Mukungu from Goma airport and will keep a standby force ready to deploy here in minutes from Heaven . . .'

Rukuba cuts in more mildly this time with another finger pointing at him. 'But my Unit 17 bodyguards and KPP workers will ensure security when they are on my land.' He waves his hand around him to indicate the farm.

'Yes, Mr President.'

The awkward meeting closes and Alex makes his way back down the hill to the car park where his helicopter is waiting. As he approaches it, he sees a large crowd of KPP youth wing members near it, staring at him with hostile expressions.

He ignores them, walks up the ramp and lifts off.

Rukuba watches him go from his hammock at the top of the hill.

Chapter Forty-Seven

Sophie is sitting on Alex's lap after dinner. He has just got back from seeing Rukuba and she from her harrowing journey through Bukavu.

'It was terrible, I was sure we were going to die. All those men shoving their faces in the window and banging on it.' She buries her face in his neck and he hugs her tight.

'It just went on and on,' Sophie mutters into his neck.

'Uh-huh.' He strokes her back and listens as she recounts her journey through Bukavu.

'I've never seen a crowd that whipped up before. The atmosphere was so hyped, I mean, we got through just but I had this feeling that we were going to die . . .' She sits up and looks at him and he nods.

She puts her head back down and they stay still for a while.

'I'm sorry I wasn't there, I feel terrible.'

''s OK,' she mumbles into his chest and then adds more clearly, 'I've had to put our alert status up to Condition Delta now, though. All the NGOs have recalled their staff to base and we're all locked down.'

'Hmm, that's sensible, things are bad. We just need to get through this visit and they'll get better.' He pauses and then says cautiously, 'I went to see him this afternoon.'

'And how was that?' she whispers.

'Not great.'

'What was he like?'

Alex takes a deep breath. 'Very touchy, very volatile. Didn't really want to hear what I had to say about having to do what the Chinese want.' He shakes his head. 'I'm sure that seeing Johnson will be good for him. I mean, he will get the biggest ego massage he has ever had, having the Secretary of State from the most powerful country in the world fly out especially to a two-bit province like Kivu.

'It's got to have some effect on him. She might not be able to persuade him to be democratic but at least he will see that he's got to cooperate with people, he can't just do the whole thing on his own, this Kivu nationalist crap has just got way out of hand. I think he's just gone off on an ego trip for a bit and needs to calm down, I think she will make him do that.'

Sophie nods; she's too shaken up to make much sense of things. She remembers something else, and sits up on his lap and looks at him. 'There was something Nicolas said on the way back here that really worried me.'

'Like what?'

'He said that he'd been listening to the radio in different parts of the province when he's been out visiting stations and he's heard these new radio stations on air.'

'Uh huh?'

'Well, he said they aren't in Swahili or French – they're in local tribal languages so he couldn't understand much of them.'

'What, you mean commercial stations?'

'No, he said they were definitely new KPP stations and they are broadcasting a lot. Most of the time he couldn't understand them but then he was in a Hunde area and he speaks that.'

'What did they say?'

'Really strong Kivu nationalist stuff – Kivu for the Kivuans, no foreigners will tell us how to live our lives all the time, and talking about the need to be organised and strong. What really scared me was that he said it reminded him of the hate radio like they had in Rwanda before the genocide broke out.'

Alex takes a deep breath. 'Shit.'

There's a long pause and then he mutters, 'We just need to get her in to see him and talk some sense to him, I can't do it. It's only the day after tomorrow. We've just got to hang on and keep our nerve.'

'Hmm.' She sits and strokes his hair, kisses the top of his head and whispers, 'Stay tonight.'

Alex is up early the next day, 6th July, and has gone for his run before Sophie surfaces. He showers in his quarters afterwards and gets dressed. It's going to be a busy day finalising arrangements for Johnson's visit tomorrow.

He spends the day in the ops room with the usual planning team, finalising details and briefing the crews who will fly the five helicopters to pick up the Americans from the airport.

Zacheus is the only person left from Unit 17 in the ops room these days; their other staff have all been withdrawn to Mukungu by Rukuba to work there. The major is as hard to read as ever but continues to do his job professionally, liaising with the Unit 17 presidential bodyguard and confirming they are ready to receive Johnson.

They get everything sorted out in good time and Alex is able to leave at a reasonable hour and go back to Sophie's. He feels awful about not being able to protect her in Bukavu yesterday and is going to cook for her tonight as a way of making up for it.

He picks up a bag of food from the mess tent and walks over to her bungalow. It's just gone six but it's dark already and her light is on. He knocks and enters.

'Hi,' he says cheerfully.

She's sitting at her desk against the wall with her back to him, her legs pulled up and her arms wrapped around them, staring at her laptop. She often sits there for hours working on things and he knows not to disturb her until she's finished.

He goes through and dumps the bag in the galley kitchen, gets a beer out of the fridge and comes back in.

Something about her rigid posture worries him. 'Sophie?'

She still doesn't respond and he comes up behind her to see what she is working on: it's just a page from YouTube.

He puts his hand on her shoulder and she flinches away from him, gets up and walks across to the table and sits down on a chair. He sees that she's been crying and he stands open-mouthed looking at her, beer bottle held awkwardly in one hand.

'Hey, what's . . .?'

She covers her eyes, refusing to look at him, and points to the laptop.

He looks at her and thinks, 'What the hell is going on?'

She curls up again on the chair and so he walks over to her desk, puts the beer down and looks more closely at the screen.

The title of the YouTube video is: 'Kivu war crime ordered by mercenary thug Colonel Devereux.'

Shit.

Alex sits down and taps the play button.

A shaky handheld video camera film starts. It swings round a steep-sided valley and pans over a bridge of girders, some of which have been blown off and sag drunkenly over a fast-flowing river.

He stares at it fixedly.

The view moves from a panning shot and looks down at the ground. For a hundred yards in front of it all that

366

can be seen are burnt bodies. The camera zooms in on them: blackened teeth are visible in a skull, rib cages stand out of the congealed mess, bodies are fused together by the heat.

The camera walks over the bodies and the screen fills with blackened corpses for a minute, a pair of black welly boots walking at the bottom of the screen the only thing breaking the view.

The shot cuts to another of men in civilian clothes wearing white facemasks as they go about picking up the bodies, loading them onto stretchers and dumping them in the river. The men call the camera over and it looks down at a row of twelve bodies laid out on the riverbank. They are blackened and distorted but it is obvious from their size that they can only be children and babies. The camera focuses in shakily on one of them and when the auto focus clears the screen it shows a tiny curled and blackened hand.

Alex hits the stop button and looks in horror at the view counter: 23,687 hits.

He looks back at Sophie, who is still curled up hugging her knees.

What do I say? I love you and want to go to you but you won't even look at me.

Thoughts whirl in his head. Part of him screams with defensive rage at the injustice of it. He had to take that action or else all the gains would not have happened. It looks bad but it was a tactical military necessity with collateral damage.

He stops the thoughts dead, he knows none of it will be any good and just starts quietly, 'Sophie . . .'

'Don't speak!'

She still won't look up at him but her voice lashes him like a whip.

'Just leave,' she says more quietly.

Chapter Forty-Eight

Joseph stands laughing on the roof of the cab of a beer truck and shouts, 'Kivu for the Kivuans!' in Swahili and waves his new Kivu flag.

He looks down and sees the large crowd of KPP youth wing swarming around the Ngok brewery. They ran out of home-brewed beer by the end of yesterday's rally and someone yelled that they should nationalise the local breweries so today a crowd of several hundred young men formed up outside their accommodation block on the edge of Bukavu. The same number of former Congolese army troops joined them from the local barracks; they had a great time at the rally as well and are excited by the wave of nationalism sweeping the country. They have brought their rifles with them.

Gabriel tried to stop them going, shouting in vain at the men and boys he recruited. He's appalled at their indiscipline but they took no notice of him – the chanting and singing drowned him out as different groups set off to take over the main breweries: Primus, Ngok and Turbo King.

The Secretary of State is coming tomorrow and Joseph and the boys are driving up to Mukungu to welcome her there. They want to take some drinks and make a party of it. The workers at the brewery were terrified and ran off when they arrived and broke open the gates.

The trucks are loaded with crates of bottled beer; they'll have a great time. Youth wing groups are assembling in Goma and other towns to travel up to the farm complex by bus again. It'll be a blast, just like the independence day celebrations.

Someone gets into the cab and starts up the truck. The roof wobbles under Joseph's feet and he nearly falls off. His friend Simon is next to him and shoots a hand onto his shoulder to steady the two of them. He laughs and shoves a green bottle of Ngok with its crocodile emblem into Joseph's face. He giggles hysterically, points at the truck and shouts, 'Alamuki!' the slogan for the crocodile – 'He's awake!'

Joseph doubles up laughing and they crouch down and cling onto the radio aerial as the truck lurches forward and swings out of the brewery.

Alex comes out of Sophie's front door and stands for a minute looking out over the lake with an agonised expression on his face.

After a while he collects himself and turns to walk away towards the ops room. His head is in turmoil as personal pain and professional disaster wrangle with each other. The phrases 'war crime', 'mercenary thug' and then Sophie's sharp, 'Don't speak!' all fight inside his head. His whole body burns from her refusal to touch him.

He doesn't know which is worse: the rejection by the person he cares for, or the fact that thousands of people view him as a murderer, with more seeing the film every minute as that view counter on YouTube ticks up.

As an exile from his social class, his whole identity is built on his professional reputation and pride and now those same exacting standards are turning in on him and jabbing unforgiving goads into his soul. His body feels like a demolition site, full of jagged pieces of rubble, bits of sharp wire, shards of glass and pieces of dirt, every part of him is in pain.

As with Achilles, his fame has become his doom.

The action of walking helps him think and the sight of the ops tent up ahead forces some control over his emotions.

Just deal with the professional problem now and talk to Sophie later.

He makes himself put on a controlled expression and ducks through the flaps into the large tent. He calls Col and Yamba into his office, sits them down and gives them the bad news.

Col is outraged. 'That bastard's stitched us up!'

Yamba looks at him and then at Alex and nods. 'Who else can it be? It was KPP workers that cleared the site and obviously filmed it as evidence. Now we are in a political battle Rukuba's released it on the net as a smear campaign to discredit us.'

Alex nods. 'That was what I was thinking.' He is sickened by the duplicity of Rukuba's actions.

He looks up at his two old friends; he is heartened by the way they both talked about 'us' and not 'you'. He looks at them both and thinks, 'God, I'm glad I'm working with you. You would never let me down.'

'Thanks, guys,' he says.

They both shrug. Their loyalty is intrinsic; they didn't even think about it.

Yamba asks, 'So what are we going to do now?'

Alex starts thinking straight. 'Well, I suppose we have to draft some sort of rebuttal and get it out to the press. We'll have to think carefully about how we frame this, we can't release details of the Lubonga operation and we can't be seen to publicly blame Rukuba. We need to try and think what the Americans are going to . . .' He groans and rests

370

his forehead on his hand as he begins to realise the issues they have to deal with. 'God, what a fucking mess!'

There is a tap on the wooden panelling that screens them off from the ops room. 'Colonel?'

'Yes.'

'President Rukuba on the line for you, sir, says it's urgent.'

Alex looks quickly at Yamba and Col and then says, 'Right, put him through.'

The phone on his desks blares, sounding unnaturally harsh. He stares at it, composes himself and picks it up. 'Mr President.'

'Colonel Devereux, are you aware of a video that has recently been posted on YouTube? My communications staff have informed me of it this morning and I am very concerned.'

Alex is speechless at the polished delivery and wonders how to respond for a moment, he wants to shout at the man. He manages to keep in control and plays the game. 'I have seen the video and it is very unfortunate. It presents an entirely one-sided view of the Lubonga action. I am very concerned about how it has come to be released by the KPP now.'

'Colonel, don't start getting accusatory with me! The source of the film is neither here nor there, the point is that it shows that a major war crime has been committed here on the sacred soil of Kivu!'

Alex loses it. 'Look, we both know full well that that incident was collateral damage as part of a necessary military strike, not some war crime. You've known that for months but have released this video now as part of a smear campaign against First Regiment . . .'

'Colonel, I will not listen to these crazed ideas! You are suspended as commander of First Regiment pending a full investigation; I am issuing this executive order forthwith.

Major Douala will take control of Johnson's visit. Thank you, Colonel, goodbye.'

The line goes dead and Alex is left red-faced and raging. He slams down the phone.

'Bastard!'

'What d'e say?' asks Col.

'I am fucking well suspended pending a full investigation. Yamba, you're in charge apparently.'

Yamba shakes his head in disbelief.

Alex tries to get a grip on things. 'Right, let's just think what we've got to do.'

'We can draft that statement for the press at least,' says Yamba.

'Yes, good idea.' He pulls a pad out of his desk and they start trying to think how to go about rebutting the accusations and dealing with the suspension.

After an hour they have a good outline defence and Alex's BlackBerry chirrups on the desk next to him. He glances at it with irritation and sees a message from Sophie. Being with the others and having to deal with Rukuba had kept him occupied.

He snatches it up and reads the message: 'Alex, I've gone to Bahomba outstation on one of Bilal's helicopters. Please don't try to follow me, I need to get away and think.'

Shit.

His face betrays his distress.

'What's up?' Col asks quietly.

Alex takes a deep breath; they know about him and Sophie and how much he cares about her.

'It's Sophie, she showed me the video today.'

They both look grave as they imagine her response to it.

'She's gone to Bahomba outstation on one of Bilal's choppers.' Alex gets up. 'Where is Bahomba?'

He walks round the partition and goes over to the large map of the province laid out on the birdtable with little markers stuck on it for the location of different units and militias. He peers at it trying to think where Bahomba is; there are hundreds of little villages in the province and a lot of projects running. Col and Yamba join him but can't find it.

Eventually Alex calls over to Zacheus. 'Major Bizimani, where's Bahomba?'

Zacheus gets up from his desk and walks over. He thinks for a moment and then leans over the map. 'It's near Violo somewhere; it's a tiny place up in the hills. Why?'

'Sophie's gone there. We might need to get some security up to her.'

Col looks at Alex. 'Is that wise? I think she wants a bit of space, like.'

Alex thinks for a moment about their earlier exchange and feels at a loss. He nods. 'Yeah, you're right, let's finish this document.'

Chapter Forty-Nine

The Fadoul refinery on the outskirts of Goma is a large complex surrounded by a high chain-link fence. The corrugated-iron sheds where the tin, coltan and gold ores are sorted are painted a faded blue with the Fadoul Ishfaqi logo on them. On a flat area of ground behind them sit Mr Fadoul's two Mi-17 helicopters.

The refinery office building is next to a dusty and deserted street and screened from it by a high metal gate. It's early afternoon on 7th July, just before the Secretary of State is due to arrive at the nearby airport. Tensions are running high in the city – KPP youth wing members have been getting out of hand here in Goma as well, with former government troops joining them. Everything is locked down and no one is out on the streets.

A minivan with blacked-out windows pulls up quietly in front of the main gate and an officer in a Unit 17 uniform gets out and walks over to it. He knocks politely on the small metal door set into the large double gates and waits. A bearded Lebanese guard pulls open the hatch in the door and peers out at him.

'Yes?' he says warily.

'I need to speak urgently to Captain Mahmood Bashoor on an official matter.'

The guard eyes him for him a moment. He has camouflage combat trousers and a baggy green shirt belted in with a wide webbing belt but is unarmed. The guard thinks for a moment; refusing to deal with these guys usually just causes more hassle.

The hatch shuts and there is a scraping as bolts are drawn back and the officer steps through the gate. Then he pulls a silenced pistol from inside his baggy shirt and motions the guard up against the wall.

At the same time the side door of the minivan slides quietly back and six men wearing black cloth hoods and armed with machine pistols run silently up behind him and slip through the open door. They quickly gag and cuff the guard hand and foot and then move on rapidly into the buildings.

Patricia Johnson is flying into Goma in her specially configured US Air Force Boeing 757. She looks at John Ciacola who is sitting across a narrow desk from her in her office at the back of the aircraft.

'OK, so what is this Colonel Devereux's response to the allegations?'

Ciacola has been busy monitoring the internet in the communications office next door towards the front of the aircraft.

'He posted a statement on the KDF website yesterday denying any allegation of war crimes, saying it was collateral damage.'

'Well, he would say that, wouldn't he?'

'But the key thing is he isn't denying that he was in control of whatever military operation resulted in those pictures.'

Johnson nods; she has seen the footage and is sickened by the pictures of burnt babies. 'I cannot believe what sort

375

would do that.' She shakes her head. 'So let's be
here, we are not having anything to do with this guy
all on the visit, right?'

'Correct. I've been in touch with President Rukuba's office
and he assures me that he has suspended the colonel and
will investigate the allegations fully.'

'Hmm.'

She looks out of the window and can only see jungle and
hills, part of the fifteen-hundred-kilometre-wide green sea
that divides Kinshasa from Kivu.

'OK, can you make that clear to the press before we land?
I don't want us getting sucked into that mess by association,
we've got enough issues to deal with as it is.'

'Yes, ma'am.'

The plane descends into Goma, touches down on the
newly repaired runway just after 3 p.m. and taxis over to
one side of it, away from the airport terminal. There is a
pause as the steps are driven up and State Department staffers
hurry down and check that all the arrangements are in place.

Johnson looks out of her window again and sees the five
camouflage-painted Mi-17s lined up on the side of the apron
near the plane. She hates flying in helicopters but has had
to do a lot of it in her job and just forces herself to get
through it.

The three staffers walk over to Major Reilly on the tarmac
and confer with him. Around the helicopters are a group of
fifteen Delta Force soldiers toting a mixture of M4 carbines
with grenade launchers and M249 light machine guns.

Reilly isn't taking any chances.

Also talking to the group is a tall, serious-looking African
major and a white sergeant major with a moustache, both
dressed in smart uniforms and berets.

She walks out of her office, through the communications

376

and staff offices to the front section of the aircraft to talk to the press. She is always very careful to cultivate good relations with them and there has been a lot of coverage of the trip, with all thirty allocated press seats booked. The gangway is crowded with people as they get up and stretch after the long flight and pull laptop cases out of the overhead lockers.

She squeezes past them down the aisle. 'Hey, Bill, good to see you.' She shakes hands with Bill Jakowski of the *New York Times*. She's known him for years.

'Did you see my headline?'

'Yeah, I caught it on the website. Bit overdramatic, don't you think?'

Jakowski smiles. 'Well, we gotta sell papers, and besides when do I ever get a front page as Africa correspondent?'

She smiles and walks on. 'Hi, Carla, how are you, haven't seen you for ages.'

Carla Schmidt is CNN's roving danger woman reporter whom they send out on high-profile assignments. She's in her forties and looks tough and drawn. 'My editor thought this might be an interesting story and pulled me out of Afghanistan for it.'

Johnson is concerned what she might mean by 'interesting' but doesn't show it. She doesn't like Schmidt but admires her professionalism. They chat for a bit and then Johnson moves on down the gangway. All the main networks have sent reporters and camera crews and there are teams from Al Jazeera, the BBC and the other big international operations.

The press disembark first and their bulky cameras and satellite equipment are unloaded from the hold and carried over to helicopters along with the Johnson team's baggage and secure communications equipment. Finally, when everyone is on the choppers, Johnson comes down the steps, strolls over to them and they take off at 3.30 p.m.

Col and Yamba and a few KDF officers accompany them but the bulk of the room is needed for the Secretary's entourage. It's forty miles to Mukungu and they make the hop in twenty minutes, landing in the stadium area at the bottom of the hill. The large stage from the independence day celebration has been left up.

Johnson walks down the ramp with her hair shielded under a UN blue headscarf and is met by KPP staff. Unit 17 soldiers with rifles ring the bottom of the hill and Major Reilly eyes them warily through his mirrored Oakley shades. His experienced eyes also scan along the terraces on the hillside behind them; they are packed with KPP youth wing members who are jogging on the spot and singing and waving Kivu flags. Joseph is amongst them and stands on tiptoe to peer over the men and boys in front of him to get a glimpse of the Secretary of State. He waves his beer bottle over his head and roars a greeting.

Johnson looks round at the loud noise and smiles and waves; she is used to excited crowds wherever she goes in the world.

Major Reilly walks up next to Staff Sergeant Moretti, who is watching the crowd, holding his rifle across his chest with his finger on the trigger. 'Must be about five hundred,' he shouts over the noise of the crowd and the choppers.

'Yeah. Can't see any weapons but a lot have got beer bottles.'

'Yeah, I think they're just sightseeing at the moment.'

'All combat-age males, though, hardly any females.'

'Yeah.'

Yamba and Col hand over control of Johnson's

entourage to the Unit 17 bodyguards, get back into the choppers and take off for Camp Heaven at 4.00 p.m. Johnson and her team load up into a convoy of Land Cruisers and drive up the hill. Carla Schmidt, Bill Jakowski and the rest of the press stand around waiting to be picked up in a second run. There is a press briefing scheduled after the meeting.

At 4.10 p.m. Johnson and Ciacola are shown through the farmyard and greeted by Rukuba on the back veranda of the farmhouse. Standing in his white flowing robes and pointed sandals, Patricia thinks he looks like some sort of African mystic.

Rukuba is all smiles and charm. 'Secretary of State, how delightful to see you!'

She can see what Ciacola means about his charisma: it is like being hit by the beam of a heat lamp and she cannot but warm to it.

They pass through the house and out onto the lawn and she admires the view down the valley. 'Mr President, this is beautiful.'

'Well, I try to maintain a connection with the rural roots of my country. Please take a seat.' He gestures to a smart set of hardwood garden furniture that has replaced the white plastic chairs. Johnson and Ciacola sit and after tea is served and niceties observed, Johnson gets down to business.

'Mr President, as you know, I have a long-standing interest in Kivu and am very pleased with the progress that you have made in combating the FDLR and bringing peace to this country.'

Rukuba smiles and nods. 'You are very kind, my people appreciate the concern that you have shown for us.'

'Thank you. How do you see the future of your people developing from here?'

379

The smile continues unbroken. 'My policy of Kivu nationalism is overcoming tribal divisionism. We are confident, we are strong and we will succeed.'

He isn't making it easy for her to approach the key issue obliquely so she has to do it directly.

'Mr President, I listened to your independence day speech with great interest and I am keen to stress that the United States and our partners in the UN and the EU would all like to see that the wishes of the people of Kivu are reflected in their new government.'

Rukuba's smile is waning. 'Well, of course and they will be. I am in constant communication with the general will of my people through my radio broadcasts and am in daily touch with the ordinary people. It is a direct democracy as outlined by Rousseau, the founding father of liberalism.' Rukuba looks at her earnestly as if he cannot understand why she should be concerned about this.

Johnson is thrown for a moment and then sits forwards on her chair. 'OK, but what we are looking for in this scenario is a representational democracy with a choice of political parties.'

Rukuba shakes his head, his smile now gone and a very grave expression in its place. 'That will not be necessary. What you are talking about in Africa just produces sham democracies, like Congo, and ethnic divisionism. The people of Kivu have expressed confidence in me, and my system will work much better.'

Johnson is getting tired of what she sees as his clever wordplay. Her neck stiffens and she places her hand slowly and firmly on the table. 'Mr President, let me put this on the line for you. If a multi-party, representational democracy does not emerge in Kivu then the United States will be minded to veto any application for full nationhood in the

UN Security Council and I know I speak for my counterparts in the UK and France when I say this.'

Rukuba's face takes on a withdrawn look and his eyelids lower. Johnson feels a shiver, as if someone has switched off the heat lamp inside him.

There is a long silence.

Johnson looks at him and is about to ask if he is OK when he finally replies in a whisper, 'I will consider your proposals overnight and respond to you in the morning.'

With that he gets up and signals to the staff on the veranda who have been watching. He pulls his robes around him, looking pained, and then walks off round the side of the house without another word.

Ciacola checks his watch out of habit; it's 4.25 p.m. The meeting lasted all of fifteen minutes.

Chapter Fifty

Alex is pacing up and down in the ops tent, his arms folded across his chest and his head down. He decided it would be politic not to meet Johnson at the airport because of his new pariah status but is still very much in command of First Regiment; no one has even questioned his authority.

The atmosphere in the ops room is tense, with none of the usual chat. Everyone is listening in to the radio desk speaker as calls come through from Yamba in the helicopters as they pick up the entourage at Goma and then fly them to Mukungu.

'Black Hal, this is Loyola, departing Mukungu now and returning to Heaven. ETA ten minutes.' Yamba's callsign is from Ignatius Loyola, founder of the Jesuits, a former soldier whom he has always admired.

Alex confirms, 'Roger that, Loyola.'

Yamba and Col touch down at 4.10 p.m. and drive fast in a jeep over to the ops tent.

'How was it?' Alex asks as they duck in through the tent flaps.

Yamba nods. 'Fine, it all went smoothly. We just wait for the press conference this evening and then pick them up tomorrow morning.'

A soldier manning the satellite communications desk calls over to Alex, 'Satellite phone call for you, sir.'

'Who is it?'

'It's Miss Cecil-Black, sir, says it's urgent.'

Alex shoots a look at him. 'I'll take it in my office.'

He hurries into the sectioned-off area, his heart pounding. The phone on the desk blares and he grabs it. 'Sophie?'

'Alex, I'm scared.'

Her voice has an edge of barely controlled hysteria and she gabbles, 'They're making howling noises in the bush around the village here; I think it's the Kudu Noir. There's a few *mai-mai* troops in the village but they're as scared as I am. Alex, get here fast, please!'

'OK, OK. I'll scramble a chopper straightaway; I'm coming to get you. I'll bring a platoon and pull you out of there, OK?' He forces himself to think about the distances and flight time: it's seventy miles to Bahomba. 'We'll be thirty minutes, I promise you.' He glances at his watch – it's 4.30 p.m. and it gets dark at 6 p.m.

'OK, OK.' She is sobbing on the phone now. He hears a sound in the background and she cries in fear and sobs, '*Jesus!* Alex, they're close, please.'

He is torn momentarily between wanting to stay in communication with her and needing to leave immediately. He blurts out, 'Stay in the village. I love you, I'm coming!'

'OK, I love you too.'

'OK, bye.'

'Yes, bye.' Her voice sounds forlorn.

He hangs up and races round his desk and into the ops room.

'Yamba! I want you to stay here and hold the fort. She's got Kudu Noir approaching the village, I'm going out with a platoon to bring her back.'

'*Shit*,' mutters Col. 'Right, I'll come with you.'

Alex looks at him. 'Thanks. OK, let's go!'

They rush out, jump into the jeep and race down to the flight line.

Alex screeches to a halt. Jean-Baptiste looks up in alarm, he has never seen Alex look so hasty.

'Major Delacroix, I want a platoon in that chopper now! We're going to Bahomba.'

Jean-Baptiste nods. Echo Company are on standby as the rapid reaction force for Mukungu and there is a chopper next to them on the pad, fully fuelled and with its engine turning over ready to go. Its wipers flick back and forth as a rain squall comes in off the lake.

Jean-Baptiste bellows to his men, 'Two Platoon, load up now!'

Stein has been promoted to Sergeant after Matt Hooper's death and he in turn gets the men on their feet and they run over to the chopper.

Alex and Col both grab rifles, webbing and flak jackets off other soldiers waiting nearby and run up the ramp with Jean-Baptiste. The chopper roars, goes through a rapid liftoff, darts away west, rising steeply to clear the mountains overlooking the lake, and disappears into the rain clouds.

In the ops room Yamba rapidly takes charge of the situation, barking out orders and the well-oiled machine goes into action around him. 'Mordechai, get me satellite shots of Bahomba! And where's Major Bizimani?' He needs Zacheus's expertise on the local *mai-mai* group.

'He left about ten minutes ago, sir. He had a satellite call from President Rukuba and said he had to go and get something urgently.'

Chapter Fifty-One

Carla Schmidt and the other journalists are still waiting in the stadium to go up the hill to the farm when a Unit 17 officer with a walkie-talkie comes over to them.

'Press conference is cancelled.'

'*What?*'

'Press conference is cancelled,' he repeats. 'You must leave now.' He turns and shouts to the drivers of three dark green army trucks parked at the side of the bowl and waves them over.

The press pack is outraged that they haven't had their chance to put questions. 'Look, we've come all the way from the United States!' Bill Jakowski remonstrates with the officer who brushes him aside.

'Maybe the President will say something to you in the morning, but now you must leave for your quarters!' The officer points west towards a hilltop half a mile away, where there is a prefab camp put up to house the large Rwandan delegation during the peace conference.

The press don't like it and there is a lot of complaining but more Unit 17 men walk over and stand with their hands on their rifles across their chests, glowering at the journalists. The crowd of KPP youth wing members stop singing on the terraces as they see the altercation going on. They stare and some jump down and gather next to the trucks, pushing and shoving and trying to see what the argument is about. Murmurs of disapproval come from them as the journalists continue to argue with the soldiers as they are loaded onto the army trucks.

Carla Schmidt glances at the crowd and then mutters to her cameraman. 'Mike, this is not good.' He nods and quietly picks up his camera gear and swings up into the truck.

Once they are in, they can see Patricia Johnson's body-guards and staffers driving back down the hill in the convoy of Land Cruisers. Carla glimpses Johnson sitting in the front seat of one, looking stony-faced as she passes. The trucks follow them and they wind along a road through open land covered in waist-high grass, that dips down and then rises up again to the hilltop encampment.

The Rwandans were keen on their security and there's a high razor-wire fence around the collection of single-storey, white, rectangular prefab buildings. There is a good view from the hilltop all around them.

The cars and trucks drive through the gate into the compound and KPP staff come out. Again their mood appears sullen and hostile as they show people to their dormi-tories and escort Johnson to a separate building. The KPP staff get back into the trucks and Land Cruisers and drive off back to Rukuba's base, leaving the Americans in their isolated encampment.

Johnson dumps her briefcase down and looks at Ciacola and Major Reilly as they come in.

'Shit,' she says quietly. The men look shocked – it's the first time they have ever heard her swear.

She presses her knuckles against her mouth and stares at the floor thinking.

'OK, so what now?'

386

'Well, he says we resume talks in the morning when he's thought about . . .'

Reilly interrupts Ciacola. 'Secretary, I have been in a lot of tense public order situations in Iraq and I see combat indicators here, the atmosphere is not good. I recommend we call in the choppers and return to Goma.'

'And stay where? Or what, get back on the plane and leave?' Johnson snaps. 'We cannot just walk out of this one – if we do that it will blow the situation completely. Imagine what the press are gonna say.' She gestures towards the journalists' huts. 'Secretary of State has ten-minute meeting and runs for it. God, we'd look total asses! We'd be backing down in front of the Chinese, they'd laugh their heads off at us!'

Reilly nods, acknowledging the wider picture she has put to him. 'OK, well, I'll set up a security perimeter and secure our communications.'

'Thank you, Major.'

Reilly leaves and Johnson looks at Ciacola who just shakes his head.

'What is that noise?' Johnson cocks an ear back towards Mukungu and they both go outside and walk round the huts, looking back down the road towards the farm. Journalists and staffers are gathering there as well and they can all hear the sound of an amplified voice booming. They can't make out any words as it's distorted by the distance and is accompanied by the shouting of a crowd in response.

Major Reilly walks up next to Johnson and they both stand listening for a moment. An angry bellow comes from the PA system. The words are garbled but the tone is clear.

Johnson's face stiffens and she goes pale.

She turns to Reilly. 'Major, I think you are right, I think we do need to extract – get the choppers back here now.'

* * *

Zacheus is in such a hurry he nearly misses the turning. He brakes the Peugeot jeep hard and then swings left off the N2 main road along the edge of Lake Kivu up the steep track into the mountains.

The jeep bounces on the rough surface and the engine roars as he revs it hard and forces it up the gradient. He hasn't got long.

After three hundred feet the track levels out and he drives parallel to the lake for a minute before he sees the back of the battered old truck in a copse of trees. He's radioed ahead and they've had the GPS coordinates for weeks now so they should be ready to go.

He brakes hard again and the jeep skids to a halt on the mud. Unit 17 soldiers emerge from the trees on either side of the road with rifles and beckon him forward. He runs around to the truck's cab. It's pointing south towards Camp Heaven, three miles away, easily in range.

He talks briefly with the artillery officer and then jumps up onto the back of the lorry to inspect the forty long barrels that are raised and swung out slightly to the left of the truck body.

He jumps down and then grabs the command console on its long wire and they all run fifty yards in front of the truck and take cover on the side of the track.

Under his expressionless exterior, Zacheus has long been a member of the Kudu Noir with its links through the charcoal burners to the KPP and President Rukuba. He has been passing on information from First Regiment's ops room ever since operations started.

He rests the command panel on his knee, casts one last quick glance at the BM-21 launcher and then looks towards Camp Heaven.

Chapter Fifty-Two

Joseph and the crowd of young men watch the American convoy drive away towards their camp and then turn and watch a pickup truck full of Unit 17 men driving fast down the road from the farm.

It bounces across the little bridge over the stream at the bottom of the hill and then the troops jump out in front of the crowd. An officer yells at them through a loudhailer, 'Go to the stage now, the President will address you!'

The men all cheer and run over to the stage waving their beer bottles. They are all drunk by now and Joseph and Simon race each other to get to the front. They look up at the farm with its Kivu flag flying, the symbol of their new identity that has given meaning to their lives, and see the bright white figure striding down from the hilltop.

A huge cheer goes up as Rukuba walks on stage, his head high and proud. He takes a radio mike from an official and walks right up to the front of the stage – no stately podiums now.

The sound system crackles and booms and then his voice bursts over them, the tone urgent and dangerous. 'Men of Kivu! My men! Have I brought you peace in this land?'

'Yeeeesss!' they roar.

389

'Have I brought you prosperity in this land?'

'Yeeeesss!'

'Do I have the right to rule this land as a free nation?'

'Yeeeesss!'

'Well, that *bitch* says I don't!' He jabs an accusing finger towards the American camp, half a mile away. 'And that we do not deserve to be a free country! She has said that she will stop us becoming a free country in the United Nations!'

Howls of rage rise up from the crowd.

'Well, that's what she says she is going to do! But I will not have it. For too long the foreigners have told us what to do here in Kivu, for too long we have been the plaything of the Rwandans, the Congolese, the Ugandans, the United Nations!' He starts punching the air with his free fist. 'Now we are masters in our own house! Kivu has stood up! Kivu for Kivuans!'

The crowd start shouting. Joseph and Simon in the front are chanting 'Kivu! Kivu!'

Rukuba is ranting at them, jabbing his arm towards the American compound with each statement. '*We* are the future, *we* are the new way, the way for Kivu, *nothing* will stop us!

He begins marching back and forth across the stage clutching the microphone. His skill with oratory begins getting the better of him; the words start tumbling out without thought, old slogans from the genocide coming back into his hate-filled mind.

'Raise your voices to protest to them! Get the foreigners out! Uproot the weeds in our field! Kill the cockroaches in our house!'

The crowd erupts; all around him Joseph sees fists raised and faces inflamed with beer and anger, eyes staring, pink mouths open and white teeth bared.

Rukuba gives one final, '*Go!*' and they turn and run towards the American compound.

At 4.52pm the remaining one hundred men of Echo Company are waiting to be scrambled to the choppers. A rain squall is blowing up from the lake and they pack into the large green, open-sided tents along the edge of the flight line. They sit on the ground and lean back on their bulky webbing packs, stuffed with ammunition and grenades. They're used to this kind of hanging around in the army and chat or doze off.

The nine remaining transport helicopters and the two gunships are all sitting on their concrete pads next to them and the large fuel depot, screened off by high, bulldozed earth banks.

Three miles north, high up on the edge of the lake, Zacheus presses the electric firing switch and the forty 122mm rocket tubes fire off in twenty seconds. Each launches with a screaming flash of white propellant and howls away over the cloudy lake.

The men of Echo Company have no chance. The BM-21 is one of the heaviest weapons in the land-based arsenal and is designed for exactly this sort of artillery ambush over a wide area. The men are grouped together and protected only by a piece of canvas.

The shells airburst over them and the heavy detonations create a dreadful fast beat for twenty seconds. Blast waves repeatedly sweep the area and razor-sharp steel splinters fizz across it. The men are stunned and then pulped and cut to pieces.

The explosions hit the helicopters and knock them on their sides, their rotors spin away and they explode. Huge bursts of flame erupt across the flight line as they all go up and then a shell hits the main fuel tanks and an enormous fireball erupts, knocking out the heavy earth embankments and sweeping a blast wave up towards the main encampment.

In the ops room Yamba looks up in alarm from staring at the satellite shots of Bahomba as the first explosion hits. He glances at Mordechai and they are frozen in shock. Then the fuel depot goes and the walls of the tent flap violently in the blast and loose paper blows about them. It sounds like the thunderclap heralding the day of judgement.

Yamba snaps out of his shock. 'Major Eisenberg, stay here! Signaller, with me!' He darts out of the tent and sees a huge dirty black cloud roiling up into the rain over the flight line.

Arkady and others run out and they stand and stare in shock.

'Come on!' Yamba leads them at a pelting run through the camp. Men are standing outside their tents staring at the chaos but snap to it and run after them.

Yamba gets to the flight line and looks at it. What was a well laid out, orderly airport is now a scene of utter carnage, covered in eleven blazing wrecks, with the bodies of over a hundred men smashed and scattered around the edge of them, severed arms, legs and heads strewn about. The whole scene is covered in drifting sheets of rain and lit a lurid orange by a hundred-foot-high wall of flame from the fuel depot.

They have arrived in hell.

Patricia Johnson, John Ciacola and Major Reilly all stare at the mob of five hundred angry drunk men running at them along the road from the farm.

They can hear them shouting and yelling.

Reilly snaps into action. 'OK, Madame Secretary, can you take shelter in your block? I will set up a cordon and get the choppers in a-sap.'

Johnson nods and turns and walks as fast as she can back to her prefab hut with Ciacola.

'Sergeant Moretti! Get that gate barred and I want five guys behind it as a show of force. Break out the spare ammo and get the other guys up on the roofs there.' He turns and points back to the line of prefabs nearest the gate in the razor-wire fence.

'Get the press people inside the huts as well, I want them outta the way, this could get ugly!' Moretti and the other fourteen Delta Force soldiers jump to it.

'Juarez!' Reilly calls his signaller over with his radio backpack. 'Get on the First Regiment command net.'

Once he's on the frequency, Reilly barks into the handset, 'Loyola, this is Bronze Six, Loyola, this is Bronze Six, do you copy?'

Yamba's signaller is standing next to him looking at the devastation in front of them. He taps him on the shoulder and numbly hands him the handset.

Yamba forces himself to look away and concentrate. 'Bronze Six, this is Loyola, go ahead.'

'Loyola, we have a riot situation developing here at our camp, request immediate helicopter extraction!'

Yamba pauses for a moment and presses the receiver against his forehead trying to think what to say. He can't believe the words he has to use.

'Bronze Six, we cannot assist you, we have suffered an artillery ambush on our flight line and all our helicopters have been destroyed plus over a hundred men dead. Bronze Six, I am sorry.'

Yamba feels the professional failure deeply.

'*Oh shit!*' He hears the tension edging Reilly's voice. He knows it takes most of a day to drive up through the mountain roads to get to Mukungu from the base.

Yamba tries to think of what he can do to help. 'Bronze Six, we will keep the drone over you and the farm and feed any intelligence to you.'

Reilly forces himself not to say anything offensive. 'Loyola, we will advise you of our situation and seek alternative help. Out.'

What help?

Chapter Fifty-Three

Alex leans over the shoulder of the door gunner and looks out of the side door of the Mi-17.

'Circle the village, I want to see the area,' he shouts into the mike on his headset.

The pilot banks and he sees a collection of round thatched huts and a few tin-roofed shacks crammed into the bottom of the valley with forested sides. Vegetable plots and meadows spread out on either side of the village up and down the flat land in the valley, and at the far end of the fields downstream is a football pitch surrounded by trees.

Half a mile away up a side valley to the west is another area of flat meadows divided from the village by bush. Otherwise the terrain is just rugged hills and trees.

He checks his watch; it's just after five o'clock. They've got under an hour until it gets dark to get in and find Sophie. It's been thirty minutes since he spoke to her on the satellite phone and he can't use it in the noisy cargo bay, so he has no idea what has happened to her in that time. The weather is closing in as well, with low rain clouds pouring out from Lake Kivu.

Every minute of the journey has been agony for him. He wants to get out of the damned chopper, get out there on the ground and find her alive and well before the Kudu Noir get to her. He cannot think about that.

Packed in the back of the troop bay with twenty-two men, Col glances over at Alex. He looks tense and angry as he stares down at the ground trying to see any movement in the village. He can't see any human figures at all, everything looks deserted.

Alex turns and leans into the cockpit between the two pilots and points down at the ground. 'OK, let's land at the end of the village in that first field.'

The chopper turns quickly and flies along the valley before going into a fast assault landing. They know there are enemy troops in the area and they cannot hang about. The pilot puts the nose up and flares the rotors, dust and mud blasting off the little field as they slide into the narrow valley. The rear wheels bang down hard on the ground and the troops run down the ramp, rifles at the ready. Alex is desperate to be out and jumps out of the side door a few feet to the ground and runs for the side of the field, Col following him.

The action saves their lives.

The pilot throws in full power and pulls hard on the cyclic and the heavy machine rises up fifty feet above the troops. Two RPG rockets streak out of the bush on the valley side and hit it, one exploding just behind the cockpit and killing the door gunner and one hitting the fuel tank near the rotor. Thousands of litres of high-explosive avtur ignite and explode in a fireball overhead spraying burning fuel into the trees. The main rotor spins away and the body of the aircraft drops like a stone, smashing into the ground. The aluminium airframe burns with an intense white light too bright to look at.

The tail boom with the rotor on it is blown backwards and lands on top of the last two men to exit the ramp who are down on their belt buckles in the defensive perimeter.

The explosion sounds like a huge clap of thunder that

rolls up and down the valley. The men on the ground all look in horror at the mangled wreckage. They are now stuck in enemy territory.

Alex and Col both put their arms over their heads as the helicopter explodes over them, lying face down on the ground. The blast waves bang down on their backs.

Burning fuel and bits of metal scatter down around them and the main airframe lands nearby with a heavy thud that they feel through the ground on their fronts.

Alex pulls up his head and looks at the flame and smoke around them. 'Shit!' He glances around trying to see who is alive. 'Major Delacroix!'

'Here!'

Jean-Baptiste's hand goes up on the far side of the field.

'Get the men into cover on your side of the valley. Signaller, on me!'

Alex dashes over and throws himself down in cover in some bushes at the side of the valley.

Jean-Baptiste, Col and Stein are bellowing and getting the shocked soldiers into cover. Two bodies can be seen sticking out from the collapsed wreckage of the tail boom; the force now numbers twenty-two men in total.

The Tac signaller runs over to Alex who is rapidly calculating what reinforcements they need. He gets through on the radio to Yamba's signaller who is down at the flight line with him.

'Loyola, this is Black Hal, we have lost our helicopter to ground fire. Request replacement with gunship and another platoon in separate aircraft be despatched immediately.'

Yamba is surrounded by the burning fires of hell and screaming wounded. He shouts into the receiver, 'Black Hal, this is Loyola, we have been hit by MLRS artillery ambush, flight line has been wiped out. All helicopters have been destroyed.'

'*What!*'

'Repeat, all helicopters have been destroyed.'

'*Fuck!*'

Yamba continues to give him more bad news. 'Bronze Six reports he is being attacked by a mob.'

Alex's mind goes blank for a moment – the scale of the disasters is catastrophic, his entire airmobile capability has just been destroyed and the global dignitary he swore to protect is now under threat. A minute ago he was in charge of the most powerful military force in the province that could handle any threat, now he is reduced to abject weakness in enemy territory.

He forces himself to think. They need more helicopters to get them out of this place and get the Americans out. Who the hell has got them?

'Loyola, I want you to contact Bilal Fadoul and get one of his choppers up here now, get the other to the Americans. We are in the main village but it's under fire. New extraction LZ is area of flat meadows half a mile away up a side valley to the west of village.'

Yamba doesn't think he will have much chance with Bilal but he repeats the instructions and then gets on the satellite phone to the Lebanese.

Alex looks round the valley and tries to see where the enemy are. They've fired two RPGs but no other rounds. He can't work out what is happening; maybe they are keeping out of the way, fearful of another gunship airstrike like the ones that wiped out their last attack on his troops.

He calls to Jean-Baptiste, 'Let's move forward into the village and search it!'

The platoon begins moving down the side of the valley staying in the cover of the trees and leapfrogging forward, one section covering another as they scramble from tree to tree.

As the commanding officer, Alex stays in the centre of the platoon with his signaller, his heart rate high and his vision adrenaline-sharp. He can't hear any enemy movement, there doesn't seem to be anyone else in the valley. They move on and then a hand signal is passed back to him from the point section and he hurries forward past the first few mud-walled huts.

He can see a dead *mai-mai* soldier lying in the doorway of one of the houses. He's wearing a tee shirt and combat trousers; it looks like he was shot as he ran out of the doorway. Blood has leaked from his chest and congealed in the red dust around him, his rifle lies in front of him.

Sergeant Stein leads the point section forward and they fan out, staying low and darting from hut to hut as Alex moves forward behind them. As he crouches next to the door of a hut, he sees more evidence of a firefight – a scattering of spent rifle cartridges and he can smell the distinctive whiff of cordite. The gun battle is very recent.

The point man uses hand signals to say that he's found something on the ground. Alex is impatient to find Sophie; he runs forwards, reaches the lead man and sees him pointing to an object in some open ground between the huts. Alex's eyes latch onto it and immediately he wishes he had never seen it. A small red Hope Street rucksack lies on the ground, its contents scattered around it. Sophie always had one with her whenever she left base.

He stands up carefully in the shelter of the hut and looks at the ground around it. The earth is scuffed and torn with boot marks and there are signs of dragging leading out of the village the way they came in, back down the valley. He uses hand signals and moves the men back the way they came. This time he goes on point, his rifle held ready; he's desperate to find her.

Jean-Baptiste moves up next to him and together they dart from tree to tree, rifle sights up and questing but still finding no targets and there is no sound, the valley is still. The tension is getting to Alex; his soul harbours a dread feeling. They scout along the side of the fields where the helicopter is still burning and then past it towards a thin line of trees that divides them from the football field.

Stein whispers hoarsely to his men, 'Charlie Fireteam, secure the treeline,' but Alex signals that he will go. The men take up positions, rifles pointing across the other side of the field and towards the trees.

Alex darts out of cover, expecting a burst of fire but none comes. He runs forward and butts his shoulder up against one of the line of trees across the valley. Still no sign of the enemy.

Jean-Baptiste scuttles up next to him, his rifle sweeping the trees around them. He nods and Alex moves on through the trees to the football field. He sees something at the far end and walks out of cover into the open.

Jean-Baptiste isn't ready to cover him yet and calls sharply, 'Wait!'

Alex ignores him and walks forward in full view of any enemy sniper. Jean-Baptiste takes up a position behind a tree and watches the figure as it walks and now stumbles forward. It drops its rifle on the ground, reaches the halfway line and sinks to its knees.

Chapter Fifty-Four

Joseph is near the front of the mob charging towards the American camp. Simon is next to him and they run as fast as they can, pushing their way through the men around them.

Major Reilly sees the mob racing at him, a line of angry men coming over the sea of green grass. As they run some make throat-slitting gestures at him and wave machetes. He stands front centre with his five soldiers and thinks, 'How are we going to get out of this alive?'

He knows they only have limited ammunition – they were supposed to be protecting an individual against an assassination attempt, not fighting a war. He scans the crowd through the razor wire for weapons. Some machetes are held aloft but he can't see any rifles.

'OK, that's far enough, fire five rounds over their heads.'

The five soldiers advance towards the thin fence and bring their rifles to their shoulders.

A fusillade of shots cracks out slowly and deliberately over the heads of the crowd. The men at the front see the shots fired over their heads and drop down into the grass fifty yards from the fence. The men behind them also duck down but cannot see the shots being fired into the air; they only see men dropping to the ground in front of them.

'They're killing us!'

The crowd stops and crouches down in the high grass, shouting 'Murderers!' 'Foreigners out!' 'Kivuuuuu!'

The men at the front stand up quickly and throw beer bottles at the Americans. A hail of them flies forward and the soldiers are forced to dodge and run for cover. Reilly gets hit by a half-full bottle of beer on the head and it gashes his brow and he stumbles and falls.

'Shit! Reilly's down!'

One of the ten men up on the flat roofs of the huts sees him fall and scans over his rifle sights for the next man to stand up in the grass and hurl a missile.

Two shots crack out and the man spins backwards.

Reilly pushes himself back up and starts shouting, 'Cease fire! Cease fire!' but it's too late.

Kudu Noir and former government troops have mingled with the crowd and crawl forward through the grass with their AK-47s. One soldier sights on the Americans on the roof and fires off a long burst. It chatters high and the bullets crack over their heads. The Americans quickly spot the sparkle of muzzle flash in the long grass and blast rounds back at him.

A firefight breaks out and Reilly abandons his attempt to cease fire. 'Everybody on the roofs!'

He runs round to the back of a hut where someone has put a white plastic chair up against it. He clambers up on it and pulls himself up onto the roof. Crouching low, he sticks his head up between bursts of fire. He can look down and see the sprinkling of heads in the grass, men crabbing around, keeping low and fanning out around the compound, surrounding him.

'All round defence! Spread out!'

Men run and jump across the roofs of huts to keep the threat back from all sides of the perimeter.

'Conserve ammunition! Only fire on targets with weapons!'

Rukuba is lying in his hammock with his arms folded tightly across his chest and a glowering expression on his face.

Zacheus and a group of government ministers stand at a distance from him, not daring to approach when he is in such a fury. Gabriel runs out of the farmhouse, pushes past the group and rushes up to the President; he is too anxious to be afraid.

He stands over Rukuba, his eyes wild and his big jaw jutting awkwardly. He flings his hands out in desperation. 'Mr President, they are firing at the Americans!'

He gestures over towards the encampment, half a mile away, from where the popping sound of gunfire can be faintly heard.

Rukuba merely turns a baleful gaze up at him and says in a quiet voice, 'She must accept responsibility for her actions. If my men want to express their patriotic anger, I will not stop them.'

Gabriel throws himself on his knees; the Unit 17 men behind him dart forward anxiously. 'But the Americans will kill us!' he wails and he grabs the President's robes. Two Unit 17 men step up, get hold of his arms and drag him back onto his feet.

Rukuba leaps up, boiling with rage. 'Get him out of here!' he roars, pointing at the farmhouse. 'Nothing will interrupt the expression of the will of my people!'

Gabriel goes limp and is frogmarched back around the side of the farmhouse and then shoved and kicked on his way on the road down the hill. He is distraught and in tears.

He stumbles along towards the village and a feeling of

doom grips his soul. What will happen to them now that they have provoked the greatest military power on Earth?

Carla Schmidt has got her satellite link set up and hauled herself and Mike, her cameraman, up onto a roof; he is filming the disaster as it unfolds.

The CNN studio in Washington DC is seven hours behind Kivu, so at 10 a.m. her editor rudely barks in the anchorman's ear as he introduces a piece on the housing market. He looks shocked for a moment and then says, 'We have just had news of an incident unfolding in the newly established Republic of Kivu in the Congo, where the Secretary of State is on an official visit. I'm live with our correspondent Carla Schmidt now. Carla, what have you got for us there?'

The screen cuts to a low-resolution shot of Carla crouching down on the roof, one hand holding her microphone in front of her and the other pressing her earpiece in. There is a delay on the satellite line and then her mechanical, distorted voice comes back.

'Rob, we have a major incident developing here. We're not sure why but the compound where the Secretary of State is staying is being attacked by a large mob, there must be five, six, seven hundred men out . . .' She cuts off and ducks as a burst of gunfire goes over her head, sounding like a faint popping noise on the TV screens all across America. The camera shot ducks down and shows a blurred close-up of the roof. Muffled sounds come from offscreen.

In the studio Rob barks, 'Carla, are you OK?'

'Shit!' she blurts out and then puts her head up. 'Mike, are you OK?'

'Yeah, OK, we're still rolling.'

She lies down flat on the roof and Mike does likewise,

404

getting the camera back up and twisting its viewfinder round until he gets a focused shot of her again.

'Sorry! Rob, we're under fire here. We have a small Special Forces team protecting us but this is a big mob we are facing and . . .' a soldier takes up a firing position on one knee next to her and bangs out a burst over her head '. . . this is serious. Rob, I have been in some tight spots but this is serious!' The panic in her voice comes through the low-quality sound.

A burst of heavy bullets smashes into the side of the hut and angles up through the thin plywood of the roof into the soldier's ankle. He screams and drops his weapon.

'Man down! Man down!' his partner on the roof is shouting.

'Stay on station!' Moretti yells. 'They're coming round the back!'

In the central hut in the compound the other press journalists are all flat on the floor as bullets smash through the thin walls over their heads and shower them in dust and splinters.

At one end of the hut the Secretary of State is also down on the floor, speaking via satellite phone to the President. She has to shout over the noise. 'Asani, this is bad here!' She hardly ever uses the President's first name.

'We're holding them but I don't know for how long. Speak to Major Reilly.'

She hands over the phone. The President has got the TV on mute in front of him and is watching what is happening; he can see the situation is grave. Admiral Harry Kruger is with him in the Oval Office listening in on a speaker phone, having run across from an adjacent building along with other key White House staff. They all know that across the country people are stopping work and switching on radios, TVs and the internet to watch the ghastly action film play out as their

405

most senior foreign diplomat and a lot of leading journalists are threatened with death.

The President tries to keep his famed calm but doesn't manage it. His voice snaps, 'Major, what is your assessment?'

'Sir, we are in big trouble here. My men are holding the perimeter just but we have limited ammunition and it's getting dark in under an hour. They're bringing up more weapons and the incoming is getting worse, sir.'

'OK, OK, soldier, Admiral Kruger will explain our options.'

'Reilly, this is Kruger.'

'Sir!' Reilly had not anticipated having to speak to the President and the senior military commander and is feeling out of his depth.

'I've got a company of Rangers taking off in a C-130 in Kenya ready to parachute in and there's a Spectre gunship going with them but it's eight hundred miles and they'll take three hours to get to you. How long can you hold?'

'That's too long, sir!'

'OK, the President has agreed another option. I can launch cruise missiles from off the coast of Somalia and they can be there in an hour and twenty minutes. We can use cluster munitions from them on the area around the compound and we can hit Rukuba's base and take the heat off you guys and try and get some in as close to you as we dare. That should give you some breathing space until the Rangers and the Spooky get to you.'

'Yes, sir, that would be good. Right now danger close is OK with me, sir.'

'OK, well, I don't want to be the guy who drops a bomb on Johnson, so you gotta hang in there.'

'Yes, sir!' Reilly glances at his watch. It's 5.10 p.m.; he's got until 6.30 p.m. before the missiles arrive and he gets any hope of relief.

Chapter Fifty-Five

One thousand kilometres away to the northeast, night has just fallen and the ships of Combined Task Force 151 cruise in darkness in the Indian Ocean off the coast of Somalia.

The multinational antipiracy squadron includes vessels from twenty-one different countries assigned to different sea areas. However, two days ago the nine-thousand-six-hundred-ton Ticonderoga Class missile cruiser, the USS *Gettysburg*, left its allotted area and steamed south with its screening destroyers, away from other national vessels, under orders from Admiral Kruger in anticipation of an incident in Kivu.

Deep inside the huge ship in her high-tech war room, officers have been scanning satellite imagery of the area of Mukungu and preparing a range of attack options for their BGM-109 Tomahawk cruise missiles. The TLAM-D version contains one hundred and sixty-six Combined Effects Munition bomblets which spray out of ports on both sides of a missile as it passes over a target.

These plans are now put into effect.

The ship turns beam on to the target to use her fore and rear deck missile launchers. A series of large armoured hatches flip open rapidly on the decks as the Vertical Launch System prepares to fire each six-metre-long missile. Technicians complete final preparations for launch in the darkened war room and the captain mutters a laconic 'Launch missiles.'

A flash of white light splits the night on the fore and rear decks, illuminating the ship's high superstructure. Fire and smoke belch out of the hatches and the missiles shoot up like demons emerging out of a trapdoor from hell. One after another, six missiles are blasted up into the air by propellant charges before their motors kick in and thrust them up and away, their exhausts burning bright and trailing a long stream of smoke. They make a hideous scraping sound like a heavy weight being dragged across the sky that fades as they disappear rapidly away southwest towards the coast of Africa and Kivu.

Yamba is on the satellite phone.

'Mr Fadoul? This is Major Douala.'

'Ah, Major Douala, what the hell is happening? The whole world has gone mad, they're rioting in Goma, you know, the Chinese have all fled back over the border to Rwanda.' He utters an Arabic expletive. 'They've taken one of my helicopters . . .'

'What? Who's taken your helicopter?'

'I don't know, soldiers, they came to the refinery this morning and stole a helicopter with Mahmood. My staff said they made him fly off but I don't know where.'

'Oh . . .' Yamba can't think of anything to say; the flow of bad news just keeps getting worse.

He's back in the ops room at Camp Heaven. Arkady and the other company majors are sorting out the carnage down on the flight line though there isn't much they can do and there are very few injured left to be saved.

'Why? What is happening with you? This whole country is going mad.'

'It's bad here as well, we've been attacked by artillery and all our helicopters have been destroyed . . .'

'*What?*'

'Yes, that's why I'm calling you. Sophie is in trouble. She went to an outstation yesterday . . .'

'Yes, I know, she called me and I sent Mahmood to take her there with those goalposts . . .' Another outburst in Arabic. 'What are you telling me? Are you saying she's in danger?'

'Yes, Kudu Noir have attacked the village and Colonel Devereux has gone there to get her out but his helicopter has now been destroyed . . .'

The sound of wailing comes down the phone as Bilal realises what has happened to her.

'Kudu Noir! *No!*'

'Look, we need to get them both out of there – do you have another helicopter?'

'*Yes, take it!*' Bilal is filled with anguish. He wanted only to impress and help Sophie with his helicopter. Now the irony is killing him. 'It's at my house here, I'll send it up to you now.'

'OK, that's good news, that's great, thank you.'

At last something has moved in a positive direction.

'Tell the pilot to land by the operations tent, the flight line is destroyed.'

He gets off the phone and calls Arkady on the radio. 'Arkady, get up here fast, we've got a chopper and I want you flying it.'

'Good! I'm coming!'

Yamba sets to work getting together the weaponry that he needs to make the trip to Bahomba. He's going with Arkady but otherwise the aircraft will have to fly out empty in order to be able to pick up Alex and Sophie and the platoon of men and bring them back.

Ten minutes later a Mi-17 with the Fadoul company logo on it thumps over the ops tent and Yamba looks up at the clock on the ops room wall to check the time. It's next to the kudu head that Col put up there and the creature looks back at him with its menacing stare.

He looks away from it and checks the clock. It's 5.25 p.m. He runs out with Arkady who takes over from the pilot and they lift off.

Alex's doom is now complete.

Sophie's body hangs on the crossbar of the new goalposts.

He is a failure: public, private, professional, personal. A pariah, a war criminal, a liar, a man who makes promises to keep people safe and breaks them; he has failed to protect his lover.

He cannot look at her like that and kneels with his head down. Jean-Baptiste appears next to him, scoops up his rifle and, seeing his immobility, is about to retrieve the body.

The movement galvanises him. 'No!' He rises painfully to his feet and walks over to her; he must do this.

They used the canvas belt on her jeans; it digs into her long slender neck. Her face is tinged blue with deoxygenated blood, her tongue is a ghastly protrusion from her mouth. Her long legs are wet with urine.

Jean-Baptiste holds her legs to take the weight off and Alex undoes the belt and between them they lay her awkwardly down on the ground.

Alex is in shock; he kneels and stares at her distorted face and cannot reconcile it with the beautiful, funny, angry, living one he knew.

Jean-Baptiste stands next to him and puts his hand on his commander's shoulder.

410

The first howl breaks out from the bush across the valley from them.

Jean-Baptiste ducks and pushes Alex down as a burst of machine-gun fire scythes across them. They crawl frantically on the ground into the cover of some trees behind the goalpost. Bullets thud into wood and shower them with wet white splinters.

Gunfire breaks out from both sides of the valley and the long howls echo back and forth across it triumphantly. The violence makes Alex focus; he's running on instinct alone now, a blind drive from somewhere under his soul that simply forces him to put one foot in front of the other and keep on doing what he knows how to do.

He is crouching behind a tree and yells across to Jean-Baptiste. He's separated from his signaller but the Frenchman has a platoon radio headset on. 'Tell them to cover us back through these trees and we'll join them. We need to extract west to the meadow!'

Jean-Baptiste relays the order to Stein who gets his sections to manoeuvre back onto the west side of the valley. Two men are killed by bursts of gunfire as they cross over. They are down to twenty men.

The remainder take up firing positions in the trees and lay down covering fire to allow Alex and Jean-Baptiste to dodge from tree to tree out of the middle of the valley and onto its western side.

Alex finds his signaller, and Col and Stein start extracting the platoon back through the trees, each section covering the other in a fighting retreat. He moves with them and his signaller tries to raise Yamba on the radio. They blunder through the dense foliage. The high tree canopy cuts out a lot of light and it's getting dark anyway. All around them are bursts of gunfire and figures darting from tree to tree.

411

The Kudu Noir on the west of the valley begin to close in around them on both sides and the ones on the east side dash over and follow after them. They are fighting on three sides now as they hack their way westwards up the half-mile slope to the meadows.

'Loyola for you, sir!'

They squat down for a moment behind a tree and Alex grabs the phone from his signaller and yells into it over the gunfire near him, 'Loyola, this is Black Hal, what is your status?'

Yamba is in the co-pilot seat of the Mi-17, his radio headset on, his voice distorted by the loud noise of the rotors as Arkady pushes the machine hard. 'Black Hal, we are inbound from the east in a Mi-17, ETA is 18.00 hours. What is your locstat?'

'Roger that, we are extracting west from Bahomba village and will RV with you in the meadow half a mile west of the village. Be advised we are in contact with enemy troops and LZ will be hot.'

'Roger that, Black Hal. Out.'

The words were easy to say but Alex now thinks, how are we going to break contact with the enemy in order to extract? Normally they would try and get an artillery or air strike to separate them and then leg it to the chopper but they can't do that now. They need to win the firefight in the bush first but it doesn't sound good – the volume of incoming fire is high and they are being hit from three sides. Bullets zip overhead and thunk into trees around him. An RPG explodes to his right and the orange flash cuts through the gloom momentarily. Alex glances towards it and sees a horned head move between two trees lit by the stabbing muzzle flash of a machine gun.

Chapter Fifty-Six

Joseph has his face pressed down into the wet grass. Bullets crack over him; the Americans have them pinned down with fire from the roofs of the huts. Every time anyone pops up to take a shot at them they are hit by accurate marksmanship.

Wild bursts of gunfire still zip over his head from gunmen further away behind him in the darkness. The tracers sweep across the huts and sometimes screams come as they find a target. The men in the grass around the perimeter roar when they do.

Joseph decides to crab sideways towards where someone got hit and take their weapon. He is a soldier and he knows how to fight. He is furious at these people who have come into this new land that has given him an identity, and insulted President Rukuba. Who are the Americans to tell Kivu if it can be a state or not? Drunken rage has replaced any thought for the consequences.

'Simon, come on!' he calls towards his friend and hears the rustle in the grass as Simon moves towards him. They crawl along together and come across the body on its back with its rifle nearby in the grass. 'Get the magazines.'

Simon pulls them out of the man's bandoliers and hands them over. 'Hey, there's a truck coming.' He points back down the road towards Mukungu, where soldiers are bringing up the three army trucks.

'Come on! Let's go!' Joseph jumps up and runs back away from the besieged base towards the trucks. Out of range of the American rifles, men are climbing up into the back of one of them, some of them Kudu Noir soldiers in their black masks. All are shouting and cheering in anger, waving their guns over their heads.

The two teenagers jump up alongside them and hold on to the metal frame overhead in the back. One of the Kudu Noir heaves a box up onto the back of the truck. 'Grenades! Everybody pass them round!' Joseph is handed four of the hard metal balls and stuffs them into his pockets, then grabs the wooden sideboards as the truck lurches forward. The engine roars, the gears grind and they gain speed along the road towards the base.

Major Reilly is crouching on a roof inside the compound and hears the truck coming through the night. It hasn't got its lights on but with his night vision headset he sees it accelerating towards the razor-wire gates intent on ramming them.

'Jackson, get over here!'

The soldier scuttles over to him and he gives him the goggles. 'I want a grenade in its cab as soon as it's in range.'

'Sir.' Jackson pulls on the headset and, in the green watery light of the image intensifier, sees the large truck driving down the road, moving at speed now.

He hurriedly slots a fat 40mm grenade into the launcher tube slung underneath his carbine and sights carefully on the cab. When it's two hundred metres away he pulls the trigger and the rifle thumps and lobs the grenade.

It strikes a glancing blow on the front wing of the long

truck bonnet and explodes. The bonnet is ripped off and the shrapnel shatters the window.

The driver is wounded in the face but ducks down under the dashboard and keeps driving with one hand on the wheel. The radiator spews steam out but the truck keeps coming.

In the back, Joseph and the other twenty men all duck down at the sound and bright flash of the explosion. Bursts of machine-gun fire crack over them and they cling onto the side as the truck swerves off the road onto the grass and then bumps back onto the road.

The besiegers around the camp hear the truck coming and increase their rate of fire at the Americans.

'Give it another one!' Reilly yells and Jackson slots another grenade into the launcher. The truck is nearly at the gates.

Chapter Fifty-Seven

A shout comes through the trees to Alex's right.

'Man down!'

Shit! They cannot leave any men behind with the Kudu Noir; he has seen the photos of what they do to their captives.

He has made his command decisions now; with nineteen men left in action he needs to join the fight.

'Right, let's get him!' he says to Jean-Baptiste and his signaller and they start moving towards the casualty. Alex pulls his machete from its scabbard on his webbing and cuts his way through a patch of hanging vines. They reach the soldier – it's Sean Potts, he's on the ground with one leg blown off at the knee from the grenade explosion and a load of shrapnel in his groin and the other leg. Arterial blood jets out of him in long regular pulses.

Jason is on his knees in front of him desperately trying to get a tourniquet on the stump, his face and front covered in blood. Sean is out of it, his head lolling back and his eyes rolled over to show the whites.

Jason is shouting, 'Yer gonna make it, mate! Yer gonna make it!' He pulls the belt loop fast on Sean's lower thigh and strips off his friend's webbing. Alex grabs his PKM light machine gun and gathers up the ammo belts.

With the strength of desperation Jason hauls his friend

up onto his back in a fireman's lift and the group of five of them set off through the foliage following the sound of Col's huge voice bellowing, 'Two Section, covering fire! One Section, prepare to move! *Move!*'

A fresh round of muzzle flashes and banging breaks out and they scuttle and stumble forward.

They get through to where Col is in cover behind a tree; Alex crouches next to him. Jason slumps down and Sean's body falls off his shoulder and lolls on the ground. Col takes one look at the white, blood-drained face, catches Alex's eye and shakes his head.

Jason is frantically fumbling in his webbing and pulls out his morphine injector. He yanks the yellow cap off the top and plunges it into Sean's thigh. Col puts his hand on his shoulder and looks at him seriously, 'Tell you what, mate, let's give him mine too, eh?'

Jason looks at his friend with tears in his eyes and knows full well what Col is saying. He can see that they're not going to get him out. He nods silently and Col thumps his injector into Sean's arm.

There's a lull in the firing and Alex and Jean-Baptiste gather the remaining men together into a better formation. It starts raining heavily and the sound of the drops drums loudly on the leaves above them. Water pours down off his helmet rim and Alex wipes it off his face and checks his watch. It's 5.45 p.m., the light is already fading fast in the trees and they've got fifteen minutes to fight their way through the remaining jungle to the extraction point. The situation is desperate and extreme measures are needed. Alex calls loudly so all the men can hear.

'Right, everybody, fix bayonets and buddy up! No one gets taken alive, if you've got to use your last bullet then do it!'

Jean-Baptiste is next to Alex and looks at him and nods. Col grabs Jason's shoulder and says, 'Right, you're coming with me, lad.'

Long bursts of gunfire start up in front of them. The reason for the lull becomes apparent – the Kudu Noir have filtered round between them and the meadow.

'Right, let's get at them! Two Section, covering fire! One Section, move!' Alex bellows and stands to fire forward. About thirty yards away he sees a black hooded figure emerge from behind a tree trunk, lit up by the strobing muzzle flashes of its rifle.

Alex leans over his weapon, squints through his sights, lines up the stub of the backsight in the circle of the foresight and pulls the trigger. The burst cuts across the man's head and he goes down.

They move forward but in the intense, confused firefight the platoon formation breaks down and the men begin pairs fire and manoeuvre. It's pitch black now and raining hard. The fighting is close quarters and vicious, randomly lit by muzzle flashes and the blast of grenades. The Kudu Noir are howling as they fire long, scything bursts through the forest.

Jason has got Sean's PKM machine gun and stands up and blasts a long burst to their rear before he takes two bullets in the face and goes over backwards. Col scuttles forwards, checks his pulse, and shouts, 'Bollocks!'

He crabs away from the body to the cover of a tree and then stands up to check forward. A bullet hits the Kevlar plate in his body armour over his heart and it feels like a baseball bat has hit him and knocked him off his feet. His ribs crack; he is knocked backward and lies on the ground winded.

The Kudu Noir soldier runs forward, his rifle up, scanning

over his sights. He gets to the tree and sees Col lying behind it on his back, one hand clutching his chest and his mouth gaping as he tries to suck in air. His other hand frantically scrabbles for the rifle lying next to him. The Kudu soldier stamps on his hand, then puts his head back and howls in triumph and others run forward to look at their prisoner.

Stein leads his buddy forward and uses the platoon AA-12 that he has taken from a dead soldier. He stands and fires a burst of six shots into a patch of bushes that strips the leaves from them and riddles two Kudu Noir men with buckshot. He charges forward and finishes them with blasts to their heads as they twist in pain on the ground.

Alex and Jean-Baptiste are doing well, gaining ground and moving expertly. The superior battlecraft of the First Regiment troops is showing through and the enemy numbers are thinning as they get towards the meadow.

The former Foreign Legionnaire expertly cracks two rounds into a man ahead of them and Alex moves forward. Jean-Baptiste pauses and lobs a grenade towards the noise of movement behind him and then waits for the loud bang and fizz of splinters over his head.

Alex loads a new magazine quickly and yells, 'Prepare to move! Move!' stands and fires forward covering him. Shots ring out behind, there's a loud crack as Jean-Baptiste is hit in the thigh and his femur snaps. He screams and falls forward.

Alex runs back to where he is twisting on the ground in agony. He gets his morphine ampoule out quickly and jabs it into his thigh opposite the wound and then whips a webbing strap around the injured leg as a tourniquet. The Frenchman makes a huge effort to get a grip on the pain, bringing all of his ferocious discipline to bear on it.

Alex bends down and starts trying to get him up into a fireman's lift. Jean-Baptiste pushes him off. 'No, you must fight! We won't make it.' The Frenchman grabs the front of his combat jacket. 'We can't both die. Give me your grenades, I will hold them!'

Alex stares back at him, he can't see his face in the darkness but he can hear the furious intensity in his voice. He glances ahead, and knows Jean-Baptiste is right, there is firing coming from ahead and he'll need to fight to get to the meadow. He checks the luminous dial of his watch, six o'clock, the chopper will be here any minute and it can't hang around with ground fire coming at it. He cannot bring himself to say yes to one more betrayal so he just fumbles in his webbing packs and hands the four hard metal grenades to him.

Jean-Baptiste groans and pushes himself up against a tree trunk. Alex is silent but the Frenchman wants to say something, 'Colonel, when I met you, you asked me why I joined the Legion?'

Alex croaks a quiet, 'Yes.'

'I did it because I killed someone.' Alex doesn't want to hear his confession, he has had too much horror. 'I loved her very much but . . .' He stops; there's no time for the detail.

'I have never told anyone that . . .' He grabs Alex's arm and hisses at him with a fury, 'Stay alive, Colonel, stay alive!' He shoves him away, pulls the pin out of the first grenade and lets the lever ping off into the darkness.

'Go, Colonel, or we both go!'

Alex puts his hand on his shoulder. 'You are a great man, Jean-Baptiste.'

'Thank you, now go.' Alex cannot see the tears mixing with the rain on his face. He gets up and runs forward, it's all he can do.

Chapter Fifty-Eight

The second rifle grenade smashes through the windscreen of the approaching truck and explodes on the back of the cab. The front of the truck pulses with the explosion, the roof is blown off and the driver killed outright. Shrapnel punches through into the troops in the back and Joseph hears three men fall down and start screaming.

He feels the truck lurch as it runs out of control, the momentum hurrying it along. It swerves off the road and crashes at an oblique angle into the razor-wire fence around the compound, smashing down the metal stanchions and tearing a long strip of wire away.

The right-hand side of the truck is now side on to the Americans who rake it with machine-gun fire. The darkness is lit by the flames from the burning cab and Joseph scrambles desperately over the wooden sideboards away from the gunfire and crouches down in the shelter of the truck.

Bullets continue to pour into the base from the darkness encircling it. Joseph presses his back up against the shot-out rear tyres of the truck and holds his rifle in front of him, ready to make a break through the broken fence.

A burst of gunfire comes from his left; Alex turns and

listens to the heavy thudding as the AA-12 fires back.

Through the rain and the trees he sees Stein's huge figure lit up by the muzzle flashes and then his weapon clicks empty. The German flings a grenade forward and then there is a bright flash as one explodes next to him.

Alex turns and runs on, bullets zipping past him from behind and hammering into a tree. He spins and fires back at the man who screams and falls. All around him in the darkness are the dwindling sounds of the gun battle as the remnant of the platoon are isolated and cut down one by one. A series of grenade explosions, shots and screams behind him mark the end of Jean-Baptiste.

The noise of the helicopter overhead cuts through the mayhem and Alex looks up. Arkady switches on the landing light to find the meadow and the single bright beam of light shoots out from under the helicopter through the darkness, lighting up each flying raindrop. To Alex, lost in a welter of darkness and horror, dazed and disorientated by pain and failure, it is the purest and most sacred light he had ever seen. The light moves on ahead of him over the trees and he stumbles forward. It steadies over the meadow and he begins to run towards it.

A shape darts between the trees on the edge of the meadow just in front of him. Backlit by the helicopter light, the figure stands out starkly – the twisted kudu horns and rifle make it look like the devil hurrying across the face of the earth. Alex brings up his rifle and fires a burst at it. It turns and fires towards him, unable to see him because of the bright light and the thrashing of the helicopter rotor wash behind it.

Alex's magazine clicks empty but he runs headlong forward, his bright bayonet on the tip of his rifle seeking out the hateful figure. It sees him too late dashing between the trees and parries the bayonet charge with its own weapon. Alex crashes into the figure and they fall onto the ground. His rifle is knocked from his hands and he punches it in the chest, the ghastly figure stares up at him and punches him in the side of the head. Alex feels the blow jar his upper teeth and it knocks him off. He yanks his machete from its scabbard, spins round to face the Kudu and they hurl themselves at each other, grappling in the mud.

Arkady holds the chopper a few feet off the ground ready for a quick takeoff. He kills the landing light so as not to illuminate them for longer than he needs to. Yamba is at the side door with a light machine gun ready to cover anyone who comes out of the treeline.

He peers through the darkness trying to see any movement. The grass under the machine is thrashing in the downdraught and he glimpses a figure as it emerges from the trees and stumbles towards him. It doesn't have a weapon but is carrying something.

Muzzle flashes burst from the trees and the figure drops onto all fours and crawls forward dragging its burden. Yamba braces the machine-gun muzzle on a door bracket and fires a long burst of suppressive fire over it and the enemy firing cuts off.

The figure crawls towards the lowered ramp at the back of the aircraft, hovering four feet off the ground, and then staggers to its legs and throws something heavy into the cargo bay. Yamba stays on his gun firing bursts into the trees but glances back at the figure as it hauls itself up onto the ramp and then crawls towards him.

He sets his machine gun down and runs back to it. In the dim light of the cargo bay he sees a sodden, mud-covered creature on the floor. It twists its face up to him and he sees crazed eyes and a blood-streaked visage. He knows it is Alex but cannot recognise him. He crouches down and shouts, 'How many more?'

Alex looks up at him and shouts weakly, 'None.'

Bullets start thudding through the side of the chopper, knocking puffs of insulation out of the walls as the remaining Kudu Noir fire at them. Yamba glances up. One round in the fuel tank and they've had it.

He looks back down at the heavy object and sees that it is a kudu mask with blood leaking out of the severed head inside it. He looks away from it in horror and shouts at Alex, 'What about Col?'

Alex slumps on the floor. 'Dead. We're all dead.'

Inside the American compound, Major Reilly yells over the din of the firefight, 'Jackson, keep them pinned down behind the truck. How many rounds have you got left?'

Jackson glances down and checks the bandolier on his chest. 'Two mags, sir!'

'Great, sixty rounds', Reilly thinks, but gives him a thumbs up nonetheless. 'Good shooting.'

He turns and crawls to the edge of the roof, swings himself over it, drops down and scuttles, bent double, back to the hut in the middle of the compound where Secretary Johnson and the journalists are all flat on the floor in the dark listening to the bangs and explosions going on around them and trying to guess if they are going to get out alive.

Reilly ducks in through the door and crawls over to Johnson. 'OK, we held off a truck assault, I think that will keep them at bay for a while.'

'Great.' She manages to sound in control. 'How long till the missiles get here?'

He checks his watch: 6.10 p.m. 'Twenty minutes till they

hit; I think we can do this. I'll check with Heaven and see if they can see any other threats on the drone. Signaller!' He yells in the dark and the man crawls over to him. 'Get me Heaven on the command net.'

The six cruise missiles scream through the night over northern Kenya at 550mph. Their terrain-following radar holds them at a hundred feet altitude and they jink and twist as they follow the contours of the land. Satellite controls direct them to fly in a V formation like a flock of geese.

Some Masai herdsmen look up in alarm from their campfire as they howl overhead, deadly and intent on their target.

Chapter Fifty-Nine

Yamba pours water from his canteen over Alex's face and wipes away some of the mud and the blood smeared over it. In the dim light of the helicopter cargo bay his commander is battered and exhausted. He's slumped on the floor, leaning against the wall, a ghost staring into space, as they thump back to Heaven in the nearly empty aircraft.

Arkady's voice crackles in Yamba's headset. 'It's Mordechai on the radio, wants to speak to you.'

'OK.' He hands the canteen to Alex who grasps it numbly and doesn't move as Yamba walks back to the cockpit.

A minute later he returns quickly and Alex is still staring ahead into space.

Yamba comes close and shouts, 'Alex, they've got Col!' His eyes are wide and staring.

Alex's eyes focus and he looks at Yamba who continues shouting, 'Bilal's pilot, Captain Mahmood, is flying him back to Mukungu now; the Kudus got Mahmood and used his helicopter to fly to Bahomba. Mordechai said Mahmood called him on the command net when no one was in the cockpit with him.'

Alex blinks and looks at him. 'Col's alive?'

'Yes, Mahmood said it was him, he saw him at the party you went to.'

Alex sits up. A pack instinct somewhere deep inside has told him to protect one of his own. 'We've got to go and get him.'

Yamba is in a more rational state than Alex. He pauses and looks at his friend, thinking about the risks of going back into Mukungu. But he hesitates only for a moment, his loyalty to Alex and Col overcomes any doubts – they cannot leave Col to be tortured by the Kudus. He knows both of them would do the same for him. He looks Alex in the eye, gives a silent nod and commits himself.

Yamba keys the mike on his headset. 'Arkady, take us back into Mukungu.' The Russian grunts with surprise but he too is loyal to Col and they have been through too much for him to abandon the man. He checks his maps and banks the chopper round on a new course.

Alex hauls himself up and starts looking around him, trying to think how he will take on a whole base full of enemy troops.

Joseph crouches behind the back wheels of the burning truck. He can't see much because he is cramped in with Simon and three other men all clutching rifles and hiding from the bullets that thud into the truck body making it vibrate against his shoulder. Black smoke pours out of the cab at the front of the lorry and flames light up the bullet-riddled prefab buildings defended by a handful of remaining American soldiers.

He is trapped in no man's land with the Americans firing at him from the front and bullets snapping around him from his fellow fighters shooting back at them from behind him. In the distance, back towards Mukungu, he hears another truck engine rev up, the engine note rising as it approaches.

Inside the camp, Reilly has just been told by Mordechai

that Alex is approaching Mukungu. 'Oh shit,' he mutters quietly – he doesn't want to broadcast the fact that cruise missiles are about to be used. 'What frequency is he on?'

He gets the frequency and his signaller raises Arkady on the radio, who calls Alex up to the cockpit.

'Black Hal, this Bronze Six, advise you should not approach Mukungu base. It will be targeted by airstrike at 18.30 hours.'

In the noisy cockpit of the helicopter Alex closes his eyes.

Reilly continues, 'What is your ETA there?'

'Bronze Six, our ETA is 18.25.'

'Negative, Black Hal, that is too short to assault and extract a prisoner. I cannot delay the airstrike, I need it a-sap, we're in deep shit here. I have ten men left and the Secretary of State to protect! You were supposed to be providing security for us!'

Alex pauses before replying and rests his forehead on his hands for a moment. 'Bronze Six, I have failed you, I am sorry.'

'Black Hal, that is no good to me now. You cannot go back in to Mukungu now, if you go back you will die!'

Alex pauses again before answering quietly, 'Bronze Six, I know. Out.'

The truck accelerates along the road towards the American camp at 6.20 p.m. Joseph and the four other men crouching behind the burning vehicle hear it coming and grip their rifles in anticipation.

Reilly is back up on the roof and directs Jackson to fire another grenade. He kneels and sights on the truck.

Joseph scrambles away from the back wheels and glances round the rear bumper. He sees the American kneeling on the roof lit up by the orange flames from the burning cab, raises his rifle and fires a long burst. The heavy slugs hit the soldier in the legs and track up across his body knocking him over backwards.

Joseph screams with victory. At last, his first combat killing!

Reilly presses his face down on the roof. A few soldiers bang out shots at the truck but the grenade launcher was the only thing that was going to stop it dead.

It roars on at the wire gate, its front bonnet looking tall and powerful. Attackers stand up in the grass and cheer as it crashes through the flimsy wire and ploughs on into the first prefab hut, smashing the walls to shards as the long nose buries into it. The crowd of men with guns on the back of it jump off and run forward.

Reilly and the others leap off the roof just in time and fall back around the next line of huts in their last-ditch defence.

Joseph roars and leads the other men out of their hiding place. They run forward, weapons raised, hunting their prey in the light of the flames.

Alex stands and stares out of the back of the helicopter at the black rain and rushing darkness below him.

He is bewildered by pain over Sophie but filled with anger as well at the betrayal of his men by Rukuba. A murderous revenge is brimming in his heart.

He has made preparations with Yamba as best they can for their two-man assault on the base but he doesn't know if they will be enough. Realistically he has a few minutes left to live but it does not bother him.

Mordechai told him on the radio that the pictures from the drone circling overhead showed Mahmood's helicopter touch down on the lawn outside Rukuba's farmhouse. A prisoner was marched off the back of it and into the house.

At least they know Col is alive and where they need to attack; whether the plan will work is another thing.

Johnson's voice blares out of the desk speaker in the Oval Office, she is desperate and shouting, 'Asani, you've gotta help us, they've broken through the perimeter, they're coming for us!'

The President, Kruger and the other officials crowding round the desk stare at the speaker ashen-faced. Though they are thousands of miles away, satellite technology has brought the battle right into the heart of the White House: they can hear the bangs as bullets smash through the walls of the hut over her head and grenades explode nearby as the attackers lob them at the remaining American soldiers.

Johnson and the other diplomats and journalists are all lying on the floor, the hut they are in is pitch black. All over America the population is getting a similar blacked-out screaming commentary on the crisis from Carla Schmidt and the other network journalists.

'How long till the missiles hit?' Johnson yells over the noise outside; she can't see her watch.

Kruger leans forward and shouts back, 'Five minutes, Patricia, you've gotta hang in there, we're pushing them as fast as we can.'

Joseph runs round the corner of a hut following the men from the back of the second truck. The first six of them are cut down in a hail of bullets from Americans firing from the top of two huts in a crossfire. The bodies twist and fall in front of him and he turns and darts back round the corner of a prefab with Simon. He pulls a grenade out of his jacket pocket.

'Here.' He hands his rifle to Simon, stands back from the

hut, pulls the pin out and pitches it forward onto the roof of the hut opposite him. In the two-second delay there is a confused shout and then a loud bang and someone starts screaming in pain.

Kudu Noir soldiers dart round the corner of other huts and spray long wild bursts of fire at the Americans. Joseph rushes forward from behind them and throws another grenade around the next corner.

Alex peers out of the side door of the helicopter as it circles over Mukungu. He can see the old farmhouse on the edge of the hill with the lawn in front of it. Lights blaze from the windows and arc lights on the roof illuminate the Fadoul company helicopter parked on the lawn.

Arkady brings the chopper in slowly towards the house and Alex sees Unit 17 and Kudu Noir soldiers run out of the farmhouse with rifles and look up at them in confusion. Some raise their weapons to fire but then an argument breaks out as they see the Fadoul company logo on the side of the helicopter. It is approaching slowly to land and doesn't seem to be a threat; an officer knocks down a rifle raised by one soldier and walks out onto the lawn, looking up and waving them in.

Alex ducks back from the door and glances at Yamba in the cargo bay who nods grimly and they make their final preparations.

The door of Johnson's hut bursts open and Reilly rushes in. 'Anybody know how to fire a weapon?'

'Yes, sir, I'm a shooter.' A journalist shouts back and stands up from the carpet of bodies.

'M4 carbine, two magazines.' Reilly shoves them into his hands. 'You take that window, I take this one. Anyone moving

431

out there now is a bad guy. We've got to hold them off for three minutes!'

The six missiles scream on through the night searching for their quarry. Technicians on the USS *Gettysburg* send out signals to them and the pack splits into two groups, three missiles diverging off towards the American base and three heading towards Mukungu half a mile away.

With minutes to go till they reach their targets, ejection ports slide open on both sides of each long missile. Bomb racks inside them whirr and click and bring the first of their one hundred and sixty-six bomblets next to the ports ready to be ejected.

The barrage of grenades and gunfire drives the Americans back towards the centre of the complex. Joseph runs forward to the corner of a hut and looks round it. Flames are pouring up from burning huts behind him set on fire by the explosions and in the light of them he sees a rifle poke out of a window in a building.

'There!' He points it out to Simon. 'You fire, I go!'

The gunman at the window sees them and fires a burst that shreds the wooden corner post over their heads.

Simon lies flat on the ground, crawls forward, pokes the end of the rifle round the corner and sprays a whole magazine towards the window. Joseph dashes forward towards the door to the hut, kicks it open and lobs in a grenade.

Reilly is firing at targets on the other side of the hut when the door is kicked open behind him. Light comes into the hut from the flames outside and someone yells, 'Grenade!'

Screams of panic burst from the people lying on the floor as they scramble over each other to get away from it.

Reilly's senses are adrenaline-fast. In a split second he

turns and sees the metal ball thump onto the floor and the space opening up around it as people scuttle away from it. He knows it's going to blow and he has to protect the people in the room. He hurls himself forward onto it and covers it with his chest.

In the Oval Office, the President, Kruger and the others all hear the blast of the grenade muffled by Reilly's body. Johnson screams, the President flinches and everyone looks aghast.

Joseph runs forward to the door of the hut with his rifle held up in front of him. He looks in and sees about twenty people scuttling on the floor to get away from him. He looks down at a middle-aged woman who has a satellite phone in one hand and her back pressed up against one wall. She looks up at him in terror, her mouth hanging open – he's seen that face of helpless fear before, it's the one that recurs in his nightmares and he hates it.

He raises his rifle and screams as he fires a burst into her and then turns the gun on the rest of the room and sprays bullets over them. President Rukuba said to exterminate the cockroaches in their house and that is exactly what he is doing.

Chapter Sixty

The helicopter settles down gently on the lawn and sinks onto its wheels. The ramp lowers slowly at the back of it and the crowd of soldiers on the veranda pushes forward curious to see who will emerge – more prisoners? A gasp goes up from them as a tall figure walks down the ramp.

It ducks its head down under the whirling rotors and then straightens up and walks towards the crowd of men and stands still in front of them.

The tall creature is half man, half beast. The massive kudu head stares imperiously at the soldiers; to the top of its huge twisted horns it is eight feet high. It wears a long army rain cape that drapes down over its front and back and flaps in the wind from the chopper. It carries no weapons but stands and gazes slowly and commandingly at them.

A Kudu Noir soldier comes out of the aircraft and stands next to the creature. He is also wearing a cape and carries no weapons. His eyes dart across the crowd from the ragged eyeholes in his black mask.

The Kudu Noir soldiers are ecstatic to see one of their commanders and start howling and yelling, 'Kuuuudu! Kuuuudu!'

Alex stares out of the eyeholes of the mask. The weight of it and its wicker frame is heavy on his shoulders. Inside it is stuffy and smells of animal hide and the blood of the man he beheaded to get it. He looks slowly across the crowd of soldiers as he counts them and assesses their weaponry. They are armed with rifles but they look drunk and excited.

Behind him he hears the helicopter wind up its engine and lift off. The wind whips his cape around him and he thinks, 'We've got five minutes before the missiles hit, how do we get Col out in time?'

The crowd presses forward towards Alex shouting excitedly, but Yamba leaps in front of them holding his hands up and yelling, 'Don't touch, don't touch!' in Swahili.

He pushes the men away from Alex who walks forward towards the veranda of the house.

Yamba yells at the men, 'Where is our prisoner? We want to see him!'

A Kudu Noir shouts back, 'He's in the cowshed out the back! We got him! We got one of those bastards!'

Alex continues to be mystically silent and walks towards the door into the house but a Unit 17 officer stands in front of him barring the way. He is annoyed with the Kudu Noir men for acting like they run the show in Mukungu. He holds his hand up in front of Alex. 'You can't see him now, the President is interrogating him.'

Alex looks at the man five feet in front of him and thinks, 'This has gone as far as it can.'

His rain cape whips back and the AA-12 machine shotgun hanging on a harness on his chest comes up in his hands. He doesn't need to bother sighting, he just fires on full auto. At such short range the fat twelve-bore cartridges blow holes in the Unit 17 officer and he then turns and pours fire at the crowd on the veranda. They stand stunned as the solemn, mysterious creature suddenly bursts into deadly life and shreds men with a fury.

Behind him Yamba also pulls his AA-12 from under his cape and fires off a full magazine. Between the two of them, sixty rounds of buckshot blast into the crowd on the veranda and the lawn in a few seconds.

Having massacred the men, Alex and Yamba quickly pull off the empty magazines, slap new ones home and then dig grenades from their webbing and throw them into the house through the door. They dart away along the veranda as the double blast blows out the windows and the room plunges into darkness.

Alex pulls the kudu mask off and the night air feels fresh and cool on his skin. He darts into the doorway with his weapon held at his shoulder. Now that they have started shooting he can hear shouts of alarm from the other side of the farmhouse. They have got to get to Col in the cowshed fast before he is killed or the missiles hit.

Nothing moves in the room so he and Yamba run on through it to the other side of the farmhouse. Alex switches out a light and they both dart across to a window overlooking the farm buildings at the back and quickly look out of it. He can see the cowshed fifty yards away and soldiers emerging from it and other buildings, looking shocked but bringing their weapons up as they stare at the now dark farmhouse in confusion.

Alex ducks back from the window. 'How many?' he says quietly to Yamba.

'Ten.'

'OK. I'll fire from here and you go right flanking round the side of the farmhouse.' He checks his watch quickly. 'We've got four minutes before the missiles hit.'

Yamba nods, ducks down away from the window and runs out of the room.

Alex gives him ten seconds to get round the side of the

building and then kneels at the window and sights on the men approaching cautiously across the farmyard with their rifles raised.

He clicks on auto again and fires off the full mag. Yamba opens up as well from his right and the crossfire cuts most of them down. Three men dart back into cover and then emerge from around a corner and fire long bursts across at them.

'Shit,' Alex thinks, 'we don't have time for a protracted firefight.' He slams in a fresh magazine and ducks over to another window before popping up and firing at the corner of the building where the gunmen are hiding and sees chunks of wood being blown off it.

He needs to change the game here and quickly. He yanks off the magazine and rummages in the bandolier on his chest. He pulls out a magazine with blue markings on its side, slams it into the weapon, gets back to his firing position and sights on the corner where the three soldiers are and pulls the trigger.

Each shotgun shell fires a three-inch-long projectile, folding fins popping out as it leaves the barrel. The mini-grenades hit the corner of the building and blow it away. Shrapnel bursts out and spatters into the heads of the three men crowding behind it.

Alex hears their screams. He grunts with satisfaction, quickly pulls off the grenade magazine and slaps a shotgun one back in the port. Then he is up and running to the door. He bursts out and his cloaked figure sprints across the open ground to the cowshed. A man emerges from behind another building and sights on him but Yamba blasts two shells into him and he goes down.

Alex kicks in the door at one end of the long low building and runs in. It is empty and lit by harsh neon striplights. A soldier is walking towards him with his rifle levelled and fires from the hip. Alex drops to one knee and blasts two rounds at him with the twelve-gauge. The man is thrown backwards and his rifle clatters on the concrete floor.

Behind him Rukuba leaps up from the chair he has been sitting on. Kneeling in front of him with his hands cuffed behind his back is Col; blood is running down the side of his face from a blow by a rifle butt.

Rukuba's tall figure is a blaze of white under the neon lights. His head darts around the room looking for another exit but the only door is blocked by the tall, bloodstained mercenary with an automatic shotgun held tight in at his shoulder and aimed at him. Alex stares at him over his sights.

Rukuba's eyes are wide with shock and desperation. His hands flutter up at his sides, like two panicking birds. 'Colonel Devereux . . .' he says, his voice high pitched with fear as he tries to think how he can talk his way out of the situation.

Alex lowers the muzzle of the gun slightly and stares at him. What should he do? Arrest him; allow the rule of law to take its course?

Two minutes until the missiles hit.

Rukuba finally finds something to say. 'It was for the good of the people, for Kivu, we needed to take control . . .'

Images flicker through Alex's head: Sophie's dead body, the artillery ambush of the helicopters, the desperate battle in the forest and the brave men that now lie there.

Rukuba looks at him with his mouth open and his hands held up in appeal. Alex lowers the muzzle of the gun and Rukuba drops his hands in relief.

The shot reverberates inside the low room. The blast hits Rukuba's left knee and nearly severs his leg. Red blood spatters up over his white robes and he collapses to one side, screaming and clutching his leg.

Alex takes one step nearer and looks down at him. He brings the gun up, fires into his body and again red bursts out on his white robes. He steps nearer and fires again and again with each step, blinded by rage and pouring his hatred into the bloody mess on the floor.

'Alex!'

Yamba's shout from behind him cuts through the mayhem and he stops firing. Blue gunsmoke hangs in the air.

'Come on! Get Col! Let's go!'

Alex looks round at the tall Angolan covering their escape route from the door with his rifle.

Alex steps over Rukuba's body and quickly cuts the plastic ties on Col's hands with his bayonet. 'Come on, let's move! Can you walk?'

'Yeah,' Col mumbles through the blood in his mouth.

Alex heaves Col to his feet and the smaller man gasps with pain. His broken ribs and battered head make him unsteady but Alex supports him with one arm and they hobble to the door.

Yamba yells, 'Come on!' and fires a long burst of suppressive fire at some movement across the farmyard.

Alex half drags Col with him to the door. 'OK, cover us!'

'Go!'

They run forward, Alex holding his weapon at his hip and firing on auto as they run. They reach the cover of the farmhouse and he reloads and fires off another full mag as Yamba's cloaked figure lopes across towards them. The two of them drag Col back into the house, desperately hoping the second part of their plan will work.

Overhead the three missiles targeted on Mukungu swirl into their preset bombing patterns with perfect choreography like angels of death. Half a mile away their companions begin bombing the area around the American compound and the flashes of the explosions sparkle rapidly in the night and then a second later the heavy repeated thudding of the blast waves arrive.

Inside the house Yamba stumbles along a dark corridor trying to find the door to the cellar that Rukuba showed them when they first visited the house. His hands search frantically along the walls for the handle.

Alex supports Col with one arm behind him but keeps his weapon free to guard against anyone following them. 'Come on!' he yells to Yamba. He can hear the bombs going off around the American encampment and hear the missiles overhead. In his mind's eye he sees the bombs tumbling down.

'OK!' Yamba finds a handle and twists it. It opens onto inky blackness and he tests with his foot. There are steps down. 'This is it!'

'Take Col!' Alex passes him over and the two of them stumble down into the cellar as Alex turns and fires at a soldier running into the far end of the corridor.

Over their heads the three cruise missiles circle the farm area and in seconds the bomb racks whirr and spew out their deadly cargo from both sides as they move over the target. Four hundred and ninety-eight bomblets shower down, blanketing the area and exploding in a rain of death that wipes every living thing off the face of the earth.

Alex throws himself down the stairs as the first bombs explode. He tumbles to the bottom and lies still as the repeated blast waves suck the air out of his lungs and pound on his head like a hammer.

Above him the wooden farmhouse is blasted apart, planks and chunks of timber flying through the air and cutting down the pursuing troops as they close in. The barns and cowsheds, the new prefab offices, the trees supporting Rukuba's hammock on the lawn, the flagpole – all are angrily smashed down by the exploding American ordnance. The heat of the blasts sets fire to the flimsy wooden structures.

In the cellar, Yamba drags Alex away from the bottom of the stairs as the door is blown in on top of him and balks of timber crash down above them.

The cellar is filled with tall computer server units and the three of them crawl between two stacks and shelter as beams smash onto the top of them and dust showers down. Still the pounding of the bombs continues as the missiles fly their patterns overhead.

The air becomes stifling as the oxygen is sucked out by the blasts and the dust builds up.

Finally the torrent of explosives stops and Alex lies on the floor and tries to heave air into his lungs whilst covering his mouth with his hand. He is battered from his fall down the stairs and concussed by the blasts.

Drunkenly he heaves himself up to his knees. He can smell smoke from above and hear the crackling of flames in the dried pile of wood over his head.

'Come on!' he croaks and breaks into a fit of coughing. 'Get out!' he mumbles. He can see Yamba lit up in the dark by a streak of light from the flames above them.

He hauls himself onto his feet, sways and steadies himself against the server stack. His rifle hangs on its harness off his chest and he and Yamba drag Col upright and up the stairs. Alex insists on going first and painfully heaves a heavy beam out of the way. The farmhouse has been completely flattened above them and he can feel the heat of the flames on his face as he pushes the beam to one side.

A bloodied and soot-stained face emerges from the burning wreckage of the house. The bodies of the soldiers they fought a few minutes ago are scattered around, blown to pieces by the bombing. Alex turns and drags Col after him and then he and Yamba support him between them as they stumble across the shattered remains of Rukuba's base and their brave new world. They stagger away from the flames and into the darkness.

Once again the bright landing light of the Mi-17 switches on above them and its pure beam cuts through the rain and flickering orange shadows around them. Arkady looks down at the devastation in horror and sees the three figures swaying in his downdraught.

Alex waves desperately to him and he brings the big machine down in a hover over the wreckage-strewn lawn where he dropped them off a few short minutes before. They clamber up onto the rear ramp and Alex lurches forward to the cockpit as they take off again, supporting himself by holding onto the struts on the wall.

He slumps into the copilot seat and puts on the headset.

Arkady looks with horror at his bloodstained, battered commander. He is soaking wet, he has wounds on his face and his clothes are burnt in places. The Russian barks over the noise of the rotors, 'What are we going to do?'

The World to Come

Epilogue

President Asani Jaafar looks ashen-faced as he walks slowly up to the podium in the White House garden. He's a well-intentioned, liberal politician who has just lived through his first firefight, a bruising encounter with the very worst of human nature. Admiral Harry Kruger and the Defense Secretary walk behind and then move to stand stony-faced on either side of him.

It's early afternoon on a warm day and the garden is in bloom, creating an atmosphere completely at odds with the appalling scenes of violence that he and the press pack in front of him have just lived through. All the sounds of the grenades and gunfire in the compound were broadcast live. Everyone is morbidly silent as they wait.

The President is a slow speaker at the best of times but now he seems to take an age as he shuffles his notes and finally looks up at the cameras. He opens his mouth and eventually says, 'My fellow Americans,' and then looks down again trying to think how to articulate the horror that the nation has just witnessed. It feels as bad as 9/11.

'What we have just seen and heard are terrible events that we will never forget. We as a country are all in a state of shock.

'What I will do in the press conference is update you on

the latest information that we have on the situation in the newly declared Republic of Kivu. Following the intervention of United States Navy cruise missiles on the area around the besieged compound, and on the nearby headquarters of President Rukuba, the siege of the compound was lifted.

'One hour and forty minutes later, at 8.11 p.m. local time, a USAF C-130 cargo aircraft dropped a company of one hundred twenty soldiers from 3rd Battalion Rangers Regiment into the area of the siege.

'With the aid of an accompanying Spectre gunship, they have now secured the area and searched it for survivors. Some have been found and are receiving immediate medical attention from army medics, including Under Secretary of State John Ciacola. But they have also reported finding numerous casualties.'

Here he pauses again and steadies himself.

'It is with extreme personal regret that I must announce to you now the murder of the following American citizens.' His voice begins to crack and he pauses to clear his throat. 'My close friend and trusted personal political comrade, United States Secretary of State, Patricia Johnson. Nine other State Department diplomats, fifteen United States military personnel and eleven press journalists accompanying the mission. A total of thirty-six people.

'The Rangers have also searched the nearby headquarters of President Rukuba. This was destroyed by the deployment of cluster munitions and burnt to the ground. However, they have recovered and positively identified the body of President Rukuba and a number of his senior security personnel.

'In the light of this disaster, I have spoken to the Secretary-General of the United Nations and agreed to the immediate deployment of a large United States military force to Kivu under a UN mandate to secure the province and take control of it from the mercenary army led by the war criminal, Colonel Alex Devereux, whose whereabouts are currently unknown.'

His voice suddenly takes on an angry tone and he glares at the cameras.

'The murder of these innocents is a crime against humanity and I pledge to you now that *I will not rest* until we have brought to justice all those responsible for their deaths! Not only those who pulled the triggers but also those who were negligent in their duty of protecting this peaceful diplomatic mission!'

Two miles away from Rukuba's headquarters at Mukungu, Gabriel and some friends listen to a simultaneous French translation of the press conference on Radio Okapi.

The five men huddle around the crackling radio trying to make sense of the madness that has broken out around them. Gabriel was so full of hope for the future and now it all seems to have gone wrong. Maybe even the FDLR will come back?

After his desperate pleading with Rukuba had failed, he fled down the hill to the temporary encampment with the rest of the KPP supporters who did not want to run out to attack the Americans. They were appalled by the violence whipped up in an instant by Rukuba's demagoguery.

When the missiles struck, he and a small group of friends looked in horror at the flames pouring up from the hilltop headquarters into the night sky.

The press conference ends and Gabriel slowly switches off the radio. There is too much to take in. After a minute of stunned silence, someone says, 'Well, at least the Americans are coming in, maybe they will be better than the UN?'

Gabriel is about to round on him for being insensitive

when an idea strikes him and he stops and looks thought-fully at the ground for a moment.

Adversity is spelt opportunity.

He reaches into the pocket of his jacket, pulls out his new mobile phone and calls his wife in their house in Goma.

'Eve, get me the number for the UN commander's head-quarters in Goma, I think I can help him.'

Alex stares out of the cockpit canopy of the helicopter as they fly into the rainy night.

Arkady's voice sounds in his headset again, harsh and mechanical against the background roar of the engines. 'What are we going to do?'

Yamba leans his head in through the door between the two pilots and looks at him as well; he heard Arkady's question on his headset. Col is huddled on the floor in the cargo bay behind him.

Alex forces himself to think. His murderous attack on Rukuba cleared some of the pent-up rage from his mind and helped him reassert some feeling of control over his shattered world.

His voice regains its hard edge of command. 'We'll make it back to Heaven and check what state the regiment is in. I'll need to see what the American reaction has been and then we may have to withdraw everyone back across Lake Kivu to Rwanda.'

'What about us?' Yamba asks. 'The Americans will come after us, they're not going to let this go.'

Alex twists his head round and looks up at his old friend; the Angolan's expression is severe but full of concern. He is worried about Alex's state of mind after all the horrors of that one day.

Alex turns away and looks out of the canopy window on

his left at the darkness outside. After a moment he narrows his eyes and frowns. The dim cockpit lights create a reflection of his face in the glass. It is the face of a man with strong feelings but he can see that they are still deeply controlled. Dark tides run just under the surface and he now understands more about what drives them.

His fame has become his doom but he has survived them both.

He stares at his war-weary but hardened expression and remembers another Devereux with a look of similarly grim determination – Black Hal.

He turns back to the other two with a straight gaze and says in a voice filled with a sudden certainty, 'We've come through worse than this, we always win in the end.'

He turns back and faces the darkness ahead.

Acknowledgments

Firstly, I am indebted to my agent Judith Murdoch for all her help and support over the years, without which this book would not have happened.

Also, a big thank you to my editor, Kate Bradley, for her hard work and creative insight as well as the Sales and Marketing team at HarperCollins, especially Claire Power.

I am particularly indebted to the following people for giving their time to talk to me:

Sarah Bailey – Humanitarian Policy Group

Tim Butcher – journalist and author of *Blood River* and *Chasing the Devil*

Katie Eves – International Red Cross

Nick Garrett – Director of Resource Consulting Services

Katy Grant – UN World Food Programme

Simon Guillebaude – Great Lakes Outreach

Zannah Jeffries – Tearfund

Sophia Pickles – UK All Parliamentary Party Group on the Great Lakes Region

Professor James Putzel and Gabi Hesselbein – LSE's Crisis States Research Centre

Susan Schulman – freelance journalist, for her intrepid

filming on patrol with the Rwandan army in Kivu.

Vava Tampa – Congo Now

Colonel Stuart Tootal – for conversations and his book, *Danger Close*, on the process of setting up a military expeditionary force in a hostile environment, in his case leading 3 Para into Helmand in 2006.

A lot of the international relations ideas behind the story are based on the work of Professor Paul Collier of Oxford University in his book *War, Guns and Votes: Democracy in Dangerous Places*, as well as Dambisa Moyo's book *Dead Aid*. Many thanks also to the LSE and the Frontline Club for their excellent public lectures and discussions on DRC and development issues.

I also made a lot of use of Colonel Mike Hoare's book, *Congo Mercenary*. This is a very well-observed and vivid account of how he put together a mercenary regiment of a thousand men, 5 Commando, from nineteen different nationalities in 1964. He was employed by General Mobutu and fought an eighteen-month-long campaign against Chinese-backed Simba rebels in eastern Congo which saved the newly independent state from collapse.

Finally, for proofreading and suggestions I am indebted to Ashley House, Charlie Leach and Alex Ingr.

Author's notes

Warlord is a complicated story that took two years to research, plan and write. In terms of style, it is what I call 'mindful violence'. The whole book was designed as a way for me to explore some big international relations issues whilst at the same time being a page-turning read. These are issues on both an international level and also a regional level in Kivu Province and reflect its complicated relations with its neighbours in the Great Lakes region.

On the international front, one of the key questions I wanted to discuss is: how do you fix failed states? This is increasingly the problem of our age. As an historian I find it interesting to note that the twentieth century was characterised by the problems of too much state power in the hands of communist and fascist dictatorships, whereas now we seem be battling to boost state power in failed states: Afghanistan, Iraq, Somalia, Pakistan and Yemen are all areas of concern. However, now these countries must choose not between capitalism or communism but between anarchy and authority.

So, why do states fail in the first place? This is a complex area but in many cases it is not because the insurgencies are strong but because the central authority is weak. What the West is currently doing in Afghanistan amounts to trying to prop up a drunk. Unless the Kharzai government rids itself of corruption it will continue to play a parasitic role on the population, meaning that they will support any insurgency as an alternative to it.

A similar state of affairs exists in Kivu Province in DRC where around thirty armed groups continue to terrorise the region because there is no effective central authority to stop them, despite the presence of a large UN force since 2003. In a number of instances, small professional military forces have had a great impact on ending wars in such chaotic circumstances, two good examples being the South African mercenary company, Executive Outcomes, that ended the long running Angolan civil war and the British Parachute Regiment in ending the reign of terror of the RUF in Sierra Leone. Both of them acted to give the weakened central authority the threat of credible force that enabled them to bring the rebels to the negotiating table to negotiate a peace deal in good faith rather than just using the talks as a respite from the fighting.

Kivu also provided an interesting way of discussing the other big issue I was interested in; the battle of social models currently going on in the world between China and the West: managed capitalism versus democracy and human rights. In many ways the biggest clash of civilisations at the moment is not between the West and radical Islam but between these two very different social systems.

Again this is a complicated issue, but in the developing world a number of countries are looking to the success that China has had in lifting three hundred million people *sustainably* out of poverty and comparing it favourably to the Western model. A lot of this interest by developing world governments is also for cynical reasons in that the government can do what it likes and is not bothered by the constraints of an opposition or human rights, e.g. in Sri Lanka and Rwanda.

However, at the same time it can also be argued that ethnically fractured, post-colonial states need managed capitalism to organise and direct the resources of the country in order to build the infrastructure that they need to develop. Only in this way can Africa achieve the capitalist revolution that it needs to move it *sustainably* out of poverty. Removal of the Common Agricultural Policy and the Farm Subsidies Bill would also be key structural developments that would be of more use than all the aid that the West gives.

In terms of my own views on the matter, I can see arguments on both sides. I didn't want the novel to be a polemic and so had to end it in an ambiguous manner. Africa has already had more than its fair share of dictators that have brought only ruin and destruction to the continent. But at the same time I wanted to ask some of the searching questions that Professor Paul Collier asks about the practical impact of democracy in fractured, post-colonial states.

Aside from this clash of social systems there is the general issue of the rise of China and the question of: can a great power rise without there being a major war? On the plus side, one can look at the rise of the US in the nineteenth and early twentieth century but on the downside we can see the emergence of Germany and Japan and two world wars before they were able to find a way of fitting into the world order.

The overall issue here is complicated; America and China are rivals who need each other. The main question is: can China balance its growing economic strength against its growing nationalism? In the absence of communism the state now relies on Chinese nationalism as its unifying ideology and this can be a very aggressive force. However, as the world's largest exporter it is not in China's interests to start a shooting war with anyone. Economic success is the main method of legitimisation of its government and it needs to maintain 8% pa growth rates just to employ the new workers coming onto its labour market every year. A war would not help this.

Therefore, for the moment, China pursues policies of peaceful rise and harmonious living that mean it tries to stay out of big international issues, rarely taking a lead. However, it currently piggy backs on American-provided security and it cannot continue indefinitely pretending that it is Switzerland. It will eventually have to take a more assertive role in the world and in *Warlord* I was sketching out one way of this happening through buying up large areas of land. The land deals mentioned in *Warlord* all happened recently: South African farmers bought two hundred thousand hectares of Republic of Congo, just north of DRC. UAE leased six thousand square miles of Southern Sudan and Daiwoo Logistics tried to buy half the agricultural land in Madagascar, which provoked a coup.

Whether China uses the land purchase route to assert its power or not it is nonetheless the case that it is having a huge influence in promoting a capitalist revolution in Africa and connecting it to world markets. This is both at a state level with massive infrastructure projects, but also through private sector purchases of raw materials and at a bottom-up level with a million entrepreneurs on the ground developing African business. Crucially here, the Chinese see Africa as a business opportunity not a charity case, in contrast to the West.

In terms of the story of *Warlord*, the plot line of the abduction and murder of albino children for black magic is unfortunately true; hundreds are killed in East Africa every year. Similarly thousands of women are raped and many suffer fistulas every year in Kivu because of the overall lack of law and order and are treated at hospitals like Panzi in Bukavu and HEAL Africa in Goma. With regard to the description of Kivu regional politics, all the details of the current situation are as accurate as I could make them.

James Steel
April 2011